A PROPER FAMILY HOLIDAY

Sisters Chelsea and Ronnie Benson haven't spoken to each other in two years. When their mother announces she wants the whole family to go on a week-long holiday in Lanzarote for her sixtieth birthday, both dread the excursion for different reasons. Sophisticated singleton Chelsea, a fashion journalist, would rather not revisit the "chips with everything" world she left behind when she moved to London. Ronnie, now a mother of two, is feeling fat and frumpy: the last thing she wants is to strip down to a swimsuit alongside her super-thin, super-chic sis. The week begins badly and gets worse, as underlying tensions and secrets are exposed. And then their mother drops a bombshell on the group. Will the holiday bring the sisters closer, or blow the Benson family apart?

SPECIAL MESSAGE TO READERS

A Proper Family Holiday

Chrissie Manby

LARGE
PRINT

First published in Great Britain 2014
by
Hodder & Stoughton
An Hachette UK company

First Isis Edition
published 2017
by arrangement with
Hachette UK

A catalogue record for this book is available
from the British Library.

ISBN 978–1–78541–331–5 (hb)
ISBN 978–1–78541–337–7 (pb)

Published by
F. A. Thorpe (Publishing)
Anstey, Leicestershire

Set by Words & Graphics Ltd.
Anstey, Leicestershire
Printed and bound in Great Britain by
T. J. International Ltd., Padstow, Cornwall

This book is printed on acid-free paper

For Penelope Alice Susan Hazel

Prologue

Of the many family photographs that graced the shelves in Jacqui Benson's living room, there were three of which she was particularly fond. The first, taken in the mid nineteen-eighties, was a photograph of an apple-cheeked baby girl, her younger daughter Chelsea, smiling in toothless delight as her grandfather Bill held her for her first paddle in the shallows of the sea. Chelsea's big sister Ronnie, just two, stood alongside, gripping their father Dave's hand for balance. Ronnie's smile was big and proud as she waved a plastic spade at her mother behind the camera. That photograph was taken at Littlehampton, on a rare bright day in a fortnight of rain. They were staying in a borrowed caravan that smelled of Benson and Hedges and wet dog but didn't they have a great time?

The second photograph had been taken four years later. Same resort. Different caravan. Chelsea was five by now and Ronnie was six and a half. This time, neither sister needed an adult for support as they dashed in and out of the sea. Together with Granddad Bill, they had built a sandcastle and were filling the moat bucket by bucket. It was a thankless task; they spent the entire afternoon going backwards and forwards, spilling more than they managed to tip into the channel and finding it soaked away altogether before they got back with another load. In the photograph, the sun was shining, though Jacqui remembered it as another wet fortnight. Stormy even. Wasn't that the holiday where the caravan's awning blew away in the middle of the night? All the same, they had a laugh.

The third photograph was taken in the late nineteen-nineties. Littlehampton again. Granddad Bill liked the old-fashioned seaside town so much he'd bought a static van on a proper full service campsite when he retired. It was a great idea — free holidays for all the family when money was especially tight. In this photograph, the girls were on the beach once more but they were too old for paddling and sandcastles now. They'd spent the morning — a brief respite of sunshine in a fortnight of near monsoon conditions — stretched out on their beach-towels, listening to music, playing it super-cool whenever a good-looking boy walked by and dissolving into giggles once he was past them. They sat up for the photograph, taken by their father. Ronnie had slung her arm round her sister Chelsea's shoulders. Chelsea's expression, eyes rolling even as she tried not to laugh, suggested their dad had just told one of his "jokes". This photograph was especially precious to Jacqui. It was the last photograph she had of her daughters together, great friends as well as sisters, enjoying each other's company on a family holiday.

Sixteen years later, Jacqui had decided that it was time to recreate that togetherness again. Only this time with more reliable weather.

CHAPTER
ONE

Chelsea

Five thirty-seven. The alarm clock on Chelsea Benson's bedside table had been going off for five whole minutes. Chelsea remained in a deep slumber, flat on her back, legs and arms spread wide like a starfish, and snoring so hard that her breath actually stirred the panels of the Japanese paper lampshade hanging above her bed.

Six twenty-three. The alarm had been sounding for fifty-one minutes. Chelsea snored on. She was finally woken by the sound of hammering on the front door of her flat and staggered to answer it, still half asleep. Her next-door neighbour, Pete, stood on the doorstep, in his pyjamas.

"You're in. I told myself she can't be in. I told myself it would stop automatically. Or the batteries would run out. Or . . . or . . ."

With a good portion of her brain still stuck in the Land of Nod, Chelsea looked at Pete in confusion.

"Your alarm clock!" Pete spluttered. "I can hear it through the walls."

"Be-be-beep, be-be-beep, be-be-beep . . ." The little clock had not given up.

As if hearing the alarm for the very first time, Chelsea turned back towards her bedroom.

"No!" She was suddenly very wide-awake indeed. "What time is it?"

"It's twenty-five past six on a Saturday morning!"

"Sorry, Pete. I'll make it up to you, I swear."

She closed the door as quickly as she could without causing offence, then raced for her bedroom, turning off the alarm clock with a slam to its button while simultaneously working out her next move. Her brand-new wheelie case, still empty and bearing its shop tags, was on the floor by the wardrobe. The pile of holiday ironing she had meant to tackle the previous night was still resolutely wrinkled. No time to fix that. Her passport was . . . Where on earth was her passport?

Now Chelsea's mobile phone was vibrating on the dressing table.

I hope U R on yr way 2 Gatwick.

It was a message from her sister, Ronnie, who, together with her partner, Mark, and their two children, Jack and Sophie, was already well on her way from her home in Coventry to Birmingham Airport. There was no time to respond.

Chelsea chewed on her electric toothbrush as she threw clothes in the general direction of the suitcase. She hopped into the dress she'd been wearing the previous evening and dragged a wide-toothed comb through her wavy brown hair. The undeniably gorgeous dress at least made her look a little more put together, and looking more put-together always made her *feel* more put-together, which was useful. Despite the hurry, Chelsea paused for a moment and looked more carefully at the clothes she was planning to pack. Her favourite Chloé tunic? Check. Hepburn-style capris by Michael Kors? Check. Three new designer kaftans that were very Talitha Getty circa 1965? Check. Chelsea wasn't sure it was the perfect holiday capsule wardrobe, but it was certainly getting there.

"Passport?" Chelsea muttered.

She spotted her passport on the table by the front door with her keys, Of course. She'd put it there so she wouldn't forget it. Six forty-five. She could still do this. She could still be on time and looking pretty stylish too, she thought, as she glanced in the mirror. The beautiful dress was made perfect for travelling with, ballet flats and a fitted denim jacket. She stuck her bug-eyed Oliver Peoples sunglasses in her hair and gave herself a quick pout. Yes. Looking all right, considering.

It was only as she got to the tube station at Stockwell that Chelsea realised her passport was still in the very place she had put it to make certain it was not left behind.

"Aaaaaaagh!"

Seven fifteen. Chelsea was back at the tube station with her passport.

"There are slight delays on the Victoria line . . ."

Eight thirty-five. Chelsea stumbled off the train at Gatwick Airport. Her new wheelie case was more unwieldy than the average shopping trolley. It had gone totally rogue. Which terminal? North or south? She didn't have a clue.

We're checking in now, said her sister's latest text message. Are you even at your airport?

Chelsea found her airline. North Terminal. She made a run for it.

The girl on the check-in desk agreed it seemed cruel that she could not allow Chelsea to board her scheduled flight even though the delayed nine o'clock to Lanzarote would be on the stand for at least another forty minutes as it waited for a take-off slot.

"But I can put you on a flight for tomorrow," the girl suggested. "I'm amazed there's space, to be honest. It is the school holidays."

"Of course," Chelsea sighed. Everybody was going away. The airport was absolutely heaving with new wheelie cases and their amateur drivers. Chelsea especially hated those stupid bloody Trunkis. Even as she stood at the check-in desk, a four-year-old boy was ramming a green one designed to look like a frog into the back of her ankles.

"Is tomorrow the best you can do?" Chelsea asked the check-in girl again.

"Unless you want to swim there," the girl joked. "Sorry. There are no more flights today."

Had she any choice in the matter, at this point Chelsea would have given up on the whole idea of a week away, cut her losses and headed home. Unfortunately, she didn't have any choice in the matter at all. "Stick me on tomorrow's flight," she said.

The girl put out her hand expectantly. "I'll need your credit card. Your old ticket isn't exchangeable."

4

"You're kidding me?"

"Oh." Having done some more tapping on her keyboard, the girl winced as though feeling the pain of what she was to say next. "I'm afraid you'll have to buy a different flight home as well. Because the return portion of this ticket is dependent on your having flown out there today."

"That can't be right."

"It's in the conditions of your fare. The only available return flight is next Sunday, so a day later. The total cost is three hundred and sixty-five pounds forty. Unless you also want to check in some luggage? That's another twenty-five pounds per item."

"For heaven's sake," Chelsea cried. She gave her credit card to the girl on the check-in desk, then turned and glared at the child with the ankle-bashing Trunki. He glared right back at her and gave her one more bash for luck.

It wasn't as though Chelsea wanted to go to Lanzarote anyway. Lanza-*grotty*, as the girls in her office all called it, had never featured high on Chelsea's list of places to see before she died. Chelsea was sure she knew everything there was to know about the tiny island. It was a volcanic dust bowl with nothing but slate-grey beaches. It was overrun with Brits. Every once passably beautiful bay or romantic cove now sported a burger bar and an Irish pub with an enormous flat-screen TV showing non-stop Sky Sports. The airlines that flew to Arrecife Airport said it all, as far as Chelsea was concerned. British Airways didn't go there. Serena,

Chelsea's colleague at *Society*, the monthly fashion and gossip magazine where Chelsea was assistant features editor, said one should never fly to an airport that isn't served by British Airways. With the exception of Mustique.

Chelsea hadn't even told Serena she was going to Lanzarote. She just said "Spain" and let Serena and the other uber-posh girls in the *Society* office imagine a carefully refurbished *finca* in an orange grove just outside Cadiz. Serena would have recoiled in horror at the very idea of the Hotel Volcan in Playa Brava, with its sports bar, mini-golf and "Kidz Klub". Its functional bedrooms with their wipe-clean walls would never feature in a coffee-table book by Mr and Mrs Smith, that's for sure. The moment Chelsea clicked on the hotel website and looked at a depressing shot of an en-suite bathroom, she fancied she could actually smell the tiny bars of cheap white soap and feel the scratchy pink toilet paper that must not, under any circumstances, be flushed down the loo. Nothing turned Chelsea's stomach faster than the thought of a holiday resort without adequate plumbing. But what could Chelsea have said when her mother, Jacqui, called so full of excitement to confirm that the Lanzarote trip was on?

"We're going to the Hotel Volcan. They can put us all on the same floor with disabled access," said Jacqui.

Same floor and disabled access. Such considerations were extremely important when your party included, at one end of the scale, an adventurous six-year-old and, at the other end, an eighty-five-year-old who was about as steady on his feet as a newborn wildebeest suckled

6

on Guinness. Five rooms had to be booked in all, for this was to be a "proper family holiday" involving the entire Benson clan — six adults and two children. No one was to be left out. No matter how much they might wish to be.

This proper family holiday was Jacqui Benson's idea of the perfect way to celebrate her upcoming sixtieth birthday. It was Chelsea's idea of pure hell.

CHAPTER
TWO

Ronnie

Ronnie Benson, Chelsea's big sister, was altogether more excited by the idea of a week in Playa Brava. After the year she'd had, she needed a week in the sun.

When Ronnie asked her mother what she would like as a gift for her milestone birthday, she had expected Jacqui to suggest her daughters chip in for a new watch or some more charms for her Pandora bracelet. Never in a million years did Ronnie think her mother might suggest a family gathering, much less a week-long family gathering in *Lanzarote*.

"You want to go *abroad*?"

"Your father and I have been planning this trip for years," Jacqui told her.

"You never said." After a second of delighted astonishment, Ronnie's thoughts immediately turned towards cost.

"We wanted it to be a surprise," said Jacqui. "And I know it sounds over the top, but you're not to worry — your dad and me are paying for everything. We just want you all to be there — you and Mark and the children. I can think of no better birthday gift than to have all my family around me. Especially . . ."

They were standing in the kitchen. Jacqui nodded through the open sitting-room door towards her father-in-law, Bill, Ronnie's beloved granddad, who was asleep in his special chair. At eighty-five, having had just about every internal organ in his body replaced with a plastic valve, Bill was constantly threatening to shuffle off this mortal coil.

"He's always said he'd like to go to Lanzarote," said Jacqui.

"Mum, are you sure?" Ronnie asked.

"Oh yes. He's always going on about it."

"I mean, are you sure you and Dad want to pay for us all? We'd love to go, we really would, but it's going to be expensive. You're talking at least four rooms. More if Chelsea's coming."

"Of course your sister's coming."

"Really?" Ronnie fought the urge to voice her scepticism. Chelsea on a package trip to Lanzarote seemed as likely as the Duchess of Cambridge rocking up at Nando's.

"Really."

"It'll cost a fortune. Mark and me will at least chip in for our lot."

Even as Ronnie said it, she wondered how on earth she and Mark could afford even four easyJet flights to the island. Their finances were more overstretched than Donatella Versace's facelift. Mark worked as a kitchen fitter. It wasn't a badly paid job, but once the recession hit, his hours had been cut from full time to just three days a week. Ronnie had picked up the slack with a part-time admin job at a funeral director's (the credit crunch could not stop people dying), but still they had had to cut back. A holiday had not been on the agenda for that financial year, not when there were school uniforms to buy. A washing machine on its last legs, gas bills, council tax, a car that needed servicing . . . Every time Ronnie thought she had the family finances under control, they were beset by some new disaster. To Ronnie's shame, she'd even considered having Fishy, the family cat, put down rather than pay for an expensive operation to fix her leg when the poor thing got run over. Things were that bad. (In the end, she'd stuck the op on her credit card). A holiday in Lanzarote was exactly what Ronnie needed and precisely what she couldn't afford.

"I know you've had a tough couple of years and that's why we're paying for you," her mother insisted. "I just want you all to be there."

"But—"

"No buts, Veronica Benson. This is important to me. The money's already in the bank and I want to take you all away. If I don't spend it on this holiday, I'll only spend it in Per Una."

"All right, Mum. Anything but more tat from Per Una."

How could Ronnie refuse?

When he heard the news, Mark also expressed concern, but underneath his polite protestations that Ronnie's parents were being too generous as usual, he seemed delighted, as did the children. A free holiday was not to be sniffed at — especially a holiday in the sun — and, unusually, Mark actually enjoyed hanging out with his almost in-laws. Sophie, who was fifteen and a half, tried to play it cool, of course, but Ronnie knew her daughter was secretly pleased and relieved to be able to tell the girls at school she would be going on a proper foreign holiday that summer after all. Meanwhile, Jack, aged six, was still at an age when the idea of a family gathering appealed to him enormously. Ronnie was sure Jack would have been equally thrilled to spend a week in a Travelodge near Wolverhampton so long as he had his family around him. His grandparents doted on him, but it was the thought of a week with Auntie Chelsea that seemed to tickle Jack most of all.

"Auntie Chelsea!" he squealed. "Is she really coming? *Really* really? She can play cricket with me," he added, remembering the last time he had seen his aunt, just over two years earlier, at a family barbecue. Chelsea had thrown a few balls for Jack that afternoon, in between turning her nose up at Mark's burgers and moaning to Ronnie about how hard she found her job at that posh magazine. She'd really hardly paid Jack any attention at all, but for some reason she'd left an indelible impression.

"I can't wait to see her," said Jack.

"If she can be bothered to come," Ronnie muttered to Mark. "I can't imagine Miss Hoity-Toity is terribly excited by the idea of a package holiday in the Canaries. What will she say to the people at *Society*? I suppose she could always write a *hilarious* article about slumming it with the working classes."

Mark just nodded. He knew better than to disagree with Ronnie where Chelsea was concerned.

From time to time you hear people refer to their siblings as their "best friends". Well, Ronnie and Chelsea definitely didn't have that sort of relationship. They hadn't spoken in two years.

It hadn't always been like that. Born just eighteen months apart, the Benson sisters had at another time been inseparable. Ronnie had doted on her sweet younger sister Chelsea and Chelsea had considered big sister Ronnie the ultimate heroine and role model. As teenagers, in their shared bedroom in the terraced house where they grew up, they had talked late into the night about their plans to escape their boring home town and make their way together in London. They'd go to university, become successful businesswomen and travel the world first class. Chelsea was going to work in fashion. Ronnie was going to have her own recruitment company by the time she was twenty-five. The sisters were each other's cheerleaders. No way were they going to get stuck like their parents had.

Those ambitions were nipped in the bud when Ronnie turned seventeen and discovered she was pregnant.

It was a disaster. Just days earlier, Ronnie and her form teacher had been talking about university applications. Her teacher had suggested a string of top colleges. "The sky's the limit for you, Ronnie Benson," were her encouraging words.

It certainly hadn't been part of the plan to become a teenage mother.

Jacqui and Dave were strangely unfazed by the news of their elder daughter's unplanned pregnancy. Ronnie had expected them to be furious. She had expected recriminations and talk of having let them down. Let herself down. In the end, there was nothing of the sort.

"We'll get through it," said her dad as he squeezed her in a bear hug. Jacqui agreed.

"We're right behind you, love," she said. "Every step of the way."

Likewise, Ronnie's teachers were sympathetic and did all they could to help her continue with her A-level courses, but Ronnie found her pregnancy surprisingly difficult and postponed her exams, with the intention of going to sixth-form college after the baby was born. However, when Sophie arrived, Ronnie was hit with a malaise she now knew to be postnatal depression. By the time Ronnie had enough energy to brush her hair in the mornings again, her brightest contemporaries were already on their way to university. Although she had actually only missed out on a year, Ronnie felt she would never be able to catch up and so she didn't bother.

Now, all these years later, Ronnie told herself that everything had turned out for the best. For a start, despite everyone's predictions to the contrary, Mark had stood by her. They'd been together since they were both fourteen. Mark had already left school and was working as an apprentice at a joinery company when

Ronnie told him she was pregnant. He vowed right away he would provide for Ronnie and his child, and he had definitely made good on that promise.

Mark moved in with Ronnie and her parents as soon as the baby was born. When Sophie was two, the little family was able to move out of Ronnie's parents' house and into a rented place of their own. With overtime and a bit of work on the side at weekends, Mark earned enough for Ronnie to stay at home until Sophie could go to school. When Sophie was nine, Ronnie considered finishing her A-levels at an adult-education college, but then she fell pregnant with Jack and the cycle started all over again. Including the postnatal depression.

But this makes it all worth it, thought Ronnie, at such moments as when she watched twelve-year-old Sophie, tall as a giraffe, make her precocious debut as goal defence in the school netball team. And what high-flying job could have been more satisfying than seeing four-year-old Jack play a sheep in his first nativity play? These were the consolations for having so spectacularly short-circuited her plans for world domination with an unprotected shag. Ronnie might not be living in a posh house or driving a fancy car like some of her old friends from school, but she had been able to see her children grow up, while her contemporaries were so scared of stepping off the career ladder they put their carefully planned babies into childcare at six months old. You never got those early years back. If you missed the first word, the first steps, that was it. Those were the things that magazine writer Chelsea didn't understand when she talked about how bored she would be if she were a stay-at-home mum.

"I don't know how you can stand not using your brain," Chelsea had said the last time she and Ronnie were together. It was at that barbecue to celebrate their grandfather Bill's eighty-third birthday (Bill was celebrated every year now, just in case). That was the comment that sparked the discussion that became a full-blown row that ended with Chelsea accusing Ronnie of having become a mummy martyr and Ronnie accusing Chelsea of having turned into a self-obsessed snob, and subsequently led to the sisters' two-year-long estrangement.

"Not using my brain!"

Mark had become used to hearing Ronnie exclaim those four words at random moments during their week. It was usually when she had finished overseeing Sophie's maths homework or had finally deciphered an incomprehensible instruction in a letter sent home from Jack's school. Ronnie would then segue into a rant about how Chelsea had no idea how taxing family life could be. Ensuring that two children and one other adult were fed, dressed, happy and healthy, all on the kind of budget that would have been tight enough for a singleton? That was no mean feat. And now Ronnie was working part time as well. She never had a minute to herself. From time to time, she really did feel as though she was running an army battalion. Chelsea did not have a clue what a mother's life was like.

Perhaps that's why she didn't see the need to apologise for her remarks, Mark occasionally dared to suggest. Only when Chelsea had a family of her own — assuming she could ever hang on to a man for long enough — would she realise the gravity of the insults she'd delivered over a chargrilled sausage in a bun.

"I don't care. I won't ever forgive her," Ronnie claimed.

Jacqui's birthday wish was to change all that. Ronnie had to promise their mother she would put her anger to one side for just this week. For what might be their last "proper family holiday".

"The best birthday present you could ever give me is for you girls to be friends again, like you used to be."

As though to emphasise her point, Jacqui looked towards that ancient photo of the sisters building a sandcastle on Littlehampton beach.

"All right," said Ronnie. "But Chelsea has to make an effort too."

"I'm sure she will," said Jacqui.

If only Ronnie could believe that. As it was, about a month before the trip, when Ronnie picked up the phone to offer the olive branch so that their first face-to-face meeting would not be too strange, Chelsea acted as though those two years of radio silence hadn't even happened. She just went straight into a story about some fancy cocktail party she had attended for work. As Chelsea twittered on about the guest list, Ronnie was mortified to realise that while she had been nursing the mother of all grudges, Chelsea had carried on regardless, not questioning her sister's absence because her swanky London life and career were just so fulfilling. She simply hadn't noticed she and Ronnie were not on speaking terms.

Reading Chelsea's text from Gatwick, as she stood in the check-in queue in Birmingham, Ronnie fumed. She was certain that her snooty sister had missed her flight deliberately. Next thing, Chelsea would claim she couldn't get another flight. Ronnie would have put money on Chelsea not coming to Lanzarote at all.

CHAPTER
THREE

Chelsea

Of course, Chelsea hadn't missed the flight deliberately. Here's what led up to her oversleeping and forgetting her passport.

On Friday — her last day at work before the flight to Lanzarote — Chelsea made careful plans to ensure she would be at the airport on time come Saturday morning. She arrived at the *Society* office a whole hour before the rest of the team to finish off all those jobs she could not safely leave to someone else in her absence. She worked through her lunch break with the intention of leaving the office at five on the dot, giving herself plenty of time to pack and prepare and get a reasonably early night in anticipation of the painfully early morning ahead. Getting to Gatwick in time to check in would mean leaving her flat at six thirty at the latest. Why did charter flights always leave so early?

By five o'clock on Friday afternoon, Chelsea was feeling quite pleased with herself. She was almost looking forward to getting back to her flat and starting the packing. Perhaps this week in Lanzarote would not be so bad after all. The weather had to be better than it was in London, and a sneaky Web search suggested there were cultural depths to the island that would give Chelsea a break from non-stop beer and karaoke at her parents' chosen resort. She was just looking at some pictures of an idyllic naturally turquoise lagoon worthy of a fashion mag swimwear shoot when Davina, *Society*'s editor, poked her head out of her office door and barked that Chelsea should join her *pronto*.

There had been a catastrophe. Eugenia Lapkiss, the actress who was to adorn the cover of the next issue, was upset about the article written to accompany the sumptuous photo shoot that would fill ten pages of the magazine. She was furious, in fact, and her PR was threatening to rescind permission for the article altogether if it wasn't rewritten in a more flattering light. Unfortunately, the piece had been written at great expense by a famously difficult artist who could not be asked to make the edits himself because a) he was on holiday and b) he would almost certainly refuse to do them anyway. No one touched his work.

"You'll have to do it," said Davina. "And you'll have to do it now."

"I'm going on holiday first thing tomorrow and I've still got to go home and pack," Chelsea tried.

"Oh, darling. I'd consider it a personal favour. We're going to lose the cover if you don't help."

Chelsea didn't even bother to protest further. She knew that there wasn't much point. Davina had already turned back to her computer screen as if to signal that the conversation was over. It was left to Chelsea to work out how to put the damage right without offending the actress or the artist.

"What was she offended by?" Chelsea asked in vain hope of an easy answer.

"All of it," said Davina. "I know you can do it, sweetheart."

So, instead of going home just after five, as she had planned, Chelsea went back to her desk. She spent the next hour and a half on the phone to Eugenia's PR, who explained in great detail exactly the image Eugenia hoped to convey with this "in-depth" portrait in *Society*. Unfortunately, the list of things that could not be mentioned was far, far longer, than the list of attributes and achievements Chelsea *was* allowed to write about. For example, Chelsea could not mention the three mega-grossing slasher movies that had catapulted Eugenia to fame, despite the fact that she'd only appeared in one other film. Admittedly that other film was a great film, but Eugenia's three-line part was generally considered to be its low point. Neither was Chelsea to mention Eugenia's love affair with the director who cast her in that three-line part. Or her brief early marriage to an adult-movie star. Or her current relationship with a huge Hollywood name widely rumoured to be gay. Chelsea should not mention Eugenia's religious conversion (lapsed Methodist to fervent Scientologist). Or her nose-job (which she had to have because she was born with a deviated septum, not because she'd sniffed it to pieces with cocaine). Chelsea should not mention the landlord who had sued Eugenia for wrecking his Hollywood condo while on a drug binge, and she should definitely not go anywhere near Eugenia's shoplifting conviction (as she had been confused into leaving a boutique without paying by the store's fire-alarm test). In short, Chelsea should not mention anything that made the young starlet slightly more interesting than the average cookie-cutter LA blonde.

"I will need approval," the PR finished.

"Of course."

Chelsea could see why Eugenia (or rather her PR) had been upset by the original piece. It was snide, and where it wasn't snide, it was damning with faint praise. But there was the added problem that the artist who had written the piece to form part of a whole issue based on the theme of "art and beauty" had an even bigger ego than Eugenia. How to change his words without him actually noticing . . .

"He won't notice," Carola, the assistant fashion editor, assured Chelsea when they met in the staff kitchen. "He won't read it. I very much doubt he wrote it in the first place."

"Oh, I don't know," said Serena. "Don't you remember what happened when someone moved a comma in that haiku he wrote to celebrate the Olympics?"

"Oh, yeah," said Carola. "That was bad."

"Thanks, girls," said Chelsea. "You've been really reassuring."

"You'll be OK. You just have to make it so good that he won't *want* to say it's not his own work. Come and have a drink when you've finished?" Serena suggested.

Chelsea had a feeling she was not going to be finished before last orders.

She delivered a first draft of the rewritten piece to Eugenia's PR within an hour. The PR sent it back covered in red edits. Chelsea made herself another cup of tea and started again. The second draft fared no better. Meanwhile, the office emptied out. Carola and Serena went for their traditional Friday-night cocktail at Browns, where they hoped to bag themselves a couple of hedge-fund managers, except that all the hedge-fund managers were in private jets on the way to their super-model wives in the South of France. Davina, the editor, swept past in a cloud of Chanel at seven without even saying goodnight, on her way to a Michelin-starred dinner somewhere. The lowly intern left as soon as Davina was safely out of sight. Soon Chelsea was alone in the office, waiting for the film star's PR to make yet more comments. Or should that be complaints?

This was not the first time Chelsea had changed her plans to sort out a potential disaster at the magazine. And heaven knew losing a cover so late in the month would be a serious disaster. When she started at *Society*, Chelsea had stepped into the breach gladly, eager to make her reputation as a hard worker, but lately she was beginning to think all she'd actually managed to do was set a dangerous precedent. Now Davina didn't think twice about asking Chelsea to stay late or blow off a long-standing arrangement to do something Davina probably should have done for herself, but that didn't translate into any greater rewards. No pay rise. No promotion. Chelsea couldn't help wondering if it was because there were aspects of herself she could never change through pure hard work: a state-school education and a family line that could only be traced back as far as the coal man. Among the daughters of aristocrats and generals who adorned the pages of the magazine and its office, Chelsea's face just didn't quite fit. In her heart of hearts she knew she would have to leave *Society* to progress. Go somewhere more egalitarian.

For now, though, she was stuck, waiting for copy approval, while the rest of London started its weekend. She used the time to browse the job ads in the *Guardian*'s media pages, making a note of a position on another mag. It was in the fashion department. Chelsea had always been in features, but she would love to be in fashion instead. That part of her teenage ambition still persisted.

More changes came through. By eleven o'clock, Chelsea had rewritten the piece eight times.

"This is hopeless," said the PR when Chelsea finally got her to return a call. "Eugenia says why don't you come to the restaurant and she'll tell you what she wants face to face."

"What? Now?"

"Yes." The PR gave the address of one of the hottest new places in town.

Thinking quickly, Chelsea grabbed a sundress from the fashion cupboard. It wasn't strictly kosher to raid the cupboard without express permission, but she was sure that Carola would understand. Carola wore clothes from the fashion cupboard all the time. There was no way Chelsea could turn up at that restaurant to meet a film star in the jeans and sweater she had been wearing all day. The dress was perfect: a floral-patterned silk sundress by a new designer called Mebus. It looked like something Audrey Hepburn might have worn.

As she took a taxi to the address she had been given, Chelsea felt her excitement rising. Perhaps it had been worth staying late after all. Perhaps this would be the moment that made her career. She was going to get a face-to-face exclusive with the biggest rising star of the year. Hopefully she was going to get something nice to eat as well.

In the end, Chelsea did get a face-to-face exclusive, but only after having waited in the restaurant lobby for another hour, suffering the pitying stares of the reception staff, who would not even let her sit at the bar. When Eugenia, accompanied by her bulldog PR, finally deigned to come and speak to Chelsea, she added nothing whatsoever to her mystique. She was stupid and vain. Mostly stupid. She misquoted several religious leaders and philosophers, attributing the words of Homer Simpson to Socrates. Finally, she dismissed Chelsea with a wave of her manicured hand.

"I know you'll do me justice because I can tell you have a kind heart," were her parting words.

Tired and hungry, Chelsea felt anything but kind. She finally got home at two in the morning. She worked on the article until three. She had to be up again at half past five.

"I better not miss my flight" was the last thought that ran through Chelsea's mind before she fell onto her mattress without removing her make-up. "I better not miss my flight".

But of course she had missed her flight, and now she had twenty-four hours before the next one with nothing to occupy her but her sister's increasingly accusatory texts.

Mum is so disappointed you're going to be late.

Dad wants to know how you managed to sleep through your alarm clock.

And best of all . . .

How did you miss that flight? Why weren't you USING YOUR BRAIN?

Needless to say, Ronnie's texts didn't make Chelsea any more excited at the prospect of spending the best part of a week in her company. Though Ronnie had made that olive-branch phone call, it was clear that she was still holding a grudge about the row Chelsea only vaguely remembered. What was all this stuff about "using your brain"? Annoyingly, Chelsea couldn't even share the real reason why she wasn't going to be in Lanzarote on time. Up until three writing up a half-witted film star's philosophy on life? Once upon a time, Ronnie would have leapt on the possibility of celebrity gossip, but these days she would just think Chelsea was showing off. Sitting in Starbucks on the wrong side of security, Chelsea deleted Ronnie's hectoring messages. Then she laid her bone-tired head on her arms and had a small cry at the thought of the money she'd had to spend on another flight, another early start and seven nights in a hotel where you couldn't even flush the loo paper.

CHAPTER
FOUR

Ronnie

Despite Ronnie having made sure everyone was at the airport a full two hours before the scheduled departure time, things were not going smoothly in Birmingham either: the flight was delayed.

When she heard the news, Ronnie bundled her family into Costa and sent Mark to the counter to get two cappuccinos and two cartons of juice. She had brought sandwiches in her bag, both to save money and because Sophie had lately become incredibly fussy. As it was, Sophie turned up her nose at the thought of her mother's lovingly made breakfast picnic. She wanted to go off and explore the shops instead. Ronnie told her she couldn't.

"The last thing we need is to be unable to find you when the flight is called."

"Mum," said Sophie, "when they call the flight, you've still got ages. Everybody knows that."

"We don't know that," said Ronnie. "We don't even know which gate we're supposed to go to yet. It might take a while for us to get there."

"You're being so lame," said Sophie. "Lame" was Sophie's new favourite word.

Ronnie was ready to give her daughter a piece of her mind, but right then Mark signalled that he needed help at the counter.

"Go and give your dad a hand," she said instead.

Sophie got to her feet in a cloud of disdain, banging her chair against the table in protest as she did so. Ronnie closed her eyes for just a second to let the urge to yell again pass. When she opened them, she saw that her daughter had rearranged her mutinous expression into something altogether sweeter for her father — as usual — and by the time the two of them got back to the table, Sophie had somehow persuaded her dad not that she should be allowed to go shopping but that he should give her some spending money with which to do it. Tenner in hand, Sophie skipped off in the direction of Accessorize.

"Ten pounds?"

"I got a tip from that job on Monday," Mark explained.

"Still, I told her she couldn't go. We don't know when our flight will be called."

"The girl at the check-in desk said at least an hour. Do you want her sitting there with a face like thunder for the next sixty minutes? She's got her phone," Mark continued. "And we're going on holiday. Let's start having a good time right here. Eh, Jack?"

Jack was busy playing a game on his DS. He looked up.

"Shall we go and get a *Simpsons* comic for the flight?" Mark suggested.

"Yeah!"

Jack handed the DS to Ronnie for safe keeping and, like Sophie, skipped off in the direction of retail heaven without so much as a backward glance. Mark was right behind him.

Alone at the table, surrounded by her family's bags and the untouched sandwiches, Ronnie tried to regain her sense of humour as she sipped her coffee. Alas, the coffee was so hot it burned her tongue. She was tired and she was anxious and suddenly her eyes were stinging with the effort of holding back tears. It was all right for Mark. He was always the good guy, dispensing gifts and overturning Ronnie's sensible decisions. Surely the first rule of parenting was not to undermine each other? Mark had no idea how hard it was for Ronnie to impose any kind of discipline on the daughter he called his "little angel" when he contradicted everything she said. Lately, it seemed almost every row they had began with something Sophie had done.

And now, just as Ronnie had feared they would, they were calling the Lanzarote flight. Ronnie stood up at once and scanned the terminal for her family. She had known this would happen. The hour-long delay had turned out to be only half an hour in the end. She looked at the departures screen. Seconds after the new departure time was revealed, their flight flashed in red for final boarding. Final boarding! They'd only just announced that boarding had begun.

Ronnie phoned Mark. She phoned Sophie. Neither of them picked up her call. She kept one eye on the departures screen and the flashing red gate number. If they missed the flight, she would never forgive Mark.

Her parents had spent a fortune on this holiday. They had to get there. She could feel her blood pressure rising. She phoned Mark again. Then Sophie.

"All right, Mum," said Sophie. "*All right*. I'm standing right behind you."

Mark, too, was striding through the crowd towards her, with Jack perched high on his shoulders.

"Come on," said Ronnie. She was starting to panic. She couldn't hold back any longer. "We need to hurry up. Has everybody got their things? Sophie, where's your jacket?"

"Er, I'm, like, wearing it?" Sophie had the jacket from Hollister, a birthday gift that had cost way more than Ronnie wanted to pay for something that already looked so worn, tied carelessly round her waist.

"Jack, where's your rucksack?"

"It's on my back."

"So it is. Now come on."

Ronnie led the charge for the gate. By the time they got there, Sophie was complaining of a stitch, and Mark, who had carried Jack all the way, said he thought he might be having a coronary.

And so much for last call. The gate area was absolutely rammed with would-be passengers for Arrecife. Despite the departure screen's insistence that the flight was closing, no one had boarded at all, and there was nowhere for Ronnie and her family to sit down until they did.

"I knew we didn't have to hurry," said Sophie. "I knew it. I could have stayed in the queue at Accessorize."

Sophie sat down on Ronnie's carry-on bag with a dramatic sigh.

"For heaven's sake. You'll squash the sandwiches!"

"Who the hell brings their own sandwiches on a flight anyway? My family is so bloody chavvy."

Luckily for Sophie, Ronnie didn't hear her above the announcement that the flight was ready to board at last.

Despite the jam at the gate, Ronnie and her family had slightly better luck with their seating arrangements. Mark somehow hustled to the front of the queue by carrying Jack, whose smile parted crowds before them. Jack was that kind of child, with a face at once angelic and mischievous. Once on board, Mark nabbed four seats in the second row. Ronnie was surprised and pleased when he wrestled the hand luggage away from her so he could put it in the overhead locker while they took their seats. She was less surprised and pleased to find she had ended up in the aisle seat, with Jack next to her in the middle seat while Sophie sulked with her head against the window. Mark, across the aisle, was sitting next to a perky twenty-something blonde who was just a bit too smiley for Ronnie's liking. Mark didn't seem to have noticed her, though; he was typing frantically.

"You're supposed to turn off your phone when you get on the plane. Who are you texting?" Ronnie asked.

Mark blushed before he answered, without looking up, "Just Cathy next door. About the cat."

"What about the cat?" Ronnie asked.

"Just telling her where the food is."

"She already knows," said Ronnie. "I told her yesterday."

"Yeah. Yeah, of course. She must have forgotten."

"Then why didn't she text me to ask? Why would she have texted you?"

Mark shrugged. "I don't know, do I?"

Sophie also sent a last few messages before a flight attendant asked her to switch off her phone. Three hours without recourse to text was going to be difficult, both for Sophie and for the people who had to sit near her.

"Can't you let Jack have the window seat?" Ronnie asked her. "It's the first time he's been on a plane."

"It's the first time *I've* been on a plane," Sophie replied. Ronnie knew Sophie still hadn't forgiven her for saying she couldn't join a school trip to Berlin. That they *really* hadn't been able to afford it had not mattered. All Sophie focused on was how much she would be missing. It was especially hard on her because Harrison Collerick, the boy she had liked for so long — the love of her life ("So far," as Mark always added. Somehow Sophie would take that from her dad) — was going to be on the trip, along with Sophie's best friend, Skyler. As it happened, Sophie's "best friend" somehow ended up snogging "the love of Sophie's life" on the coach on the way back from a day trip to the Jewish Museum. Skyler later claimed it was the heavy emotional vibe of the history laid before them that had rendered her vulnerable to the awful boy's charms. Sophie had forgiven her best friend and Harrison but it seemed she wasn't about to forgive her mother. If

32

Sophie had been allowed to go to Berlin, none of it would have happened, after all.

"I don't mind having the middle seat," said Jack.

Jack was so easy-going compared to his big sister. Perhaps that would change when he hit puberty too, but for now Ronnie was grateful she had at least one laid-back child.

"It's still exciting," he assured her. "My first time on an aeroplane."

"Guess what?" said Ronnie. "It's practically my first time too. And Daddy's."

Ronnie and Mark had flown only once before. It was before Sophie was born. Ronnie had joined Mark's family on a trip to a resort in Portugal (against her parents' better judgement). It was on that trip that Sophie had been conceived.

The stewards began the safety procedure. Ronnie forced Sophie to put down her gossip magazine and pay attention.

"Nobody else is watching," said Sophie.

"Nobody else on this plane matters to me except you, your dad and Jack. Will you please listen to what they're saying?"

Jack was much more attentive. He wanted to know whether he could wear his oxygen mask regardless of the pressure on the plane, just in case. And when the safety briefing was over, Jack slid his hand across the armrest into Ronnie's lap. She linked her fingers through his.

"I'm holding your hand in case you're afraid," he explained.

"Thank you. Though there's nothing to be afraid of," said Ronnie, more to convince herself than her son. Since she'd last flown, things had definitely changed. The whole business of going to an airport and getting through security had become decidedly grim.

"I love you, Jack." Ronnie kissed her son on the top of his head. "You too, Sophie. I love you too."

"Right," Sophie grunted back. Sophie didn't do familial love any more. Like so many things Sophie had once enjoyed, these days she considered time spent with her family as "lame". Nevertheless, Ronnie noticed that Sophie had taken Jack's free hand.

Across the aisle, Mark was still fiddling with his phone.

"Mark," Ronnie hissed. He hurriedly switched it off.

"I love you," Ronnie mouthed across the aisle at him.

He mouthed it back. Ronnie had told all her family members that she loved them. Whatever happened now, they would know what they meant to her.

But of course the take-off proceeded without incident. As soon as the seatbelt sign was switched off, Mark reclined his chair and inserted his iPod headphones in his ears. With Sophie sulking and Jack asking questions all the way — "If heaven is in the sky, how come we can't see it now we're up here?" — by the time Ronnie and her family were landing in Lanzarote, Ronnie definitely felt a little bit less inclined to tell Mark again that she loved him.

CHAPTER
FIVE

Chelsea

While Ronnie was in the air, Chelsea was settling in for an unexpected day in an airport hotel. She flicked on the television. Hundreds of channels and nothing she wanted to watch. She stared at her iPhone as if staring might cause it to beep with a new message. It was nearly midday and there was not so much as a single word of acknowledgement from Davina that Chelsea's hard work on the Eugenia Lapkiss article had been worth it.

After an hour spent watching *The Jeremy Kyle Show*, Chelsea began to think she should have gone back into London after all. She certainly could have done without spending the extra money on this coffin-like room at the Gatwick Shangri-La, but in her panic at the thought of a second early morning with its attendant potential for missing another flight, she had shelled out £100 for the privilege of being just thirty minutes away from the airport rather than an hour and a half. The salesgirl hadn't mentioned that this particular "airport hotel" was closer to Brighton than Gatwick. Chelsea would still have to get up before seven to get the complimentary bus to the terminal.

Chelsea slumped back against the pillows.

Sometimes it felt like she never got a break. How had she ended up at this place? Not just at an airport hotel but at this place in her life. Supposedly "successful" with her sophisticated London magazine career but somehow still skint and living in a dump and absolutely single. An unwanted memory of Colin the banker, her last boyfriend, came to Chelsea's mind. What was Colin doing that morning? Not eating stale biscuits from a minibar, that was for certain. His lovely fiancée was probably squeezing him some fresh juice. Yep, that waste of space Colin Webster, who always claimed he would never marry, had recently become engaged to some stick-thin 24-year-old model whose father owned a chain of clothing stores, just three months after dumping Chelsea. How come he got to find love again when Chelsea was stuck in a nightmare of Internet dates that inevitably made her feel worse than getting no dates at all?

Chelsea's phone chimed. As though someone had read her mind — someone with a nasty sense of humour — she had an email notification of a new "fan" on one of the dating sites she had forced herself to sign up to. Feeling momentarily hopeful that this could be the email that changed her life, she clicked through the link to discover that her new fan was an unemployed IT specialist who still lived with his mother. He looked like Beaker from *The Muppets*. The mere fact that he thought he might have a chance with Chelsea was profoundly depressing.

I must stay optimistic, Chelsea told herself as she deleted her new fan. She needed a new plan. That's what she would do with her free day at Gatwick: think about her future and make plans. She'd been so busy lately that she'd lost sight of where she was going. That was all. She had a pile of self-help books in her hand luggage (including *From Booty Call to Bride*, a manual dedicated to "helping a woman move from one-night stand to wife material"). She could use this time in the airport hotel to do some reading and refocus, the importance of which she had only recently explained to the readers of *Society* in a three-page article illustrated with pictures of £500-a-night spa suites. None of which she could afford to visit . . .

Chelsea picked up the pad and pencil that had been thoughtfully provided by the hotel and began to write a wish list of all the things she hoped to achieve this year. A promotion would be a great start. She definitely deserved one. A move to the fashion department would be even better.

Lately, Chelsea felt like she'd been living at the *Society* building, covering for one colleague after another as pretty much the whole office went on maternity leave. Not only was she having to work crazy hours, Chelsea was practically bankrupt from all the baby showers. She was sick of cooing at flat-headed newborns, while listening to the patronising prattle of the new mothers who insisted that it wasn't fully possible to be a woman until you'd forced something the size of a grapefruit out through your nether regions. Something, Chelsea observed, the average battery hen did several times a day without complaint or expectation of beatification. Chelsea was especially sensitive to being patronised by parents, having received the "you just can't understand" speech for the first time when she was only fifteen and a half from her seventeen-year-old sister. Trust Ronnie to spin having been too stupid to take the Pill properly into a vaulting achievement.

Anyway, it was time that Davina and the Mothers' Union at *Society* magazine recognised Chelsea's contribution to keeping the magazine going while they spent six months decorating paint-your-own-pottery plates with baby footprints. Once she got the promotion, she'd move out of her poky little flat into something that fit better with her image as someone who wrote for such a glossy mag. At the same time, she'd start taking better care of herself physically. She needed to get fitter. She'd sign up for Pilates again. She'd go out more, with people other than Serena and Carola, who were as toxically single as she was. She needed to widen her social circle. The only events she got invited to outside work these days were sodding baby showers.

So . . . Get a promotion. Get fit. Get some new friends. Chelsea wrote out her ambitions and outlined small steps for achieving them, just as she'd encouraged her readers in that three-page article. She could do it. In a year's time, she could be a different woman. A happy woman. And all in time for her thirty-first birthday.

For about an hour, Chelsea kept herself reasonably optimistic with the thought of everything she could do over the next twelve months or so, but when it came down to it, her wish list was not so very different from the wish lists she had been writing for the past five years. And realistically, she knew she would probably write the exact same list again in another year's time. One thing she knew for certain was that her wish list would not contain the words "holiday in Lanzarote with my parents".

It wasn't that Chelsea didn't love her family; it was just that she found it increasingly difficult to be around them for any length of time. The unease she felt when she was with them had been growing in tiny increments since she first left Coventry to go to university in London. When she came back home for Christmas, after her first term there, her parents had made fun of her "new posh accent". Ronnie had commented meanly about her new look. It had continued in the same vein for years, so that now whenever she saw any of the Bensons, Chelsea would count the minutes until they made a comment along the lines of "I bet they don't do things like that in London." Chelsea just wished she could believe that the teasing was good-natured and not some sort of rebuke. She wished she thought her family was proud of her.

She looked at her watch. Her sister would have landed by now. She could imagine the scene of jubilation at the cheap hotel their mother had probably found on Teletext. She could almost hear what Ronnie would say about her missing her flight to their mum and dad, who had flown out the day before. Ronnie, who was always right even when she got everything wrong. Ronnie, the golden child. Not even her getting pregnant in the middle of her A-levels had drawn their parents' disapproval. She'd always been their favourite.

Ronnie texted: We're here. Mum's looking forward to seeing you tomorrow. You are actually coming tomorrow, right?

Chelsea replied, Unless I can arrange a bomb scare. Then she lay back on the suspiciously shiny coverlet and prayed for a strike by air-traffic control.

CHAPTER
SIX

Ronnie

By the time she and her family arrived at the Hotel Volcan, Ronnie was just about ready to collapse. She had not slept much the night before. Unlike Chelsea, Ronnie had way too much at stake to sleep through her alarm.

It was only when they finally arrived at the bright white-painted hotel that Ronnie could relax. Actually, forget it. She couldn't relax even then. There were still rooms to find and cases to unpack. Her mother, Jacqui, and father, Dave, were waiting for them by the main pool (there were three), having saved four extra sunloungers. They had the room keys. Jacqui said she had opened all the windows to air the rooms.

"Thank God you're here. Hanging on to these sunloungers was like defending the Normandy beaches," said Dave. "This whole resort is full of Germans."

Sophie drew breath sharply. Born more than half a century after the end of the Second World War, she was well drilled in political correctness and made it clear without saying a word that she found her grandfather's xenophobic humour embarrassing. Sophie found an awful lot of things embarrassing. It was a condition of being a fifteen-year-old girl. Her pain was almost visible as Jacqui gave her a squeeze and commented on how "big" she was getting.

"Big?" Sophie was horrified.

"Your grandma means 'tall'," Ronnie chipped in quickly.

"Tall? Yes. Tall. Of course I meant tall. That's exactly what I meant," said Jacqui. "You're turning into a real beanpole."

Sophie shook her head. She didn't actually say "lame" in response to her grandmother's embarrassment, but Ronnie heard it all the same.

"Am I getting tall too?" asked Jack, pulling himself up to his full height. Unlike his sister, Jack couldn't wait for his grandmother to sweep him into her arms. Ronnie smiled at Jack's unselfconscious delight as Jacqui blew a raspberry on his neck.

"Where's Bill?" Ronnie asked.

Jacqui jerked a thumb towards the bar. Granddad Bill, Ronnie's grandfather and the family patriarch, was inside in the shade. Jacqui explained that she and Dave had found him a nice spot beneath the wide-screen TV, which was permanently tuned to Sky Sports, and instructed the barman to make sure he was kept well lubricated. But not *too* well lubricated.

Ronnie found Granddad Bill exactly where Jacqui said she'd left him. He was wearing a Coventry City football shirt, a pair of ancient Bermuda shorts, which showcased his knobbly knees to perfection, and his carpet slippers, which were dark red velvet with a gold-embroidered crest. Very regal if totally inappropriate, not to mention at least twenty years old and with soles full of holes. Still, he refused to wear anything else on his feet these days.

"All right, Granddad?" Ronnie pressed a kiss to his cheek, which was as dry and papery as an autumn leaf. "You OK in here on your own in the dark?"

"I've got an armchair, I've got a bottle of beer, and I'm watching lovely young women play beach volleyball on Sky. I've won the bloody lottery," said Bill.

Ronnie laughed. Her grandfather was having a good day.

"I've won the bloody lottery" was Bill's catchphrase. Two Christmases ago, while staying at Ronnie's house for a family celebration, Bill had fallen out of bed and been unable to get back up from the floor. When Mark went in to help and asked whether he was all right, Bill had said, "I've won the bloody lottery. What do you think?" He'd actually broken a rib. Ronnie was glad to hear him use the phrase in altogether better circumstances.

Jack wheeled into the bar. He was followed by his sister at her usual emo shuffle. Ronnie shook her head indulgently as she watched her son's chaotic approach. Why walk in a straight line when instead you could skip and skitter and bounce off every piece of furniture you passed, was Jack's philosophy. He was already wielding an ice lolly, and a big orange stain spread across the front of his T-shirt like a paintballing wound.

"Jack! That shirt was clean on," Ronnie sighed. He'd spilt Coke over the shirt he'd been wearing on the flight. Ronnie had made him change on the resort bus so that he'd look his best for his grandma. What a waste of time that turned out to be.

Jack didn't care what he looked like. Now he was dripping melting orange ice over his great-grandfather. Jack was so free with his hugs. Bill was delighted to receive one. Sophie, meanwhile, muttered her hellos and made it clear she wanted to go upstairs asap. There was nothing more embarrassing than being seen in the company of a great-granddad. It was almost as bad as being seen with your parents. The previous Christmas, Mark had bought Sophie a knitted balaclava so she could still go shopping with her mum and dad without being recognised by her peers. Needless to say, Sophie had not seen the joke. Maybe if the balaclava had come from Hollister . . .

Fortunately, Jack was soon listening, rapt, as Bill explained the rules of the game on the screen, leaving Ronnie and Sophie free to find their family's rooms and decant the contents of their four suitcases into the wardrobes. The main room — the one that Ronnie would share with Mark — had a balcony overlooking the hotel's largest pool and the beach, just a few feet beyond. Ronnie stepped out and took a look at the view. It was exactly as she had imagined. The sea shimmered on the horizon like a sheet of blue silk shot through with silver thread. The air was soft and warm and scented with exotic flowers. It was Ronnie's idea of heaven, this place. A week of warmth and relaxation at the edge of a bright blue swimming pool. A simple white-painted bedroom. The rustle of palm leaves in

44

the wind. No cooking, no cleaning, no school run and no work. Well, there would always be work for Ronnie. She looked down at the poolside, where Mark was already cracking open a beer as he reclined on one of Dave's fiercely defended sunloungers. Mark seemed to think suitcases packed and unpacked themselves by magic. Ronnie stepped back inside and asked Sophie to help her carry the two smaller cases next door.

"Hold on," said Sophie. "Why do we need both these cases in here? Are you telling me I'm sharing with my brother?"

"Where else is he going to sleep?"

"You told me I wouldn't have to share with Jack."

"I never told you that," said Ronnie.

"Dad did," Sophie insisted. "When you said I couldn't go to Berlin, which, by the way, has totally ruined my life, he said that to make up for it, I would definitely have my own room in Lanzarote. Sharing with Jack is not the same as having my own room. Duh."

"I know, sweetheart, but Grandma and Granddad have paid for this trip and—"

"You could have given them some extra money. Or Jack could go in with you. Why can't he go in with you?"

"Sophie, you're just being difficult. Take this bag. You're sharing with your brother. Like you did in Cornwall."

"Yeah, and that was terrible. It was like sharing a room with a chimpanzee."

"You're only going to be sleeping in here. You don't have to spend all day with him."

"I did last year."

It was unfortunate that the weather in Cornwall the previous summer had meant there was little to do but stay in their tiny rented cottage all day long, playing Connect Four and Pictionary until a fight broke out.

"Sophie, I don't know what I can do about it," Ronnie pleaded. "We've only got two rooms."

"You don't understand me. You make no effort to understand me. First, you stop me from going to Berlin. The only other person who didn't go to Berlin was Shelley Tibbetts, by the way ..." Sophie's lip curled in disgust as she named the least popular girl in her school year, a poor girl who had such outrageous BO that even some of the teachers gossiped about her. "And now you're going to force me to share with my brother and he'll see me in my bra and he'll tell his school friends all about it."

Ronnie closed her eyes. "He's six, Sophie. Jack's not going to talk about your bra to anybody. He still thinks babies are delivered by Amazon." That was Mark's joke.

Sophie wasn't listening. "You treat me like I'm still a child, but I'm not. I'm nearly sixteen years old, for God's sake. I need my independence."

"All right, all right, I'll see what I can do."

What could she do? In desperation Ronnie called reception and asked for a collapsible bed to put in the corner of the room she and Mark would be sleeping in. It wasn't as though they were planning to have a load of hot sex anyway. Ronnie got no joy from the

46

receptionist, though. This being the school holiday season, the hotel was full and every spare bed had already been pressed into use. Sophie would have to share.

"You're ruining my life," was Sophie's measured response again. She refused to utter a further word to her mother while they unpacked the suitcases.

When Ronnie and Sophie finally got back outside, Sophie stormed to the low wall that surrounded the hotel complex and sat there looking out to sea in grand dudgeon. She refused even to join her family for lunch. Some holiday this was turning out to be. They'd been in the resort for less than two hours and already Ronnie's daughter wasn't speaking to her. And then Chelsea texted in response to Ronnie's question about her flight: "Unless I can arrange a bomb scare." What was that supposed to mean? Could she make it any more obvious that she didn't want to come?

The day didn't get much better. Sophie managed to sulk for the best part of six hours without a break. She didn't even change out of her black skinny jeans, despite the blazing sunshine. Jack, meanwhile, would not stop asking when Auntie Chelsea was going to arrive. It was "Auntie Chelsea this, Auntie Chelsea that" all the long afternoon. And of course Mark got right into the holiday spirit by tucking into the beers as though it was New Year's Eve. By the time the family had finished dinner, with Sophie refusing to eat anything except three chips and Jack having a choking fit when he tried to emulate his father downing a pint

47

by knocking back his own overly large glass of fake Coca-Cola, Ronnie was almost ready to go back to Coventry.

She fell into bed.

"I think we're going to have a good week here," said Mark, as he flumped down on the mattress beside her.

"Hmmmph," said Ronnie from the depths of the pillows. It was all right for Mark. The minute he stepped off the plane, he'd shed his responsibilities. Meanwhile, Ronnie already felt as though she wanted to go back to work for a rest. She may have travelled almost as far as Africa to "get away from it all", but she'd brought her biggest stressors with her. If only Chelsea were the kind of sister whose arrival would make everything easier.

CHAPTER
SEVEN

Chelsea

Sunday

Chelsea's free day at Gatwick had actually ended up being another workday. When Davina finally woke up and looked over the changes Chelsea had made to the Eugenia Lapkiss article, she had plenty of suggestions of her own, which Chelsea had to implement from the dressing table in her hotel room. There were other pieces to be worked on too. Chelsea's boss obviously hadn't registered the fact that it was a Saturday, or that Chelsea was technically on annual leave. When another email from Davina titled "Just one more thing" appeared on Chelsea's iPhone, she almost responded by pointing out that she was on holiday, but she didn't. Until she could find the time and energy to apply for a new post, she still needed her job at *Society*, so instead she responded with her usual efficiency and ended her email by wishing Davina the lovely weekend she didn't deserve.

As soon as it seemed decent, Chelsea treated herself to a couple of glasses of wine in the hotel bar. Two glasses of wine turned into three. They were big glasses and so, without even really noticing, Chelsea had soon drunk the equivalent of a whole bottle of Sauvignon Blanc. Rough Sauvignon Blanc with extra sulphites, at that. No wonder she felt like something the cat had sicked up when she was woken by her alarm the following morning. Sunday. Still half asleep, she climbed back into the outfit she had been wearing since Friday night and headed for the shuttle bus.

When Chelsea had been buying her replacement ticket, the check-in girl had offered her the chance to have "priority boarding" for an extra £50 on top of the eye-watering fee. "It'll save you having to scramble in the queue," the girl had said. "There are three hundred people on the flight, but we only sell sixty of these passes." Chelsea had declined.

Standing at the gate with her fellow passengers, however, Chelsea wished she'd forked out the extra money. Though she could be pretty damn sharp-elbowed on the first day of the Harvey Nichols sale, Chelsea didn't fancy her chances with this gang. They were, to a man, woman and child, the most horrible bunch of people she had ever laid eyes on. Nearly all of them were dressed in football shirts. How different they were from the Boden-clad queue waiting to board the flight to Pisa, which departed from the gate next door.

As the crowd shuffled towards the desk, Chelsea found herself behind a hen party, all wearing pink T-shirts saying, "Lanzarote 2014. Lock up your sons." They handed round two large plastic cups filled with cava from the terminal bar. It wasn't long before they started singing. Worried that it was just a matter of time before one of those plastic cups of cava was spilt in the direction of her borrowed dress, Chelsea decided her best strategy was to wait until everyone else had boarded. She stepped out of the queue and sat back down on a bench, trying to block out the horror of her flight-mates by starting *From Booty Call to Bride* (carefully tucked inside a copy of the weekend *FT* magazine). She had her boarding pass, so there would definitely be a seat for her, right?

"There's room at the back of the plane," the steward explained when Chelsea finally boarded.

"Where?" Chelsea looked down the cabin. She couldn't see a single empty spot.

"By the toilets."

Of course. But at least the whole row was empty. That was much more than Chelsea could have hoped for. She wriggled her way down the length of the aisle and squeezed herself into the window seat. There was no room for her luggage in the overhead locker, so she dragged her wheelie case into the row alongside her, risking the wrath of the steward. Still, Chelsea told herself, as soon as the plane took off, she would be able to put her bag on the empty seat beside her as a kind of barrier against the people queuing for the loo. All she wanted now was to get this flight over with.

But Chelsea was not to have a whole row to herself after all. Just as she was settling in, a final passenger was hustled on board.

Chelsea felt slightly better when she noticed that the man walking down the aisle towards her was a dead ringer for Hugh Jackman. He was over six feet tall and looked as though he was no stranger to the gym, so he wasn't going to spill over the armrest. He was dressed pretty well, in a blue linen shirt, and he looked half-intelligent. Tired and fed-up as Chelsea was after twenty-four boring hours at Gatwick, she found herself straightening up a little in anticipation of her good-looking row-mate's arrival. She quickly hid *From Booty Call to Bride* in her handbag, pulled out the new Malcolm Gladwell instead and surreptitiously checked her reflection in the screen of her phone. Maybe Chelsea and this handsome stranger would get talking.

What Chelsea didn't realise was that the man was not alone. His travel companion was too small to be seen over the headrests, but the Hugh-alike ushered ahead of him a blonde-haired child, about six years old. She had the sweet and gentle face of one of Cicely Mary Barker's Flower Fairies and was dressed in a pink party dress and a pair of silver tulle wings. As she walked the length of the plane, the little girl dispensed fairy luck with her pink plastic wand. Everyone was charmed. You could hear the cooing that followed her progress. Then at last the girl stopped level with the row she and her father would be sharing with Chelsea. She looked at Chelsea. She looked up at her dad. She looked back at Chelsea and her big blue eyes narrowed alarmingly.

"You told me that *I* would have the window seat."

"Lily," said the Hugh-alike, "that lady is already in the window seat. Go in the middle. Quickly."

"No." Lily stood her ground in the aisle. She folded her arms. "You said I could go by the window."

"That was when I thought we would have more choice," said Lily's father. "These are the last two seats left on the whole aeroplane. Everybody is waiting to go on their holidays. Get in."

"I won't," Lily insisted.

"*Lily*," Her father tried a different tone of voice. It didn't work. The girl pushed out her bottom lip and stood her ground.

"Is there a problem?" a steward asked.

The passengers in the rows to the front and side strained to get a better view of the unfolding situation.

"No," said Lily's father, "there isn't a problem."

"Yes," said Lily, "there is." She turned to the steward with all the confidence and entitlement of Anna Wintour discovering a civilian in her front-row seat at Chanel, then pointed back at Chelsea with her wand. "She's in my seat. I was promised the window seat. I was told I would be able to see my house when we flew over it."

"Aaaah." The steward at least seemed to find Lily's truculence charming. "You want to see your house, do you?"

"I do," said Lily. "I've been looking forward to it all week."

Chelsea smiled but didn't move. She really did not want to be on the aisle for three hours. No way. This princess Lily would doubtless want to get up and down the whole flight long and Chelsea didn't want to have to keep getting up and down herself to let the little girl out. But Lily was not about to quit. She folded her arms and gave Chelsea a death stare. Lily's father and the steward also looked at Chelsea now, though in a slightly more imploring way. The steward cleared his throat and raised his eyebrows. It took less than ten seconds for Chelsea to cave.

"OK," said Chelsea. "I'll swap."

Chelsea dragged her luggage out from beneath her seat and shuffled out into the aisle. Lily sprang past her without so much as a "Ta very much" to acknowledge her sacrifice. Still, Lily's father at least seemed grateful.

"Thank you," he said. "Really, thank you. It's just that . . . I know I shouldn't have promised her, but . . ."

"It's OK. I understand," said Chelsea.

"It's very good of you." The dad smiled at Chelsea as he squeezed himself into the middle seat. The pitch between the rows was so tight, he had to fold himself like a collapsible umbrella. "Saved me a whole lot of earache."

"I bet."

"Are you sure you're going to be all right in the aisle?"

"Of course."

"I'll make sure I don't nick your armrest."

"I think that middle armrest is technically yours," said Chelsea.

"We can share," said Lily's dad with a grin that left Chelsea surprisingly flustered. Chelsea noted his perfect, straight teeth. This guy really was impossibly handsome, which made Chelsea all the more disappointed that her one hope of an airborne flirtation had turned out to be a dad. Chances were, there was an older version of the entitled little blonde now in the window seat sitting further forward on the plane.

"Madam, if you'd just stow your luggage," said the steward to Chelsea as though this last-minute hold-up was entirely her fault.

With Lily's dad's assistance, Chelsea crammed her handbag into the overhead locker, but they failed once again to get her wheelie case put away. The steward took it from her with a sigh.

"This should have been checked in," he said, "but I suppose I'll take it to the front of the plane. Then we can be on our way."

"Why aren't we on our way already?" Lily asked. She occupied the window seat like a queen on her throne.

"The pilot has to make sure everyone is safely in their seats," her father explained.

"I would have been in my seat ages ago," said Lily, "if that silly lady wasn't already in it."

"Lily," said her father, "that's not kind. You mustn't say that sort of thing."

"But it's true," Lily insisted.

Chelsea smiled as brightly as she could. "Children say the funniest things."

CHAPTER
EIGHT

Ronnie

In Lanzarote, the rest of the Benson family were gathering for their first holiday breakfast. It was a beautiful day. The wispy clouds over the sea were purely decorative and the wind was as warm as a lover's caress. The view from the restaurant terrace was picture postcard perfect.

Ronnie had woken in a much better mood than she went to bed in. Amazing what a difference a good night's sleep could make, and it had been a very good night's sleep, considering. The bed was comfortable, and Ronnie had been tired enough to fall asleep *before* Mark started snoring. Jack, of course, was always full of beans, but even Sophie seemed transformed that morning. She'd decided that she was speaking to her mother again. Well, grunting to her at least.

Breakfast, in the hotel's poolside restaurant, was a buffet affair. Ronnie's stomach rumbled appreciatively as she saw and smelt the vast vats of fried eggs and bubbling beans. She took two bits of toast from the counter and piled them high with bacon and sausage and cooked plum tomatoes. She loved plum tomatoes, but no one else in her family would touch them, so she rarely had them. Anyway, sod the calories. This was her first holiday breakfast and she was going to enjoy it. Meanwhile, Mark was assembling a sausage sandwich for Jack and Ronnie was glad to see Sophie wasn't skimping on breakfast either. Lately, Ronnie had been concerned that Sophie didn't seem to be eating as much as she used to. She had grown almost ten centimetres in height the previous year but did not appear to have put on any weight. That morning, however, she had perched two fried eggs on top of two pieces of fried bread. Ronnie didn't say anything in case drawing Sophie's attention to her eating habits sent them haywire again. Back at the table, Sophie picked up a fork to break an egg yolk. Everything was right with the world until . . .

"Look at that," said Granddad Bill, pointing at his great-granddaughter's carefully laid out breakfast. "Sophie's made a model of her chest."

"Oh my God!" Sophie screeched her indignation. "I can't believe you just said that. You're so disgusting." Sophie pushed her plate away from her and got up so abruptly that her chair fell over. She didn't pick it up. Instead, she stormed out of the restaurant, almost knocking over an unattended toddler as she thundered by.

"Granddad Bill," said Ronnie, "what did you have to say that for?"

"I was only having a laugh," he said.

"For God's sake. You can't say that sort of thing. She's sensitive. She's a teenage girl."

So much for a quiet breakfast. Ronnie got up to go in search of her daughter. Meanwhile, Mark just shrugged and dipped a piece of toast into the yolk of one of Sophie's discarded eggs.

"She'll get over it," he said, catching Ronnie by the hand as she passed him. "Leave her be."

"Mark, she's really upset."

"Leave her to calm down for a bit. She'll see the humour. It's only the dementia talking. Eh, Bill?"

"All right, Mark." Bill raised his cup of tea. He'd already forgotten what he'd said.

"I'm going to find her," said Ronnie.

"You've got to take her less seriously and she'll take herself less seriously too. It's you who makes her so moody by indulging her. It was only a joke. If the rest of us don't take any notice, she'll get it into perspective that much quicker."

"What?" Ronnie snarled. "What do you know about parenting teenage girls?"

"I'm just trying to make your life easier. I'm saying you don't need to take responsibility for her feelings all the time."

Ronnie glared at Mark while she formulated a stinging reply.

"I like these sausages." Jack broke the silence.

"They are nice, aren't they?" said his grandmother, leaping on the opportunity to talk about something other than Granddad Bill's faux pas.

"So, what are we going to do today?" Jack asked. He was the consummate diplomat, always ready with small talk.

"You could play in the swimming pool again," Jacqui suggested.

"Maybe Auntie Chelsea will play with me when she comes."

"*If* she comes," said Ronnie, momentarily distracted from concern for her daughter by disdain for her sister.

"Chelsea will be here," said Jacqui.

Sophie returned to the table. Her eyes were still glistening with rage and upset. She sniffed theatrically.

"Your great-granddad is very sorry," Ronnie prompted.

"Am I?" asked Granddad Bill.

"Of course you are."

"Sorry, sweetheart."

Sophie grunted her acceptance of his apology.

"Anyway, we all know this is much closer to a representation of Sophie's chest," Mark interrupted. He held two grapefruit halves up to his own man-boobs.

Sophie was gone again.

"This time, *you're* getting her back here," Ronnie told Mark. "For pity's sake. Try to have some sensitivity." She turned to Jacqui. "You see what I have to deal with, Mum? I haven't got two children, I've got three, and Mark is the worst of the lot. My life is a warzone with added cooking and ironing and cleaning. Chelsea is so right not to bother with men and kids."

If only Chelsea wasn't bothered about getting herself a man. As it was, the arrival of her row-mate on the plane to Arrecife had thrown her into something of a spin. Every time she tried to sneak a look at him, she caught

59

him sneaking a look back at her. Was something happening between them? Something like chemistry?

The take-off was relatively smooth. Lily, happily installed in the window seat, gave a running commentary on what she could see below as the plane reached its cruising height.

"Is that our house, Daddy? Is that our house? Is that our house, Daddy? Is that it? Is that our house?"

Lily's dad turned to Chelsea and shrugged apologetically as his daughter chuntered on. Chelsea smiled to let him know she was absolutely charmed by his darling child just as she was ready to be charmed by him. Assuming he was alone. The seat-belt signs had been switched off but Lily's mother hadn't yet appeared to check on her, which was what Chelsea had thought might happen.

"Sorry," said Lily's father. "About the chatter. I know you're trying to read."

"That's OK."

Chelsea half-closed the cover of her book to indicate that she might actually be happy to be interrupted.

"Oh, Malcolm Gladwell," Lily's dad observed. "I've been meaning to read that one too. It's supposed to be great."

Chelsea was very glad she had hidden away her self-help book.

"Have you read his other stuff?"

"I read *Blink*," Chelsea told him. She hoped he wouldn't ask her any questions about it. She couldn't remember a word.

"How about that one about success? What was it called?"

Chelsea didn't know.

Fortunately, before Chelsea could show her ignorance, Lily interrupted, demanding a book of her own. Her father dug into his rucksack and handed over a book of fairy tales. With Lily taken care of, he turned straight back to Chelsea. Chelsea tucked her hair behind her ear in a manner her ex, Colin, had once pronounced "adorable". Perhaps she would get her flirtation after all.

"I'm Adam," he said, extending his hand.

"Chelsea."

"Like the football team," Adam grinned. "Was your dad a fan?"

"Ha! No," said Chelsea. "Mum chose my name because she liked the sound of it. Dad's more of a rugby man. He played when he was younger."

"I used to play too," said Adam. "Haven't for years. As you can probably tell." He pantomimed a bloated stomach.

No, thought Chelsea. You look pretty fit to me. Very fit indeed. She felt herself begin to grow warm in the cheeks and looked at her book cover so he couldn't see her blushing. She racked her brains for something clever to say next but Lily saved her the trouble.

"Daddy, stop talking to that lady and read this book to me."

"Duty calls."

Adam excused himself and started reading to his daughter.

Though she opened the Gladwell again, even after such a brief exchange, Chelsea wasn't really in the mood to concentrate on social science. Instead, she listened to Adam reading aloud from the tale of the Three Little Pigs. He was very good at it. He put plenty of character into the voices of the hapless piggies and their lupine nemesis. Chelsea had the idea that he was making an extra effort for her benefit.

She wondered what Adam's own story was. Was Lily's mother somewhere else on the plane and just taking advantage of the break from her daughter? Or was he travelling alone? If so, why? Divorced? Separated? Because he had been flirting with her, hadn't he, when he talked about sharing the arm-rest and drew attention to his rugby player's physique? How to find out the real situation? Chelsea longed for Lily to get tired of her father's reading so she could get to know more.

Eventually the pigs worked out the value of building in brick and the story ended. Lily busied herself with colouring in the accompanying illustration using a packet of crayons retrieved from the cavernous rucksack.

"I always travel with crayons," Adam explained. "I can't tell you the number of times a packet of crayons has literally saved my life."

Chelsea nodded. "I can imagine." She was thrilled to have Adam's attention again. Thank you, Crayola.

"So, what do you like to read apart from Gladwell?" Adam asked.

Chelsea cast her mind back over the last five books she'd bought: *Why Men Love Bitches, He's Just Not Into You, Make Every Man Want You, Men Who Can't Love* and *From Booty Call to Bride*. Her colleague Serena had recommended that particular one to help Chelsea understand why her confirmed-bachelor ex should have changed his mind about marriage so quickly when he met the model. But the last thing Chelsea wanted was for Adam to know about her self-help habit, so she told him, "I bought the new Alex Marwood at the airport."

"Love those books. Really chilling."

"And I loved Hilary Mantel."

"*Wolf Hall*," Adam agreed. "Excellent novel."

Chelsea hadn't ever cracked the spine on her copy, but why did Adam need to know? This was going well. Really well. Chelsea didn't think she'd had such an easy conversation with a man she actually liked the look of since she first met Colin. And they were flying to the same island. She was so pleased with the thought that she even smiled at the steward when he clipped her elbow with his trolley.

Adam continued. "Reading is massively important to me."

"Oh, me too," said Chelsea. "Me too."

"You can tell such a lot about a person from their bookshelves."

"You're absolutely right."

"A shelf full of self-help is definitely a bad sign."

"Indeed," Chelsea nodded, as she thought of her shelves at home.

"I really love being able to discuss a good book with friends. I know that might seem nerdy."

"Not at all."

With such a lovely face, Adam could be excused any amount of nerdiness. Chelsea wondered if she could download some crib-notes on *Wolf Hall* when they got to the island, just in case she bumped into him again. Just in case he asked to see her. Maybe she should just throw caution to the wind and ask to see him? Chelsea's imagination raced ahead. She thought of that fabulous blue lagoon she'd seen on the Internet. Now that would be the perfect spot to share a passionate kiss. Assuming Adam was travelling alone with his daughter, of course. Surely he wouldn't be making conversation like this if he wasn't . . .

But while Chelsea nodded enthusiastically and did her best to look charming and charmed as Adam extolled the virtues of Lionel Shriver, Lily was getting restless.

About halfway through the flight, and long after the catering trolleys had been stowed, Lily insisted she needed another drink. Chelsea patiently stood in the aisle while Adam rifled in the overhead locker for the bag that contained the juice he'd bought after security. She took the opportunity to admire his back view, which was every bit as good as the front. At last Adam found the drink and sat back down. As he fitted a straw into the carton of blackcurrant juice, Chelsea sat down too, smiling at Lily as she did so. Lily narrowed her eyes in return. Then Adam handed the carton to Lily, who squeezed it as she took possession of it so that a

64

fountain of sticky black juice escaped the straw and arched right over her father to land with a splatter on Chelsea's Malcolm Gladwell book, from where it dripped onto the lap of the dress she had borrowed from the fashion cupboard.

"Shit!" Chelsea tried to get to her feet, only to be foiled by her seatbelt, which she always wore when sitting down on a plane.

"That lady swore!" Lily pointed out.

As far as Chelsea was concerned, there was every reason to. There was a bright purple puddle in the middle of her borrowed dress's skirt. Much flustered dabbing of paper towels and apologising by Adam followed. The book seemed relatively unscathed, but God knew what would become of the sundress.

"It's fine, it's fine, it's fine," said Chelsea, when Adam impulsively offered to buy her a new one. She was certain he had no idea he was offering to replace a dress that would cost more than a car when it hit the shops the following summer. She batted away his hands, sure that he was only spreading the mess with the wet-wipes he had pulled from his jacket pocket. "It can be dry-cleaned."

"I'll pay for that, then," Adam insisted. He fished £20 out of his wallet. "Will this cover it?"

"No. Really. Don't worry about it. It's OK. Accidents happen."

Chelsea pushed the money away. The juice spill was an accident. She knew she should be more laid-back about it, especially if she wanted to continue the good work she'd been doing with Adam so far. But she wouldn't have been surprised if that child had squeezed the juice carton deliberately. Chelsea did a bit more cursing as she flapped her skirt about in an attempt to dry it off a little. In the window seat, Lily was wide-eyed.

"She keeps on swearing."

"I can understand why," said Adam. He attempted another conciliatory smile. "It's not OK, is it? That dress was new."

Chelsea assured him once again that accidents happen, but also knew that her face when she looked at Lily did not quite match the levity of her pronouncement.

"I'm scared of that lady," said Lily suddenly, pointing an accusatory finger.

Chelsea gave a stiff grin. She half wanted that devil child to be scared. But she didn't want Adam to know it.

"She's frightening me!" Lily continued.

"Lily," said Adam. "Just sit still and be quiet, please. You've caused enough trouble already." He turned to Chelsea. "I am so, so sorry. I usually take a sip out of the carton first to make sure that doesn't happen, but—"

"It's OK," said Chelsea.

"She scared me," Lily insisted from her seat by the window. "She looked at me like a witch."

"Lily," Adam laughed but without much conviction. "Please don't be silly."

Within seconds, Lily was howling as though Chelsea had pinched her. As Adam employed every trick in the book to quieten his daughter down — even going so far as to stick two crayons up his nose, which seemed risky — it became clear that there was no chance that he and Chelsea would resume their conversation. Chelsea escaped to the loo to examine the borrowed dress for damage. She couldn't see much in the fluorescent light but she feared the worst.

Alone in the cubicle, Chelsea knuckled her forehead in frustration. She might have known her one chance at a flirtation in months would end in sticky disaster. But cruel fate wasn't quite finished with her yet.

At last the flight landed. Chelsea got to her feet to grab her handbag from the overhead locker as soon as the seatbelt lights were switched off. Adam jumped up too and practically wrestled the bag from her hands in an attempt to be chivalrous. As he did so, the unzipped bag went flying and the contents of Chelsea's hand luggage spewed half-way down the aisle. Adam picked up Chelsea's copy of *From Booty Call to Bride* and handed it back to her. But not without taking a quizzical look first. Self help. A very bad sign.

"Research," she said. "I work for a women's magazine."

Adam nodded but he didn't look convinced.

That was it, Chelsea told herself. The flirtation was officially done. She stuffed the book back into her bag.

Lily waved Chelsea off.

According to Jacqui, Chelsea should wait for the hotel bus to take her to the resort — a free transfer was included in the price of the holiday. But after such a fraught ending to the flight, there was no way Chelsea was going to wait around while the tour rep did ten head counts, got a different number every time and had to make a tannoy announcement for a pair of pensioners lost in baggage reclaim. Chelsea was going to take a taxi. Her shins were still sticky with blackcurrant juice, despite her having tried to wipe them clean with her ridiculously expensive Chanel eye make-up remover pads. The dress, too, needed to go straight to a dry-cleaner.

Oh, the dress. As she stood in the taxi queue, Chelsea was able to examine the skirt of the Mebus extravaganza more closely. Thankfully, the dress had a pattern, so the stain wasn't as obvious as it might have been had the fabric been plain, but Chelsea knew there was no way she would be able to sneak it back into the fashion cupboard as though nothing had happened. Apart from anything else, the spillage had left Chelsea smelling like some cheap bath foam: sweet and cloying as a jelly baby. She was actually starting to attract flies. And it was so hot in this place! Chelsea felt her make-up melting. Please let the cab have air-conditioning.

Chelsea texted her mother and sister as the taxi with no air-conditioning sped towards Playa Brava. The countryside rolled past in a relentless ribbon of dust, punctuated by the odd low white house and what seemed like hundreds of petrol stations. They passed a field where a group of forlorn-looking camels waited to be loaded with tourists after the *Lawrence of Arabia* experience. According to the taxi driver, who simply would not shut up, a camel ride was on every visitor to Lanzarote's list of "must-dos".

"Camels are very intelligent creatures," he said.

"Yes, yes," said Chelsea. She was too busy catching up on the emails that had come in while she was flying to ask exactly how camels showed their vast intelligence.

A text came through.

We're having a walk around the town, said her mother, but we'll try to be at the hotel when you arrive.

"Try?" Chelsea snorted. After all the effort she had made to come on this stupid trip. Using a whole week of her precious holiday time?

"You got a boyfriend?" the taxi driver asked, catching her eye in the rear-view mirror. "I show you the town if you like." The taxi driver had no front teeth.

When at last the taxi pulled up at the resort, Chelsea's first instinct was to say, "Are you sure this is the right place?" but she knew, with a sinking heart, that there was no mistake. The terrible pictures on the hotel's website had actually been rather flattering. Chelsea paid the taxi driver, declined to give him her phone number in exchange for a five per cent discount and stood on the pavement, surveying her home for the week ahead. What a dump. She looked up and down the street. Amusement arcades. Fast-food shops. A restaurant across the street promised chips with everything. Chelsea was only glad that her colleagues from the magazine couldn't see her now.

"I am in hell," Chelsea whispered to herself as, taking a deep breath, she stepped into the lobby of the Hotel Volcan.

CHAPTER
NINE

Ronnie

Ronnie was the only adult member of the Benson clan to be in the hotel at that moment. The rest of the family had gone to explore the town, but Jack wanted to stay by the pool and somebody had to keep an eye on him.

"Come in the pool with me, Mummy," Jack begged, but Ronnie was staying resolutely on dry land. She was, as Jack reminded her in an attempt to win her round to his point of view, already wearing her swimsuit, but Ronnie kept a sarong firmly tied round her waist and refused to budge from her sunlounger. She did not feel like stripping off, despite the fact that the mercury must be nudging forty degrees.

Ronnie hadn't felt much like stripping off in a long time. Not since Jack was born, When she had Sophie, the weight just fell off and she was soon back into her pre-pregnancy clothes, but with Jack, it had been different. Ronnie was a teenager when she became pregnant with Sophie. Her body was ready to be stretched beyond anything she might have imagined possible and yet spring straight back into shape within a fortnight. She was eight years older when she conceived Jack. Her life had changed so much in the meantime.

When you had a small child and no money, there was little to do but stay home and comfort-eat. Two children and no money? More of the same. Much, much more.

As a result, one of the things Ronnie had been dreading most about this holiday was having to wear a bathing suit in the vicinity of her stick-thin younger sister. That said, Chelsea hadn't always been the skinny one. When the sisters were children, Chelsea had been as soft and round as a Cabbage Patch doll. She'd hated sport, preferring instead to stay inside and read. When puberty came, Ronnie had quickly developed a model figure. A tiny hand-span waist complemented her new breasts, while Chelsea had continued to be, well, a little bit lumpen into her teenage years. There was one especially embarrassing moment when a neighbour who had heard that one of the Benson girls was pregnant had collared Chelsea on her way back from school and asked how many more months she had to go before the baby was born. There were tears when Chelsea got home that afternoon.

The situation reversed quite dramatically when Chelsea went off to university in London. Away from home and their mother's carb-heavy cooking for the first time, Chelsea had transformed herself. While the average fresher put on half a stone in the first year, Chelsea had done the exact opposite. The year in France her language degree required had brought about the final polish. When she got back from twelve months in Grenoble, no trace of the dumpy little girl who'd begged to borrow Ronnie's clothes remained.

Ronnie doubted very much that Chelsea would ever covet any of her clothes again. She certainly wouldn't covet Ronnie's body-control swimsuit, which seemed to be exercising about as much control over her body as a sleeping bag might have done. That was the other thing Ronnie was dreading: Chelsea's designer wardrobe.

Since Chelsea had been working on *Society* magazine, she'd been dressed like an oligarch's missus. Ronnie remembered when Chelsea turned up at Jack's third birthday party wearing a black Chanel jacket with her designer jeans. Genuine Chanel. Everything about it breathed quality, from the real horn buttons to the delicate little chain that weighted down the hem at the back. Anyone with half a brain could tell the difference between the Zara knock-offs all the girls in Coventry were wearing that year and this piece of authentic fashion art. While wearing it, Chelsea hadn't let her nephew or his preschool friends come anywhere near her for fear of their sticky little fingers. Eventually, unable to bear the tension any longer, Chelsea took the jacket off and put it in Ronnie's bedroom for safe keeping. Unfortunately, Fishy the cat, who had also been put in the bedroom to protect her from Jack and his marauding pals, made a bed of it, her claws pulling threads in the pristine camellia-embossed silk lining as she scrunched the fabric together to make it more comfortable. Chelsea had not seen the funny side.

Then there were the handbags. At the barbecue where they had last seen each other, Chelsea had been toting a real Louis Vuitton. Ronnie had looked it up on the Internet a couple of days later. Even second hand on eBay, those bags cost more than Ronnie earned in half a year. What would Chelsea think of Ronnie's beach bag, which had come free with a magazine several years before?

Then there were the shoes. Chelsea had a real pair of Louboutins long before the Wags even knew they wanted them. When both sisters were visiting their parents one Christmas — before they fell out, back when Chelsea still couldn't believe her luck that she'd landed a magazine job at all — Chelsea had let Ronnie try on her red-soled treasures. (Shoe size was the one size they still had in common.) Chelsea looked so nervous when Ronnie got her feet in them, as though the delicate stiletto heels might break under her weight, that any potential sisterly-bonding joy of the moment was extinguished in a puff of self-loathing. Ronnie kicked the petrol-blue patent shoes off seconds later, claiming they pinched her toes.

Though once upon a time they had made plans for a fabulous future together, Chelsea's figure, her clothes and her lifestyle were a million light years away from anything Ronnie could aspire to now. Chelsea wore Chanel and Prada and Louboutins, and went to cocktail parties where supermodels rubbed shoulders with movie stars. Her day job was to interview celebrities and review five-star spa resorts. Even Chelsea's voice had changed when she moved away from Coventry; these days, she had the polished vowels of a girl who'd spent her formative years at Cheltenham Ladies' College, rather than the local comprehensive she and Ronnie had actually attended. She'd once

74

joked that her colleagues assumed she was called Chelsea because she had been born in the smart London borough, and Ronnie could tell she was proud to have convinced them. There was no trace of the Midlands left in Chelsea's accent any more. There was no trace of Benson left . . .

Jacqui insisted that Ronnie and Chelsea would always have a special bond as sisters, but Ronnie had come to think that had they not been related, they would not have naturally become friends. Not these days. They moved in different circles. Different worlds.

"Mummy! Watch me!"

Jack broke into Ronnie's thoughts by demanding her attention for a half-dive into the pool, which basically involved pointing his hands above his head before jumping in feet first as usual. Ronnie felt her heart leap as her son sprang into the air before she could say, "Make sure it's deep enough!" Her heart stayed in her throat until Jack came up spluttering. When he could take a breath again, he gave his mother a huge grin.

"How was that?" he asked.

"Just like Tom Daley," Ronnie assured him. "You'll be in the next Olympic team."

Jack climbed out of the pool for another attempt. He was so happy. Why was it so hard to hang on to childish confidence and enthusiasm? If children knew what being an adult was like, they wouldn't bother to grow up at all.

A text arrived on Ronnie's phone. It was Chelsea.

Ronnie steeled herself for a meeting with the sister she hadn't seen in over two years.

CHAPTER
TEN

Chelsea

It was not the kind of welcome Chelsea had hoped for. Having imagined the whole family being there to greet her, she was disappointed to find just Ronnie and Jack in the advance party. Ronnie didn't seem exactly overjoyed to see her either. Having perceptibly stiffened in Chelsea's air-kissing embrace — "You've gone very media" — she gave Chelsea the usual once-over and immediately commented on her luggage.

"I bet that's the first time they've had Louis Vuitton on easyJet."

"And how are you?" asked Chelsea, to make a point.

"All right," said Ronnie. "You remember your nephew, Jack."

"Of course I remember my nephew."

"Well, it's been a long time."

Jack was hiding behind his mother's legs. Though he had talked about nothing but the imminent arrival of his aunt for the past twenty-four hours, now that she was here, he was suddenly shy.

"Hello, Jack."

Chelsea had forgotten how cute her nephew was, with his big eyes and white-blond hair. It was a shame that Ronnie had given him a thuggish buzz cut and he was dressed in a Coventry FC T-shirt four sizes too big for him. Chelsea bobbed down to greet him. She stuck out her hand. Jack stared at it.

"How are you?" Chelsea asked.

"Shaking hands is a bit posh for him," Ronnie suggested. "He's not a London child."

First reference to "fancy London ways": approximately ten seconds in.

"A hug, then?" Chelsea suggested. "Have you got a hug for your auntie?"

Jack tucked himself further behind his mother. His eyes were wide, as though he had never seen anything quite so exotic as his aunt before and the sight of her had rendered him speechless. When Chelsea told him she'd brought him a teddy bear (a last-minute airport purchase to make up for missing his birthday), he actually covered his eyes to lessen the intensity. Chelsea straightened up. She wasn't in the mood to try to coax Jack out from hiding. All she wanted was a shower and a nap. It felt like she'd been travelling for a week.

"He'll get used to you," said Ronnie.

"Sure. Where's everybody else?" Chelsea asked.

"They're exploring the town," said Ronnie. "Except for Granddad Bill. He's in the bar."

"I'll see him later," said Chelsea. She wasn't especially looking forward to seeing how far he'd declined in the two years since she'd last seen him and felt that a moment or two in her room first would make it easier. "Have you got my room key?"

Ronnie handed it over.

"Thanks," said Chelsea. "I guess I'll see you later."

"OK," said Ronnie. "We'll be by the main pool."

That was that. It had not been as painful as Chelsea had expected or as warm as she had hoped. Ronnie turned round to go. Chelsea picked up her bag and headed in the opposite direction, for the lift. Before she got that far, however, she was almost knocked off her feet by a low-flying missile. Jack had decided he would give his aunt a hug of welcome after all. He wrapped himself round her legs and looked up at her in adoration. Chelsea closed her eyes and sighed inwardly as he buried his pool-damp head in her skirt. Blackcurrant juice and now wet hair. Perfect. Just perfect. Why didn't people keep children on leads?

"I'm really happy you're here, Auntie Chelsea," Jack told her with great sincerity. "Now that you're here, I've got someone to play with."

Not if I can help it, thought Chelsea, as she peeled Jack off her thighs. After the plane ride over, she had resolved to steer well clear of the under-tens. "Better catch up with your mum," was what she said out loud.

At last, twenty-four hours later than planned, Chelsea pushed open the door to her hotel room. First impression: bad. It was small, cheaply furnished and smelly. The ensuite bathroom was a former cupboard that had been hastily converted into a "wet room". The toilet roll had unravelled and was soaking up the dampness greedily. Whoever invented wet rooms should be shot, Chelsea observed. In a wet room.

Next, Chelsea examined a painting of a sad-eyed donkey on the wall between the twin beds. Less "Conran" than "car-boot sale". There was no balcony. No proper view.

She opened the wardrobe. There were just three coat hangers, left behind by previous guests. Chelsea had to hang her favourite summer dress — a white smocked affair by Chloé — from a plastic hanger that bore the legend "6–7 years". She opened a drawer to find a space for her underwear, but quickly thought better of it as a musty aroma billowed out. Even if she wasn't going to be getting any action, she didn't want her lingerie to smell as though it belonged in a museum.

Having given up on unpacking her case, Chelsea observed the twin beds with their thin, well-worn sheets and scratchy-looking blankets. Bed bugs, was the first thought that sprang to mind here. There were already faint firework splatters of red on the walls where several dozen mosquitoes must have met their deaths in seasons past. Chelsea pulled back the covers of the bed that looked less lumpy. She moved quickly, dreading what might lie beneath.

Oh, it was awful. The pillow had the look of the Turin Shroud about it, stained by the sweat and dribble of heaven only knew how many hotel guests over the years. The thought of having to put her head on it made Chelsea shiver with misery. What was she doing here? Why hadn't she just said she was too busy at work to spare a week? God knows she really was too busy at work. Oh well. There was not much she could do about it now.

At the very least, Chelsea had consoled herself when she bowed to the inevitable and agreed to this trip, she could get a bit of a suntan. Though she had embraced the fashion for alabaster-pale skin over the winter months — it was rare for Chelsea to feel naturally fashionable — she could not quite bring herself to stay deathly white for the whole summer. Not when she was still carrying six pounds more than she thought she ought to be.

Though her packing had been somewhat rushed, Chelsea had managed to bring six bikinis. Earlier that month, *Society* had run an article that said that the ideal summer wardrobe should contain a bikini for every day of the week. Preferably two a day, so you could change into a new, dry bikini after swimming. The readers of *Society* didn't go to lunch with wet bottoms.

In her horrible room, Chelsea changed into a pale blue bikini by Eres. Like the dress, this bikini was "borrowed" from the fashion cupboard. It had been too big for the model in the bikini spread it was picked out for, but on Chelsea it was just right. She felt a little surge of happiness as she checked her reflection and noted that not having eaten anything but a burger without the bun since the previous day, her stomach was pretty well perfectly flat.

Unfortunately, Chelsea knew the second she stepped out through the double doors that packing her fabulous bikini wardrobe had been an absolute waste of time. The pool was surrounded by men, and women, in football shirts. No one above the age of twelve was able to see their own toes for the enormous stomachs they sported, and nobody seemed at all bothered. A man the size of a killer whale belly-flopped into the pool as Chelsea walked by, splashing her from head to toe.

"Sorry, love," he said. "You might as well jump right in now, though, eh? I'll catch you."

Chelsea pretended not to have heard him. She just wiped her face dry and carried on. The killer whale confirmed that there was going to be no chance whatsoever of a holiday romance here. Not at the Hotel Volcan.

Chelsea scanned the poolside for her family. She saw them at last arranged around the five sunloungers closest to the bar. Ronnie was hunched over a gossip mag. Beside her sat Sophie, who looked like her mother seen in a fun-house mirror. The elongating type. She was wearing a voluminous black T-shirt that did nothing for her at all. Seeing Chelsea arrive, Ronnie and Sophie managed identical snorts of greeting before Ronnie went back to reading and Sophie went back to texting. Mark was asleep. Jack was once again shy. He watched Chelsea from behind a parasol stand.

Still, at least Chelsea's parents seemed completely thrilled to see her. Her mother leapt up to grab her for a cuddle, and her father pinched her cheeks.

"Won't be able to do that to you much longer," he said.

"You should probably have stopped fifteen years ago," said Chelsea.

"We're just so glad you're here at last," said Jacqui.

"Wouldn't have missed it for the world," Chelsea lied.

"Fancy a beer, love?" asked her father. "I'm going to the bar."

"Not a beer, Dad."

"One of those cocktails, then? With an umbrella in? And a cherry?"

"Just sparkling mineral water, please," Chelsea replied.

"Very posh," said Dave. "Is that what they have down in London?"

"London ways" reference number two.

"Where's Granddad Bill?" Chelsea asked her mother.

"Watching Sky Sports," said Jacqui. "Oooh. That's a lovely kaftan you're wearing. Did I see that in Next?"

"Something like that," said Chelsea. If only Jacqui knew. Chelsea could have bought just about everything in the Next catalogue for the price of that one piece of Melissa Odabash.

Jacqui cooed over the rest of her daughter's outfit: her bikini, her sun hat, her custom Havaianas. "You always dress so well," she said. "Even by the pool. That'll be that magazine's influence, I suppose. So what do you think of the hotel, then? I know it's not up to your usual fancy London standards, but . . ."

From the corner of her eye, Chelsea noticed Ronnie perk up and tune in to the conversation. As if Chelsea was going to say something bad. Chelsea certainly felt bad. Here she was, the London snob, come to pass judgement on them all.

"Mum, it's lovely. Really. It's perfect." Another lie.

"It's all right, isn't it? For the money, I mean. I know you would normally stay somewhere a little more—"

"It's great," said Chelsea. Her mother's insistence on pointing out that this was not Chelsea's usual scene was getting painful.

"How's your room?" Jacqui asked.

"Lovely," Chelsea insisted. "Plenty of space. Comfortable bed. It will suit me just fine."

"We've got one of those wet rooms. Have you got one? Dead fancy."

"Yes," said Chelsea. "They're very trendy. All the rage in London."

From the corner of her eye, Chelsea noticed Ronnie's mouth twitch in amusement.

Dave returned from the bar with the mineral water.

"So, come on, Chelsea, tell us how come you missed your plane," he said.

"I slept through my alarm."

"Slept through your alarm?" Jacqui tutted.

"Up drinking the night before?" Dave suggested.

"She won't have been drinking! She's been working too hard," said Jacqui. "I told your sister you'd have been working too hard. You don't take proper care of yourself, you don't." Jacqui tucked a stray strand of hair behind Chelsea's ear. The gesture, which was so reminiscent of her childhood, brought a sudden prickle to Chelsea's eyes. She quickly sniffed it back.

"I do, Mum. Of course I do. But I was actually only ten minutes late to the airport, FYI, Dad. There was a massive queue. Only two check-in desks open. I bet half the people waiting missed their flights. They do it deliberately so you have to fork out for another ticket."

"You didn't have to buy another ticket?" Jacqui breathed.

"I got it on my Air Miles," Chelsea lied again. The last thing she wanted was for her mother to offer to pay the difference. Chelsea knew her parents didn't make much in their respective jobs as a school cook and a part-time delivery driver. She was embarrassed that she'd let them pay for the trip at all. But then she didn't actually get paid that much either. Not by London standards.

"Well, you're here now and it's lovely to see you," said Jacqui. "We don't see enough of you by half. Your dad and I understand that you're busy down there in London, but you know you can come home whenever you want, don't you? There's always a room for you. The bed is always made up."

"Of course."

"We don't like not being able to look after you from time to time, like we do for your sister. I worry that you work too hard. Are you sure you're eating properly? You're looking very thin."

"Am I?" Chelsea asked.

"Yes, you are. Your hip bones are jutting out. I can see your ribs. You look like a xylophone."

Jacqui's eyebrows were knitted with worry, but Jacqui's concern was Chelsea's compliment. Chelsea hugged the news that she was looking thin close, even as she assured her mother that she always ate three good meals a day. Though three good meals a day

84

would turn out to be very hard to come by at the Hotel Volcan.

CHAPTER
ELEVEN

Chelsea

That night, the Bensons had their first meal as a complete family since Granddad Bill's eighty-third birthday party and the sisterly estrangement that had ensued.

The Hotel Volcan had three restaurants. Guests on a half-board package, such as the Benson family were on that week, could choose to eat at any one of them each evening. Jacqui had chosen the hotel's "traditional" restaurant, the Jolly Pirate. As far as Chelsea could tell, it was traditional in the sense that the restaurant catered specially for the British holidaymakers in the Hotel Volcan's clientele. There was not so much as a Spanish omelette on the menu which promised "chips with everything". What an indictment of Brits abroad, was Chelsea's thought as she picked up the menu and saw what the locals thought the British ate: chips, chips and more chips.

Sitting down between her sister and her nephew, on a broken plastic seat that threatened menace to her thighs each time she shifted, Chelsea couldn't see a single thing she wanted to order.

"You're allowed three courses every night," said Dave. "That's what we've paid for. And as much salad and side dishes as you can eat from the buffet bar. Might as well get your money's worth."

Unwilling to upset her father or seem ungrateful, Chelsea eventually ordered tomato soup followed by the fish and chips. At least she could pick the fish out of the batter. She said she would decide on a pudding later, hoping that no one would notice if she didn't. On the other side of the table, Sophie looked on the verge of tears.

"You know I'm a vegetarian," she told her mother. "I only want the chips."

"You'll get anorexic," Ronnie told her. "You read too many of those stupid magazines." As she said that, Ronnie cast a dark look towards Chelsea. It was starting already. Chelsea wondered how many times Ronnie would get a dig in about her job before the holiday was over.

"In any case," Ronnie continued, "you can't be a vegetarian and still eat your dad's bacon sandwiches."

"That's the only meat I can eat!" Sophie protested. "Everything else makes me feel sick."

"I don't suppose this is the kind of food you eat in London, is it?" Having failed to persuade Sophie to order a burger, Ronnie suddenly turned her attention to Chelsea.

"Not often," said Chelsea.

"Neither do we," Ronnie snapped back. "We don't eat chips every night, do we, Mark?"

"I wasn't suggesting you did," said Chelsea.

"It's what everybody eats here. There isn't any choice."

"Which is exactly why this place wasn't on my holiday wish list," said Chelsea, low enough so that she thought no one would hear.

Ronnie heard. "I'm sure it wasn't," she hissed back. "You've already managed to get out of one night. And I know it may not be the kind of holiday a *Society* reader would go on, but Mum and Dad saved for years to pay for this trip, so you might at least pretend to be grateful. I hear you didn't exactly fall over yourself to offer to pay your share."

"And you did?" said Chelsea.

"I would have—"

"And so would I."

"Are you all right down that end of the table, girls?" Jacqui called down to them.

Ronnie and Chelsea turned to their mother with big smiles.

"Yes, Mum," they chorused in unison.

Oblivious to the simmering resentments among the younger members of his family, Granddad Bill was on fine form. He sat at the head of the table and used his best Spanish on the waitress.

"Grassy-arse!" He elbowed Jack in the ribs. "Grassy-*arse*! Fancy having 'arse' as your word for 'thank you'."

"You said 'arse'," said Jack, with horrified delight.

"Granddad," Ronnie reprimanded him, "Jack doesn't need encouraging."

"Tell her, Jack," Granddad Bill nudged him. "Say it loud."

"Grassy-arse!" Jack shouted at the top of his voice.
"Jack!"

"I'm only learning Spanish," was Jack's defence.

"Bill," said Jacqui, in an attempt to change the subject, "are you sure you want a steak? You wouldn't prefer something a bit softer? You know, for your teeth?"

Bill responded by taking his false teeth right out. He clicked them above his head like castanets.

"Look at this, Jack," he mumbled without the benefit of dentition. "We're on a Spanish island here. *Olé!*" He got to his feet and danced a short flamenco before stumbling over his chair and ending up on his backside. Mark and Dave leapt to haul Bill back up from the floor.

While all this was going on, Chelsea wanted to put her forehead on the table and weep. The waitress returned with their order. Chelsea gave her an embarrassed smile.

"*Gracias*," said Chelsea, hoping she'd got the pronunciation right. She knew the locals in the Canaries spoke a very different Spanish from the people in Madrid. "I'm sorry our Spanish isn't great," she added for good measure.

"That's OK," said the waitress. "Neither is mine. I'm from Poland. The fish and chips is for you, right?"

Chelsea stared at the plate before her. The batter was radioactive orange. A teaspoon of Day-Glo mushy peas garnished a potato-chip mountain that could have fed a whole village. All around her, other holidaymakers were tucking in with relish. No wonder they were all

"Matalan sizes", as the X-ray-thin *Society* magazine girls nastily referred to anyone over a sample-size eight. While Ronnie berated Sophie for failing to clear her plate, Chelsea could feel Sophie's pain.

"Grassy-arse!" Bill continued to chime to his granddaughter's decreasing amusement. Even Jack was starting to look slightly embarrassed. Bill hadn't been such an idiot two years earlier, had he? Chelsea wondered when her grandfather had turned from a loveable and elegant elderly man into an annoying old nutter. The change was alarming. What was with the Coventry FC shirt and the slippers? There was a time when Granddad Bill wouldn't have been seen outside the house without his regimental tie. Now he was dressed like a refugee from a charity shop, and his exclamations were drawing attention from everyone in the pirate-themed dining room. The wrong kind of attention.

Meanwhile, Dave, Chelsea's father, was complaining about his steak. It had come with some sort of gravy that definitely wasn't the Bisto he was used to.

"I can't touch it. There are bits in it," he explained to his wife.

"I think it's just onion, love," said Jacqui.

"I can't eat onion. You know I can't eat onion, Jax. It'll only give me heartburn."

The Polish waitress was called over. She took the plate away and promised the chef would start again from scratch. Chelsea imagined the waitress rinsing the steak under a tap in the kitchen and bringing it straight back out.

Jacqui was complaining now. She would deign to try the dodgy continental gravy with its daring vegetable bits, but her steak wasn't hot enough.

"And it isn't properly cooked," Jacqui told the patient waitress. "It's still pink on the inside. Look."

"You asked for medium," the waitress reminded her.

The waitress wasn't to know that the Benson family's idea of "medium" was the average professional chef's idea of "cremated".

Who are these people? Chelsea asked herself, as her mother marvelled at the lack of "basic cooking skills" found in the hotel restaurant's kitchen, her father downed half a pint and belched to make room for the rest, her grandfather sang a loud, lewd song about loose knicker elastic, while her sister tried to force-feed her niece half a ketchup-smothered burger in the name of "health".

Chelsea brought her focus back to the table just in time to hear, "Well, I'm sure that's how they do it in London, but they've got much more money than we have. We can't all have Chanel tea towels like auntie Chelsea."

"Chanel tea towels," said Chelsea. "I know several people who would buy one."

It was the closest Chelsea would come to making a joke that night.

"Well, if you've got money to burn," Ronnie sniped, "you could use some of your old Prada vests for dusters. Or rather, get your cleaner to use them. Don't want to ruin your manicure, eh?"

Chelsea didn't bother to protest her lack of domestic staff. Or her lack of manicure, for that matter.

Chelsea had known this would happen. When she was away from her family, in London, she could kid herself she was doing OK. Now that she was back with them, she felt just as she had done at the age of sixteen. Perhaps how Sophie was feeling right now.

Chelsea thought she had escaped when she went to university, but sitting here now, she realised she hadn't made it far. She'd swapped a council house in Coventry for a studio flat with chronic damp in Stockwell. Every night she ran the gauntlet of drug dealers and dropouts on her way home from the Tube. She had an ancient fridge that shook the whole house when it rattled. She had no car. The fabulous wardrobe her sister was now belittling was the only thing she had to show for her hard work, and most of that was borrowed. Chelsea's family had no idea that the remuneration at *Society* reflected the title's "prestige" and thus was little more than the minimum wage. It was pin money for the heiresses who worked there while they waited to marry well, pop out two kids and get a Labrador. Heiresses like her ex-boyfriend Colin's new fiancée, because of course he'd had to pick an heiress.

The Polish waitress reappeared to clear away the plates.

"Grassy-arse," said Bill. Again.

The waitress's smile said, "If I didn't need this job, I would kill you all."

"Put me out of my misery while you're at it," said Chelsea's smile in return.

"I will never escape," said Chelsea's inner teenage self, still alive and kicking beneath her new accent and the London polish her family found so funny. "These people who have come all the way to a Spanish island off the coast of North Africa to eat exactly the same food they eat at home will always define me."

With her Louis Vuitton bag tucked between her feet, Chelsea had never in her life wanted less to be a Benson.

CHAPTER
TWELVE

Bill

Tired from a long day of travelling and the horror of her first family dinner in two years, before long Chelsea was yawning. Sophie and Jacqui quickly followed suit. Jack snuggled up against his grandmother as he ate a huge ice-cream sundae. He was soon struggling to keep his eyes open.

"Time for bed," Jacqui announced as the clock struck ten. Both her daughters greeted her words with silent relief. They had been waiting for Jacqui, as the family matriarch, to make the first move to end the excruciating evening. Ronnie and Chelsea had hardly addressed a word to each other for the past hour, not since the "Prada dusters" wisecrack. Sophie couldn't wait to get to her room to text her best friend, despite the fact they had been texting each other all evening already. Mark said he'd carry Jack upstairs. Only Bill wanted to party on.

Unfortunately, like Jack, Bill could not be left on his own. Dave had to keep Bill company while the old man had a nightcap. Jacqui insisted her husband stay with his father. The last thing they needed was for Bill to drink until he fell off a barstool. He was in that kind of mood, Jacqui could tell.

Thankfully, the bar was relatively quiet. Most of the hotel's guests retired to their rooms straight after dinner to put the children to bed. Hotel Volcan was very much a family establishment. It prided itself on being such. Nevertheless, along the bar from Dave and Bill, two distinctly un-motherly women shared a bottle of rosé wine. Dave didn't really notice them until Bill commented that the blonder of the two had a "cleavage like the flippin' Grand Canyon".

"Look, look." Bill nudged Dave with all the subtlety of a Benny Hill sketch. "You could park a bicycle . . ."

Dave studied the bottom of his glass. His father had made his comment loudly enough for the whole hotel to hear. The two women at the bar had definitely heard it.

"Give it a rest, Dad. Please."

Unfortunately, there was no chance of that.

"I haven't seen a cleavage of that quality since Carol Roberts moved in next door."

Dave nodded in agreement at the memory of his father's former neighbour and hoped that would be the end of the conversation.

But worse was to come.

"That's a beautiful dress you're almost wearing," said Bill, in an attempt to strike up a direct conversation with his fellow bar-fly. Unsurprisingly, the blonde woman looked affronted by Bill's cack-handed compliment. She screwed up her nose as though she had smelt something bad and turned back towards her companion with an audible tut.

"Dad, I think those ladies want to keep themselves to themselves."

Bill had become a liability where women were concerned. Once upon a time, he had been the perfect gentleman: opening doors, carrying shopping, unfailingly correct and polite. Jacqui had read something somewhere that said certain types of dementia were accompanied by a lowering of inhibitions. Dave suggested that Bill had just decided he was too old to be polite, but that evening in particular — after what seemed like three hours of "grassy-arse" — Dave knew his wife was right. Bill wasn't himself any more. They were losing him.

"I was only saying that—"

"You can't say that sort of thing, Dad," Dave interrupted him before he could get the words out.

"Bloody PC brigade," said Bill. "If you can't tell a woman she's got a lovely chest—"

"Right. That's it." Dave took the glass from Bill's hand. "Time for bed."

"But I haven't finished my drink yet."

Dave stood up and started helping — or rather manhandling — his father down from his stool. Old age had left Bill too frail to struggle.

"Come on, son. Just one more pint."

"We'll have another one tomorrow, Dad. I promise."

In his hurry to get out of there, Dave accidentally left a fifty-euro note instead of a five for the barman.

With Bill and Dave gone, Gloria Smith, the woman with the "lovely chest", felt free to vent her outrage.

Her holiday companion, Lesley Beard, a woman without such obvious charms as Gloria's blonde locks and magnificent cleavage, nodded in disgusted agreement as Gloria complained to the barman that a woman should be able to have a drink without facing such harassment, no matter what she was wearing. The barman agreed that a proper gentleman would be able to focus on a woman's personality rather than her body. The barman was fishing for tips.

"Who does that disgraceful old man think he is?" Gloria asked no one in particular.

"He's a lottery winner," said the barman.

"What?"

Their interest suddenly piqued, Gloria and Lesley leant over the bar to hear more.

"I hear him say it," the barman confirmed. "He say it all the time. Every time I talk to him, he say he win the lottery."

"Never," Gloria breathed.

Gloria and Lesley shared a look.

"Oh yes. That's why he bring his whole family here. They have whole floor in the hotel for themselves."

"Well, I don't believe it," said Lesley. "I'd never have guessed. He's obviously not spent his winnings on his wardrobe. But he's brought his whole family here, you say?"

"Oh yes. They take eight rooms," said the barman erroneously. "And that old man, he pay for everything. Everything. All the rooms. All the beers. Everything they like. And they drink all the day. Believe me. I have to serve them. And look at this. Fifty euros tip on an eight-euro bill."

"It must be true," said Gloria. "I wonder how much he won?"

"One of the granddaughters," the barman continued, "she is carrying a *Louis Vuitton* handbag. I know. My brother, he work in Louis Vuitton in Marbella. That bag, he tell me, it cost as much as my house."

"I did see that bag," said Lesley. "It was in my magazine. Madonna's got one. I assumed that girl was carrying a fake."

"No, it's real," the barman confirmed. "She put it on the bar earlier on. I had real close look. I know all the signs of the designer. Is no mistake."

"Well, well, well," said Gloria. "A genuine lottery winner here in Hotel Volcan. And he said I looked good in my dress . . ."

"He might at least have offered to buy you a drink," Lesley pointed out.

"He don't just want to splash his cash around. That way, you get gold-diggers," said the barman wisely.

"A good point," said Gloria. "A man like that has got to be very careful. He needs to know a woman likes him for himself, not just for the money. He's obviously a simple man of classic tastes and he must find it hard dealing with the unwanted attention such unexpected wealth brings. Poor chap."

From disgusting old man to an object of empathy in a matter of moments. Gloria did not seem in the least bit uncomfortable with her sudden and dramatic change of heart.

"How long's he staying here?" Gloria asked the barman. "Do you know?"

"I think he's staying for the whole summer," said the barman. In reality, he didn't have a clue, but in Gloria's eyes the idea of such a long stay added yet more weight to the compelling picture of Bill Benson as bona fide lottery winner. How else could his entire family afford to take so much time off work? If they ever had worked, thought Gloria unkindly. Apart from the one with the Louis Vuitton handbag, they looked like a right bunch of benefit scroungers.

"The whole summer? Plenty of time to get to know him properly, then," Gloria concluded. Lesley gawped. The disgusting old man had suddenly become a most eligible catch indeed.

CHAPTER
THIRTEEN

Ronnie

While Bill was terrorising the ladies in the bar, Ronnie lay awake in bed. Though she had felt so tired towards the end of dinner she could barely keep her head out of her plate, now she could not sleep at all. The events of the past two days were buzzing round in her head. Sophie's stroppiness about the food and the palaver over the bedrooms. Mark starting drinking at eleven in the morning. Granddad Bill's embarrassing behaviour. Her own humiliation when it was time to put her swimming costume on. Chelsea's arrival . . .

Ronnie might have known what it would be like when Chelsea finally deigned to show up, wafting in like she was Jackie Kennedy with her ballet flats and her big sunglasses and her posh designer handbag dangling from her elbow. She was the prodigal daughter. Josephine in a Technicolor sundress. Ronnie knew from Jacqui that Chelsea hadn't been to Coventry in over a year but having finally shown her face, she was the favourite child once more and Ronnie was left on the sidelines, feeling and looking like the fatted calf.

How aloof Chelsea had been. She had looked pained from the moment Ronnie first saw her standing in the lobby, regarding the other holidaymakers as though they were on day release from prison. Ronnie half expected Chelsea to clutch a handkerchief to her nose to avoid breathing in their chavvy germs. The way she tried to shake hands with Jack was excruciating. Any normal woman would have given the poor boy a cuddle. It didn't get any better. It had broken Ronnie's heart to see Jack try and fail to engage Chelsea in conversation all afternoon and evening. She hadn't even looked up from her iPhone to see him do his "best ever" dive. And how about the way she had just raised an eyebrow when Sophie went into meltdown over the menu in the Jolly Pirate? Any caring aunt would have backed Ronnie up when she insisted Sophie had to eat more than just chips. Not that Chelsea was much better than Sophie. She had picked at her food as though it was poison. Ronnie knew their mother had noticed and would take it personally. The food at the Hotel Volcan was not good enough for someone like Chelsea, whose body wasn't just a temple; it was the fricking Taj Mahal.

As Ronnie had feared, Chelsea did not look as though she had just turned thirty. Chelsea was as slim as a breadstick. Her hair looked expensively coloured. Her skin was perfectly smooth and entirely unlined, though maybe that was down to Botox. In the edition of *Society* Ronnie had flicked through in the doctor's waiting room, she'd found an article written by her sister saying you should start doing Botox in your mid-twenties to ensure that lines never formed in the first place. Ronnie had no doubt that Chelsea would be taking her own advice. Perhaps that was why she couldn't raise a smile for poor Jack. And how about Chelsea's holiday wardrobe? In that blue bikini, Chelsea knew she had a better body than any other guest at the hotel. There was absolutely no chance Ronnie would take her sarong off once Chelsea had arrived.

It was agony to sit by that pool and be unable to jump in, but it wasn't just Chelsea that Ronnie felt like hiding from. Ronnie had heard two young guys in the bar talking about a "whale" who had almost emptied the pool of water when she dived in. She did not want them to say the same about her. She just wanted to stay out of their line of sight. Under the radar. Safe.

Did Mark fancy Chelsea? Earlier that evening, when Ronnie had commented that her sister was in "good shape", Mark had said, "She's a bit thin," but did he really mean that? It wasn't possible to be too thin, was it? Whatever he thought of Chelsea, Mark certainly didn't seem to fancy Ronnie any more. Within minutes of getting back to their room that night he was asleep. Or pretending to be. Ronnie had forgotten the last time he had cuddled up to her in bed. There had been times when he couldn't seem to get enough of her. Increasingly of late, however, Ronnie felt as though they were just lodgers in the same house. Ronnie worried that Mark would get fed up and start to look elsewhere, but she herself would never initiate sex any more for fear of being actively rejected. She couldn't bear that on top of everything else.

Mark rolled onto his back. In just a few moments he would start to snore. Tonight would be worse than usual because he had had at least four pints of lager with dinner and those were just the ones Ronnie had counted. He'd been drinking by the pool since eleven. Ronnie had told him before that his snoring got worse the more he drank, and she was the one who had to suffer — he slept through it, after all — but he still had not tried to cut down his intake in any way. If it didn't matter to him that she lay awake all night, then why should she be surprised that he didn't seem to want to make love to her any more?

She looked at Mark's profile, silhouetted by the light coming in from the pool outside. Even when his snoring was as loud as a Jumbo coming in to land, he seemed so utterly at peace. In sleep, he looked somehow younger too, as though the cares of the past few years had fallen away and he was once again the cheeky teenage apprentice she had fallen so deeply in love with. Ronnie felt a sudden stab of affection for him. She remembered the young man — still a teenager himself — who had thrown himself into parenthood so fully and so lovingly when Ronnie herself was finding it such a struggle. Just then he gave a snort and rolled over, taking the whole of the thin cotton sheet with him so that Ronnie was left naked but for the enormous jersey nightshirt she always wore to bed these days. Her mum-wear. Her camouflage. Ronnie shook her head. This was not the life she had signed up for. She wanted her life to be like Chelsea's.

But what was a life like Chelsea's really like? Alone in her room, Chelsea knelt over the toilet that wouldn't take toilet paper and flushed away that disgustingly carb-heavy dinner at last.

CHAPTER
FOURTEEN

Ronnie

Monday

As it happened, Chelsea was not the only member of the Benson family who would spend part of that night at the Hotel Volcan throwing up. Having finally managed to drop off, Ronnie woke again just half an hour later with tremendous stomach cramps. They were almost as bad as being in labour. Each violent contraction of her bowels knocked the breath right out of her body. Something was obviously going very badly wrong.

Ronnie hauled herself out of bed in a panic. Her stomach hurt so much she could hardly see straight. It could only be appendicitis. When she blundered to the bathroom, however, she discovered that Mark was already in there, kneeling on the floor in front of the toilet, groaning like a wounded bull elephant. He refused to give up his position for his wife.

"I can't," he said. "I just can't."

"But I need to . . ."

Mark waved her away.

Ronnie had no choice but to throw up in the basin. She was both impressed and frightened by the amount that came out in one go. Had she really eaten that much? What was going on? Mark was having a similarly awful time of it. Whenever he tried to get up from the cold white floor tiles, he had to sit straight back down again.

"At least it isn't coming from both ends," he managed to joke during a brief moment of respite.

And then it was . . .

"For heaven's sake, Mark," Ronnie begged him as he went from kneeling in front of the toilet to sitting on it, eyes scrunched tightly shut as his intestines rebelled. "I need to use that thing too."

"Use the basin," Mark instructed her.

"I can't . . . You've got to—"

"I'm not moving."

Ronnie sank down on the bidet in defeat.

"You utter, utter—"

Worse was to come. It wasn't long before Ronnie heard a faint knocking on the door.

"You get it," she said.

"I can't move," said Mark.

"I can't move either!"

"Mummy!" a child's voice called in the corridor. "Mummy! Mummm-eeeeee!" Compelled by motherly instinct, Ronnie had no choice but to answer.

Half sobbing, she staggered to the door and opened it to find Jack, looking terribly grave.

"Mummy, Sophie won't stop being sick," he said.

Though she herself was drenched in cold sweat and could barely stand, Ronnie had to follow Jack into the children's bedroom next door. Sophie was sitting on the very end of the double bed she'd been sharing with her brother, crying like it was the end of the world. She hadn't even managed to get as far as the bathroom. What little she had eaten of her all-inclusive dinner was splattered across the green tiled floor.

"Mum," she whispered, "I think I'm dying."

"You're not dying," Ronnie promised her, as she tried not to heave at the sight of so much more sick.

"It's like *28 Days Later*," said Mark, when he felt well enough to stand and join his wife in surveying the carnage in the children's room.

"We must have eaten something funny," Sophie suggested when she heard she wasn't the only one evacuating dinner.

"Too right. I'm going to sue this bloody hotel," was Ronnie's response. "I bet they've been reheating that buffet all week." Then she covered her mouth and made a dash for the bathroom again.

Jack perched on the wide windowsill, with his legs well clear of his sister's vomit. He had his arms wrapped tightly round himself to make up for the fact that everyone else was too covered in puke to give him the hug he really needed.

"I'm frightened," he said to his father. "What's wrong with you and Mummy?"

"It's just a little tummy upset," said Mark with a queasy smile. "We're all going to be perfectly fine."

Jack could be forgiven for thinking it didn't look that way. In the corner by the door, Sophie had rolled herself into a ball round the wastepaper basket, which was unfortunately made of raffia and, as such, was far from being the ideal barf receptacle.

"For heaven's sake, use this carrier bag," Mark suggested, handing her the Hollister carrier that had formed part of Sophie's luggage.

"No way," said Sophie. That bag was a totem for her. It was proof that she owned something cool, even if it had been bought in the sale. She wasn't going to waste it. She wasn't *that* ill.

"But—" Just as Mark was about to point out the obvious folly of a barf bucket with great big holes in it, Sophie discovered its limitations for herself, getting sick all over her favourite pyjamas. Seeing it happen, Jack jumped down from the windowsill and started to have a proper freak-out, skipping from one foot to the other as though the whole room was swimming in vomit.

"For God's sake, Mark, take him to Mum's room," Ronnie called from her place on the bathroom floor. The echo chamber of the toilet bowl made her voice sound subterranean.

Mark, who had managed to stay remarkably clean, picked Jack up and carried him down the corridor. Alas, the scene in Dave and Jacqui's room was not an awful lot better. Dave was curled up on the bed in the foetal position. Jacqui was next door, trying desperately hard to make sure that Bill stayed in his en-suite bathroom until the danger had passed. All three of them were also afflicted.

"We must all have food poisoning," Jacqui groaned. "Did you have the prawn cocktail, Mark? I bet it was the prawns."

"I didn't have the prawns," said Jack. That seemed to confirm it. He was the only one who wasn't ill.

"Ronnie says can you take him?" Mark asked.

He held Jack out in Jacqui's direction.

"Do I look like I can take him? You'll have to take him down to Chelsea," Jacqui said. "She might still be OK. She won't have touched the prawn cocktail. She hardly ate a thing."

"God, please let her be all right," said Mark, who felt another wave of horror coming on. "Which is her room?"

"She's near the lift."

Jack, thankfully, knew the way, and further cause for thanks, Chelsea was unafflicted. Having vomited to order for her own reasons before the bugs in the hotel food started to act, she had escaped the very worst of the sickness that was bringing everyone else down. She felt no more ill than she would have expected to feel after four glasses of the hotel's non-specific house red. Still, she took a little while to open her door, having to find a place to hide *From Booty Call to Bride* first.

"Hurry up!" Mark hammered on the door.

"What's happening?" asked Chelsea as she observed Mark's grey face. "You don't look very well."

"I'm not. None of us is. You've got to take him."

"Who?" For a moment, Chelsea was confused.

"Me."

Mark pushed Jack ahead of him. Jack gazed up at his aunt with his big blue eyes as though he were a Victorian orphan and she his last chance of staying out of the workhouse. Chelsea looked down upon him as if he were an urchin covered in coal dust and snot and she had no intention of letting him and his dirty feet into the manor.

"What?"

"He's going to have to sleep in here with you," Mark persisted.

"Won't he be happier with his sister?"

"He can't. Please, Chels. We're all ill. Me. Ronnie. Bill. Your mum and dad. His sister's ill too. There's puke all over their bedroom floor. He needs to sleep in here while we get everything cleaned up."

"It's true," said Jack. "Sophie's puking, and Mum's got the shits."

"Jack," Mark and Chelsea said in unison.

"Please," begged Mark. "I need to get back and help Ronnie. Sophie's in a right state, but Jack's all right. Being with you is his best chance of staying that way. You've got to take him. He'll be good."

"I *will* be good," Jack confirmed.

Chelsea looked unconvinced.

"Please, Chelsea . . ."

With his pallid face and quavering voice, Mark endowed the moment with near-apocalyptic portent. Meanwhile, Jack was wavering between seeming suitably upset at his parents' sickness and being extraordinarily excited at the thought of getting to stay with his aunt as a result. He had been trying to get her attention all evening, telling her his best jokes, explaining *Doctor Who*, asking her about her favourite animals. Nothing seemed to interest her. Was she softening now? It seemed she might be. Jack piled on

110

the pressure by making his eyes big and round like a puppy's. He waggled the teddy bear she had bought for him in her direction.

"I'll be so good you won't even notice me," he promised.

"Oh," said Chelsea. "All right."

She opened her door wide enough for Jack to step inside.

And that is how Jack ended up spending the night with his auntie Chelsea. He crawled into the spare twin bed, which Chelsea had been using as a makeshift open wardrobe, and pulled the scratchy sheet up to his neck. Mark tucked the new teddy in beside him before making a swift exit.

"I can't stay in my room, because it smells of sick," Jack explained. "Sick isn't very nice, is it?"

Chelsea had to agree with him.

"Well, there's no sick in here. Now, you'd better get some sleep," she said.

"I think I'd prefer it if you talked to me for a bit," Jack told her. "I've been having a very worrying time tonight."

Where did he get a phrase like that from? Chelsea wondered.

"It's two o'clock in the morning," she said.

It was one thing having to share her room with a child. Having to entertain him was out of the question.

"Two o'clock is early," said Jack.

"No," said Chelsea, "it's late."

"I'm not usually allowed to stay up past two o'clock in the morning."

"And you're not going to start tonight," Chelsea assured him.

She lay down on her bed and switched out the light to draw a line under the conversation that Jack seemed determined to have. It didn't work.

"But tonight is different, isn't it? Tonight there's an emergency."

"The emergency is being sorted out by the grown-ups. You can go to sleep."

There was a half-minute of silence.

"Do you watch *Doctor Who?*" Jack asked.

"Lights are out, Jack. That means it's time to sleep."

"Do you prefer Doctor Who or Captain Jack?"

"It's the middle of the night. If you're staying here with me, then you're going to have to be quiet."

"Just tell me which one is better."

"I don't know which one is better."

"You must do."

"No, really, I don't," Chelsea snapped. "I don't even know who Captain Jack is. In fact, I really don't have an opinion on any form of children's television at all, as I told you over dinner."

"Shall I tell you which one is better?" Jack asked regardless.

"Please don't," said Chelsea. "Just go to blinking sleep."

Chelsea's prayer as she fell asleep that night was that her sister would be well enough to resume parental duties *first* thing in the morning.

CHAPTER
FIFTEEN

Chelsea

Jack was up bright and early the following morning, much to Chelsea's chagrin. It was confusing enough to wake in a room she didn't immediately recognise. To wake to find a small boy standing right over her, his button nose just an inch away from her own as he stared into her sleep-filled eyes, was something else again. It was borderline terrifying.

"What on earth are you doing?" Chelsea scrambled into a seated position.

"I was just checking you're alive," said Jack.

"Well, I am," said Chelsea, attempting to gather herself. "But how come you're in here?"

"Don't you remember, Auntie Chelsea? Daddy brought me in the night."

Ah yes. It was all coming back to her now. Mark, grey-faced and desperate, dumping Jack on the spare bed before making a dash for the nearest suitable loo. Thank goodness he'd been clever enough not to use Chelsea's en suite for fear of passing on whatever was ailing him to the only adult in the Benson family still in any kind of fit state to take care of his son. How bad a mess must they all have been in?

"Do you think everyone else is dead?" Jack asked.

"Someone would have come to tell us—"

"Not if they're *all* dead," said Jack.

"Good point," said Chelsea. "Then maybe they are all dead. Yes, that's probably what's happened."

Jack paled at the thought.

"What's the matter? You're not feeling ill too?" Chelsea asked Jack then. She didn't want to have to deal with small-boy sick first thing. It didn't occur to her that her comment might have drained the colour from his face. "If you're going to be sick, you need to go to the bathroom."

"I'm OK," said Jack. His bottom lip quivered.

"Then why don't you get back into bed and have a nice lie-in?"

"I don't want to lie in. I want to see Mummy and Grandma. You've got to get up and help me."

Jack climbed onto his bed. He pulled the flimsy orange curtains apart so that the room was suddenly flooded with sunshine. Chelsea screwed her eyes tightly shut.

"Heaven's sake, Jack. What are you doing?"

"This will help you be awake more quickly," he said. "Mummy always opens the curtains when it's time to get up for school."

"Well, there's no school today. Worse luck. What time is it anyway?" Chelsea asked. She dared not look at her watch. Whatever time it was, it was too bloody early. "Look, why don't you go and knock on Mummy and Daddy's door? Maybe they'll be awake by now."

"Because I'm not allowed in the corridor on my own," said Jack. "Except in an emergency like last night. It's in case of baddies."

"Baddies? Really?" Chelsea rolled her eyes. What kind of horrors was Ronnie filling Jack's head with? "I don't think there are any baddies here in the Hotel Volcan."

"I know. I told Mummy I could get them with my sonic screwdriver anyway, but she said it wouldn't work against baddies on Earth. I told her that's stupid, because the sonic screwdriver works everywhere. It even works in outer space. Have you been to outer space, Auntie Chelsea?"

"I haven't," she had to admit.

"I want to go there for my birthday. Do you know when my birthday is? It's the sixteenth OF May. That's after Granddad's birthday, but before Grandma's and Sophie's. When's your birthday, Auntie Chelsea?"

"Not today, it seems," said Chelsea. She realised with a sinking feeling that Jack was not going to go back to sleep. If there was no chance of that, she had to get rid of him pronto. The clock on her phone said it was six forty-five, and Chelsea had had nowhere near enough shut-eye. If she was going to waste a week of her annual leave in Lanzarote, then she at least wanted to spend a significant part of it asleep.

"Just run down the corridor and knock on their door. You know where it is. You'll be OK."

"I'm not allowed to. I've got to have an adult."

"Oh, for heaven's sake. Then wait there for a minute while I put on some clothes and I'll take you to your parents."

Chelsea didn't want to get out of bed at all, but she would do whatever it took to pass responsibility for Jack straight back to his mother as soon as humanly possible. She made a halter-necked dress from a Melissa Odabash sarong and slipped on her flip-flops. "Come on. I'm sure they'll be delighted to see you." Chelsea would certainly be delighted to hand him over so that she could go straight back to sleep.

"Excellent," said Jack. He reached for his aunt's hand to hurry her along. Chelsea reluctantly took Jack's little paw and tried not to look too disgusted at the unmistakeable sensation of a bogey stuck between their palms.

Ronnie and Mark were not answering their door.

"Knock harder," Chelsea instructed.

"They might be asleep."

"I don't care." If Chelsea was awake, she wanted her sister to be awake too.

Jack rapped double hard.

Still no answer.

Losing patience and eager to get back to bed, Chelsea went ahead and simply opened the door. As soon as she did so, she was greeted by the smell of vomit and something far, far worse. Instinctively, she blocked Jack from going any further in as she put her own head round the door. This was looking bad.

"Why can't I look?" Jack asked her.

"Mummy and Daddy might not be dressed."

116

"I've seen them when they're not dressed before."

"I don't want to think about that. Just stay there," said Chelsea. "Ronnie?"

There was a moan from one of the two mounds of clothing on the bed.

"Ronnie?"

"What is it?" Ronnie groaned at last. Jack pushed at the back of Chelsea's legs when he heard his mother.

"It's me, Mummy! Me and Auntie Chelsea."

"Wait there, Jack," Chelsea insisted. She stood Jack next to a plant pot in the corridor while she stepped into the room to talk to his mother. Jack set his sights on an imaginary baddy and fired off a couple of rounds.

"Ronnie," Chelsea hissed from the furthest point of the room from the bed, "what's going on? It smells like something died in here."

"I *am* dying," Ronnie announced.

"Me too," said Mark.

"Great. I hope you're joking, because I've got your son in the corridor. What am I supposed to do with him?"

Ronnie struggled to pull herself upright against the headboard. Chelsea's mood fell further when she got a good look at her older sister's face. There was no way that Ronnie was faking how ill she felt. She looked as though a mad professor had reanimated her after she'd been lying dead for a week. She was actually the exact pale shade of Colefax and Fowler green on the walls of the *Society* office.

"You'll have to look after him," said Ronnie. "The doctor is coming to see us later on. We must have a twenty-four-hour bug."

117

"What?"

"A twenty-four-hour bug."

"No. The bit before that. The bit about looking after Jack."

"You'll have to. I'm sorry. Just give him some breakfast. I wouldn't ask, but— we can't—"

Chelsea protested. "Are you expecting me to amuse him all day?"

"I don't know, but he can't come in here," Ronnie told her. "I wouldn't ask you if I didn't have to, Chelsea. Please, you've just got to take him away while we get a bit better. I can hardly keep my eyes open."

At the same time, Mark let out a fart so noxious that Chelsea couldn't have stayed in the room to argue even if she'd wanted to.

Chelsea wasn't going to leave it at that, though. There had to be someone better qualified at knowing what to do with Jack than she was. Looking after her nephew had never been part of Chelsea's holiday plan. Alas, as soon as she opened the door to her parents' room, she knew she was going to get no joy there either. Chelsea's mother, though she made more effort to get up than Ronnie had, still looked like death warmed up. Her father, being a man, was suffering far more dramatically. He waved a floppy arm in Chelsea's general direction.

"We're not moving. And your granddad couldn't help even if he wasn't shitting for Great Britain," Dave announced with charm.

"You can't ask Sophie," Jacqui added. "She's not well either. In any case, I don't think a fifteen-year-old can be left in sole charge of a minor."

"But," Chelsea tried again, "I don't know what to do with him all day."

"It's easy," Jacqui echoed Ronnie's opinion. "Jack's a lovely, easy child."

Chelsea looked back down the corridor to where Jack was fiddling with the handle on a fire extinguisher.

"I'm sure he is, but— are you sure this is just a twenty-four-hour bug?"

Twenty-four hours suddenly sounded like a very long time indeed.

"Just get him out of here," said Jacqui. "Get him away from all these germs. Give him some breakfast. Take him out into the sunshine. There's no point the two of you hanging around us and ending up with what we've got. It's a lovely day out there. You can still enjoy yourselves."

As far as Chelsea was concerned, babysitting Jack and "enjoying herself" were mutually exclusive activities.

"Mum, this is ridiculous. I don't know what to do with him. And what if it isn't a twenty-four-hour bug we're looking at? You don't seem to be taking this seriously. What if you all end up going to hospital?"

"Then it's a good job we've got you here to help us," said Jacqui, attempting a smile. "You'll work it out, love. Just get out of here before you get sick too. Take Jack down to breakfast. He'll tell you what he wants."

"I can't—"

But Jacqui was already sinking back into the pillows. "Mum?"

Jacqui feigned sleep. Dave was snoring.

Chelsea closed the door on her parents' room and stood with her hand on the handle for a moment, taking in the horror of the task ahead. So much for her plan to stay in bed until midday, then spend the afternoon reading. She really was going to have to look after Jack. She turned to find him, catching sight of him again just as he knocked the fire extinguisher off the wall. It fell with a clatter, missing his feet by a matter of millimetres.

"Jack!" Chelsea called to him. "For goodness' sake, you could have broken your toes."

Jack stood in the middle of the corridor, hands behind his back, the very picture of innocence.

"I was only reading the instructions," he said. "I need to know what to do. In case there's a disaster."

"The disaster has already happened," said Chelsea.

"Is Grandma going to look after me?" Jack asked.

"Unfortunately Grandma is not going to look after you. She's not very well."

"What about Granddad?"

"He's not well either."

"Sophie?"

"Nope."

"Mummy and Daddy?"

"You know they're not well."

"Granddad Bill can't look after me. Granddad Bill's a dementor."

"You mean he has *dementia*."

"Does that mean you are looking after me?" Jack couldn't keep the excitement off his face.

"Seems that way," Chelsea sighed.

"It's the best thing ever!" said Jack. "We can go in the swimming pool. We can play cricket. I can tell you some more about *Doctor Who*."

"*Doctor Who?* Please, no . . ." Chelsea groaned.

"Yes. Hang on. What have I done with my sonic screwdriver? I've left it in your room. We need to get it, Auntie Chelsea. Come on!" He grabbed her by the hand.

Chelsea felt exhausted already.

CHAPTER
SIXTEEN

Chelsea

Breakfast in the Jolly Pirate looked no more appetising than the previous evening's dinner, and given the state of every other adult member of her family at that moment in time, Chelsea was rather disconcerted to see several items she thought she recognised from the night before back beneath the greasy heat lamps. Jack wanted Rice Krispies, thank goodness. They were in an individual mini-box. Couldn't go too wrong there. Still, Chelsea sniffed the milk before she let him have it. The milk was UHT. Chelsea had no idea whether it was off or not. Wasn't UHT supposed to be bug-resistant? She let him have just a little.

Chelsea herself stuck to a piece of dry toast. She'd never heard of someone contracting food poisoning from toast, especially if you eschewed butter and the marmalade pot that had been stirred by a thousand dirty knives. Chelsea shuddered. People really were disgusting. The guy behind the counter offered Chelsea a spoonful of scrambled eggs. Chelsea saw them as though in one of those advertisements for germ-killing bathroom cleaners. The eggs were crawling with bacteria. They might as well have glowed radioactive green to show exactly how quickly the bugs were proliferating.

"It's all-inclusive," the chef reminded her, as the yellow mass wobbled on the spoon.

"No, thank you," said Chelsea. She was tempted to add, "My family will be suing as it is."

With their breakfast tray loaded, Chelsea and Jack found themselves a spot at the only empty table in the restaurant, which was sticky with spilled coffee. Ugh. The whole hotel was filthy. If the Bensons did decide to sue for contracting food poisoning, it would surely be a slam dunk.

All the while he was supposed to be eating his Rice Krispies, Jack kept up a ceaseless monologue regarding the characters of a children's action adventure series that Chelsea had never heard of. Captain This. Princess That. King So-and-So battling the baddies. Chelsea felt her brain softening with every potted storyline he offered her. Meanwhile, she kept an eye on the comings and goings by the lift that led up to the hotel bedrooms. At about nine o'clock, a man in a smart suit arrived. He was carrying a large briefcase. Must be the doctor, Chelsea decided. Not even the hotel manager wore a proper suit. Chelsea continued to watch the lift for his return. He was only upstairs for twenty minutes in total. That had to be a good sign. Especially if he had visited all six patients in that time. Jack finished his Rice Krispies.

"Right," said Chelsea, abandoning what remained of her toast. "Let's go and see what the doctor said to your mum." There wasn't a moment to waste. Chelsea had been awake and in sole charge of her nephew for less than three hours, but she already knew she would go insane if she had to listen to another episode synopsis of *Captain Tim and His Space Bimbo*, or whatever that kids' show was called. If there was a chance to hand back Jack, she was going to grab it. She practically ran to the lift. Jack followed, still talking about space dust. Though he had to sprint to keep up with her, he didn't even draw breath.

By now Ronnie and Mark were sitting up in bed with the sliding doors to their balcony open, so the room smelt slightly less fetid. It was still pretty disgusting, but Chelsea decided that Jack could go in there. *Should* go in there. Even breakfast with Jack had been enough to convince Chelsea that if they spent all day together, she would end up going more than a little insane. Perhaps if Ronnie saw her son, she would be encouraged to get better and take him off Chelsea's hands much more quickly.

"It's a twenty-four-hour bug," Ronnie confirmed. "The doctor said it's nothing to do with the hotel food, though. It's all round the resort: hotels and self-catering places. We might have picked it up in the toilets at the airport, he said. People flush with the seat up; the germs go all over the place. You might as well spray the walls with diluted poo."

Jack squeaked his horror at the thought.

"Too much information," said Chelsea. "What else did he say? When will you be able to come downstairs?"

"He said we've got to stay in bed until lunchtime at the very earliest and drink Diet Coke to get our electrolyte balances right. We can't eat anything but dry toast. The hotel doesn't do room service, but they're making an exception. I don't think we'll be up before dinnertime, to be honest."

"And what's Jack supposed to do until then?" Chelsea came straight to the point.

"What he'd normally do," suggested Ronnie. "You can take him down to the pool, but you have to keep an eye on him. You don't have to go in with him, but don't let him out of your sight. Seriously, do not let your attention wander for a moment. I'm not kidding, Chelsea. You've got to watch him all the time. It's not just the danger of drowning; it's the—"

"Baddies," Jack elaborated.

"Ronnie, I — I really didn't intend to — I've actually got some work to do. On my laptop. I've got to write a piece and mail it back to London as quickly as possible. Can't he just sit in here with you and read a comic?"

"He might get ill," said Ronnie.

"I might," Jack echoed.

"We're really grateful to you, Chelsea," Mark interrupted. "You'll have a good time together. Give you a chance to bond with each other, like."

"Please get my son out of here," Ronnie begged her. "You've got no idea what this bug is like."

Chelsea had some idea that her sister was exaggerating how bad it was, but finally she accepted that she had no choice other than to take care of Jack until the rest of the family got better. She shuffled him out into the corridor.

"Are you all right, Auntie Chelsea?" Jack looked up at her, concern etched on his face.

"I'm fine," said Chelsea. "Mummy and Daddy need their rest, but we'll both have a lovely morning."

"Are you still looking after me?"

"I am."

Jack gave a little skip of delight.

Chelsea was aware that the whole family thought of her as something of a joke when it came to life's practicalities. She had often been frustrated by their inability to grasp how well she had actually done since leaving university. At best, they seemed to picture her life as an extended episode of *Absolutely Fabulous*. They imagined she worked with people like Patsy and Bubble. They had no idea that Chelsea's world was populated by women with the best degrees from the best universities, who could have run a PLC as easily as they ran a magazine. The world of magazine publishing was cut-throat and Chelsea had succeeded entirely on merit. She had hardly been able to rely on nepotism. She thought of her dad as she had seen him when she first saw him yesterday, lazing on a sunlounger with a copy of the *Mirror* draped over his face to keep the sun off his nose, his belly undulating with each snore. Chelsea had definitely not been able to tap up any of her father's friends for useful work experience. More than half of them had been unemployed since the last recession. Or even the one before that.

Well, perhaps looking after Jack would give Chelsea a chance to put this bizarre notion that she couldn't cut it in "normal life" to rest at last. Really, how hard could it be to keep a six-year-old entertained for a morning? (Chelsea was sure her mother would have pulled herself together by lunchtime, even if Ronnie hadn't.) At least there would be no nappy-changing. She was going to look after Jack for the morning, and she was going to do it well. Perhaps it would encourage Ronnie to drop the constant sniping about Chelsea's lifestyle, her clothes and her love life as well.

"What do you want to do first?" she asked her nephew, accepting her fate.

"I'd like to go in the pool. Will you come in with me?" Jack asked. "Mummy won't ever come in."

"I'll dangle my feet over the edge," was Chelsea's compromise.

Pool duty was not as much fun as the laughter and shrieking that came from the water suggested. Chelsea struggled to keep her hair dry with all the splashing that went on. She needed to keep it dry because she'd had it finished with a hideously expensive new Japanese blow-drying technique the previous week and she wanted to keep it looking perfect for as long as possible. None of the other punters in the Hotel Volcan pool seemed to appreciate the problem.

Thankfully, it wasn't long before Jack decided that he was fed up with being in the pool if Chelsea wasn't going to join him properly. And she wasn't. She really did just dangle her feet over the edge. So Jack took up a position on the sunlounger next to the one Chelsea had draped with a Pucci towel. She hoped it would be easier to keep an eye on him on dry land.

Wracking her brains for the sort of thing a parent would think of at this point, Chelsea told Jack he had better put on some more suncream since any earlier application would have been washed off while he was swimming. She handed him the bottle of Ambre Solaire Factor 50. Jack just looked at it.

"Auntie Chelsea," he said after a little while, "I don't normally do this myself."

"What?"

"Mummy does it for me."

"Oh, of course she does," said Chelsea.

She squirted cream over Jack's skinny little back and rubbed it in. He sat still and patient while she covered his arms and legs and applied a white stripe of total block to his nose as the finishing touch.

"Easy," she said when she'd finished. "You're done."

"You missed a bit." He held out his arm.

"Well, you can get that bit, can't you?"

"I might not do it right."

"It's very easy." Chelsea squirted some more lotion onto Jack's spindly little forearm, trying not to show her irritation when he told her, "You've got it."

"Now it's reading time," she told him. "Don't you think?"

Right then, Chelsea was still pretty sure that Ronnie had exaggerated the degree to which Jack required constant monitoring and attention. At least, when he was out of the pool and away from danger of drowning.

128

She settled back down on her sunlounger with *From Booty Call to Bride*. She had decided that she could read all the self help she wanted at the Hotel Volcan. There was no one she needed to impress. Jack, lying adjacent, opened up a copy of the latest *Simpsons* comic. That was better. This wasn't going to be so difficult. Chelsea was looking forward to getting stuck into her book.

No such luck. She had time to read just half a sentence before she was interrupted.

"Auntie Chelsea?" said Jack.

"Yes, Jack," said Chelsea.

"Which would you rather be, a rhino or an elephant?"

Remembering that she was being a good aunt that morning and for that morning only, God willing, Chelsea momentarily closed her paperback.

"That's a very good question," she said. "An elephant, I think."

"Wrong," said Jack, as though he were surprised she could be so stupid. "A rhino is way better." He declined to give his reasons why.

"Oh," said Chelsea. "OK. Then I'd rather be a rhino. Of course. I don't know why I didn't think of that."

Jack nodded in satisfaction.

Chelsea reopened her book. She managed another half-sentence before Jack interrupted again.

"Auntie Chelsea?"

"Yes."

"Which is better, a rhino or a giraffe?"

"I'd rather be a giraffe, if that's what you're asking."

"I'm not asking that. It's a rhino again. Why did the giraffe cross the road?"

"I don't know. Why did the giraffe cross the road?"

"I don't know. I thought you did."

"Riiiii-ght."

Chelsea focused on her book again. One second, two seconds—

"Auntie Chelsea?"

"*What?*"

"What if there was a fight between a rhino and a bear—"

"The bear. The bear, definitely," Chelsea snapped.

"No, the *rhino*. It's *obvious*."

"OK. So it is."

This was getting a bit Dada-esque. All Chelsea wanted to do was sit and read, but it was clear that simply wasn't going to happen while Jack was around and awake.

"Do you ever take a nap in the middle of the morning?" she asked hopefully.

"No," said Jack. "I'm not a *baby*." He seemed quite affronted.

"Then don't you want to play in the sandpit?"

Chelsea could see the sandpit from where she was lying. It didn't look busy. Surely that would be safe.

"Will you come with me?" Jack asked eagerly.

"No." Chelsea shook her head. "I don't want to get sand all over me."

"Then I don't want to either. I'll just stay here with you."

130

"Well, I'm being really boring. You might find the sandpit more interesting. There are children there. Look. You could play with them. I'm just going to read my book."

"Read it to me," Jack suggested.

"I don't think you'd like it."

"What's it about?"

"I can't tell you."

"Is it like *Doctor Who*? I like *Doctor Who*."

"It's not like *Doctor Who* at all."

Jack titled his head to read the title. "What's a booty call?"

"Jack, this is a book for grown-ups."

"Is it scary? I won't get frightened. I like scary things."

"You won't like this," Chelsea insisted.

"Then make up a story," Jack suggested. "That's what Mummy does."

"Does she?"

Jack nodded.

Well, anything Ronnie could do . . . Chelsea didn't have the faintest idea where to start. Jack looked at her expectantly.

"Oh, all right. Er . . ." Chelsea began. "Once upon a time, there was a princess."

"Not a *princess*."

"A prince, then."

"No, not a prince."

"A witch who lived in a castle?"

"Witches don't live in castles."

"Then where do they live?"

"They live in caves. Or in cottages in the woods. Made of gingerbread."

"OK. There once was a witch who lived in a cottage in the woods. It was made of gingerbread—"

"I don't want a story about a witch."

"Fine. In that case, it seems to me you don't really want a story at all."

"Not really. You're right."

Chelsea put her book down.

"Jack, what do you actually want to do?" she sighed.

Jack beamed his most winning smile at her. "We could always go to the Kidz Klub?"

As a child, Chelsea had been filled with horror at the idea of anything remotely resembling organised activity during the school holidays, and as an adult, she found her feelings hadn't changed in the least. Jack, however, was delighted by the idea of the Kidz Klub, and assuming she would just be able to drop him off and get back to her reading, Chelsea decided she was happy to take him right to the door. And make sure it was firmly locked behind him. Genius. Why hadn't she thought of using the hotel's childcare facilities before? Why hadn't Ronnie reminded her they existed? It was a win-win situation.

The location of the Kidz Klub was extremely easy to find. All you had to do was follow the noise. When Chelsea and Jack arrived at the picket-fenced enclosure, which contained a pretty large playground and another swimming pool, they found a gang of children racing around as though they had been fed nothing but additives for the past six months. In the middle of the chaos stood a young man and two young women wearing bright yellow T-shirts that announced they were the "Kidz Klub Ko-ordinatorz". Chelsea was relieved to see that they hadn't taken the "K" theme right through their job titles. The male coordinator bounced over.

"Hey there, little buddy," he said to Jack with the kind of creepily patronising friendliness that would have made a six-year-old Chelsea run and hide behind her mother's legs. Jack, to his credit, looked equally dubious at this overly familiar approach. "And what's your name?"

"Jack Benson-Edwards," said Jack.

Chelsea snorted involuntarily. She hadn't realised her sister had double-barrelled the children in lieu of actually getting married. And Ronnie thought Chelsea was a snob?

"Are you coming to play with us, Jack Benson-Edwards?" the coordinator asked.

"I'm thinking about it."

The coordinator feigned amusement. "We have a whole lot of fun here at the Kidz Klub, you know."

Chelsea tried to place the man's accent. Danish, perhaps? He looked as though he had been raised on state-sponsored coordinated fun.

"We play games. We have competitions. Sometimes we go to the beach—"

"That sounds good. So what do you think, Jack Benson-Edwards?" Chelsea pushed her nephew for an answer. "Are you happy to stay here for the rest of the morning?"

Jack surveyed his fellow underage holidaymakers. For the time being, they looked quite nice. No one was indulging in especially feral behaviour. Jack turned back to his aunt and nodded. "I think so."

"Great," said Chelsea. "I'll just find out what time it finishes so I can come back and collect you when you're done."

"You're not *going*, Auntie Chelsea?"

"Well, of course I am. I'm not a kid. I don't think I'm supposed to be here at the *Kidz* Klub," she added.

"Parents are allowed to stay if they want to," said the coordinator. He helpfully pointed out a gaggle of bored-looking adults at the playground's perimeter.

"Ah, but I'm not a parent, you see," Chelsea tried.

"She's just my auntie," Jack concurred.

"I won't tell anybody," the coordinator promised with a wink. "I'm sure we can make an exception for an auntie."

"My favourite auntie," Jack added.

"That's great. But why do you want me to stay?" Chelsea asked her nephew then. "You'll be perfectly safe here. I'll only cramp your style."

"Well, I think I'm going to like it," said Jack, "but I'm not completely sure. What happens if you go and I only like it for ten minutes?"

"You'll *love* it," said the coordinator.

"I might not," Jack warned him.

"Then I can come and fetch you earlier," said Chelsea. "Simple as."

"But how will I get hold of you? I don't have a mobile like Sophie. It would be easier if you just stayed," Jack announced.

His logic was flawless. It *would* be easier if she just stayed.

"How about I stay for fifteen minutes? Then, if you still think you're having fun, I can go and get a cup of coffee and read my book by the pool," Chelsea bargained.

"You can read your book there," said Jack, pointing towards a row of uncomfortable-looking plastic chairs. There wasn't a single sunlounger. Or any shade.

"You want me to sit there?"

"Yes." Having sorted that out, Jack took off the sweatshirt he had been wearing tied round his waist and handed it to Chelsea. "Thank you. I'll go and play now."

As serious as he had been while negotiating the business of Chelsea's staying to watch over him, he skittered off into the crowd without seeming in the least bit nervous at all.

"Come on, Jack." The coordinator skittered after him. "Let's pretend we're aeroplanes!"

"No, thank you," Jack called out politely. "I can make up my own games."

"Fine," Chelsea muttered as she looked for the least broken chair. "I guess I'll stay." She laid Jack's sweatshirt over the splintered plastic seat so that it wouldn't catch against her bare legs and flipped open her book. Trapped in the bloody Kidz Klub. If the girls at the office could see her now . . .

CHAPTER
SEVENTEEN

Ronnie

By lunchtime, the members of the Benson group who had been so ill the night before were starting to feel a little better, not least because the hotel manager himself had visited them in their sickbeds, and while he agreed wholeheartedly with the doctor's view that the gastrointestinal distress the Bensons were suffering was absolutely one hundred per cent not related to the hotel buffet, he had been keen to offer the family free vouchers for the bar as a goodwill gesture. Mark in particular was very pleased with that. Nothing could have improved his prospects of recovery more than the thought of a cold beer or two at the end of the ordeal.

Ronnie was much less certain.

"You realise that if we take those vouchers," she said, "we are basically waiving our right to compensation. Our holiday could have been ruined by this, you know."

"Relax," said Mark. "We've only lost a morning. When we get back to England, we'll have something to talk about. Plus, we've got Chelsea babysitting and we've got free beer. In my view, that's something of a result."

"What about Sophie?"

"She's fine."

Sophie had texted her parents to say as much. She was very happy so long as she had phone credit and a room of her own.

"Well, I want to get better as soon as I can before Chelsea loses Jack in the hotel minimarket or something equally half-arsed," said Ronnie.

"They'll be OK," said Mark. "I say we stay in bed for as long as we possibly can. Make the most of it." Mark rolled so that his head rested on Ronnie's shoulder. He stroked the side of her neck.

Though she had convinced herself so recently that Mark no longer ever touched her except by accident, Ronnie ignored his gesture of affection and looked straight up at the ceiling.

"I find it hard to relax when I think my child may be in danger."

"For God's sake, he's with your sister. What on earth could possibly go wrong?" Mark asked.

Ronnie was acutely aware of all the things that could go wrong. That was the worst part of being a mother.

"I've been more relaxed at work," she sighed.

Parenthood didn't seem to have changed Mark's life anywhere near as much as it had Ronnie's. Neither had getting a decade and a half older. Mark stuck to the routine he had always followed their whole life together. He went to work at eight. He came home at five. On Wednesday, he played skittles with Dave and Jacqui. On a Friday night, he went out with the guys he worked with. On Saturdays, he ordered in a curry. He lived just as he had done when Sophie was still a baby. These little pleasures were his release valve, he explained. And Ronnie could hardly have argued with that when he was the only one bringing home the money.

The ongoing recession and Ronnie's new job had redressed the balance just a little.

Ronnie had gone to the job centre without a clue as to what she was looking for. There wasn't a lot of choice. It seemed an HGV licence was a pre-requisite for just about anything. Those jobs that didn't require an HGV licence were in childcare. Ronnie had quite enough of that at home. The only thing she saw that looked remotely interesting was a part-time admin position.

"This job," said the woman behind the counter, "is a little bit unusual. They're looking for someone mature and unflappable. You've got to be good with people when they're at their very worst."

"What is it?" Ronnie was intrigued.

"You'd be working for an undertaker. Do you still want to be put forward?"

Ronnie shrugged. "Why not?"

She had an interview two days later. Not having interviewed in such a long time, she wasn't sure what she should wear.

"Wear what you wore for your great-auntie's funeral," Jacqui suggested.

"What, my funeral outfit?" Ronnie blurted before she saw the funny side.

It would certainly be a convenient job. She could walk to work, which was great given that the Peugeot

205 Ronnie had been driving since she passed her test eight years earlier was pretty much on its last legs and there was no hope of a replacement. The hours were convenient. She'd be able to drop Jack off at school on her way in. There was just the dead-body thing.

"Once you've seen one . . ." her prospective boss, Mr Jason, joked. "Would you like the position?"

Ronnie had been in the job for two weeks before she saw her first body. Mr Jason was right. In the end, it was a total anticlimax. The old lady really did look as though she had fallen asleep. There was nothing scary about it at all. And eventually, Ronnie got used to seeing the grieving relatives and learned the best way to help them deal with the miserable process ahead. Mr Jason was impressed with her empathy and Ronnie allowed herself to be a little bit proud of her people skills. Perhaps all those years at home with the children hadn't made her unemployable after all.

But it wasn't her dream job, that was for certain. There was nothing about Ronnie's current life that fitted "the dream". Even this holiday, a free holiday, was already a disaster with half the family stuck in bed.

And then Mark got a text. He rolled over onto his side to read it, shielding his phone from Ronnie with his back.

"Who's texting you now?" asked Ronnie.

"Cathy next door," Mark answered quickly.

"Again? What does she want? Is something wrong with Fishy?"

"No, she just wanted us to know that everything's OK," Mark replied.

Ronnie nodded, but she couldn't help wondering once more why Cathy had texted Mark and not her.

CHAPTER
EIGHTEEN

Chelsea

For Chelsea, sitting on the sidelines at the Kidz Klub was about as much fun as sitting in a doctor's waiting room. Still, Jack seemed to be enjoying himself. Despite his concern that he might be fed up after ten minutes, he had not so much as glanced in his aunt's direction for the past half-hour. He was having fun with his peers. Perhaps she could sneak off and get herself a coffee, Chelsea thought after forty-five minutes. She half stood up.

"Auntie Chelsea!"

Too late. Jack had spotted her.

"Are you going somewhere?" he asked. Clearly her presence was making a difference to him after all. Chelsea gave him a little wave and sat back down.

"I was only stretching my legs," she reassured him.

Damn. She was going to be there for the duration, sitting on an uncomfortable plastic chair, trying and failing to concentrate on *From Booty Call to Bride* what with the shouting and the shrieking and somebody asking her to throw back a ball every fifteen seconds. And no matter how much she wanted to be the kind of person who let the children come and fetch the ball themselves (most of them looked as though they could do with the exercise), Chelsea couldn't really ignore their squeaky requests.

"Too quick to offer help," was one of the cardinal sins of dating according to Chelsea's book. And indeed she'd been like that with Colin. Always quick to make his life easier. She'd never been a challenge. She had a lot of work to do.

Just then, however, something happened to make the Kidz Klub altogether more interesting. Chelsea looked up from beneath her wide-brimmed sun hat to see the man from the plane — Adam — talking to the chirpy club coordinator. Little Lily was swinging from his arm. What were they doing there? Had she waited to catch the resort bus rather than take her own taxi, Chelsea would have known that Lily and her father were also inmates of the Hotel Volcan.

Chelsea was a little embarrassed to see her aeroplane acquaintances. The incident with the blackcurrant juice and then the horror of the upturned handbag made her shudder. Talking of which, she quickly stuffed *From Booty Call to Bride* back into her beach bag. What should she do? Should she acknowledge Lily and her father? Should she wave?

Adam chose a seat on the other side of the playground while his daughter ran off to explore. Shaded by her enormous hat, Chelsea didn't think he'd seen her yet. While he sorted through the available chairs to find the one that was least broken, Chelsea studied him from behind her sunglasses. Were those shorts he was wearing Vilebrequin, that crazily

142

expensive French brand? Chelsea thought they might be. That would be a first for the Hotel Volcan. Adam certainly had style. Or maybe the woman in his life did. And what raw material Lily's mum had to work with. Adam was extremely well toned, and his chest had just a smattering of hair, the way Chelsea liked it. She looked back at the other book she'd put in her beach bag that day — the respectable Alex Marwood thriller — before Adam caught sight of her ogling him. Sod's law that the only remotely good-looking man she'd seen since she arrived in Lanzarote was a dad and she'd already embarrassed herself in front of him.

Best to pretend she hadn't seen him. That way, she could save herself the possibility of rejection. But Adam had seen her. And now he was getting up and walking towards her. Flippin' heck.

When he got close enough to her, Chelsea feigned surprise.

"Hello!" said Adam. "Fancy seeing you here. I didn't know you were staying at the Volcan."

"I didn't mention it," said Chelsea.

"We didn't see you on the bus."

"I didn't know there was one," Chelsea lied.

"So . . ." Adam gestured to the playground.

"I'm looking after my nephew," Chelsea explained. "That's him on the slide." She pointed Jack out. Jack waved. "Thank God for the Kidz Klub," she added.

"Indeed," said Adam. "It's the only reason I picked this hotel. It's hard work, entertaining a six-year-old all day, especially when you're on your own."

On his own? Chelsea sat up a little straighter.

"I'm glad I've bumped into you," Adam continued. "I wanted to check about the dress. I've been feeling really guilty."

"Oh, it's fine. I dunked it in the basin in my room and all the juice came out," she lied.

"Phew," said Adam. "It was a very pretty dress."

Chelsea blushed as though he had complimented her directly.

"Thank you."

"I like your hat too," said Adam.

Chelsea adjusted the wide brim. "Hard to see where I'm going when I'm wearing it," she said. "I'm always bumping into things."

"You have to suffer for style," Adam joked.

Chelsea found herself liking him more and more.

"So, what do you think of this place so far?" he asked. "Lanzarote? The Hotel Volcan?"

"It's . . ." Chelsea struggled to think of the right word. "It's OK. I didn't actually book it. My mum did. We're here en masse, for her birthday. Me, my sister, her kids. Even Granddad."

"That's lovely," said Adam. "I wish Lily and I had a bigger family. It would be great for her to have cousins to play with."

Again, no mention of a Mrs Adam. Chelsea allowed herself to think that things might just be going her way.

"So, where are they?" Adam asked. "The rest of your gang?"

"Would you believe, they're all laid up in bed," said Chelsea. "Twenty-four-hour tummy bug."

"No way! From the food here?"

144

"That's my guess."

"Mine too, if breakfast was anything to go by. Your sister's lucky she's got you here," he continued. "If I get food poisoning, we're stuffed."

He was definitely on his own! Oh joy! Chelsea was delighted. All she had to do now was follow the rules of *From Booty Call to Bride*. Act natural. Act normal. Act like talking to a good-looking single bloke is something you do every day of the week. Don't. Screw. It. Up.

Just then, Lily and Jack both appeared in front of their respective carers. Jack regarded Adam with suspicion. Lily looked similarly unimpressed to see Chelsea again.

"Lily," said Adam. "You remember the lady from the aeroplane."

"Yes. She scared me," said Lily.

"She's my auntie," said Jack. "She's not scary."

"Well, I can be," Chelsea joked, making her hands into claws for a laugh. Jack winced. Lily frowned.

"And you must be?" Adam asked Jack.

"Jack Benson-Edwards."

"Well this is Lily Rose Baxter," said Adam. "Perhaps you two can play together today?"

Chelsea smiled somewhat desperately at Jack, as though willing him to say "yes" through the strength of her grin.

Jack hesitated.

"No thank you," said Lily, as she headed for the Wendy House.

"I'd rather play with boys," Jack concurred.

"Ah well," said Chelsea, once the children were gone again. "I'm sure they'll warm up to each other later on."

Like we're warming up to each other, was the thought on Chelsea's mind.

Chelsea didn't mind in the least that she was stuck at the Kidz Klub now that she had a new friend. Adam was lovely. He was so funny and intelligent. And he laughed whenever she made a lame joke (which was less frequently than usual because the very first chapter of *From Booty Call to Bride* had informed her that men don't really like funny women). She was glad that she had worn the Melissa Odabash kaftan that morning. It was definitely the most flattering beach cover-up she'd brought with her. It covered her thighs, so she didn't have to worry about flashing cellulite, but it had a very flattering neckline that gave just the right hint of décolletage (sexy but not slutty, as *From Booty Call to Bride* would recommend).

Adam seemed just as enchanted as Chelsea. Within half an hour, they were talking as if they had known each other for years. The children were no obstruction to their flirtation whatsoever as they busied themselves in the playground. Jack had found himself a couple of playmates. Lily was arranging the patio furniture outside the Wendy House. Who would have thought that the Kidz Klub could be the perfect place to start what Chelsea was increasingly sure would be her holiday romance? Maybe her luck was changing.

It wasn't. Glancing up to check on Jack while Adam went to fetch a bottle of water from his bag, which was still on the other side of the playground, Chelsea saw that her nephew was at the top of the slide. He wasn't preparing to slide down, however; he was just standing there, delivering some sort of soliloquy to the small group of boys he had gathered around him. Chelsea couldn't help feeling proud of Jack's obvious popularity. Now that her babysitting had been rewarded with another chance to get to know Adam, Chelsea felt more kindly than ever towards the little boy.

But there was trouble ahead. Lily, bored of playing house-wife, was climbing up the ladder behind him. It took her a while to get to the top, and when she did, Jack was still standing there, addressing his new "friends, Romans and countrymen". The little girl was not best pleased to find her path to the exciting slide blocked by Jack in full flow. She waited patiently, staring at his back. Well, she didn't wait *patiently*. She waited for exactly two seconds before she gave Jack an almighty shove that was designed to send him down the slide whether he wanted it or not.

Thank God Jack didn't just pitch sideways off the top of the slide straight onto the tarmac below. He did at least manage to go down the chute, but the unexpected timing of his downhill ride rattled him. As did the fact that having shoved him, Lily followed seconds later and landed on top of him before he could get up and dust himself off.

A wail went up from both children. Chelsea abandoned her chair and raced to Jack's side.

"She pushed me!" Jack was astonished.

"He was in the way," Lily replied.

"Are you hurt?" Chelsea asked Jack urgently.

"Did he hurt you?" Adam was asking his daughter.

"Did *he* hurt *her*?" Chelsea exclaimed. "Didn't you see what happened? She pushed him down the slide."

"She never would have pushed him," said Adam. "She must have lost her balance and fallen into him. Lily, tell Jack you're sorry you accidentally hurt him when you slipped."

"Sorry." Lily tossed the word over her shoulder. She was already headed for the swings. Adam followed her. Jack and Chelsea stared after them, open-mouthed.

"I hope he's telling her off," said Jack.

Chelsea strained to see what was going on. A little later, Adam returned.

"I'm sorry about that, Jack," he said. "Lily says she's very sorry but accidents happen, eh?"

"I suppose they do," said Chelsea. She was still a little rattled by what she thought she'd seen, but her desire to continue her conversation with Adam soon overrode that uncomfortable feeling. She thanked Adam for his apology.

"It's OK," said Jack. After Chelsea gave him one more check for bumps and bruises, Jack was ready to go back into the fray and Chelsea and Adam were back in conversation.

CHAPTER
NINETEEN

Chelsea

Chelsea and Adam swapped details of their lives back in London. Chelsea told Adam about her job at *Society*. Adam told Chelsea that he was an architect. They'd both lived in Clapham when they first moved to the Big Smoke.

"We must have passed each other on the street," said Adam.

"And we finally meet on an aeroplane bound for Lanzarote," said Chelsea, wishing straight away that she hadn't said it at all. It sounded a little bit as though she was already mythologising the beginning of a relationship. Not cool at all when they'd only had two conversations.

But if the comment was a little prophetic, Adam didn't seem to have noticed. He started to tell Chelsea about his university days, which was when he'd played rugby. Chelsea attempted to impress him with reminiscences about her time as an exchange student in France, which seemed so much more romantic now as she looked back on it. At the time, she had been desperately homesick and made very few friends.

While the adults talked, Jack was playing with two of the boys who had attached themselves to him before

149

the Lily incident. They roamed almost the entire playground, but they all avoided the slide. Lily was back in the Wendy House. She seemed to be playing at running a café.

Half an hour passed. A whole hour. Adam was telling Chelsea about his horrible boss. Chelsea sympathised. Davina would definitely fit the same category. Chelsea had no doubt that her iPhone was full of messages from the office but with Adam to talk to, she no longer felt the slightest inclination to check. As Adam and Chelsea shared career horror stories, the incident on the slide was long forgotten. By the grown-ups, that is.

It was almost midday. Jack and his new friends were playing on the roundabout. Jack was standing in the middle, singing at the top of his voice, while the two other boys took it in turns to spin him round.

Meanwhile, Lily had come out of the Wendy House. She hop-skipped her way along the painted hopscotch grid. Next, she picked up a plastic hula hoop and used it to skip round the perimeter of the playground. As she came within six feet of Chelsea and her father, Lily narrowed her eyes at Chelsea. From behind the safety of her sunglasses, Chelsea narrowed her eyes back. Lily wrinkled her nose and skipped onwards.

It was a matter of seconds later that Lily made a beeline for the roundabout. With half an ear still on Adam's work stories, Chelsea watched. She could see, even from a distance, that Jack was suddenly nervous. He'd stopped singing. His body had stiffened. His facial expression was serious. Lily said something to the

150

two boys who were pushing Jack round. They immediately brought the roundabout to a halt. Jack stepped off and Lily stepped on. Chelsea was relieved that Jack had stepped aside and out of trouble without a murmur. Adam, who had looked up to see what had attracted Chelsea's attention, was relieved too. He shrugged and shook his head.

"Good move, Jack," he said.

Chelsea had expected Jack to come straight across to her, but he was not hurrying to be back by Chelsea's side after all. Jack and his two companions were still standing by the roundabout. Lily was sitting in the very middle now. She had taken Jack's place like a conquering general. She had her arms raised above her head. She was exhorting the boys to do something. Ah. As she watched the situation unfold, Chelsea was impressed by the natural justice of children. Lily wanted the boys to give her a push and they weren't going to do it. They may have conceded the roundabout, but they sure as hell were not going to become slave labour while they were at it.

Imperious little Lily crossed her arms in a very disgruntled fashion. The boys weren't pushing, but nor was she climbing down. The stand-off continued. Chelsea and Adam watched. How long would it be before Lily capitulated to the three boys? Surely they had strength in numbers. Lily would have to give up. The seconds seemed to pass like hours. After what seemed like ten minutes but was probably only thirty seconds, Lily got to her feet again. She did some more pointing and some shouting. She put her hands on her hips and leant right over Jack's face. Jack closed his eyes.

"Good for him," said Adam. "She gets what she wants far too often, that daughter of mine."

Chelsea was impressed by her nephew. He seemed to be doing really well.

However, Jack's saintly forbearance was in fact wearing thin. Lily continued to shout her demands, growing increasingly shrill and red in the face. What Chelsea couldn't see from her seat by the fence was that Jack's hands were now clenched into two little white-knuckled fists. His jaw, too, was solid with the effort of not shouting back.

"Push me! I said, *Push me!*" shouted Lily. She pointed to each of the boys in turn. "You do it. And you. You pushed him." She jabbed her finger at Jack. "You have to push me too."

At which point, Jack suddenly stepped forward. He put his hands on one of the roundabout's bars and began to push with all his might. Lily, who had not been expecting her demands to be met quite so suddenly, had not been hanging on and the force of Jack's efforts sent her crumpling against the middle post. That was bad enough, but even after she had fallen to her knees in the centre of the roundabout, Jack would not stop pushing. Then the two other little boys joined in. Soon, the roundabout was a blur of pumping legs and flying hair. Chelsea watched in horror. It wasn't long before the boys were pushing so fast she couldn't see which was Jack and which a stranger.

152

Lily was screaming at the top of her lungs, "Stop, stop, stooooooppppppppp!"

Adam dropped his water bottle and ran to the roundabout, shouting instructions as he ran.

"Stop that at once!" he yelled.

Chelsea, too, had no choice but to intervene.

"Jack! Jack! Let Lily get off. Stop pushing!"

The KK coordinators followed suit.

As it happened, the adults didn't need to stop the roundabout. Before they could get there, one of Jack's accomplices tripped, causing a dramatic three-boy pile-up on the special soft play surface that turned out not to be all that soft after all.

"Oh Christ," Chelsea swore. There was going to be trouble.

Adam was already scooping his darling from the centre of the roundabout. Meanwhile, Chelsea checked the tangle of limbs on the ground. Total carnage. It took a little time to work out which one was actually Jack. Eventually, he crawled out from the very bottom of the heap. His knees and the heels of his hands were scraped raw. His chin, too, bore a bloody graze. Chelsea helped him to his feet, while other adults dealt with their children, Jack's friends.

"Are you all right?" Chelsea dabbed at Jack's chin with the edge of her kaftan. It had cost more than three hundred pounds and the last thing she wanted was to get it covered in blood, but . . . needs must. She had nothing else to hand. She couldn't *not* try to stop the blood. Could she? She couldn't. Gingerly, she wiped Jack's face clean.

Jack's eyes were glittering. Chelsea waited for the tears, but they didn't come. Eventually she realised that his eyes were glittering with triumph as he watched the little girl he had unseated so dramatically being carried, crying, back to her father's chair. Chelsea set her jaw and inspected Jack's injuries more closely. She brushed gravel from his knees.

"What were you thinking?" she asked in a whisper.

"I didn't say anything to her," said Jack. "She was calling me names, but I didn't say anything back."

"Well, that's good, Jack. Well done. But someone who didn't know you might think you were pushing the roundabout extra fast because you wanted to frighten her."

Jack smiled a slightly wicked sort of smile.

That was exactly what Adam thought. Leaving Lily wrapped up in a towel on his chair, he strode over to Chelsea and Jack.

"That was a very silly thing to do," he began to tell Jack. "Someone could have broken a bone."

"But they didn't," said Chelsea quickly.

"You should tell your nephew —"

Chelsea cut Adam off before he could say something awful. "Everyone is going to be perfectly fine."

Adam nodded. "You're right but, Jack, you've got to be more careful. And Lily mustn't be so bossy."

Chelsea seconded Adam's view. "But now I think we had better go and get some lunch, don't you, Jack?"

Chelsea did not want to stick around for the post-mortem. Wasn't that how lawsuits got started? Better to pretend it was really no big deal.

154

"We'll see you later, perhaps?" she said to Adam. But he was already distracted by Lily, who seemed to think that only an ice-cream would cure her ills.

Chelsea walked Jack away from the playground at a clip. "Please, God," she muttered, "let your mum and dad have recovered by now."

CHAPTER
TWENTY

Chelsea

What a disaster! Just when it was all going so well. While Jack was having his ice-cream, Chelsea took the opportunity to phone her sister in her room. Ronnie didn't answer the first time. Or the second. Or the third. In the end, Chelsea resorted to texting, FFS. Are you dead?

No, Ronnie responded.

Then why the f- don't you pick up your phone?

Ronnie called Chelsea. "You'll have to call me back," she said. "I'm nearly out of credit."

Chelsea did as Ronnie asked.

"Are you better yet?" Chelsea began.

"No," said Ronnie. "If anything, I feel a bit worse."

"Right. So you're not coming down here to take over the care of your son anytime soon? I've got work to do, you know."

"I know. But I can't move six feet from the bathroom . . . Is Jack all right?"

"Yes, of course he's all right. I just—"

"I'll be down as soon as I can, I promise."

"What am I supposed to do with him in the meantime? I feel like I've exhausted all the options."

"You've only had him for four hours. Have you taken him to the Kidz Klub?"

"Yes, I've taken him to the Kidz Klub."

"He stayed there all afternoon yesterday."

"I know. But he seemed to take a dislike to one of the other children."

"Oh, don't take any notice of that," said Ronnie. "That happens all the time. They'll be best friends before you know it."

"I'm not sure . . ."

"Why don't you ask him what he wants to do? I've got to go, Chels. I think I'm feeling sick again."

Chelsea hung up.

Ronnie wasn't exactly feeling fantastic, but after that call from Chelsea, she decided she could not stay in bed a moment longer listening to Mark belching and farting as the last of the twenty-four-hour bug took its deeply unpleasant course. She got up.

"I should go and check on Jack," she said.

"He'll be OK," said Mark. "Make the most of the free babysitting."

"He hardly knows his auntie. He might not be happy. She certainly didn't seem happy at the prospect of having him all day."

"Give them a chance to get to know each other," Mark suggested, "while you relax. Come on."

Ronnie snorted at that. How could she relax while one of their children was unwell and the other one was in the care of a woman who would probably swap him for a Gucci handbag if the opportunity arose? Mark tried to pull Ronnie back down on the mattress, but she resisted.

"You never give yourself a break," he said. "Let Chelsea take the strain."

"I wish I could," she said.

Mark rolled onto his back and sighed, but then his phone beeped. He had another text. That soon made him sit up. He grabbed his phone with astonishing speed.

Ronnie watched him read the message.

"You never get texts. Who's texting you now?" she asked.

"Cathy again," he said. "Wants to know if Fishy has a whole or a half-tin in the morning."

"A half-tin," said Ronnie. "She knows that. I told her three times."

"She's a bit forgetful," said Mark. "You know what she's like."

"I thought I did," said Ronnie.

Ronnie dropped in on Sophie on her way down the corridor. Though she had claimed to be on the point of death the night before, Sophie seemed to be doing all right. She was sitting up in bed with a new gossip magazine on her lap (courtesy of the hotel manager) and her smartphone in her hand. Her texting thumb moved constantly all the time Ronnie was in her room. It was as though her phone were a mere extension of her arm.

"I'm surprised you've got any credit left," Ronnie told her.

"Dad said I could have some extra since I'm stuck in my room being ill."

"Of course."

"Does Jack have to come back in my room tonight?" Sophie asked then. "Only, if I'm not a hundred per cent better, I think it would be a bit of a risk to expose him to my germs."

"You'll be better by tonight," said Ronnie.

"Oh, Mum, I don't know if I will." Sophie clutched her stomach.

"You can't expect your auntie Chelsea to have him in with her again. She doesn't want to share with a six-year-old."

"I bet she would," said Sophie, "if she knew how ill I am. My stomach still really hurts. Seriously, Mum, I'd be putting Jack in danger."

Ronnie shook her head.

"Please, Mum. Honestly. I'm not kidding."

"You are just like your father," said Ronnie. "I'll nominate you for a BAFTA."

It was time to rescue Jack.

Ronnie did not rate Sophie's chances of having her bedroom to herself for another night. Chelsea could not have made it clearer that morning that she did not relish being lumbered with a child.

It hadn't always been like that. As she walked down to the pool, Ronnie remembered how happily Chelsea had played with Sophie when she was a baby. She had seemed interested enough in her niece, doted on her even. Chelsea was always buying Sophie little presents with the money she made at her Saturday job. She had adored Sophie as a six-year-old, and yet she hadn't even sent a birthday card on Jack's all-important birthday. Perhaps she'd got bored of being an aunt. Ronnie's secret hope that Chelsea might relieve her of some of her burden on this trip had died a death in the hotel lobby when Chelsea had recoiled from Jack's hug. The sooner Ronnie relieved Chelsea of her emergency childcare duties, the better. Apart from anything, Chelsea seemed so ridiculously scared about looking after Jack. She could only make a hash of it.

Ronnie's worst fears were confirmed when she found her sister and her son sitting at a corner table in the Jolly Pirate restaurant.

"What the hell happened?" Ronnie asked without preamble. She dived on her son and started doing a damage assessment. She examined his chin, his hands and his knees in growing horror. "He's covered in blood."

"Not *covered*, exactly."

"I fell over in the playground," said Jack.

Chelsea concurred. "He was pushing the roundabout with a couple of other boys. They were running quite fast. Someone tripped and—"

"Oh dear God. He looks like he's scraped his face across the whole Kidz Klub."

"Yeah, that's what happened," said Jack, nonchalant as an action hero.

"Does it hurt?" Ronnie asked her son.

"It was worth it," said Jack cryptically.

"What do you mean, it was worth it?" said Ronnie.

"What do they ever mean?" asked Chelsea. "If there's one thing I'm learning very quickly, it's that you can never know the working of a child's mind."

"He needs some Dettol on those grazes," said Ronnie.

"Not Dettol!" Jack squealed. "I'm OK."

"You're not OK. You've got grazes and they might get infected. I still don't understand how he got in this state," Ronnie said again.

Jack was happy to fill her in. "Well, first of all, a little girl pushed me off the top of the slide."

"What?"

Ronnie's stomach lurched as she pictured her precious child pitching straight off the top of the ladder onto the tarmac. She glared at Chelsea. "He was pushed off the top of the slide?"

"Not *off* the slide. He came down the slide itself," Chelsea quickly explained. "I think he was shocked more than anything."

"What was the girl doing pushing him?"

"I think she was impatient for her turn."

"Then I pushed her really fast on the roundabout until she started screaming really loudly and fell off onto the ground," Jack concluded.

"She didn't fall off—" Chelsea interjected.

"Where were you while all this was happening?" Ronnie turned to her sister and moved straight to accusation mode. "Weren't you watching him?"

"That wasn't what happened and of course I was watching him! I got up and ran over there the minute I realised what was going on."

"Then Auntie Chelsea nearly got in an argument with the little girl's dad," said Jack. "He was telling me off. I thought he was going to shout at me."

"There was *no* shouting," said Chelsea. "I totally defused it. The girl's father and I agreed it was an accident. It was just the sort of thing that must happen in playgrounds every day. Everything is fine."

Ronnie didn't seem to think so.

"Was the little girl hurt?"

"I think she broke her arm," said Jack.

"She did *not* break her arm," said Chelsea. "He's exaggerating. She looked all right to me. She's fine. Everybody's fine."

"For pity's sake, I can't even be ill without something going wrong. Couldn't you just keep an eye on him for one morning without him almost getting killed?"

"I was watching him all the time."

"You let that girl push him off the slide."

"How was I to know that psychos come disguised as six-year-old girls wearing fairy wings?"

"If you had spent any time at all in a school playground, you would know all psychos start out exactly like that," Ronnie replied.

She was still checking Jack for cuts and grazes. "What's this?" She pointed to a graze on his elbow.

"I did that in the garden on Friday," Jack reminded her.

"You need to be more careful," said Ronnie, in what felt like her constant refrain.

"Can I have some lunch now?" he asked. "I'm starving. I'm going to sit next to Auntie Chelsea. She's my hero."

162

"Oh right. She let you fall off the slide and scrape half your face off on the roundabout and she's your hero," Ronnie echoed.

"She protected me from the man."

"Who is this man?" Ronnie asked Chelsea.

"It's fine, Ronnie. He's talking about the girl's father. I sat next to them on the plane coming out here. He's all right. He would never have shouted at Jack. He was just a bit stressed about his daughter. I had everything under control."

"Why don't you run over to the buffet and see what there is to eat?" Ronnie told her son.

"OK." Jack scampered off in search of chips. The two sisters watched him without speaking. They could each tell that the other one was getting ready to blow.

"Well, thank you, Chelsea," Chelsea broke the silence at last, saying the words that Ronnie wouldn't say. "For looking after my son all morning while I lay in bed."

"I wasn't just lazing around, you know. I was *ill*."

"I know. I stepped in to help you."

"Yes, and I'm very grateful."

"You've got a great way of showing it."

"My son is covered in scrapes and cuts. Another child's parent verbally abused him. All that happened on your watch. Do you want me to be happy about it?"

"There was no verbal abuse. I stepped in at once. I did my best." Chelsea folded her arms and looked away.

"You were probably emailing. Your work is the most important thing in life after all."

"In *my* life, yes, since it's all that I have, as you're always pointing out."

"Ah well, better than my boring life as a stay-at-home mum, eh?"

"It's not a competition."

Jack had returned to the table carrying a tray, in the middle of which was a plate piled high with chips. The woman behind the counter had clearly given him a double portion. Jack's face could make people do that. Both Ronnie and Chelsea turned to smile at him, and both could tell by the watery smile he returned that he somehow knew they'd just been having a disagreement.

"Those look good," said Chelsea, pinching a couple of chips from the top of the pile.

"Mummy," said Jack, "you can have some too."

"I don't think I'm quite up to it, sweetheart," said Ronnie. "My tummy's still a little bit tender."

"Will you be better soon?" Jack asked her, full of genuine concern.

"Of course I will. I just need to take it easy this afternoon. No running around for me."

"Oh!" Jack suddenly exclaimed. "Tomato sauce! I forgot the tomato sauce."

He headed back to the buffet at high speed.

"Is it all right if I leave him with you now?" Chelsea asked. "I mean, you can sit by the pool and watch him, I assume?"

"Yeah," said Ronnie. "It's OK."

"Good, because I really do have work to do."

"I think it's probably safer in any case."

"Thanks a lot."

Chelsea headed for her room without looking back.

"Where's she going?" Jack was very disappointed to see his auntie leave.

Chelsea had to walk past the Kidz Klub to get to her room. She pulled her hat down low as she neared the picket fence. She wasn't sure she was ready to see Adam. What a disappointment. She'd thought Adam was great but after the antics in the playground, she was left thoroughly confused. Lily had definitely shoved Jack. Jack had definitely deliberately pushed the roundabout too hard. Did that make them quits?

Adam was there. He was standing by the picket fence, talking on his phone. Chelsea thought perhaps she could get past without attracting his attention. All she had to do was keep walking. But Chelsea had reckoned without her stupid sun-hat. While she was studiously ignoring Adam, who had spotted her and was actually waving, Chelsea walked straight into the metal post that held the Kidz Klub flag.

If only Chelsea hadn't been walking so fast, she might have been able to stay on her feet. As it was, the collision knocked her straight to the floor, where she lay spread-eagled to the enormous amusement of at least a dozen other holiday-makers.

Seeing Chelsea wipe out, Adam vaulted the short fence. He helped her into a sitting position.

"Are you OK?" he asked her. "How many fingers am I holding up?"

Chelsea assured him she was fine. Her mortification was far more painful than the bump on her head at this point.

"That hat is bloody lethal," said Adam.

"You've got to suffer for your style," Chelsea echoed his comment of earlier in the day.

"Do you need someone to walk you back to your room?" Adam asked.

"No," Chelsea told him. "I can manage on my own. You need to keep an eye on Lily."

"Look, I'm really sorry about this morning. Kids just take against each other sometimes. I suppose it's understandable. I mean, we grown-ups make snap decisions about people too."

"I suppose we do," said Chelsea.

"Let me get that."

Adam helped Chelsea to stand up and then went to pick up her bag, but only got one of the straps so the contents spilled onto the floor again. And there was *From Booty Call to Bride*.

"You're really reading that stuff?"

"Like I said, it's for work."

"Daddyyyyy!" the cry went up from the playground. "Leave that horrible lady alone."

Chelsea snatched the book up and made as fast an exit as her dizziness would allow.

CHAPTER
TWENTY-ONE

Chelsea

When Chelsea came down to the bar ahead of dinner that evening, with a bruise the size of an egg on her forehead (though thankfully no concussion, according to the hotel doc), she drew a round of applause from the next table, where two of the Kidz Klub dads sat with their grubby brood.

"Yeah, thanks," said Chelsea.

"It was better entertainment than the club puts on," one of the dads explained to his wife. "You should have seen it. Straight into the post and flat on her back. I haven't laughed so much in years."

"He's not got much to laugh about," said his wife. She raised her glass at Chelsea.

"Glad I could brighten your day," said Chelsea tightly.

She got a round of applause from her own family too. Having for the most part recovered from their tummy bugs, they were keen to replenish the calories they had lost, starting with a liquid infusion. Chelsea regarded the row of beers set out before the adults. Sophie was drinking a Diet Coke the size of a bucket.

"The warrior returns," said Jacqui. "Jack's told us all about your morning at the Kidz Klub. I think you deserve a drink."

"I certainly need one," said Chelsea.

"I'll get it," said Mark.

"A glass of wine. Rioja if they've got it," she added, though she knew it was unlikely there was a choice beyond colour. "Red."

Jack touched Chelsea's bruise tenderly.

"Does it hurt?" he asked.

"I expect Auntie Chelsea's pride hurts more than her head," said Jacqui.

"No. My head hurts like shit as well."

Jack's eyes widened.

"I mean, my head hurts like billy-o," Chelsea corrected herself. "I know I mustn't swear."

"Auntie Chelsea swears a lot," Jack observed.

"Auntie Chelsea often feels the need to," Chelsea said.

That night, the family Benson ate at Roma Roma, the resort's Italian-style trattoria, which promised proper pizzas from a proper wood-fired pizza oven. The twenty-four-hour bug was long forgotten as they arranged themselves at a huge circular table covered in a plastic chequered cloth. Jack was delighted at the prospect of pizza. He ordered a twelve-inch Margherita.

"He'll never eat all that," said Chelsea. "Surely?"

"No," said Mark, "but it's all-inclusive, isn't it? So it doesn't matter. You order what you want, Jack. Go wild."

168

Mark ordered a twelve-inch American hot for himself. Bill followed suit.

"Pepperoni gives you wind, Bill," Jacqui reminded him.

That prompted Bill to give a demonstration of his prodigious ability to fart to order anyway, pepperoni or not.

"My old man's a dustman . . . Thrrrruuuppp . . . He wears a dustman's hat . . . Parp," Bill farted at the end of every line.

Wanting with all her heart to be able to sink under the tablecloth while her grandfather broke wind at will, Chelsea stared at the menu as though something that didn't have a dough base might suddenly appear. There was a salad. She ordered that. When it arrived, it comprised a small breakfast bowl filled with iceberg lettuce topped with grated carrot and a teaspoon of tinned sweetcorn. It was the least appetising salad Chelsea had seen in a long time. She hated tinned sweetcorn, and the grated carrot looked as though it had been in the dish for a week. At the same time, Jack's twelve-inch pizza appeared. It was glorious. The smell filled Chelsea's nostrils and set her mouth watering. Worse still, Jack asked her to cut it into segments for him.

"You can have a piece," he told her.

Chelsea could not resist. She hadn't eaten pizza in a good four years, but that night, she was unable to hold herself back. Jack gave up after three slices, leaving more than two-thirds of the pizza on his plate. While he tucked into an ice-cream sundae, Chelsea found herself finishing off the pizza. She told herself it would have been obscene to leave so much food uneaten. It was flat out wrong to order something that would end up in a dustbin half an hour later.

"I wouldn't have thought you'd eat pizza," Ronnie commented. "Not the best way to keep slim."

"Well, you can't eat pizza every day and expect to keep the weight off, but every once in a while—"

"I don't eat pizza every day."

"I wasn't saying you do. I didn't say anything about you. I was talking about me."

"It's impossible, you know, to make a meal that everyone in the family will eat. I've got one who says she won't eat meat, except her father's bacon sandwiches, and another one who won't eat fresh fruit or vegetables."

"That's Dad," Jack chipped in.

"The only thing they will all eat is chips and pizza. What am I supposed to do? Cook four different meals every night?"

Chelsea shrugged.

"I do the best I can."

"Nobody's judging you," said Chelsea.

"Well, that isn't how it sounds."

"It was you who said *you* were surprised I ate pizza."

"Well, I am. Still, I suppose you've got time to go to the gym. I haven't."

"I don't have that much time to go to the gym. I've got a full-time job, and trust me, no one in my office knocks off at five."

"Magazines like yours make life hard for people like me," said Ronnie. "You keep banging on about 'having it all'. Well, the truth is, that's impossible. You can't have children and work *and* stay a size ten. Not unless your husband's a banker, like the kind of blokes you seem to go out with."

Chelsea felt a small stab of pain at the thought of Colin, the only banker she had ever been out with. Colin was engaged. He had well and truly moved on. Even so, a part of her, even now, wanted to keep the door open for him, just a crack.

Ronnie carried on. "I suppose you've got to keep yourself a size ten to be with a man like that or he'll trade you in for a slimmer model."

Chelsea had not told her sister that was exactly what had happened as far as Colin was concerned. She'd been traded in. Having said that, it was a long time since Chelsea had been a size ten. She had got herself down to an eight, a six in some brands, some five years earlier and she never wanted to see double figures on the label of one of her outfits again.

"I like my job," said Chelsea, carefully avoiding the subject of her single status. She wasn't sure Ronnie even knew Colin was no longer on the scene. "And I like to think our readers are intelligent enough to pick and choose the things that apply to their lives from each issue we produce."

"What about all those PhotoShopped models making young girls think they're fat?"

"I can't believe there's a single woman left on the planet who doesn't know what PhotoShop is. But people want to see beautiful pictures. Whatever they say to the contrary, they don't want to see fat models, and they don't want to see their celebrities with spots."

"I do," said Ronnie.

"Which celebrities have spots?" asked Sophie, suddenly interested.

"Some of them. Quite a few of them."

"Name names."

Chelsea thought about Eugenia Lapkiss, who wore so much make-up over her acne scars she could barely move her face. She didn't share the thought. She did not want Sophie to post the information straight into the cyber-world.

"I still think what you do is irresponsible," said Ronnie. "I don't see how it adds anything to the greater good."

"The fashion and beauty industries employ hundreds of thousands of people," said Chelsea, trotting out her usual justification. As her adrenaline rose in anticipation of having to defend herself yet again, Chelsea folded the last piece of Jack's pizza into her mouth. Feeling attacked always made her hungry. She hated that about herself and often wished she could be like Carola, who dropped a dress size if anyone so much as looked at her funny on the Tube. Carola had almost physically vanished when her husband left her for the nurse. "The one consolation is that I can wear sample sizes again," she'd confided to Chelsea.

"The arms industry employs hundreds of thousands of people as well," Ronnie carried on the argument.

"I really don't think you can compare women's magazines with making guns."

"They both cause misery," said Ronnie. "People die starving themselves to look like models."

"It's not that simple," said Chelsea. "Eating disorders have all sorts of causes, and I doubt that most sufferers would say reading *Society* magazine was the main one."

Ronnie would not give up. She continued to harangue Chelsea about the magazine world's irresponsibility for what seemed like another hour. Sophie watched in awe. Jack tried to change the subject to one of his kids' shows, but Ronnie wasn't having it.

"I'm going upstairs," said Chelsea at last. "I've had a long day."

"Are you taking me up?" asked Jack. He jumped off his chair.

"I don't think you're staying with me tonight," said Chelsea, "not now your sister's better."

"Awwww," said Jack.

"Actually—" as if on cue, Sophie clutched at her stomach — "I don't think I should have eaten that pizza, Mum. I don't think that bug is completely out of my system. I think eating pizza might have reactivated it."

"Sophie's going to be sick again," said Jack, unable to disguise his glee. He knew exactly what Sophie was trying to engineer with her display of gastric distress. To maximise his chances of benefiting, he made a shot for his own Oscar nomination. "I'm afraid she's going to be sick on me!"

"Oh, Jack," said Jacqui. "You'll be all right, dear. Your sister isn't going to be sick."

"I don't know that for sure," said Jack, with plenty of vibrato. "I'm frightened."

"She's just having a twinge, aren't you, Sophie?"

"I don't know, Mum. I think . . ." Sophie covered her mouth and started to heave.

"Oh no!" Jack wailed as Sophie made a run for the nearest loo.

"All right, your mum can bring you up to my room in half an hour," Chelsea told her nephew.

"Thanks," Jacqui mouthed at her. Ronnie just nodded.

"But I need half an hour, OK?"

What had Chelsea been thinking? Why had she said that Jack could share with her again when Sophie was so obviously faking? She needed some space for herself. The pizza seemed to have stuck halfway down Chelsea's oesophagus as though it knew it would be coming straight back up the moment she was alone. She stuck the handle of her toothbrush down her throat to help it on its way. She didn't have long before Jack came upstairs.

Chelsea knew her desire to stay thin had nothing to do with an early love of fashion magazines. She wasn't a slim teenager, but she'd not been particularly bothered by her weight. The moment she decided she was going to do something about it came when Ronnie got pregnant with Sophie. The news soon spread around school and subsequently the whole neighbourhood.

174

Chelsea still flushed hot and cold as she remembered the afternoon a neighbour had stopped her in the street to ask when the baby was due. Chelsea could tell that the woman thought she was being so "right on" about it, talking to Chelsea as though she were a fellow adult rather than a teenage girl.

"You must be very tired," the woman said, "still having to do all that schoolwork. When I had my first, I hardly showed at all but your—"

Chelsea didn't let her finish the sentence. She didn't want to hear her say, "Your stomach is so fat." Chelsea ran home to find her mother and sister in the kitchen, making baby plans. They were always making baby plans. No one seemed interested in what Chelsea was up to any more, nor now Ronnie was pregnant. Chelsea could have got a tattoo on the middle of her forehead and she didn't think Jacqui would have noticed.

Ironically, at six months gone, Ronnie was still scarcely showing. Chelsea blurted out the source of her pain. Her mother tried to put a positive spin on it.

"She's just a silly old woman, and your school jumper is a bit baggy."

It didn't help Chelsea feel any better. She went upstairs to her bedroom and cried for a while. Then she stood in front of the mirror on the back of the wardrobe door for hours, turning this way and that, examining her body from all angles. Every angle said she was fat. The mirror in the hotel room in Lanzarote still said exactly the same.

CHAPTER
TWENTY-TWO

Ronnie

Chelsea's sudden departure had brought that evening's family dinner to an end. Jacqui was upset that Chelsea seemed to have left in a mood. Ronnie was indignant. As far as she was concerned, Chelsea had been picking on her.

"She's got so superior since she's been at that magazine."

"She can't help what her job is," said Jacqui.

"She's not interested in anything that doesn't come out of London. She thinks hanging out with her family is beneath her. She's not interested in her niece or nephew."

"Rubbish!" said Jacqui. "She helped you out today."

"I'd have done the same for her," Ronnie protested.

The men didn't dare say anything. Sophie buried herself in texting. Jack played with his DS. Only Bill seemed entirely oblivious to what was going on.

"Now I've had my dinner, I want that pint Dave promised me," he said. Bill's memory was perfect when it came to remembering who owed him a drink.

Quick as a flash, Mark volunteered to help Dave chaperone the old man in the hotel bar.

"Fine," said Ronnie. "I suppose I'll take Jack up."

"Dave needs some support," Mark explained.

"And I don't?"

"Oh come on, Ronnie, we're on our holiday."

"You're on *your* holiday. I'm continuing to do everything I do back home here abroad, and more."

"Chelsea doesn't want me in her room while Jack's cleaning his teeth and that," said Mark.

"I don't think Chelsea wants me in there either, but that's what she's going to get while you're otherwise occupied with another bloody pint. Jack, say goodnight to your grandma."

Exactly thirty minutes after Chelsea went up to bed, Ronnie knocked on her bedroom door. She was surprised when Chelsea opened it with a bright smile on her face, though perhaps that smile was more for Jack than for Ronnie.

"All right, Auntie Chelsea?"

"Hello, Jack. I've made up your bed. I bet you're tired after such a busy day," Chelsea said. There was hope in her voice.

"Not really," said Jack. "I don't want to go to sleep yet."

"But you *are* going to go to sleep," Ronnie reminded him, "because otherwise you'll be miserable in the morning. OK? You know how you get when you don't have enough sleep. No chatting."

"No chatting," Jack promised, but he attempted an ostentatious wink in Chelsea's direction that suggested he had other ideas.

"Don't let him chat," said Ronnie to Chelsea.

"I'll do my best. He does seem to like to talk."

"Go and get yourself sorted out in the bathroom, Jack."

Jack took his toothbrush from his mother. She had already squirted a squiggle of paste on the bristles.

"Make sure you clean every single tooth!"

Jack started running the taps.

While Jack was cleaning his teeth, Ronnie sat down on the end of Jack's bed and let out a deep sigh. It was the kind of sigh that spoke of decades of disappointment. Ronnie lay back on his mattress and covered her eyes with her arm.

"Mum thinks I was picking on you tonight," she said.

"Really?" said Chelsea, voice dripping with sarcasm. "I didn't notice."

"I know you can't help what goes into every magazine, but I worry for Sophie, you know. She's really changed over the last few months, and I don't think she eats as much as she should."

"She looks OK to me."

"Yeah? That's because you spend every day surrounded by anorexic models."

"Right," said Chelsea.

"Look, I'm sorry if you think I was unreasonable back there, but I've got a lot on my mind. I still feel bloody awful from that stomach bug, and I've been getting it in my ear left, right and centre. Mark doesn't seem to understand Sophie is at that difficult stage. He thinks he can still joke with her the way he used to, but

178

she takes everything anyone says so personally and she vents her frustration on me. It's driving me mad."

Chelsea's iPhone buzzed. Her attention was immediately diverted.

"I don't know why I'm bothering to tell you this anyway," said Ronnie, clocking that Chelsea was distracted. "You've obviously got more interesting things to think about."

"No, not at all." Chelsea put down her phone. "I'm listening. Look, I'm sorry you're still not feeling well, but Sophie seems very grown-up. She'll be fine. I can't believe how much she's matured. I was quite shocked when I first saw her yesterday afternoon."

"Well, if you'd been to see her more often, perhaps the difference wouldn't seem so dramatic."

"It's not that long since I was last at your house."

"You haven't been to see us in over two years."

"You didn't exactly bombard me with invitations."

"Well, you know why that is . . ." said Ronnie.

"No," said Chelsea.

"Like you don't remember? The last time you saw me, you told me that I'd given up on myself since I became a mother."

"I never said that."

"You did. You told me it must be awful never having to use your brain, and then you said perhaps that suited the kind of women who become mothers anyway. They can't wait to stop using their brains."

Chelsea rocked back as if to get out of the line of fire. "I never said any of that. You're misremembering."

"I'm not."

"Well, I don't remember saying any of it, but if I did, it sounds like I was making a general point anyway. I wasn't having a go at you personally."

"Oh really?"

"Yes, really. Perhaps all I was saying is that there are a lot of women out there who make out that motherhood is some great sacrifice, when, for the most part, it looks like an extended holiday to me. The women who've gone on maternity leave from my office seemed to spend all their time posting Twitter updates from paint-your-own-pottery cafés."

"And that makes you think it's easy?"

"Maybe they just make it *look* easy," said Chelsea. "Like you do."

Ronnie thought she heard sarcasm again.

"Well, let me tell you, it is not easy," Ronnie replied. "Not in the least. Can you even begin to imagine what it's like to have to worry about the welfare of another human being twenty-four-seven, three hundred and sixty-five days a year?"

"I have some idea after this morning at the Kidz Klub," said Chelsea.

"Well, it's not much of a holiday for me, that's all I'm saying. I'm not off duty when we get to the hotel. I've still got to make sure they're all washed and dressed and fed and happy and not bloody drowning in the pool. There's no chance of me swanning off on a spa break with a bag full of paperbacks. I didn't even have time to read the emergency card on the aeroplane. Every time I want to relax, somebody needs me to do something, or somebody's making someone else cry.

Between housework and homework and going to work and making sure the family runs like clockwork, I don't have a second to think of myself. I don't even have time to be ill."

"Fine," said Chelsea, holding up her hands. "I get it."

"I don't think you do."

"I *do* get it."

"You called me a 'mummy martyr' at Granddad Bill's birthday."

"I genuinely don't remember saying that, and I swear I didn't mean it if I did. I do get it. Your life is *so* much harder than mine. It doesn't count for anything that you have Mark while I have to do everything on my own. I work *full* time. I do *all* my own housework, and I pay *all* my own bills. I don't have anyone to help me unblock the toilet in the middle of the night. There's no one to so much as make me a cup of tea if I'm ill. You think that's having it easy? You have no idea what my life is like."

"And you have no idea what my life is like, so perhaps we should leave it at that rather than getting into a contest as to who's having the more shit time. I'm going to see if Jack's finished his teeth. You can go back to reading your emails."

Chelsea had picked up her iPhone in response to another ping. Like Pavlov's dogs, she couldn't *not* respond to the bell. She put it down again.

"OK," she said. "I'll do it."

"Do what?"

"I'll look after Jack again tomorrow morning so you can have some more rest. You clearly need it. Like you said this morning, he's a good kid. He's really no trouble. I'm sure I can manage a couple more hours."

"Are you serious?"

Chelsea nodded.

"I don't want you to put yourself out."

"I won't be putting myself out. It'll be my pleasure," Chelsea assured her.

Ronnie frowned. She couldn't believe what she was hearing. Chelsea must have been expecting her to say, "Don't bother," thinking she would get the brownie points anyway for having volunteered. She decided to call her bluff.

"Well, if you really want to—"

"Of course I want to. You have a lie-in. I'll get him dressed and take him down to breakfast. Then we'll find something to do until lunch time. You can spend the whole morning in bed."

Jack came out of the bathroom, grimacing to show his mother that his teeth — at least the ones at the front — were sparkling clean.

"Auntie Chelsea is going to look after you again tomorrow morning," Ronnie told him.

"Yay!" Jack pumped his arms. "Aun-tie Chel-sea, Aun-tie Chel-sea." He sang her name as though it were a football chant.

"I suppose that means he's pleased," said Chelsea.

"Oh yes," said Ronnie, "he's delighted."

CHAPTER
TWENTY-THREE

Bill

The three men in the Benson party took up a small table in the corner by the TV screen. It was Dave and Mark's usual preference to stand at the bar, but as they walked in, Dave spotted the two women Bill had insulted the previous evening and decided it would be better they stayed as far away from them as possible. Mark had heard the story of the previous night's incident and understood Dave right away. Mark went up to the bar to get the drinks in, while Dave installed Bill and his walking stick safely in the corner under the enormous wall-hung television.

"I can't see anything from here," Bill complained.

"That's probably for the best," said Dave.

Over at the bar, Mark kept his head down, but just as the barman was pouring out the third and final pint, one of the women Bill had insulted — the blonde one — gave a little "ahem" to catch his attention.

"Having a nice evening?" she asked.

"Er, yes, thanks," said Mark.

The woman adjusted the front of her blouse as though to make sure her cleavage wasn't showing, with the result that Mark couldn't help but stare at the expanse of slightly crêpey, bronzed flesh she'd revealed. She'd done it deliberately, of course. Mark snapped his eyes back to the three pints arrayed on the counter. Was she coming on to him? The last thing he wanted was to be set upon by a cougar. He had a feeling he was already in Ronnie's bad books. Besides, the texture of the blonde woman's cleavage made him think of a perfectly roasted chicken.

"Is that your dad?" the woman asked, indicating Dave, who was semaphoring that Mark should get out of there pronto.

"Father-in-law. Well, sort of. I'm not actually married to his daughter, but . . . You know. We've been together a long time. We've got two children."

"Aaaah," said the woman. "You don't have to explain it to me, love. Nobody gets married first these days, do they? So that's not your granddad?"

"Bill? No. He's my partner's granddad."

"Lovely man," said the woman. "Really gentlemanly."

Mark wasn't sure he'd heard right.

"We met him last night," the woman continued. "Will you tell him 'hello' from me? My name is Gloria, and this is my friend Lesley."

Mark and Lesley nodded to one another.

"Pleased to meet you," Lesley said.

"Yeah," said Mark. "The same."

What was going on? Mark looked to Dave for reassurance. Dave was busy fishing about on the floor for something Bill had dropped. Either that or he was hiding.

184

Mark gathered up the three pints. It was going to be tricky to carry all three at once without spilling anything, but he didn't want to have to make a second trip. Gloria was scary. It was hard to believe that anything Granddad Bill said could have bothered her overly much. There was something of the shark beneath her rainbow eyeshadow and false lashes.

"I was wondering . . . Do you mind if we join you?" Gloria asked.

"Join us?" Mark squeaked.

"Yes. Come and sit with you and your in-laws. I mean, Lesley and I love each other to bits, but we can't help getting bored of each other, stuck with no one else to talk to all week. Isn't that right, Lesley?"

Lesley nodded enthusiastically.

"Well," said Mark, "I — My partner's grandfather is a bit—"

"—of a card! Oh, we know. That doesn't matter to us. We like a laugh, don't we, Lesley?"

Lesley nodded again.

"In that case . . ." said Mark. What else could he say?

Mark suspected having the ladies join them at the table was far from a brilliant idea, but he had no idea how to put them off without sounding rude, and so Gloria and Lesley gathered up their bottle of rosé and two glasses with unseemly haste and followed Mark over to the corner. As he saw all three make their approach, Dave's eyes widened in horror. Bill, on the other hand, seemed delighted.

"Well, would you look at this," he said, regarding the two *femmes d'un certain age* as though they were supermodels. "Now I really have won the bleeding lottery."

"Oh, you're making us blush," said Gloria. "I'm Gloria."

"You're glorious," said Bill.

She held out her hand to him and he kissed it. Gloria giggled.

"I hope you don't mind us joining you. I was telling your grandson it gets a bit boring being two single ladies holidaying alone."

"You're never single?" asked Bill.

"To my eternal disappointment," said Gloria.

Mark gulped down a mouthful of beer before he choked on it. Dave just sat there saying nothing, looking as though he had been hit around the head with a wet fish.

"Which isn't to say that I haven't had offers," Gloria continued. "It's just that a woman in my position has to be careful. I'm sure you know what I mean, Bill."

Bill nodded. He didn't take his eyes from her cleavage.

"So where are you gentlemen from?" Lesley asked.

"Coventry," said Bill.

"Oh, I don't know Coventry," said Gloria. "I've always wanted to visit, though. You'll have to show me around one day."

"There's not much to see," said Mark.

"Not since the war, I suppose. Were you in the war, Bill?"

Dave and Mark groaned inwardly. She'd said the magic word.

186

"Man and boy," said Bill.

"I'd love to hear all about it," Gloria insisted.

"I don't think these ladies really want to hear how you killed an enemy soldier with your bare hands," Dave interrupted. "Not when they've just had their dinner. Not even if it was true," he added in an aside to Mark.

"You're right," said Bill. "I'll save it for another time."

"I'll look forward to it," said Gloria. She gave her empty glass a meaningful glance. Bill leapt to pick up the bottle of rose and spilt a good deal of it over the front of his own trousers as he did so. Everyone affected not to have noticed.

"So, what does one do around these parts for a good time after the bar shuts?" Gloria asked then. "Any ideas?"

"Wahey!" said Bill. "Let's all go down the disco and get grooving." Bill got to his feet and managed a couple of seconds of thrusting that would have made even the average rap star blush before he had to sit back down again.

"Careful, Dad," said Dave. "You need to pace yourself. He's had some trouble with his heart," Dave explained to the women.

"You poor love," said Gloria, placing a hand on Bill's knee.

"I think I'm having a heart attack again now," Bill responded. He fluttered a hand against his chest.

"But dancing's supposed to be good exercise," Gloria winked.

"I'm up for that," said Bill. "You, me and the girls." He nodded towards each of Gloria's considerable breasts.

"Oh, Bill!" She patted his knee again.

"Do you know what, Dad?" said Dave. "I'm going to bed. Come on up with me. I'll help you to the lift."

"It's only eleven," said Gloria.

"We've got an early start," said Dave. "A coach trip."

"Are we going on a coach trip?" asked Bill. "Nobody tells me anything."

"Jacqui told you this morning. Come on."

"Yeah," said Mark. "I should be going too." None of the men had finished their drinks. "I'll help you get up, Bill."

"Goodnight, Bill," said Gloria. "Have sweet dreams."

"Now you've given me something to dream about, I will."

It was hard for Dave to persuade his father to go to bed that evening. Bill dug his heels in halfway down the corridor, saying he'd changed his mind and wanted to go to the disco with the "lovely young ladies" downstairs.

"Not tonight, Dad," said Dave. "I've got to get up in the morning."

"What for?"

Bill had forgotten all about the imaginary coach trip, so Dave gave him an entirely different reason.

"Because Jacqui wants to go for a walk along the beach at sunrise, and it is her birthday week after all."

Bill snorted. "I can go dancing on my own."

188

"No, Dad," said Dave, "you can't."

Dave hated to watch his father's decline. There were evenings like tonight when for the most part he seemed to be his old self again, flirting with the ladies and cracking the odd joke that actually made sense, but then he would do something like that awful hip-thrusting dance, something that once upon a time would have made him blush with embarrassment if he'd even seen it on TV, and Dave was reminded that Bill's brain was breaking down. Those mental fences that had kept him from being rude or lewd ever since he understood what the word "rude" meant, now had great big gaps in them, allowing the worst of Bill to slip through and cause havoc.

On nights like tonight, Bill's old self would want to know why he was being treated like a child and it was hard to have to remind him that he needed supervision these days. Bill might think of himself as an adult, perfectly capable of going out alone, but that was because he seemed to have no memory of the numerous times lately he had been found wandering around Aldi in his dressing gown. The last thing Dave needed was for Bill to forget where he was, here in Lanzarote. Who knew where he might end up? Floating face down in the sea?

No, Bill was best tucked up in bed. Dave counted out his father's bedtime medication and turned back the sheet. The room Bill was sleeping in adjoined Dave and Jacqui's. They kept the connecting door ajar. If Bill decided to go anywhere, they would know about it.

"Night, Dad," said Dave.

"Night, son," said Bill.

"How was the bar?" Jacqui asked, when Dave finally climbed under the sheet and lay down beside her.

Dave told her about their female company.

"What, someone chatted you up?"

"Not me. It was weird. She kept talking to Dad."

"To Bill?"

"Yes. Perhaps she likes the company of older men?" Dave suggested. "Nothing so unusual in that. But Dad?"

"Exactly," said Jacqui. "What does she want with that doddery old git? She was almost certainly after you."

"I didn't encourage her if she was," said Dave.

"Hmmm. Some women don't need any encouragement," said Jacqui. "I don't think you should go to the bar on your own again," she teased. "I think I'll have to come with you."

"She wasn't after me, I'm telling you. She was full tractor beam on Dad."

"Strange woman," said Jacqui. "Still, there's no accounting for taste or I wouldn't have ended up with you, would I?"

Dave snuggled closer.

"Are you having a good time?" he asked.

"Yeah. It's lovely to have everyone around me."

"You seem a bit distracted."

"Do I? It's just . . . You know, I keep thinking about what we said we were going to do this week and I wonder if it wouldn't be a mistake."

190

"We don't have to tell them yet," said Dave. "Not if you don't think it's the right time."

"But there's never going to be a right time, is there? Not for what we've got to let them know. No. We've got to do it as soon as possible. I want to tell them while we're all here in the same place. Then Ronnie and Chelsea will at least be able to talk about it together. Think about what it means for them both, as sisters. Oh God. What will it mean to them?"

"It might bring them closer together," said Dave.

"It might. That would be a silver lining. They've been bickering like they're teenagers again." Jacqui rolled over onto her back. "Oh, I don't know. Maybe now isn't the right time. Ronnie is so worried about money and Sophie, it's making her really scratchy, and Chelsea . . . well, I really hoped she would be in a better place. I hoped she would have another boyfriend by now. Someone to help her take it all in. She's trying to make out she's happy on her own, but I don't really believe it, do you? She's so thin, and those circles under her eyes. She looks like she's not looking after herself. I don't want her to go back to London on her own, thinking the worst and not having anyone to turn to."

"She can always turn to us. She can talk to us about it as much as she wants."

"She might not want to, Dave. We've got to be prepared for that. She might not want to have anything to do with us at all after she hears what we've got to tell her."

"She's not like that. Not our Chelsea."

"I don't know, Dave. People react differently when they're shocked."

"She might not be shocked. She's a woman of the world. They both are, her and Ronnie."

"God, I hope you're right."

"Look, whatever you decide, I'll be right there with you," said Dave.

Jacqui kissed him on the forehead. "I am so lucky to have you, my loveliest love."

"Then you'd better keep kissing me," said Dave, "now you've got competition from Glorious Gloria down in the bar."

CHAPTER
TWENTY-FOUR

Chelsea

Tuesday

After the humiliation of her collision with a pole outside the Kidz Klub and her subsequent, bad, decision to get over some of that humiliation with a glass or three of wine and two-thirds of Jack's pizza, Chelsea did not feel like making a properly early start. Unfortunately, Jack woke at seven on the dot. Chelsea opened her eyes to find him leaning over her face again.

"Why do you keep doing that?" Chelsea asked him.

"I was checking to see you were breathing," he said.

"Am I?"

Jack backed off a little. Yep, she was definitely breathing. Morning breath. Chelsea dragged herself into a seated position. Her head was banging. She might have known that the Hotel Volcan's house red would be rank. It was going to give her a hangover far out of proportion to whatever small amount of pleasure she thought she'd gain by drinking it. This was despite the fact that Chelsea had done another purge once Jack was asleep. How was it possible there was even any wine left in her body after that? Chelsea clutched her forehead. She clutched it harder when she remembered that in a fit of alcohol-fuelled altruism the previous night, she had promised to look after Jack this morning.

"Are you all right?" Jack asked her.

"I'll be better when I've had a cup of tea," Chelsea told him.

"We can get one in the restaurant."

"What time is it?"

Chelsea picked up her phone and looked at the clock.

"Jack, it's still only seven o'clock in the morning. What do you want to be up so early for? You don't have to go to school."

"I don't want to miss a single minute of our holiday," he said.

"Can't you go back to sleep for just another half an hour?"

"No," said Jack. He climbed onto his bed and opened the curtains. "It's a spectacular day."

It's a spectacular day? Where on earth had Jack got that? Probably one of the cartoons he talked about endlessly. But Chelsea was not in the mood to talk about Captain Dick and Chief Space Bimbo Wee-Wee, or whatever Jack's heroes were called. She was in the mood for a couple of aspirin followed by another hour in bed. That wasn't going to happen, not if she didn't want to give Ronnie another stick to beat her with by going back on the offer of babysitting. So by a quarter past seven, Chelsea and Jack were the first two people in the breakfast queue at the Jolly Pirate. Chelsea wasn't sure whether that was a good thing or a bad

194

thing. On the plus side, the food would not have had long to fester under the greasy heat lamps. On the minus side, that was assuming the food currently being placed under the heat lamps had not already had an outing the day before.

"What are you having?" she asked Jack.

"A sausage sandwich."

Chelsea grimaced as the chef plopped two glistening logs made of pigs' snouts and tails onto the plate she held out to him. The sausages made her want to puke as she sliced them onto two pieces of bread. Still, Jack seemed to enjoy them. He assured Chelsea that it was one of the best sausage sandwiches he had ever eaten, even though Chelsea "did the spread wrong".

"I did the spread wrong?"

"Yes. The margarine. You didn't get it right to the edges," Jack explained.

"I see."

"You can try again tomorrow," Jack assured her.

"I think your mum will have to do your breakfast tomorrow," said Chelsea. This one morning was going to be enough to make her point. That was Chelsea's plan.

At eight o'clock, Jack and Chelsea were joined by some of the others. Mark was in search of a hangover cure, as was Dave. Only a proper English breakfast would do. Meanwhile, Jacqui needed to make sure Bill was fed and watered on time. She and Dave had discovered that one of the best ways to keep Bill on an even keel was to ensure his blood sugar and hydration levels stayed relatively constant.

"You're up early," Dave commented when he saw his younger daughter already at the breakfast table. "Bet you've never seen eight o'clock before."

"I get up this early every day to go to work," Chelsea reminded him. "At my *full-time* office job."

Why did everyone seem to have the impression that Chelsea didn't work for a living?

"Has he had enough breakfast?" Jacqui asked of Jack.

"I had the best sausage sandwich ever," Jack assured his grandmother. "Auntie Chelsea made it. She didn't get the spread right, but she did OK with the sauce."

"Oh," said Jacqui. "You did all right, Chelsea. Jack's very particular about his sandwiches."

"I am," Jack confirmed. "I'm very *per-tic-alar*."

Breakfast over, it was time to make plans for the day ahead. To Chelsea's chagrin, Jack insisted he wanted to go back to the Kidz Klub.

"No way," said Chelsea. "You may be ready to go back, but I am definitely not."

She'd decided it was best to stay away from the Kidz Klub for as long as possible. She didn't want to have to keep Jack from fighting with Lily. As it was, she'd spent most of breakfast anxiously watching the restaurant door for a sighting of Adam and his daughter. So far, so good. It was a pity she'd had to give up on any chance of continued flirtation with Adam as a consequence, but it was probably for the best.

"What are we going to do instead, then?" Jack asked.

196

Chelsea plucked an idea from thin air. "I thought we might go on a trip?"

"Ha!" Mark laughed out loud. "You'll have your work cut out, taking Jack on a trip on your own. Do you want me to put him on a lead for you?"

Jacqui pulled a face that suggested she wasn't sure it was such a grand plan either. Jack was only slightly less judgemental.

"What kind of trip?" he asked.

"Well," said Chelsea, "I'm sure we'll be able to find something really interesting. Lanzarote is an island of natural wonders after all."

"What sort of natural wonders?"

"Let's go and see what's available," said Chelsea.

"Rather you than me," said Mark.

CHAPTER
TWENTY-FIVE

Ronnie

Later that morning, Ronnie was attempting and failing to relax by the pool. Once again she was worrying about one of her children. Though Sophie said she was feeling better and had had a good night's sleep because Jack was in with Chelsea again, Ronnie hadn't seen her daughter smile in hours. At least she had stripped off that huge black T-shirt at last, though. Three days of baking-hot sun had won out over Sophie's determination to make herself look like a bad mime artist at all times. It was way too hot to be dressed from head to toe in black.

Ronnie watched her daughter carefully. It was so hard to believe when a tiny baby was born that it would one day be its own person, but Sophie had had plenty of personality from very early on. Ronnie had been proud to notice how alert Sophie had seemed compared to the other babies in the toddler group they attended. She spoke early. She walked early. She seemed especially sensitive, picking up on the moods and emotions of the people around her. Was that why she was such a miserable teen?

Ronnie felt a pair of eyes on her. She turned to find her own mother regarding her as closely as she had been watching Sophie. Jacqui smiled. She was clearly a little embarrassed to have been caught in the act.

"Are you all right, Mum?" Ronnie asked.

Jacqui nodded. "Yes. Just looking at my little girl. I can look at my little girl, can't I?"

"Ha. If only I could still claim to be little." Ronnie pulled out the front of her T-shirt. "I need to lose four stone."

"You're perfect as you are. I was just thinking how much you look like my mum," said Jacqui, "your Grandma Dot."

"Great. Now I look like a grandmother."

"That's not what I was saying. She was always very elegant, your grandma. She had lovely thick hair, like you do, and she didn't need to wear make-up. She had your colouring. She had your dark eyelashes and your blue eyes. She was considered very beautiful when she was young, you know."

"It's a shame we didn't get to meet her," said Ronnie.

"Yes, it is. I'm sure she would have loved you — you and Chelsea both." Jacqui looked off into the distance with a sad smile.

"You must think about her a lot."

Jacqui nodded. "I do, though not as much as I thought I would after I realised I'd seen her for the very last time. It comes and goes. Sometimes I can go for weeks and weeks without thinking about her once. Other times she's on my mind all day. I can almost hear her voice."

Ronnie proceeded carefully. Her mother had very rarely talked about her parents. Chelsea and Ronnie had never had the chance to meet them. They had both died long before the girls were born, as had their paternal grandmother. The only grandparent they had known was Granddad Bill. He'd done his best to make up for the lack of the others. He was always there, happy to eat mud pies in the Wendy House "café" Dave had built for the girls in the garden. Always ready with a packet of sweets in his pocket along with a big, soft cotton handkerchief to dry any tears.

Ronnie had always assumed her mother never talked about her parents because the memory of their deaths was too painful. It must have been especially lonely for her, not having siblings with whom to share the happy stories of her childhood. Perhaps she would share one with Ronnie now, though. Ronnie liked to think she knew a little better what people needed to help them open up since she'd been working at the funeral home. No matter how sad people were when they came in to say goodbye to their loved ones, Ronnie could generally coax a smile from the most downcast of faces by asking them to share a happy memory of the deceased. It was important to remember better times.

"Did you go on any good holidays with your parents?" Ronnie asked her mum. "Go anywhere nice?"

Jacqui looked at the ground. "Not that I can remember," she said.

It was a strange sort of answer. Who couldn't remember their childhood holidays? There must have been a couple. Still, Ronnie understood it was supposed to bring an end to that topic of conversation. She didn't push it.

"Well, I'm having a wonderful holiday now," she said instead. "Thanks, Mum, for bringing us all out here."

"It's important for a family to spend time together," said Jacqui.

Ronnie agreed.

"I'm glad you and Chelsea are both here this week. I know you aren't close like you used to be, but it's kind of your sister to look after Jack so you can get a bit of rest, isn't it?"

"Yes, it is. I suppose I had better make the most of it. Who knows what kind of trouble they'll get into today?"

"They'll be fine," said Jacqui. "That was a good idea of Chelsea's, taking Jack on a trip."

"It's certainly brave," said Ronnie.

"Who wants a cocktail?" asked Dave then, as he loomed over his wife and daughter and blocked out the sun with his belly.

"Dave," Jacqui scolded, "it's not even time for elevenses. We can't start drinking yet."

"We're on our holidays! It's always cocktail o'clock when you're on holiday. 'If you like pina colada . . .'" he began to sing. The smile came back to Jacqui's face as he pulled her to her feet to dance with him.

"You're a lunatic," Jacqui told her husband. "It's lucky I love you."

Ronnie shook her head affectionately. When she was Sophie's age, seeing any demonstration that her parents were so obviously crazy about each other had been mortifying. Now she was truly glad they had found each other all those years ago. Love like theirs, lasting over the decades, surviving the stress of having two children, was a real achievement. Ronnie glanced over at Mark. He was asleep beneath his newspaper, sleeping off the night before. The delicate pages of the *Sun* ruffled with each snore. Ronnie had a sudden stab of fear that perhaps they weren't going to dance into their twilight years together.

"I'm going for a walk," Sophie interrupted her thoughts.

"Don't go any further than the harbour," Ronnie instructed.

"Yeah, Mum. Whatever."

One day in the not-too-distant future, both Sophie and Jack would be off leading their own lives. What would Ronnie have left then? Did she and Mark have enough to carry them through?

Ping!

Mark had another text. He snorted into wakefulness and made a grab for his phone. What was so urgent? Ronnie stared at him. He noticed.

"Cathy. About the cat," he said unconvincingly.

CHAPTER
TWENTY-SIX

Chelsea

Jack had changed his mind about the trip. He wanted to go back to the Kidz Klub. Chelsea, however, would not be diverted from her plan. The lump on her forehead was still throbbing. That was the only reminder she needed as to why she would not be going anywhere near that picket-fenced patch of hell ever again. He could ask Ronnie to take him tomorrow. Chelsea ignored Jack's whining and handed over her credit card to the hotel receptionist.

"It will be exciting," Chelsea said to Jack. "We're going to see the Blue Lagoon."

"That doesn't sound very exciting," said Jack frankly.

"It is," said Chelsea. "It's where pirates hang out. I'm sure there are actual sea monsters too. We just have to spot them."

"Sea monsters?" Jack perked up. "Nobody told me there were sea monsters. But don't worry — I can protect you, Auntie Chelsea."

Jack was suddenly very much on board with the trip. Chelsea was relieved, thinking it would make her having rashly volunteered to look after Jack for the morning so much easier. It would get them out of the

203

resort for a couple of hours, and if Chelsea was going to be in Lanzarote until Sunday, then she might as well see some of its fabled cultural highlights. In reality, Chelsea had little more hope than Jack did that the Blue Lagoon would turn out to be as good as it looked in the pictures, but that was the trip that was on offer on a Tuesday.

It seemed an awful lot of the hotel's residents had had the same idea. By the time Jack had finished packing for the trip (he said he would need a lot of things, including his sonic screwdriver), the holiday rep had given up waiting for them. The bus driver had just pressed the button to close the doors when Chelsea hammered on the glass. He let them on.

"You're late," said the holiday rep, a woman who seemed so far from excited about her job that Chelsea wondered why she had ever left her native Scotland. She was the sort of woman who would have been more at home as a receptionist in a central London A&E department, asking people if their broken necks really warranted urgent attention.

"I'm sorry," said Chelsea, knowing there was little point doing anything but sucking up to the slab-faced cow. "You know what it's like, getting kids ready." Chelsea indicated Jack and his full-to-bursting rucksack with a dismissive wave of her hand.

Jack stared at her, so that she felt him silently berating her for her betrayal. Wasn't it a good thing that he was properly prepared for this trip? If there were going to be sea monsters, then a sonic screwdriver

204

could come in very handy indeed. He started to tell her as much.

"Come on," said Chelsea, cutting him off. "Let's find somewhere to sit. Quickly."

There wasn't much choice. It was the flight out to Lanzarote all over again. Chelsea could see just one empty double seat, which was in the row in front of the toilet. Who ever used the toilet on a coach? Chelsea wondered. She didn't even want to sit in the row in front of the thing, imagining every pothole in the road causing a dreadful sloshing of ordure in that tiny cabinet with its badly fitting door. But again, as with the flight to the island, Chelsea had no choice but to take her place next to the thunderbox. Manoeuvring Jack ahead of her, she directed him to the back of the bus as the driver began to rev the engine impatiently. Jack slid into the seat nearest the window. As Chelsea was sitting down beside him, she was curious to see Jack's mouth form a horrified "O".

"What's the matter?" she asked.

Chelsea followed the direction of Jack's stare. Oh no. How had she not noticed? Sitting right across the aisle from the empty row were Lily and her father. Adam gave them a friendly sort of greeting, but Lily's eyes were narrowed in that way which was becoming all too familiar. The previous day's incidents had obviously not been forgotten. Jack too, looked less than thrilled to see his playground nemesis. Chelsea sat down on the aisle side, shielding her nephew. She told Jack to look out of the window.

"There's nothing we can do about it," she whispered in his ear as she fastened the safety belt across his lap, "But we've got every right to be here, just as much as they have. Don't forget that."

Jack nodded, full of solemnity. He sat up straighter in his seat and crossed his hands in his lap. He looked dead ahead at the dirty antimacassar on the back of the seat in front of him.

"You can look at the view," Chelsea reminded him.

On the other side of the aisle, Lily and her father were tactfully looking out of their own window.

This was going to be fun.

CHAPTER
TWENTY-SEVEN

Chelsea

Lanzarote was a strange sort of island. It was certainly unlike any place else Chelsea had visited before. The volcanic landscape was more reminiscent of the surface of the moon than anywhere on Earth. Inland, the bright summer sunshine was absorbed by glowering grey mountains that undulated along the length of the island like the backs of sleeping dinosaurs. The coach passed a vineyard, also unlike any vineyard Chelsea had ever seen. Rather than being planted in regimented rows, the grapevines in Lanzarote were planted so that they grew low to the ground, surrounded by windbreaks of grey lava rock. In a voice that suggested the very opposite of enthusiasm, the Scottish guide assured the passengers that the wines of Lanzarote were superb. Chelsea wished she could have taken the tour that included a wine-tasting, but that probably wasn't such a great idea with Jack in tow. She was in loco parentis after all.

While Jack chattered on about another episode of *Captain Tim and the Brain-Melting Bobulons*, Chelsea chanced a glance across the aisle. Adam was treating his daughter to a very detailed analysis of the view from the window. He was talking about Lanzarote's dramatic volcanic past.

"Remember Vesuvius?" he asked her. "The volcano we saw last year? Well, Timanfaya, the volcano that erupted here, was about the same size as that."

"Were lots of people killed, Daddy?"

"I think most of them managed to get away," Adam assured her.

Lily wrinkled her nose as though that wasn't such good news as far as she was concerned.

"Is the volcano going to go off while we're here on holiday?" Jack asked Chelsea.

"No," said Chelsea, "it won't."

"How do you know?"

"Well, I don't know for certain."

"So it might go off." He pressed for details.

"Yes, I suppose it might."

"Cool. That would be exciting," said Jack. "I would like that."

Children were perverse little creatures, Chelsea decided. Across the aisle, Adam suppressed a smile. He must have been listening in, just as she had been eavesdropping on him. He glanced in Chelsea's direction. She allowed the corner of her mouth to twitch upwards in response. A shared joke. Perhaps when they got to the Blue Lagoon, they could encourage the children to make up and resume their cruelly curtailed flirtation. But as the tour's destination drew nearer, Chelsea grew tense as she realised that the Blue Lagoon car park would just as likely be the next potential flashpoint between Jack and Lily. When it came to getting off the bus, who was going to go first?

As it happened, Adam unbuckled his seatbelt as soon as the bus swung through the car-park gates, then reached for his daughter's seatbelt. His actions would give him valuable seconds to get ahead, but there was no way Chelsea would actually undo Jack's seatbelt until the bus had stopped moving. She couldn't. It would have been irresponsible.

When the bus did finally stop, Adam leapt to his feet. Chelsea did so too, forgetting that she still had her belt on. Jack was paralysed with embarrassment as Chelsea crumpled back down into her seat.

"You forgot to take off your seatbelt." Jack slapped his forehead. "Duh."

"I did it deliberately to make you laugh," Chelsea told him.

"It wasn't very funny," was Jack's verdict.

"At least I didn't bump my head on the ceiling at the same time," said Chelsea, indicating her bump.

"Looks sore," Adam commented, as he waited for Chelsea to unclick herself. Then he ushered her and Jack into the aisle ahead of his own daughter. Lily observed the gesture with a scowl.

"Thanks," said Chelsea.

"My pleasure," Adam said.

Once outside the coach, Chelsea made sure the entire coach party separated Jack from Lily as the holiday rep gave a short talk about safety procedures in the event that the caves should need to be evacuated. The short talk became a long talk. Jack, who had complained a little already about the heat on the bus, tried to shade himself by standing behind his auntie. He took off his hat. Chelsea insisted he put it back on.

"I don't want to," he said. "My head is boiling."

"You've got to. You'll get sunstroke otherwise."

"What's sunstroke?"

Chelsea realised she wasn't entirely sure.

"It's not nice. Jack, just put your hat on, will you?"

Jack refused, so Chelsea helped him edge back into the shade of the coach while the holiday rep continued her interminable speech. Didn't she realise she was forcing her party to stand out in the full glare of the midday sun while she droned on and on and on?

Chelsea was gratified to see they weren't the only people who had decided to dive for cover. Lily and Adam had slunk back into the shade too. Adam rolled his eyes at Chelsea, as if to say, "That rep woman is an idiot."

The children continued to ignore each other studiously until at last, the safety speech was over and the coach party made its way towards the entrance to the caves. Once again, Adam, ever the gentleman, indicated that Chelsea should go first.

The tour of the caves itself started off fairly promisingly. Jack was relieved to be out of the blazing sun and found the idea of going underground quite exciting. It wasn't long, however, before the spectacular vaulting space that housed the Blue Lagoon started to seem just a little, well, cavey in a boring sort of way and Jack started asking about the pirates. Where were they?

210

Why hadn't they seen them yet? Were they going to see them any time soon? And at what point would he have to fight a sea monster?

Chelsea realised that she had broken one of the cardinal rules of parenting in her attempt to make the day trip seem worth taking. You should never over-promise. Ronnie could have told her that. You may think it's harmless enough. You promise pirates and sea monsters for short-term compliance. Unfortunately, children aren't quite like goldfish and they don't forget what you've told them in the space of thirty seconds. Or even thirty minutes, if you've told them something even slightly compelling. Of course Jack wanted to know where the pirates were.

"Perhaps the pirates are out marauding on the high seas today," said Chelsea.

"Bor-ing," was Jack's response.

"I don't know why they'd ever leave these caves, though," Chelsea soldiered on. "How about that rock? It looks like an elephant's head."

"No it doesn't."

"Yes it does. Look."

Chelsea made Jack tilt his head to one side.

"No. I still can't see any elephants."

Jack wasn't the only one who was finding the natural beauty of the caves somewhat lacking.

"You said there would be mermaids," shouted Lily.

"I said there *might* be mermaids," said Adam. "That's different."

"No it's not."

"Look, Lily, look — can you see the strange white shellfish down there in the water? They're all white like that because they don't get any sunlight. They're extremely rare. Do you know, this is the only place in the world where you can see them?"

"Shellfish are boring," said Lily.

Jack, who actually had been peering closely at the curious albino creatures, sighed heavily and straightened up as though he had absorbed Lily's opinion.

"Aren't those shellfish amazing? You can tell all your friends you've seen something that exists nowhere else in the world," Chelsea suggested.

"They won't believe me," said Jack. "I'm too hot."

Jack dragged his feet for the rest of the trip. What was the fun in a blue lagoon if you couldn't wade right into it? Despite the proliferation of small white lobster-type creatures, the water looked so inviting, especially given the tremendous heat outside. Chelsea was beginning to understand why so many people didn't bother to move from the hotel pool. She would have paid good money to be able to dive in as well.

"Why can't we swim in it?" Jack asked a third time.

"In case the water's dirty," Chelsea told him.

"It's not dirty. It's completely clean. You can see right to the bottom."

"OK. In case we make the water dirty. We might kill the rare shellfish with our human germs."

"Shellfish are boring." Jack echoed Lily. "Why don't they take the shellfish out and make it into a swimming pool?"

212

"Because the shellfish in that pool are an endangered species. They're unique. They exist nowhere else in the world and this is their exclusive habitat." Chelsea tried to make it sound exciting.

"What's a habitat?"

"It's the place where they live. Coventry is your habitat. London is mine."

"Oh." Jack sighed. "I'm tired." He hung from Chelsea's elbow and twirled listlessly, as though her arm were a ribbon on a maypole. He pulled his T-shirt up to expose his comical little belly in an attempt to cool down. Then he pulled his hat right down over his eyes and asked her to lead him as though he couldn't see at all.

"OK, OK," said Chelsea eventually. "How about we get you an ice cream?"

Jack did a little dance of excitement and they headed for the kiosk, which was situated on a platform that would have made the perfect spot for an enchanted evening spent drinking champagne and watching the water. As it was, Chelsea would have to content herself with an instant coffee that smelt as though it had been made from ground-up dung. Chelsea immediately regretted having ordered it, though she could use the caffeine hit. The heat and the stress of looking after her nephew were making her long for her bed.

Jack deliberated for some time before he picked an ice cream, and when he did make his selection, Chelsea was quite surprised by its sophistication.

"I would like one of those," he said, pointing at a very grown-up-looking Cornetto-style affair.

"It's Black Forest Gateau flavour," said Chelsea. "Are you sure that's what you want?"

"Yes," said Jack. "Mummy has them in the freezer at home."

"Really? It's got cherries in it, soaked in something horrible."

"I know. I like them."

"Very well," said Chelsea. "Perhaps I'll have one too."

"This is actually the last one," said the girl behind the counter as she handed Jack the cone.

"OK," said Chelsea. "I'll have one of those instead." She picked out a plain orange ice lolly. It was probably a better idea than the Cornetto in any case. It would certainly contain fewer calories.

"Orange lollies are boring," said Jack.

"Thanks. Then perhaps you'll share your *not*-boring ice cream with me?"

"No way."

Chelsea helped Jack to unwrap his very grown-up Cornetto. He seemed delighted by the cone in his hand, filled as it was with soft white ice cream topped with chocolate and a dark cherry sauce.

"That does look good." Chelsea agreed with him. "Shall we find somewhere to sit? It'll be easier to eat sitting down. You might get a bit less of it down your T-shirt."

Chelsea was getting the hang of at least one aspect of this parenting lark. If she could get Jack back to the hotel without needing to change his clothes the minute they arrived, she was sure she would get some kudos.

214

Jack agreed that it would be a good idea if they could stay clean because "Mummy hates ironing."

"She ironed that?" Chelsea thought out loud. Chelsea had previously wondered if the one excuse for sending your kids out dressed in nylon was that it saved on ironing.

Jack made a start on his ice cream with exaggerated care. He held it so far away from himself that he had to poke his tongue out to its full length to lick it.

"Watch that drip on the other side, Jack," Chelsea warned him.

"I've got everything under control," he said. It was a phrase he had picked up from his father.

Adam, on the other hand, seemed to be struggling to maintain control in his world.

Like Chelsea, Adam had given up on trying to interest his charge in the wonders of evolution in isolation. No albino shellfish on earth was ever going to be as interesting to a six-year-old child as the prospect of a nice big hit of sugar and additives. In the queue for the kiosk, Lily was shouting at the top of her voice, "I want an ice cream!"

"I would never shout like that," said Jack.

"I know you wouldn't," said Chelsea, "because you have been brought up properly. And because we have both been brought up properly, we're definitely not going to stare while Lily has a tantrum." For a tantrum was definitely brewing, Chelsea decided. Both Chelsea and Jack pretended not to be watching while both, independent of the other, were actually keeping a very close eye on proceedings.

"I want an ice cream like that one," said Lily.

Jack froze as he realised that Lily was pointing at his Black Forest Cornetto.

"She's looking at my ice cream," Jack whispered to Chelsea.

"It's OK," said Chelsea. "Just keep eating."

"I don't think you'd like an ice cream like that one," said Adam. "It's got alcohol flavouring in it. I wouldn't say it's suitable for children at all."

Chelsea winced as she considered Adam's point. Still, a little bit of booze wouldn't do Jack too much harm, would it? He probably got a bigger hit of alcohol fumes each time Mark kissed him goodnight.

"I would say it *is* suitable," said Lily. "It's exactly what I'd like."

"It's got cherries in it, and dark chocolate."

"I like dark chocolate," said Lily.

"No you don't."

"I do. And I love cherries. Get me one of those."

"A Black Forest Gateau Cornetto, please." Adam caved in.

"That was the last one," said the girl behind the counter, nodding her head towards Jack.

"Lily," said Adam, "you're going to have to choose something else."

"But that's the one I want," said Lily, as though her intransigence would simply manifest another Black Forest ice cream.

"The lady says she hasn't got any more."

"He's got one." Lily whirled and pointed straight at Jack. Jack shuddered in response.

"He had the last one," said Adam. He shrugged at Chelsea and mouthed, "Sorry".

Chelsea mouthed back, "It's OK."

"I wanted the last one!" Lily continued.

"We didn't get to the kiosk in time."

"Why didn't we get here in time? Why did he get here first?"

"Lily, you can have something else. You can have anything you like. Look at all these lovely different flavours."

Lily, however, was not to be placated, not even with a mint-choc-chip version of the cone Jack was now almost too frightened to finish. While Adam peered at the list of available ice creams in search of something, anything, that might please his daughter and yet be relatively free of additives, Lily marched in Jack's direction.

"I want to taste it," she said. She almost, almost looked sweet as she asked him.

"She didn't say please," Jack appealed to Chelsea. "I don't want to let her have a taste of it."

"That's all right, Jack." Chelsea put her hand on his shoulder. "You don't have to. I'm sure her daddy's buying her an ice cream of her own."

"Please," Lily said sharply.

"No," Jack snapped right back.

Lily stared at the ice cream. Chelsea didn't know what to do. She looked to Adam desperately, but he was still studying the ice-creams that were available. Chelsea would not have been in the least bit surprised if Lily suddenly shot two laser beams from her eyes and melted the Cornetto into a puddle. Lily stood her ground. Jack stood his. Why should he let Lily try his ice cream? Perhaps subconsciously, Jack's free hand went to the hardening scab on his knee, the scab caused when he tripped over while pushing the roundabout.

Having recited the entire list of available ice creams for Lily's convenience, Adam finally noticed his daughter was no longer standing next to him. He reacted at once, turning to look for her, seeing her standing in front of Jack and moving in her direction as quickly as he could. Unfortunately, though, not quickly enough to stop Lily bringing her hand up beneath the hand in which Jack held his ice cream so that the Cornetto briefly collided with his face before sliding all the way down the front of his clean T-shirt.

"Oh my God," said Adam. "Lily, you . . ."

Jack, Lily and Chelsea all stared at the spot where Jack's ice cream lay. Now nobody was going to get to taste it.

Jack sat very still, but even Chelsea, with her limited experience of children, knew something was going on inside him. Something was building, something that would make the eruption of Timanfaya seem like a wisp of steam from the spout of a kettle. She had to react quickly. What would Ronnie do? Jack was clenching his fists. His face was twisting.

"Come on, Jack. Quick march."

Chelsea put her arm round Jack's shoulders and whisked him in the direction of the loos.

"I'm sorry," Adam called after them. "I'm so sorry. She's just hot and tired and . . ."

218

Chelsea didn't turn round. She exhaled hard. She didn't know what to say to him.

"Jack, count to ten, Jack. Count to ten." Chelsea needed to count to ten too.

"Mummy will be angry." Jack was starting to cry. "I've got ice cream on my clean T-shirt."

"I'll tell her what happened. You won't get into trouble."

"Why did she do it?"

"Lily? I don't know. I guess she must have been angry about yesterday, about the roundabout."

"But I was angry about the slide."

"I know. This is what happens, Jack. Anger spreads from one person to another. It's how wars begin."

"Are we in a war?" Jack asked.

"No, no, of course we're not," said Chelsea. "We're going to take the moral high ground."

"Where's that?"

"You mean, what's that. It's a turn of phrase. It means we keep calm and carry on. Or something like that."

"Carry on fighting?"

"Carry on being calm. Definitely not fighting."

Chelsea glanced back towards Adam, who was crouching down with his hands on Lily's shoulders. She could only imagine the conversation they were having now.

Chelsea had to clean Jack up before they got back on the bus. His T-shirt was covered in ice cream. Absolutely covered. Chelsea rinsed the worst of it out in a basin, but there was no way he could put it back on. Though it would dry soon enough outside, on an air-conditioned coach it would remain uncomfortably wet and cold. So Chelsea, who fortunately was wearing a pair of T-shirts layered, stripped off the outermost one and offered it to her nephew.

"It's orange! That's a girl's colour," Jack protested.

"Nonsense," said Chelsea as she wrestled him into it. The T-shirt almost reached Jack's knees. She tried to tuck the excess into his shorts. "Orange was all over the catwalks at the men's Paris shows. Give us a twirl."

Jack was unconvinced. He followed Chelsea to the coach with his head down.

"He could borrow one of Lily's T-shirts," Adam suggested when they were back in the car park. "I've got two spares in my bag."

"That's OK," said Chelsea. She knew there was no way Jack would be any happier in the pink T-shirt Adam was offering than the midi-length orange top he was already wearing.

"I'm very sorry. Lily knows what she did was wrong."

"Does she?" Chelsea hoped her look said everything. Lily was standing by the coach. Her face was red, as though she had been crying, but she didn't seem especially contrite.

"She does. We had a conversation and she is sorry. Believe me."

"Then shouldn't she say it herself? She doesn't need a conversation. She needs a telling-off."

"Look, don't go judging me about disciplining children. Your nephew is hardly a paragon of virtue. After what I saw on the roundabout yesterday . . ."

"You're bringing up yesterday? The roundabout? After what Lily did on the slide? Jack could have fallen off sideways and cracked his head open, and you tried to pretend that was an *accident*? What kind of thug are you bringing up?"

"Don't you dare call my daughter a thug."

"What else do you expect me to call her? She deliberately and spitefully pushed Jack's ice cream into his face."

"She was hot and tired and she wanted to try the ice cream he had."

"And that makes it right?"

"Of course it doesn't make it right, but . . . for goodness' sake. She's only a kid. She knows she did wrong. I've apologised on her behalf and I'll deal with it from here without any help from you. Look . . . just buy him a new T-shirt." Adam thrust a twenty-euro note in Chelsea's direction.

"Spend it on some lessons in manners," Chelsea suggested, as she thrust it right back.

"Why don't you spend it on a self-help book?" said Adam. "So you can be even more sure you're right about everything. No wonder you're single."

"Oh!" Chelsea let the note drop to the floor.

Unfortunately for Chelsea, Jack, Lily and Adam, the holidaymakers on the coach trip had all chosen to travel back to the resort in the same seats as on the journey out to the caves. The driver need not have bothered to turn on the air-conditioning. The back two rows of the coach were arctic, as the two adults and two children ignored each other even more emphatically than before. When the coach arrived back at the Hotel Volcan, Adam dispensed with etiquette, leaping to his feet and shuffling his daughter into the aisle before Chelsea even registered that the coach had stopped. She flicked the Vs at his retreating back, imbuing the gesture with all the anger that had been bubbling inside for the past few days. Adam got Colin and Davina and Ronnie's share of the Vs as well.

"That's rude," Jack breathed in awe.

"And you didn't see me do it."

"Auntie Chelsea," said Jack, as she helped him down from the coach, "you are awesome."

"Really?" Chelsea couldn't help preening.

"Yes. You're better than Captain Jack."

"I'll take that as a compliment," she said. But the good feeling didn't last. As she helped Jack down from the coach, she watched Adam heading into the hotel lobby. He glanced back in her direction. His expression was furious. That had to be the end of any chance of friendship now.

CHAPTER
TWENTY-EIGHT

Ronnie

Around lunchtime, Ronnie caught Jacqui staring at her again. It wasn't exactly annoying, but it was certainly unnerving. Her mother was looking at her in such an odd way, as though trying to form a mental picture of Ronnie's face that would last for ever. When Ronnie looked back at her, her brows dipping in a questioning way, Jacqui just smiled.

"Is everything OK, Mum?"

"Of course."

Then why was she being so odd? Ronnie wondered.

Perhaps she was just feeling nostalgic. Perhaps Jacqui really had been thinking about her own mother more than usual lately. But Ronnie did not consider her mother to be an especially nostalgic sort of woman. Jacqui was loving but practical. She wasn't much given to sentimentality. After thinking about it for a little too long, Ronnie decided there had to be a reason behind Jacqui's sudden spate of soppy gazing and she could only come up with bad ones. She wondered exactly when her grandmother had passed away. Had they inadvertently missed the anniversary? Perhaps it had happened in August.

"Mark," she said later on, "have you noticed my mum being a bit, well, odd these past couple of days?"

"What, odder than usual?" Mark responded. Ronnie swatted him with a newspaper, though she knew he only ever thought about her mother in the most affectionate terms. Ronnie had always been grateful for the fact that Mark and her parents liked each other. She knew that was relatively rare.

"I'm serious, Mark. Don't you think she's been acting a bit funny? She keeps grabbing hold of the children and kissing them."

"Isn't that what grandmothers do?"

"I mean she's been doing it more than usual, and I keep catching her looking at me in a funny way. It's as though she thinks that after this holiday she's never going to see us again or something."

"If only that were true. Your mum's round so often, I've been thinking of asking her if she wants our garage converted into a granny flat."

"Mark, be serious."

Mark merely looked blank. Ronnie pressed him for a more considered response to what she'd just said.

"So?" she asked. "Why do you think she keeps doing that?"

Mark shrugged. "I dunno. Maybe she wasn't looking at you. Maybe she needs new glasses. Maybe you're getting paranoid. It's all the formaldehyde you're inhaling at work."

"Oh for heaven's sake," said Ronnie. "I don't know why I ever bother to talk to you about anything serious at all."

"Well, what was I supposed to say?"

"How about something thoughtful? Or useful?"

"Bloody hell, Ronnie. Sometimes talking to you is like doing an exam. I don't know why your mum keeps looking at you. I don't know why anyone does anything. I'm just a man. Everything you women do is a mystery to me."

"Fine," said Ronnie. "I'm going to see what my sister is doing with our son."

"She'll come and find us when she's ready to hand Jack back."

"Assuming she hasn't lost him in a cave."

"Ronnie," said Mark, "you've got to learn to delegate. Trust your sister. You're on holiday. Make the most of it. Accept help when it's offered."

"Like it's ever offered."

"Chelsea offered to babysit this morning and that's what she's doing. I'm always offering to help around the house. You can't say I never ask what needs doing. You just keep turning me down."

"Because I'd only have to do everything again when you'd finished."

"If you think I'm that useless, I don't know why you bother with me at all," Mark sighed. He turned back to his paper. Then his phone chirped.

Ronnie glared at Mark's mobile. Once again, Mark scrambled to pick it up with the kind of speed that instantly betokened guilt.

"Who's texting you now?" Ronnie asked. "No one ever texts you. Now you're getting texts all the time."

"It's nothing," said Mark. "It's just one of those texts that tells you to remember it's expensive to call from abroad."

Ronnie snorted. "You're sure it's not from Cathy next door?"

"It's a bloody marketing text," said Mark, waving the phone at her. "See?"

"Then why did you look so guilty when your phone beeped?"

"I did not look guilty," said Mark.

"Could have fooled me."

"I've got nothing to be guilty about," Mark protested, lodging more firmly in Ronnie's mind than ever before the idea that he must have reason to feel very guilty indeed.

CHAPTER
TWENTY-NINE

Chelsea

Chelsea and Jack were back from the coach trip. Though Chelsea had only offered to look after Jack for the morning, she found she was unable to resist when he asked if she would take him to lunch. After that — Jack had a chip butty — they had gone to investigate the slightly smaller playground at the other end of the complex from the Kidz Klub. It was nowhere near as exciting. It was really a playground for toddlers. Chelsea and Jack ended up sitting with their feet in the paddling pool, discussing that morning's events as they stirred the sand that dirtied the pool's bottom with their toes.

Jack wanted to talk about the ice-cream incident again. He simply could not understand why Lily had taken against him in such a big way.

"I don't think you should take it personally," Chelsea assured him. "She spilt a drink all over me on the aeroplane."

"But that was an accident," said Jack.

"I'm not so sure." Then, realising that she probably shouldn't be quite so judgemental about a child, Chelsea added, "Perhaps Lily isn't very happy, or perhaps she's just been badly brought up and doesn't know right from wrong like you do."

Jack nodded in satisfaction. "She definitely doesn't know right from wrong, and I do, but I still feel like I want my revenge," he said.

"There will be no revenge," said Chelsea. "This isn't *Doctor Who*. You just have to try to forget what happened. And avoid the Kidz Klub for the rest of the week."

"But why should I avoid the Kidz Klub? Why should I have to go in the rubbish playground instead?"

Chelsea's heart went out to him. The hotel's other playground was indeed rubbish. Even the toddlers were turning up their noses at the battered old plastic slide. Why should Jack be the one who suffered because Adam couldn't keep his daughter under control? Chelsea felt her blood pressure rise as she remembered their altercation outside the coach back from the caves. He was such an idiot. Either he reacted badly because he was truly mortified his parenting skills were leading straight to an ASBO or he really was so blinkered he couldn't see that his beloved daughter was a proper little madam. Chelsea wondered where the child's mother was. She was almost certainly as much to blame. Or maybe she had left Adam because he was so spectacularly wet he had turned their only child into a monster.

"What are you thinking about?" Jack asked.

"Nothing," Chelsea lied. At least, for once, she wasn't thinking about Colin or her horrible boss at *Society*. Adam had given Chelsea a new focus for her bile. She winced as she thought of their exchange in the car park at the Blue Lagoon.

"If we can't have revenge," said Jack, "then we could beat them in the sandcastle competition?"

"There's a sandcastle competition?"

"At the Kidz Klub. They made an announcement."

"I didn't hear it."

"You were probably on your iPhone. The sandcastle competition is tomorrow and we could win a prize . . . but you said we can't go back there."

Jack's shoulders slumped.

"Well, maybe we can if there's a competition," said Chelsea. She realised as she said it that she'd unwittingly signed herself up for more babysitting. She was surprised to find she didn't mind.

Jack was delighted.

"Auntie Chelsea?"

"Yes?"

"Can I ask you another question?"

"Not if you're going to ask me if I'd rather be a rhino or an elephant again."

"I wasn't going to ask you that."

"Good," said Chelsea. "Because I don't know how I'm supposed to get the answer right."

"It's the rhino," said Jack. "Of course."

"Of course."

"But, Auntie Chelsea?"

"Yes?"

"Who lives at your house?"

"I do."

"Yes, but who else?"

"No one, Jack. I live on my own."

"No," Jack laughed as if the very idea were absurd. "Who lives in your house really?"

"Me. Just me."

"But Grandma's your mummy?"

"Yes."

"And Granddad's your daddy?"

"That's right."

"So why don't you live with them like I live with my mummy and daddy?"

"Because I'm a grown-up and I live on my own."

"People don't live on their own," said Jack.

"I assure you, Jack, they do. Hundreds of millions of people live on their own. The man who lives in the flat downstairs from me lives on his own. The lady across the corridor lives on her own. Lots of my friends live on their own too."

Jack was silent for a while.

"Auntie Chelsea?"

"Ye-essss?"

"Do you really live on your own?"

"I really do."

There was another pause while Jack took on board this unlikely news.

"But who looks after you?" was what he said at last.

Chelsea laughed. Jack sounded so very grave. She explained to him that she looked after herself and had been doing so for years, long before he was even born. She went to work to earn the money she needed. She paid the rent on her flat. She paid the bills. She did her own washing. She bought her own food and knew how

230

to cook it. OK, so perhaps the cooking bit was a stretch, but yes, she was perfectly capable of looking after herself.

"Will I have to look after myself one day?" Jack asked her. He didn't seem too happy at the prospect.

"I expect so," said Chelsea. "Unless you find yourself a nice wife."

"I'm going to do that. I'll get a nice wife. I know! You could be my wife," said Jack. He sounded very pleased with the idea. It was the perfect solution. "I will get the money and you can do the cooking."

"Sounds like a deal," said Chelsea. "Except it's not allowed."

"Why not?"

"Because I'm your auntie."

"But you're a lady and you haven't got a husband already."

"I'm your relation, though."

"What does that mean?"

"It's just the rules, Jack." Chelsea did not want to have to get into an explanation of the real reasons with a six-year-old. "It's basically because I'm too old."

The thought of Colin's much younger fiancée popped unbidden into Chelsea's mind.

"You're not too old, Auntie Chelsea."

"I'm thirty."

"Oh. That is quite old," Jack had to agree. He flippered his feet in the water to move a dirty seagull feather out of the way. "How long is it until you're a hundred?"

"Seventy years," said Chelsea.

"Ha! You're nearly a hundred!"

Jack seemed to have a loose concept of numbers.

"I don't know why you find that funny," said Chelsea. "When I'm a hundred, you'll be seventy-six. That's much older than Grandma is. That's nearly as old as Granddad Bill."

"I'm never going to be that old," said Jack.

"I hope you will be," Chelsea told him. "I hope you will be."

CHAPTER
THIRTY

Ronnie

Seeing Jack and Chelsea so deep in conversation by the paddling pool, Ronnie had decided not to disturb them. What she'd seen had been more than a little surprising. They looked so happy in each other's company. As Ronnie watched, Jack said something that made Chelsea rock backwards with laughter. Chelsea was obviously enjoying herself. As soon as she got bored, she would bring Jack back. Until then, Ronnie decided, she should try to do what Mark suggested and enjoy the peace and quiet. She took herself for a walk. It was ironic. All those days when Jack's constant yakking did her head in and now she was finding it difficult to relax without the soundtrack of his high-pitched chatter in the background. She missed the constant whine of "Mummyyy" going up like an air-raid siren every half an hour. Though she couldn't have put it into words, Ronnie needed to be needed.

Sophie certainly seemed to need Ronnie less and less. She had changed quite dramatically over the past eighteen months. Ronnie had known it would happen, of course. It was inevitable. Every mother of daughters she had spoken to said the same thing — girls hit their teens and became strangers — but Ronnie still missed the little girl who was interested in what she had to say about life. Being the constant target of Sophie's scorn was making Ronnie feel old. And God knew she wasn't really old. She'd become a mother almost two decades earlier than many women did these days.

Sitting on the sea wall, Ronnie was stung by the sudden unbidden memory of Sophie, aged three, coming out of playgroup clutching a picture she'd drawn especially for her mum. She was such a sweet toddler. Very sensitive. Always thinking of others. It had really helped that she was such a loveable child because it hadn't been easy, being a mum at such a young age.

There were so many things Ronnie had had to give up to become a mother. Not only did she have to give up her academic ambitions, she had quickly found herself losing her social life too. The friends she'd had all through school started to fall away when Ronnie could no longer be relied upon as a fixture in their gang for girls' nights out. For a while, some of them would come over to the Benson family's house. Baby Sophie was a novelty, like a new puppy. Unfortunately, like a new puppy, the baby could only hold their attention for so long, especially when she refused to be treated like a living, breathing doll and instead screamed her lungs out when someone tried to change her outfit for the third time in an hour. That was no fun for anyone. So gradually, Ronnie's old friends moved on with their lives. They went off to university, left Coventry and didn't come back except at Christmas.

The truth was Ronnie felt a bit lonely now that Sophie seemed to need her less and less. She also felt as though she was disappearing. Seeing Sophie blossom into a beautiful young woman was like a cruel cosmic joke when Ronnie felt herself becoming increasingly invisible with age. Even Jack didn't need her so much any more. He had quickly transferred his affections on to Chelsea. Ronnie realised to her shame that she had half wanted Jack to have a miserable time with his aunt and come running back to her as soon as he could. That was messed up.

To make matters worse, it seemed something was going on with Mark. He had looked so guilty when he got that last text. He had practically leapt off his sunlounger to get to his phone before Ronnie had a chance to pick it up and pass it to him. He'd never been so precious about his phone before. Never. Back home, he would usually leave it on the side in the kitchen so that Ronnie could have easily scrolled through his call log and texts had she felt so inclined. She'd never felt so inclined. She'd always trusted him. Ever since they'd been on this trip, though, he hadn't let that phone out of his sight. What was the reason? Was Ronnie's fear that Mark was getting fed up with their sex drought and looking elsewhere as a result finally coming true?

Ronnie looked out to sea and took a deep breath. What could she do about it if Mark was having an affair? Should she confront him, or was it better to turn a blind eye and hope that it didn't last long? Her natural instinct was to confront him, but that might force him into choosing and he might not choose Ronnie. If he didn't choose her, what then? The children would be devastated. They'd have to sell the house. Ronnie's imagination soon had her and the kids living in a tenement, while Mark lavished love and attention on a faceless blonde in a penthouse flat overlooking the sea.

She exhaled hard as though to force the image out of her head.

Then her phone chirped. She had a text. It was from Mark.

Quiz by the pool in ten minutes. Prize beer. Can't do without you.

He meant to put an "it" in there, Ronnie thought, but she tried all the same to be pleased.

CHAPTER
THIRTY-ONE

Bill

Of course, after dinner that night, Bill insisted that he needed a drink. Once again, Mark and Dave were drafted in to make sure he didn't wander off and end up *in* the drink instead. This time, Gloria and Lesley were waiting for them at the corner table.

"We wondered when you'd turn up. We've saved you some seats," said Gloria. "And," she added, clearly knowing this would make it impossible for them to refuse, "we've lined up three pints. It is Fosters you drink, isn't it, boys?"

"Wahey!" said Bill. "Grassy-arse."

"Oooh! He speaks Spanish as well," Gloria cooed. "You're a man of culture, you are, Bill. So, what have you boys been up to today? We went to the volcano, didn't we, Lesley? Lesley is very interested in natural history. I am too, of course, but my thing is more social history. Like the Second World War. You promised to tell us your war stories, Bill."

"And so I shall," said Bill, "and so I shall, but not until I've wetted my whistle."

Mark and Dave shared a worried look.

"Who is that strange woman who keeps making a beeline for Granddad every time he's in the bar?" Ronnie asked, having walked through the bar on her way back from the ladies' and seen her grandfather's curious new friends. Gloria had practically been draped across Bill's lap.

"God knows," said Jacqui, "but if she's keeping him amused, that's perfectly fine by me."

"But what's in it for her, Mum? Do you think she's up to something?"

"Perhaps she just likes his company," Chelsea suggested.

Jacqui and Ronnie shared a look.

"She's more likely to be trying to talk him into buying a timeshare," said Ronnie.

"Well, she'll be lucky, won't she?" said Jacqui. "Seeing as how he hasn't got a penny to his name."

"Do you think we ought to find out what she's been telling him?" Ronnie asked. "I mean, I saw something about timeshare scams on *Crimewatch*. They target the old and the vulnerable, and I'd say Granddad's both of those. It doesn't matter whether you've got the money or not. They get you to sign up and then chase you for cash to pay for buildings that haven't even been put up yet. I heard about one couple who had to sell their detached house in Birmingham to pay for two weeks a year in Tenerife."

"I'm sure that kind of contract isn't legally binding anymore," Chelsea chipped in.

"Oh, and you would know, wouldn't you?" said Ronnie. "Living in London as you do."

"I don't see what my living in London's got to do with it."

"Girls, I don't think there's any reason to worry," Jacqui interrupted. "Your grandfather is a grown man. I'm sure he won't get into any trouble. Not least because whoever she is, she'll be off once she's heard his Second World War stories a half-dozen times."

"I like Granddad Bill's war stories," said Jack. They had forgotten he was listening. He was sitting under the table near Chelsea's feet, playing with his DS.

"I don't," said Sophie, without looking up from a text.

"Chelsea," said Jacqui, "will you go over and talk to your granddad? Try and find something out about that woman. The men never find out anything useful."

"Why me?" Chelsea asked.

"Because it won't look so obvious. Take Jack with you. Her suspicions won't be raised by a boy wanting to say goodnight to his great-granddad, will they?"

In the bar, Chelsea hovered while Jack clambered onto Bill's lap to give him a goodnight kiss. She had said hello to the woman, and they'd exchanged names. Now she tried to get her measure without making it obvious that was what she was doing. Gloria was of indeterminate age — either an old fifty or a young sixty. She dressed on the youngish side. Her clothes were tacky, but Chelsea didn't think that meant they'd been particularly cheap. Chelsea also thought she recognised the telltale signs of Botox. When Gloria smiled, her eyes didn't crinkle, but she got "bunny lines" radiating from the bridge of her nose. Nothing but Botox caused those bunny lines. She'd obviously had a boob job too. Her breasts were unfeasibly perky even for a woman at the low end of her possible age range. So Gloria was someone who cared about appearances and obviously spent a fair amount of money on preserving them. Why she would choose to accessorise her ageless looks with an octogenarian in a Coventry FC shirt and carpet slippers was anybody's guess.

At the same time, Gloria was clearly sizing Chelsea up too.

"That's a lovely bag," said Gloria.

"Thank you," said Chelsea.

"It's Louis Vuitton, isn't it?" Gloria's eyes widened. "They cost a fortune."

"It was a present," Chelsea said. Davina had given it to her the previous Christmas. Davina hadn't actually paid for the bag, of course — as a magazine editor, she was always being showered with fancy freebies — but Chelsea hadn't complained.

"Nice present," Gloria breathed.

Chelsea saw at once that Gloria knew how to read the markers of money as well as any of her colleagues on *Society* did, but Gloria also knew that her best way to ingratiate herself with the women of the Benson family was not going to be by talking fashion; it was going to be by ingratiating herself with the apple of everybody's eye: little Jack.

240

Jack clambered down from Bill's lap.

"Now, young man," said Gloria, "I don't believe we've been properly introduced. I'm your great-grandpa's friend Gloria, but you can call me Auntie Gloria if you like."

"But you're not my auntie," said Jack.

"Not technically," said Gloria, "but I could be your pretend auntie, couldn't I? While we're all here in Lanzarote."

Jack looked doubtful. "I've already got an auntie," he said.

"There's always room for another one."

"I don't want another one."

"Everybody needs an auntie Gloria." She offered Jack a Polo mint.

"I'm not allowed to take sweets from strangers," Jack announced.

"I'm your great-granddad Bill's friend. I'm not a stranger."

"You are strange!" Jack exclaimed.

"Time for bed," said Chelsea quickly. "Come on, Jack."

"Aren't you going to give me a kiss goodnight as well?" Gloria asked as Jack tried to get past her. She grabbed him round the waist. Doubtless she thought she would give him a playful tickle, but Jack screamed at the top of his lungs.

"Help! Help!"

Gloria let go of him at once. Jack ran straight to Chelsea and threw his arms round her legs. He would have jumped straight into her arms had he been able to.

"Steady on," said Chelsea.

Jack looked up at her. His eyes were wide and frightened.

"I was only trying to be friendly," said Gloria.

"He's tired," said Chelsea, by way of explanation.

"No, I'm not," Jack cut in. "I'm not tired at all."

"Regardless, it is time for bed."

"That's right, sonny boy," said Bill. "Off to bed with you."

For once, Jack didn't have to be told twice.

"He'll get used to me," Gloria said confidently.

CHAPTER
THIRTY-TWO

Ronnie

About an hour after dinner, Ronnie wondered whether she should go down to the bar and drag Mark back upstairs. She had been reading an article in a magazine that suggested most relationship breakdowns could be averted if you just made the decision to make an effort again. Maybe it was Ronnie who had stopped making the effort first. Perhaps Mark no longer made any moves on her because he assumed she would rebuff them, just as she had taken to assuming that he would rebuff her. The article went on to quote a woman who claimed she had rescued her husband from the clutches of an affair by paying him more attention. Most men didn't want a new woman; they wanted new affection from the old one. Ronnie still hoped of course that she was wrong about Mark and his secretive texts, but there was no harm in acting as though there was a battle to be won. It couldn't make things worse.

There was no better time to start. Ronnie got out of bed. She stripped off her ancient jersey nightdress and started to run the shower. It took a while for the water to warm up. In the meantime, she examined herself in the mirror. Her body might be a disaster zone, but her face wasn't bad. A few days in the sun had given her a glow.

She washed carefully, moisturised and finished off with a squirt of the perfume that Mark had bought her for her twenty-fifth birthday. She still had half a bottle left, nearly seven years on. The occasions she deemed special enough to warrant perfume had been few and far between.

Then she arranged herself on the pillows and sent Mark a text.

When are you coming up to bed?

In a minute, was Mark's response.

As though he would literally be there in a minute, Ronnie watched the seconds tick by on her travel alarm clock. Of course, he wasn't there in a minute. She hadn't really expected that, but once five minutes had passed, Ronnie was already finding it hard to hang on to the fluffy feeling of expectation and hope she had gathered around herself in the shower. After ten minutes, she was starting to get annoyed. After half an hour, she got back out of bed to retrieve her nightdress from the chair by the dressing table.

Mark's "minute" eventually became "seventy-two". To make things worse, Ronnie could tell just from the sound of his struggle to find the keyhole in the door that her plans for a night of passion would not come to fruition even if Mark had been willing. Full of disappointment and on the verge of saying something vile out of anger, Ronnie quickly rolled over so she was facing the wall. The only possible way to deal with this was to pretend she was already asleep.

244

There were very few pieces of furniture in the room, but Mark managed to ricochet off all of them on his way to the bathroom. Ronnie heard him exclaim in muffled pain as he stubbed his toe against something.

Serves you right, she thought.

She heard him pee. It seemed to go on for ever, another indication of just how much beer he must have put away while he was down in the bar. He made a half-hearted attempt to clean his teeth, and then he was on his way to bed. Ronnie closed her eyes tightly as he weaved his way to her side of the double, which was really two single beds shoved close together. He practically fell on top of her.

"For Christ's sake," Ronnie exploded, "how much have you had?"

"Sorry, love," said Mark, crawling over her to get to his side.

"I was asleep."

Mark cuddled up to her. "You smell really lovely."

Ronnie shook him off.

"Is that the perfume I bought you?"

"Seven years ago? Yes, it is."

"I'm sorry I haven't bought you any more since then."

"Ah well, it's only scented alcohol, isn't it? God knows you've bought enough of that."

"I've upset you, haven't I? I'm really sorry, love. That woman kept buying us drinks. We had to stay with Bill in case she made a move on him."

Ronnie pushed Mark away from her.

"Mark," she said, "I really couldn't care less."

CHAPTER
THIRTY-THREE

Chelsea

Somehow, over the family's evening meal in the Jolly Pirate, Sophie had managed to convince Chelsea that she needed her room to herself again. She'd told Chelsea all about the Berlin trip that hadn't happened and how her father had promised her a room of her own in Lanzarote to make up for it. Then she explained how the family just couldn't afford it, and she understood, but —

"Jack can stay with me," said Chelsea before Sophie could finish her sob story.

It was worth it to see him pump the air with delight. Chelsea was surprised at how much it lifted her mood to be appreciated in such a heartfelt and demonstrative way.

But later, in their shared room, Jack grew serious.

"Are you not going to play with me tomorrow?" Jack asked.

"What's that?" Chelsea asked.

Jack sat up in bed. "I know that you've only been looking after me to help Mummy and Daddy get better. Now they're completely better — Mummy said so. That means you've finished looking after me.

246

Does it mean you won't play with me any more either?"

"Oh, Jack!" Chelsea felt her chest ache at the sound of his voice. "Of course it doesn't mean I won't play with you any more. It just means that perhaps you'll play with Daddy sometimes too, while I'm doing some work."

"I play with him all the time at home. He's boring. You're different. I feel like I'm on an adventure with you. Will you be my friend after this holiday?"

"Well, of course I'll be your friend."

"For ever?"

"For ever. I'm your auntie. You'll never get rid of me. Even if you get fed up."

"I'll never get fed up of you."

"Good," said Chelsea. She gave him a hug.

Now that Jack was finally asleep, Chelsea crept into the bathroom to purge. When she came out, feeling so much better for it — God knew why she had eaten a burger that night — she stood for a moment next to Jack's bed and looked down at his sleeping face. She found herself thinking about the conversation they'd had by the paddling pool that afternoon, when Jack asked who looked after her. Chelsea was not overly shocked to find the amusement she had felt earlier that day had dissipated and been replaced by a feeling that was almost an ache. In the centre of her chest, Chelsea had a sensation of actual emptiness. Jack's question seemed to have uncovered a big hole in her heart.

Who was there to look after her? No one. No one. That was who. Even when she and Colin were together, she'd always been the one offering the cups of tea and the back rubs. It was so unfair. The French have a saying that in any relationship, there is the lover and the loved. There was no doubt in Chelsea's mind which role she had taken with Colin. In all of her relationships, in fact. She was always the one dancing attendance, trying to be perfect, trying to be good enough to be loveable. No one seemed to take her needs into consideration at all. And judging by the way things had gone with Adam, the universe wasn't about to send her a change in luck any time soon.

Chelsea lay back down on her bed. The backs of her eyes prickled. She tried to shake the sensation off, but eventually she could hold it back no longer and the sob she had been struggling to keep inside came out in an enormous snorting honk.

Jack was immediately awake.

"What was that?" he asked.

It had indeed been an unearthly sound.

"Nothing," said Chelsea unconvincingly.

"You were crying," said Jack.

"Only a little bit."

Chelsea heard him get out of bed and pad across the bare lino between them. He sprang onto the middle of her bed, landing so that he squashed the air right out of her. Chelsea struggled to sit up. Jack sat cross-legged on her outstretched legs and looked straight into her face as though examining her for hidden clues. He shone the torch part of his sonic screwdriver in her eyes.

"Tell me what's making you sad," said Jack.

"Who are you? The Gestapo?"

"Are they in *Doctor Who?*"

"I don't think so."

"Tell me what's wrong with you."

She could hardly tell him the truth. Jack's world was as yet untainted by the mysteries of love and the agonies of its demise.

"I was thinking about a dog that your mummy and I had when we were little," Chelsea lied, as she gently directed the glare of the sonic screwdriver away from her pupils.

"What kind of dog?"

"It was a small brown dog, made up of all sorts of bits and pieces. It was a bit Alsatian, a bit collie and a bit sausage dog."

"Sausage dog?"

"Yes. It had sausages instead of a tail."

"That's just silly."

"OK. It didn't really have sausages for a tail, but we loved it just the same. We called it Pebble."

"Have you still got it?"

"No," said Chelsea. "Pebble would be very old by now."

"What, as old as thirty?"

"In dog years, yes. But she got run over by a car when she was very young. That is why I was crying."

"Did she just pop into your head?" Jack asked.

"Yes," said Chelsea. That much at least was true.

"That happens to me sometimes too. Mummy says if something bad pops into my head, I should think about SpongeBob until the bad thing goes away."

"If only I knew who SpongeBob was," said Chelsea.

"I'll tell you," said Jack. "He's a cartoon and —"

"It's OK. You don't have to tell me," Chelsea assured him. "I'll think about . . . um . . . Garfield instead."

Jack touched Chelsea's cheek with careful little fingers.

"Your eyes have been leaking," he said.

Chelsea wiped her cheek dry with the back of her hand. "Better now."

"When I grow up, I'll get you another dog," said Jack.

"You're a very thoughtful boy," said Chelsea, "but now you should go to sleep."

"And I'll always look after you," Jack assured her.

CHAPTER
THIRTY-FOUR

Ronnie

Wednesday

Mark was especially contrite the following morning, not least because he had the kind of hangover he deserved. It was so bad he couldn't even face a cooked breakfast, and Mark had never knowingly turned down a cooked breakfast. Especially a cooked breakfast that was part of an all-inclusive package. Still, as bad as he claimed he was feeling, Mark dragged himself from bed at nine, by which time Ronnie had been up and about for two hours. Her activity made him feel very guilty indeed.

While Mark was busy trying to regain some kind of balance, Ronnie composed and deleted at least twelve texts to Cathy Next Door, in an attempt to get to the truth.

"What are you doing, Mum?" Sophie asked her. "I've never seen you and Dad so, like, stuck to your phones before."

Evidently Sophie had noticed Mark was doing a lot of texting too.

"I'm just making some notes for things I've got to do when we get back home," Ronnie lied.

"Why don't you use a pen and paper?"

"Because I couldn't find a pen and paper," Ronnie snapped.

"All right, keep your hair on. God, I was only making conversation."

"I'm sorry, sweetheart. I'm sorry." Ronnie was horrified that she had ruined a chance to actually have a conversation with Sophie. "It's just that I've got a lot on my mind."

Ping!

Mark made another comical dive for his phone. This was ridiculous. Ronnie had to know who was keeping him on his toes. Could it really be Cathy? She had to get hold of his phone. When Mark sank back down on his sunlounger, though, he had his phone tucked in his shirt pocket. Mark, who once upon a time was absolutely convinced that putting a mobile phone in the front pocket of your jeans could lower your sperm count, was wearing his phone next to his heart.

CHAPTER
THIRTY-FIVE

Chelsea

There was much excitement at the Kidz Klub that morning. As the parents dropped their children off, they were asked to sign slips saying that the Kidz Klub coordinators had permission to take their children across the quiet road from the hotel complex to the scrubby strip of grey sand that passed for a private beach. The children were going to have a picnic by the sea, because today — cue the fanfare — was the day of the Kidz Klub sandcastle competition.

"Amazing!" breathed Jack.

"Yep," said Chelsea. "You could say that." She wished she had Jack's enthusiasm for the little things in life.

"We're going in for it, aren't we?" he asked.

"We most certainly are," said Chelsea. Building sandcastles didn't sound too difficult, and an organised activity would at least remove the opportunities for free association and fighting that clearly came from the children being allowed to run wild in the playground. Chelsea and Jack went back to their room to gather Jack's sandcastle equipment. Jack had brought a bucket all the way from Birmingham Airport. It had come in a kit along with two different-sized spades and a rake. The rake was already broken when Jack got it out of its packet, but that was not to put him off.

"I can use my sonic screwdriver to make it brilliant," he told Chelsea.

Chelsea nodded. She knew better than to question the plastic screwdriver's powers by now. She'd even let Jack hold it to the bruise that had developed on her forehead.

At the appointed time, Jack and Chelsea joined the other Kidz Klub members on the sand where they were appraised of the rules of the competition. There were to be two classes of competitors: children competing alone and children competing with their accompanying adults. Despite Chelsea's assurance that he would certainly come up with a castle worth shouting about on his own, thus saving his aunt's nails, Jack insisted Chelsea help him. They would be building their castle together in the "accompanied" group.

When they had worked out how many people would be competing for the Kidz Klub sandcastle prize, the two coordinators on duty that day set to work on dividing up their part of the beach accordingly. Using a broom handle, they drew out a grid and allocated numbered spaces by pulling names out of a hat. It was all very democratic. Chelsea and Jack were allocated a patch near the water's edge.

Jack was not best pleased.

"Our castle will get washed away before we've finished it!" he said.

"No," said Chelsea. "This is a fine spot. The tide doesn't come up this far, see, and it's good to be close to the sea in case we need some water."

Jack was quickly mollified.

Lily and Adam were late to the party. They chose a patch well away from Chelsea and Jack, thank goodness, though Jack kept craning over his shoulder to look at them. Chelsea reminded Jack that he had promised he would ignore Lily. Just as she would ignore Adam. She was still smarting from that crack about self-help books and her single status. As far as she was concerned, there was no point trying to mend that bridge. In any case, they had building to do.

"You've got an hour," said the Kidz Klub coordinator.

"An hour! Oh no!"

Jack went into a frenzy, jumping up and down as he tried to work out where to start.

Chelsea had not built a sandcastle for over two decades. The theory was simple enough, but it soon became clear that filling the bucket with wet sand and banging it out again was not going to be good enough to win the Kidz Klub competition that day. The neighbouring father-and-son team spent the first five minutes of their building time deep in a huddle discussing their plan. After that, they sketched out a blueprint on the sand and actually dug foundations with perfectly straight sides, using the handle of one spade as a guide.

In contrast, when Jack came out of his frenzy, both he and Chelsea had gone for a manic bout of bucket-filling and they now had eight crumbling turrets on their patch. Chelsea thought they looked good in an arty, Stone-Age settlement sort of way, but she had a feeling the judges would not be so impressed. The castle next door was growing steadily. Chelsea suggested to Jack that they start again.

"Why?" Jack asked.

"I don't think the coordinators are as artistically minded as we are. We see perfection. They'll see eight random mounds."

Jack was nonplussed.

"We need to think about a real castle and model ours on that," she said. "We've got time for a rethink."

"Yes. We need a drawbridge that will go up and down!" said Jack.

"Going to be difficult with sand," said Chelsea, "but we could shape something that looks like a drawbridge."

"Will we be able to open it?"

Chelsea shook her head.

"Then that's rubbish."

"How about we go for something more like . . . like a cathedral?"

"What's that?"

"You know, Jack. You've got one in Coventry. A big church. How about St Paul's Cathedral in London? That shouldn't be hard. We need an oblong base and then we'll put a dome on top."

"But I don't know what it looks like," said Jack.

"Hold on," said Chelsea. She fired up her iPhone and within seconds she had a picture they could use as a handy template.

256

Jack studied the picture gravely.

"But it isn't a castle."

"Sand*castle* is a generic term," Chelsea assured him. "It just means a sand *building*. This is going to be so much more original than anybody else's. No one else will think to build a cathedral. No one else will have a dome. We'll have the only dome on the beach. It could be a winner."

"OK."

Jack was convinced. They smushed the eight average-looking turrets into one big mound of sand that Chelsea set about shaping into the base. She had Jack put another two buckets' worth of sand on top of that and showed him how to create a passable dome. They carved windows and doors into the sides of the building using a lolly stick. Chelsea mused on the possibility of using little bits of plastic found on the beach — crisp packets, for example — to make "stained glass".

"We could use this," said Jack, handing Chelsea the bright red wrapper of a condom. Chelsea buried the wrapper deep in the sand and covered both herself and Jack with hand-sanitiser.

It wasn't long before the St Paul's sandcastle was finished. Even if Chelsea said so herself, it looked fantastic. It was certainly a one-off. Without exception, everyone else had gone for old-school castles with square towers, crenellations and lollipop stick flags. Boring. Boring. Boring. They had to be on to a winner.

Chelsea suggested she and Jack use two lolly sticks to represent the cross on top of the cathedral as a final flourish. Jack agreed that was a great idea. Chelsea used a bit of blue nylon string — why was there always blue string on beaches? — to tie the lolly sticks together. Jack was delighted. But calamity was to accompany the placing of the lolly-stick cross. By this point in the competition, Jack was so excited he could barely keep still. He was certainly incapable of doing anything slowly. The base of the castle was so wide that Jack had to stand on tiptoes to lean far enough to place the sticks on top of the dome. And of course, as he did so, he toppled forward.

Unlike the dome of the real cathedral in London, which survived the Blitz of the Second World War, the dome of the sandcastle St Paul's did not survive this unfortunate aerial attack. Jack put his knee right through it. The sandcastle was ruined in an instant.

"Oh no!" Jack was so shocked that at first he couldn't cry.

"It's OK," Chelsea told him. "We can fix it. Quick, quick."

"But I've ruined it. I've ruined our cathedral!"

He wasn't wrong. Together they surveyed the wreck of their afternoon's efforts. Chelsea thought it could be salvaged but right then there was no point trying to smush the castle back into shape. The Kidz Klub coordinators had blown the whistle to announce the end of the hour and they were already beginning the judging. A minute later, the coordinators passed right on by the damaged dome without even stopping to commiserate. Jack would not be consoled.

"We worked so hard!" he said.

"We did," Chelsea agreed.

"It's not fair! We had the best castle. We would have won."

Worse was still to come.

Lily and her father won the sandcastle competition for their traditional medieval extravaganza complete with crenellations and — a working drawbridge. Adam had somehow rigged a piece of driftwood with a broken shoelace so that it could be lifted up and down. The judges clapped their congratulations and Lily grabbed the bag of sweets they offered as a prize.

"She doesn't deserve those sweets," said Jack, with unexpected venom. "She didn't help build that sandcastle at all. I was watching her. She didn't do a single thing. Her dad made all of it."

"It doesn't matter, Jack," Chelsea assured him. "I'll buy you a packet of sweets in the bar."

"It won't be the same. We should have won them. If I hadn't fallen over, we would have won."

Chelsea shared her nephew's disappointment, but there was nothing she could do. She hadn't even had the foresight to take photographs during the building process. No one would ever know how brilliant the castle had been. And it had been brilliant.

Chelsea and Jack could not avoid passing Lily and Adam on their way back into the hotel. Chelsea did not even look at Adam. Lily made a show of shoving three sweets at once into her mouth. She might as well have made the "loser" sign as far as poor Jack was concerned. Adam offered his commiserations. Chelsea pretended not to hear them.

"Next year," she said to Jack, "we'll build the Coliseum."

"The Closs-eum is rubbish," said Jack.

CHAPTER
THIRTY-SIX

Sophie

Sophie had decided that Playa Brava was well lame. Her parents had granted her permission to explore the town by herself during daylight hours and she had taken advantage of that permission to spend as much time apart from them as possible, but really there were only so many hours you could spend in a gift shop, trying on sunglasses you couldn't afford to buy on your puny allowance. Why did her mum and dad have to be so badly affected by the credit crunch? Sophie's sense of injustice was made even worse by the regular updates from Skyler, who was on holiday with her dad and his new girlfriend in the South of France. Skyler's dad worked for a big insurance company. While Sophie was wandering aimlessly around shops that sold Chelsea FC tea towels and all manner of tat stamped with a misspelt "Lanzarotte", Skyler claimed she was strolling around the boutiques of Cannes, trying on and, later, actually *buying* a dress by D&G.

When Sophie relayed this information to her mother by the poolside, Ronnie snorted that Skyler's dad was trying to buy her love because he didn't see her from month to month. Sophie should be grateful she had a father who actually spent time with her instead. Looking at her father snoring beneath that day's copy of the *Sun*, Sophie could not see the benefit of having such a present dad.

She stayed by the pool for another half an hour, then excused herself to go for a walk again. This time she turned left instead of right as she exited the hotel. She didn't hold out much hope for more excitement in this change of direction, and indeed she wasn't surprised. This new direction offered another parade of gift shops purveying more of China's finest Lanzarote-themed tat. But just as Sophie was texting Skyler to say, "My life is so shit," something happened to make Sophie think that maybe this holiday wasn't going to be so bad after all.

"Well, *hel*-lo, beautiful."

A low whistle came from a darkened doorway that led to a currency-exchange booth. Sophie stopped, but she didn't turn round. Not at first.

"Yes, beautiful girl, I am talking to you. There are no other beautiful ladies around here."

Sophie turned, with her best disdainful look already in place. She and Skyler were well practised in telling teenage boys where to get off, but this wasn't a teenage boy.

"Don't frown," said the man in the doorway. "Your face is way too lovely to be spoilt with that kind of look."

Sophie continued to pout. She'd been told she looked like Tulisa when she pouted.

The man stepped out of the darkness. Once in the light, he cut a more interesting figure than Sophie had hoped for. She had grown used to being catcalled by the waiters at the seafront restaurants, but they were easy enough to ignore. They were all old and short and only really interested in getting her to look at their menus. This man was different. For a start, he wasn't that old. She estimated he was twenty-one at most. He also looked a bit like Robert Pattinson.

"What's your name?" he asked.

"Sophie," she said.

"Pretty name for a pretty lady."

Sophie rolled her eyes.

"I can't help it," said the man. "It's hard to find a compliment that is as individual as a girl like you deserves. My name is Luca."

"Do you chat up every girl who passes by?" Sophie asked him.

"Have you seen the state of most of the women who pass through this town?" Luca replied. "I do not chat up everybody. Are you always so suspicious of someone who pays you a compliment?"

"Depends." Sophie's posture relaxed a little.

"Where are you from?"

"England. Coventry."

"I know it," said Luca. "I'm half English. My mother is from there. From London."

"Really?"

"Really. She came out here on holiday in the 1980s, met my father and never went home."

"And you live here in Playa Brava?"

"All my life. Running the family business." He indicated the currency exchange behind him. "Tell me, Sophie, how old are you?"

"Eighteen," she said automatically. She and Skyler always said they were eighteen if anybody asked. They'd been served in a pub once. Sophie had been staying at Skyler's dad's place for the weekend. Ronnie and Mark were under the impression that Skyler's father would be looking after them. Instead, Skyler's father had filled the fridge with ready-meals and gone to spend the weekend with his girlfriend.

"Eighteen, eh?" Luca's expression didn't suggest he disbelieved her.

"How old are you?" she asked him.

"How old do you think I am?"

"Twenty-one?" she suggested.

Luca laughed. "Close enough. I'm happy with that. Do you want a Coke?"

He beckoned her into the darkness.

"Why not?" Sophie asked. Why shouldn't she accept a Coke from the best-looking bloke she'd seen since arriving on the island?

Sophie had two Cokes and a can of ready-mixed gin and tonic that made her eyes smart. Thankfully, Luca didn't seem to notice how unused she was to the bitter taste of gin. He would certainly never have guessed that she'd never tasted any alcohol except cider or lager watered down with lemonade on very special occasions such as her family's New Year's Eve party. Sophie spent almost three hours with him in the darkness of the currency exchange that afternoon. He asked her about the things she liked. She told him about her favourite bands and about her ambition to become an actress. He listened carefully and asked all the right questions. He paid her even more compliments. That afternoon was definitely the best part of the holiday so far, but eventually, Sophie couldn't ignore the texts on her phone any longer. Ronnie wanted to know where she'd got to.

"I have to go," said Sophie to Luca. "I said I'd meet my . . . friends at half past five."

Luca stood up and waved Sophie towards the door.

"Well, I've had a most interesting afternoon. I hope I'll see you again," said Luca.

"You might," said Sophie, hoping she sounded cooler than she was feeling.

"Can I have your number?" Luca asked. "So I can text you?"

"Sure." Sophie told him her number without hesitating.

"Lovely Sophie from Coventry," Luca murmured. He picked up Sophie's hand and placed a kiss on the back of it. "The most beautiful English woman I have ever seen in Playa Brava."

Sophie's face was still radiating heat when she found her mother and father by the poolside.

"You're late," said Ronnie.

"Only two minutes," Sophie pointed out.

"Did you find anything interesting?" Mark asked.

"No," said Sophie. "I just walked up and down the main street. There isn't much to do here."

She hoped her father wasn't going to try to engage her on the subject. She was itching to text Skyler with developments, even though she was almost out of credit thanks to all her texting from abroad.

Skyler had sent another text already, outlining the rest of that day's purchases: two new pairs of shoes and some real Chanel lipstick. Ordinarily, Sophie would have died with envy at the idea of such sophistication, but that afternoon, she had a secret that would blow Skyler's shopping exploits out of the water when it came to glamour and that all-important maturity.

Someone asked me out, she wrote. He's twenty-one.

CHAPTER
THIRTY-SEVEN

Ronnie

Fortunately for Sophie, Ronnie was too distracted to give her the third degree as to how she had really spent her afternoon. Mark had been receiving texts all day.

At one point, in response to a text, Mark had disappeared from the poolside without telling Ronnie where he was going. When he came back, he claimed he had been inside to answer a call of nature. Number two. Ronnie was unconvinced. Since when had Mark been shy about his bowel movements? Ordinarily, he'd have made an announcement *ahead* of going inside. He was up to something for sure.

When Mark got back from the loo, Ronnie told him that she was going inside for a lie-down and there was no need for him to join her.

It was while she was on her way back to the bedroom that Ronnie thought to look in on her parents and ask them what the plan was for that evening. Their bedroom door was slightly ajar. Ronnie went to knock on it, but hesitated for just long enough to catch the tail-end of a half-whispered conversation. She paused.

Her mother's voice sounded worried. Though nine-tenths of her knew she shouldn't, Ronnie decided to listen in. One-tenth of her wanted to know what her mother was worried about. Maybe listening to this conversation would answer the questions raised by how strange her mother had seemed over the past few days.

"I don't think we can tell them," said Jacqui. "It doesn't seem fair. Not while they're all supposed to be enjoying themselves."

"Then don't tell them here," said Dave. "We don't have to."

"But when are we going to tell them?" came Jacqui's anguished response. "We've kept this to ourselves for long enough, Dave. There's going to come a day pretty soon when it will be too late to let them know and too late for us to do anything about it or help them get through it."

"Don't get yourself upset," said Dave.

"How can I not get upset? We've gathered everyone around me for my sixtieth birthday and all I can think of is an empty space at the table where . . . I—" Jacqui sobbed.

Ronnie immediately visualised a table without her mother at one end of it.

"Oh, Dave, I don't know what to do for the best. We haven't got for ever. They should know as soon as possible. I want them to. They deserve to know, but—"

"Not this week," Dave suggested. "When we get back to Coventry, eh? You can get Chelsea to come up one weekend in the next month or so and we'll tell everyone then. We don't have to let it spoil your birthday. Now, you need to try to enjoy yourself, love. You need this break as much as anyone. More, if anything. Much more."

"I know. I'm trying, but how can I enjoy myself with this hanging over my head?"

"It's hanging over my head too," said Dave.

"Oh, sweetheart, I know."

"Come here and let me give you a cuddle."

Ronnie heard her parents kiss.

"I should go downstairs," said Jacqui. "I told Bill I'd find his glasses for him."

Ronnie heard her mother coming towards the door. She straightened up and skipped off down the corridor just in time.

In the room she shared with Mark, Ronnie went over the conversation she had just overheard. As far as Ronnie was concerned, everything confirmed her worst fears. This family trip to Lanzarote was not just about celebrating her mum's birthday. Jacqui had wanted to gather everyone around her because she had bad news to impart. That had to be the reason. And in Ronnie's mind, the bad news had to be health-related. What else could it be? Dave and Jacqui were hardly about to announce they were getting divorced, were they? It must be a health thing, and from the way her mother seemed to be the more anguished of her two parents at the thought of sharing the news, Ronnie deduced that it must be her mother who was ill. She hadn't seemed ill, but then neither had Linda, the woman who had lived next door to her parents back in Coventry, until she was diagnosed with breast cancer. Linda was dead within a year.

Ronnie sat down on the bed. She put together the conversation, this extravagant trip and the way her mother had been the past few days, and came to a horrible conclusion. Not only was her mother ill, she must have discovered there was nothing that could be done for her. She'd said they didn't have for ever. Exactly how long did they have? Ronnie wanted to know at once. She wasn't going to wait for her mother to tell her what was happening; she was going to have to ask.

The opportunity didn't arise that evening, though. Ronnie couldn't seem to get her mother alone for even a second, and Jacqui went to bed right after dinner, claiming that she thought she was still tired from the twenty-four-hour bug.

CHAPTER
THIRTY-EIGHT

Ronnie

Mark didn't ask to stay down in the bar with the guys that evening. Instead, he said he was ready for bed as soon as Ronnie was. They walked upstairs together. Mark chanced a quick squeeze in the lift. Ronnie pushed him off.

"You smell of garlic," she said.

Ronnie spent an age in the bathroom. It wasn't that she needed to spend any extra time in there. Her aim, her hope, was to stay in the bathroom for long enough that Mark would be asleep by the time she came back out. She didn't want to speak to him. Though he hadn't gone to the bar after dinner, he had sunk three pints while eating his evening meal, and ordinarily that was enough to send him straight to the Land of Nod. He had sat down on the bed upon entering the room — there was nowhere else to sit — and Ronnie felt sure he wouldn't be able to resist the urge to stretch out, and as soon as he stretched out, he would be out like a light. That's the way it always happened at home.

Having cleaned her teeth and taken off her make-up, Ronnie listened at the door for clues that it was safe to come out. She could hear nothing. Mark hadn't switched on the television, which was a good sign, but neither could she hear him snoring. It didn't take long for him to start snoring once he shut his eyes.

Ronnie took a deep breath. She couldn't stay in the bathroom all night. She turned the door handle as quietly as she was able and pushed the door open slowly so that it emitted just the slightest of squeaks. Even a dog would have had trouble hearing a squeak so very tiny.

"All right?" Mark piped up.

Damn, thought Ronnie, he wasn't asleep.

"What are you creeping about for?"

"I was trying not to wake you," Ronnie explained. "I thought you might have already nodded off."

"Not tonight," said Mark. He had stripped down to his boxer shorts. He was propped against the pillows with his hands folded across his ample stomach. He patted the empty side of the bed.

"I'm not feeling great," Ronnie told him before she even sat down. "I think it must have been something I ate from the buffet."

"Again? What did you have?" Mark was immediately concerned.

"I don't know. The chicken curry? I had some of that."

"I did too," said Mark. "I feel all right."

"Well, it won't have been the whole batch that had something wrong with it. It might have been just one piece of chicken."

"Do you want me to call for the doctor?"

272

"No, I'll be fine. I'll just lie down. I'm sure it will pass."

"We ought to tell somebody. If you've got that bug again, like your mother thinks she has, then somebody needs to know. We might get compensation."

"I don't want to think about that now. I just want to go to sleep."

"Do you want me to rub your stomach?"

"That's the last thing I want," Ronnie snapped. "I mean, just because it's feeling a bit tender. That's all I meant. Thank you, love."

Mark stood up. He pulled on a T-shirt.

"I suppose I'll get ready for bed, then."

He shut himself in the bathroom, leaving his phone on the bedside table.

Ronnie wrestled with her conscience for a matter of seconds. She knew she shouldn't check the messages on Mark's phone, but how could she possibly resist this opportunity? Besides, there were so many uncertainties in her life at the moment, not least her mum. It would be good to get at least one of them straightened out. In all probability, Mark had been texting some competition line or something like that. That would be a stupid thing to do, given that it was probably costing him a fortune, but it wouldn't be so bad. Slowly Ronnie reached for the phone.

The phone was locked, but luckily Mark was not the kind of person who bothered to change the passcode from the factory setting. Four zeros gave Ronnie access to everything. She started with his call log. Mark didn't seem to have called anyone except Ronnie and his boss for the past two weeks. At least he hadn't been calling another woman, assuming he wasn't having an affair with his boss's wife, the dowdy fifty-something who ran the office. But his texts . . .

Ronnie went into Mark's text messages. The majority were from Ronnie herself or from Sophie, There was nothing in his inbox more recent than a week old. Ronnie scrolled down, down, down. Mark must have been deleting the messages he'd been receiving all week. She could find nothing incriminating and yet someone other than Ronnie or Sophie had obviously been texting him. Ronnie didn't know whether finding nothing was worse than finding screeds of love notes. In Ronnie's case, it was probably worse. Her imagination knew no bounds. And then it happened. Mark got another text.

Ronnie immediately jabbed to open the message. It was from Cathy, their neighbour back in Coventry. What did she want this time?

Have you done it yet? Cathy's text asked him. I'm in your house, feeding your cat, looking at a photo of the pair of you with your arms round each other and wondering when you're going to put me out of my misery.

Oh God. Ronnie covered her mouth. She heard Mark flush the toilet. Quickly she went to mark the text as "unread" but managed to delete it in the process. Had Mark heard the text alert sound? Ronnie put the phone back on his bedside table and prayed he had no idea that an SMS had come in.

Mark did not look in the least bit shifty when he emerged from the bathroom. Neither did he rush to look at his phone. Ronnie lay on her side, turned away from him, her mind racing as she tried to remember exactly what the text had said. It was unbelievable. Right then, Cathy, the woman Ronnie considered her friend, was in her house, staring at her photos, wondering when Mark was going to tell Ronnie he was leaving her so that he could move in next door.

CHAPTER
THIRTY-NINE

Chelsea

Thursday

Chelsea had not had much sleep. Jack had kept her awake until late, endlessly replaying the sandcastle disaster. It had taken her a long time to persuade him that he wasn't the loser he seemed to think he was. He'd just been unlucky. When he finally fell asleep, Chelsea leapt from the bed with relief. She held down the back of her tongue with her toothbrush and got rid of that evening's dinner: fish and chips from the Jolly Pirate, followed by half an ice-cream sundae. Jack's ice-cream sundae.

Jack's late night did not stop him from waking up early. Once again, Chelsea woke to find him standing over her, examining her for signs of life. He reminded Chelsea of a cat the Benson sisters had shared when they were little, after Pebble the mongrel dog died. At first, Chelsea had found it endearing the way that cat would stand on her chest when he wanted her to wake up. Then she saw some horror film in which a cat sucked a baby's breath out of its lungs. She felt very differently after that.

276

"Jack," she said to her nephew, "you really can't just stare at someone to make them wake up."

"It works on you," was Jack's rationale.

That much was true.

They went down to breakfast. Jack had two sausage sandwiches. By now, Chelsea knew how to do the spread "properly" and Jack pronounced her sandwiches "perfect". After that, they discussed their entertainment options for the day. Chelsea was keen to keep Jack well out of Smug Dad — as she had come to think of Adam — and Lily's way. She suggested another day trip. They could go to the volcano. As they were discussing the merits of going before or after lunch, one of the Kidz Klub coordinators came through the restaurant, trying to drum up custom for the day. Jack didn't even look up, but then—

"Ladies and gentlemen, boys and girls, today it's the Kidz Klub Olympics!" the coordinator announced. "We're going to have races and team games and plenty of prizes, but we need contestants. Who's going to join us? Who thinks they're fast enough to be a Kidz Klub winner?"

The coordinator looked around. Several children were already getting to their feet. The triumphs of the London Olympics were still relatively fresh in their young minds. Chelsea was suddenly aware that Jack was standing up too.

"It's another competition, Auntie Chelsea, and this time we could definitely win!"

Or perhaps not. An hour later, and against Chelsea's better judgement, they were back in the Kidz Klub, and unfortunately, Jack was not much of an athlete. Chelsea's heart ached to see him attempting to take part in a potato and spoon race. (Of course, egg and spoon races had been banned on the grounds of health and safety.) It took him for ever to get the potato properly balanced, and when he did, there was no chance he would be able to move an inch without dropping it, let alone run to the finish line. The same three children seemed to be winning everything. They were covered with cheap plastic medals. The only consolation was that the races were split by sex, so Jack didn't have to compete directly with Lily, who was cleaning up in the girls' contest.

It would not have been so heartbreaking had Jack not been too bothered, but Chelsea knew that he was trying so desperately hard. Why couldn't they have had a competition that played to his strengths, like solving a puzzle? Jack was so much brighter than the other kids, she was sure.

"That's it," said Jack, as he limped home from a race that had involved skipping with a hoop. Jack could not seem to get through the hoop without bashing himself on the forehead each time. "I didn't win anything. Lily won more sweets."

"She had less competition in her races," Chelsea tried. "The girls' races were much slower."

Jack shook his head. That didn't matter to him.

"Shall we go and find Grandma?" Chelsea suggested. "We can see if she wants a walk on the beach."

"No," said Jack. "The Olympics haven't finished yet."

278

There was one more race to go.

"Ladies and gentlemen, it's time for the parents' race."

"Jack, I'm not a parent," Chelsea pointed out.

"Please," said Jack. "No one will know. You could win it, Auntie Chelsea."

"I've never won a race in my life. Your mum was the athlete in the family."

"Mum can't run," said Jack flatly.

"She could," Chelsea assured him. "Once upon a time, she was the fastest girl in school."

"Then you must be the second fastest. Auntie Chelsea, please. The winner gets a massive prize."

Chelsea looked at her nephew. She looked at the prizes on the Kidz Klub coordinators' desk. They didn't honestly look worth breaking into a sweat for, but Jack . . . It was worth breaking into a sweat for Jack, wasn't it?

"Pleeeeeeeese?"

His eyes were big and round, just as they had been that first night, when Mark dumped him in her room. Chelsea felt her own eyes prickle. How had he managed to get so far under her skin?

The chief coordinator explained what was required for the parents' event. It was quite simple, he assured them. Except that it wasn't so simple at all . . . The challenge had been honed over many years. The parents' race would encompass each of the various disciplines in which the children had competed that afternoon: swimming, sprinting, skipping with a hoop, balancing a potato on a spoon and jumping in a sack.

"I can't do all that," said Chelsea to Jack. "I'm sorry. There's really no point. You know I'm not going to win. I'm hopeless at sport."

"But you're good at cricket," Jack protested, remembering that long-ago barbecue. "That's sport. And look at everyone else. They're fatter than you are. You could totally be the winner."

"Jack, please —"

Jack pushed his aunt towards the coordinators.

Family honour was at stake.

So Chelsea found herself lining up at the starting line with the three other parents who had been unable to think of a plausible reason why they shouldn't make fools of themselves in this pantomime pentathlon. Chelsea regarded her competition. All three of the other contestants were men. Two of them looked as though they got most of their exercise lifting a pint glass between table and mouth. There was a chance Chelsea would leave them both standing. The third contestant was Adam. Adam caught Chelsea looking at him and returned her stare impassively. He was trying to psych her out. Well, he'd have to try harder than that. It was Adam who made Chelsea realise exactly what she had to do. Her heart actually squeezed as she remembered the previous night's conversation with Jack.

"Maybe we're just not meant to be winners," was what he'd said at one point.

How could a six-year-old think that? Six-year-olds were supposed to be full of irrepressible optimism and enthusiasm. They were meant to think they would grow up to be astronauts and movie stars. No ocean was too wide for a six-year-old to swim. No mountain was too high for a six-year-old to climb. And yet Jack had allowed the thought of failure to enter his tiny, pure mind. It was all downhill from there until he wound up failing all his GCSEs and ended up on benefits. Chelsea could not let that happen to her nephew. She was going to have to show him that determination and true grit still counted for something. She was going to run this stupid parents' race as though it was possible to win it.

Jack was standing to the side of the starting line with his fists curled into little balls through the strain of it all. Chelsea winked at him.

"Think, 'winner'," she said, making her thumbs and index fingers into the shape of a W.

"Winner," Jack responded in kind, though he had a bit of trouble with the thumb-and-forefinger thing. He got it close enough.

CHAPTER
FORTY

Sophie

While Jack had spent the morning exerting himself in the sunshine, his sister, Sophie, had not moved from her room.

Sophie was extremely happy with how the room arrangement had panned out that week in Lanzarote. She felt very grown-up indeed as she lazed in the bedroom she now had to herself. She held her iPhone at arm's length and captured herself luxuriating against the pillows on her bed, wearing nothing but her bikini. She pouted and turned her head, regarding the lens through downcast eyes and long lashes. The photo looked fantastic.

Sophie attached the picture to a text message for her new friend and pressed "send".

He responded at once. U R so hot. Come see me tonite.

What time? Sophie responded.

6. Outside the bar. Clubbin later?

Yeah. Sure was Sophie's reply.

Sophie hoped her response had seemed suitably casual, but in reality she felt anything but casual about the arrangement she had just made for that night. Forget about Harrison Collerick back in Coventry. As far as Sophie was concerned, Skyler could have him now. Sophie wasn't going to waste her time on little boys like Harrison any more, not when she knew she was attractive to a real man. A grown man. A man who had a job, a car and a place of his own. At least, that's what he'd told her that afternoon in the back of the currency exchange. Harrison was just a baby by comparison. A kid.

The only problem was that Sophie would have to get permission to stay out late enough to go clubbing. Her curfew back at home was nine o'clock. Ten o'clock on very special occasions only, and even then her father would insist on picking her up, which always cramped her style. Why couldn't he be like Skyler's father, who preferred to stay home in front of the TV rather than act as his daughter's taxi service?

"Because I love you and I want to know you're home safely," was Mark's reply.

Well, maybe the rules could be stretched a little that week. They *were* on holiday. Sophie didn't have to go to school for another three weeks, so a couple of late nights now wouldn't do her any harm. And she had heard her mother commenting that it seemed really safe in Playa Brava. Certainly it had to be safer than the centre of Coventry on a Saturday night. Plus, it wasn't as though Sophie would be on her own. She would be with Luca. He would know the right places to go.

With all her arguments carefully worked out, Sophie plastered on her best smile and headed down to the poolside, ready to ask her mother if she could stay out until midnight.

Ronnie's mind was on just about anything but her daughter that morning.

Cathy's text to Mark had blown a hole in every certainty Ronnie ever held. It was a double betrayal. Mark was supposed to be her partner. Cathy was supposed to be her friend. She could hardly believe that Mark would have fancied Cathy in the first place. Cathy was loud-mouthed and dumpy and smoked fifty cigarettes a day. (Mark claimed he hated smoking.) Then there was the way that Mark hadn't even bothered to lie about who the texts were coming from. He must think Ronnie was an idiot.

Added to that, Ronnie still had to talk to her mother about her concerns for her health. There just hadn't been a moment. That day, Jacqui and Dave had taken advantage of Gloria's curious insistence that she wanted to hang out with Bill and gone on a wine-tasting trip before Ronnie had a chance to say she needed to talk.

Ronnie's stomach churned as she thought about the conversations ahead of her. She would need her mum so much if Mark really was having an affair. She felt sick in this limbo. Nothing confirmed and so much to fear.

The only silver lining was that Ronnie and Mark wouldn't need to waste money on getting divorced because somehow they had never got round to getting married. They had the children; they had the joint mortgage; but they had never tied the knot. When you were inextricably linked in so many different ways, what was one more piece of paper?

"Exactly," was Mark's response whenever Ronnie suggested how simple it would be to legalise their relationship. "It's just a couple of signatures. Why bother?"

Even so, over the years it had gnawed at the back of Ronnie's mind that Mark's resistance to commitment was down to something more than a hippyish aversion to convention. Now, having read Cathy's text, she thought she knew for certain.

Ronnie's anguished inner dialogue was interrupted by the appearance of her daughter. Sophie was carrying a bottle of water, which she handed over with a smile. Ronnie plastered on a smile of her own. She had a feeling she was going to be doing a lot of pretending everything was OK for the sake of the kids in the near future.

"I thought you might want a drink," said Sophie. "It's hot out here."

"It is. Thank you." Ronnie regarded her smiling daughter with suspicion. "What's the matter with you?"

"What do you mean? You think something's wrong because I brought you a drink?"

"You look very happy all of a sudden."

"Mum, I'm allowed to look happy, aren't I? I'm on holiday with my family."

"I thought you would rather have stayed in Coventry with Skyler and your mates?"

"Yeah, well, I didn't know what it was going to be like out here, did I? I thought it would be really boring and stuff, but the hotel's all right, and the people are friendly."

"They are," Ronnie agreed.

"And I've made a new friend," Sophie said then.

"Oh?" This was the first Ronnie had heard about it. She had assumed that when Sophie disappeared on her walks, she was just mooching around on her own, plotting revenge for having been made to come away with her parents, her grandparents and her doddery great-grandfather.

"Yeah. A local kid who works in the arcade," she said.

"Really?"

"Yeah. He's my age. He's working in his school holidays."

Ronnie nodded. That didn't sound too bad.

"He's been teaching me some Spanish. I've been thinking I could do a GCSE."

"That's a great idea," said Ronnie. Previously, Sophie had resisted the idea of having anything to do with languages. Whoever this local kid was, he was obviously working some kind of magic: Sophie was talking about her education. Ronnie had never managed to engage her on that subject before. Never. God knew she had tried to. It wasn't long before Sophie had to make some decisions about whether or not she would stay on to do A-Levels.

"It's really good to have an extra language," Ronnie went on. "It gives you so many other options. Half of America speaks Spanish for a start."

"That's what I thought. It would be so useful for me to have some languages, and meeting people from other countries is the best way to learn really quickly, right? So, I was wondering . . ."

286

And here comes the punchline, thought Ronnie.

"Yes?" she said.

"My friend's invited me to go to a club with him tonight. Him and some of his mates. I really want to go. It starts at ten o'clock."

"Nine o'clock is when you have to be home," said Ronnie.

"In England, yes, but we're not in England now. We're in Lanzarote, and you said yourself that you think Playa Brava is really safe, and I'll be with a big gang of people and so everything will be fine."

"No, Sophie. Not after nine."

"But it's not as though I have to be at school tomorrow morning."

"It's not you getting up in the morning that I'm worried about. Ten o'clock is too late to go out. You're only fifteen years old."

"I'll be sixteen in December."

"That doesn't make any difference. What kind of mother would I be if I let you go out at night in a strange town in a strange country with a whole bunch of people I haven't even met?"

"The kind of mother who lets her daughter have her independence?" Sophie tried.

"You'll have all the independence you want soon enough."

"When?"

"When you're old enough to use it properly. I can't just let you go out unsupervised with people I don't know. I'm sorry, Sophie, but that's the end of it."

"You never let me do anything!" Sophie quickly lost her cool.

"The only things I don't let you do are the things I think will get you into trouble. I'm only looking after you. You're my little girl."

"I am *not* a little girl."

"Sophie, I don't want to get into an argument about this. You're not going clubbing tonight and that's final. I don't mind you going off on your own a bit during the daytime, but you are not going out after dark."

"You treat me like I'm some kind of idiot! I can look after myself."

"Perhaps you can, but until you're sixteen, I'm not going to take that chance."

"You're being so unfair."

"I'm not trying to be unfair, Sophie. Look, how about you ask your friend from the arcade to come and meet you here? He could hang out with you in the games room. I'm sure that's allowed. Then your dad and I could meet him and perhaps we'd let you go out until ten."

"That's no good. He won't want to meet you."

"Why not? Are we that embarrassing?"

"No one else's parents vets their friends. Skyler's mother doesn't. She doesn't keep tabs on her every move."

"Of course she does. You think Skyler's mother doesn't text me to make sure Skyler's round at our house when she says she is?"

"You spy on us?"

"No, we just make sure you don't get lost on the bus," said Ronnie. "We need to know where you are."

"I'm asking Dad."

"Look, you know your father is going to say the same thing as me. We don't want you hanging around after dark with people we don't know."

"He's really nice."

"Then he must be willing to come and meet us."

Ronnie thought this was a reasonable concession, but Sophie was not happy with the idea at all. She continued to rage, accusing Ronnie of behaving like Big Brother, monitoring her every move, word and thought. Sophie concluded that there was no way she would make her new friend do something so "lame" as meet her parents.

"Well, I can only think that your new friend is not the kind of person you want me to meet. Who is he really? Are you sure he's your age?"

"What does it matter if he isn't?"

"I thought so. You're definitely not going clubbing with anyone older than you," said Ronnie. "Who is he? Where did you really meet him? What are you up to?"

"Why do you always have to accuse me of being up to something?" Sophie raged.

"I'm just trying to make sure you don't make the same mistake I made."

"You mean having me? I'm a mistake?"

"Sophie, you know that isn't what I meant."

"You're full of shit," Sophie told her. Then she was gone. Back inside to sulk. Leaving Ronnie with yet another thing to worry about.

CHAPTER
FORTY-ONE

Chelsea

Back at the Kidz Klub, there was much excitement as the adults taking part in the parents' race gathered at the starting line.

"Is this all the entrants for the parents' race?" one of the female coordinators asked. "Come on, there must be some more ladies out there willing to stand up for the girls."

The female coordinator had failed to notice that Chelsea was actually the only female adult holiday-maker in the whole Kidz Klub. The rest of the children's female relatives had very sensibly delegated the childcare to their husbands and boyfriends, who were probably usually as hands-off as Ronnie claimed Mark was.

"OK," said the coordinator to Chelsea, "We'd normally have one contest for the men and another for the women, but—"

"It's fine," said Chelsea. "I'm happy to race the men if they don't feel they'll be disadvantaged."

The two fat fathers laughed. Adam remained stony-faced. He was taking this competition very seriously indeed. He stood on one leg while he pulled the other foot close to his buttock to stretch out his quadriceps. He did a couple of squats and a few bounces on the spot. Chelsea, not to be outdone, raised her arms high above her head and bent from the waist. She was pretty damn flexible. She hoped that would translate into speed. She bent from side to side. Click. Something cracked. Maybe she wasn't as flexible as she thought . . .

"All right, everybody!" The coordinator blew her whistle. The two fat dads leapt into action. "Stooooppp!" the coordinator called. "That was just the whistle to tell everybody to pay proper attention. You make a false start, you are disqualified. Like Usain Bolt."

"For crying out loud," said Fat Dad One. "It's the Kidz Klub, not the bloody Olympics."

"No swearing, please. You can also be disqualified for swearing."

Chelsea shook her head in sympathy.

"*Lady* and gentlemen, get into your places, please. As you know, the first lap is a straight sprint. At the end of the sprint, you get into the sacks; you jump in the sacks back to this end of the racecourse; then you pick up your potato and spoon."

"Potato and spoon?" said Fat Dad Two. "I ask you."

"Salmonella," the coordinator explained. "So you pick up your potato and spoon, and you race to the other end. Then you pick up your hoop for the skipping. After that, you jump into the pool and swim two lengths. The race finishes when the first person gets out of the pool and rings that bell." The co-ordinator indicated an old-fashioned desk bell, which had been placed on the middle of the see-saw. "Providing they have completed every stage of the race correctly, the person who rings this bell first is the winner."

"Got it," said Fat Dad One.

"All right. Is everything clear?"

"Except the potato," said Fat Dad Two.

"Everything's perfectly clear," said Adam.

"You're going to win, Daddy," Lily piped up from the sidelines.

"My auntie Chelsea is going to win," said Jack. His teeth were gritted, his eyes narrowed with determination. Chelsea silently promised him that she would do her very best or die trying. She conceded to herself it was more likely she would die trying.

"On your marks . . ."

Chelsea and the two fat dads adopted the standing start position that the children had been using all morning. Only Adam crouched down in a proper racing start. Chelsea raised an eyebrow at that. They were going to run for barely fifteen metres. Lily's dad would probably have driven his head straight into the fence before he had time to straighten up.

"Get set . . ."

"Hang on," said Fat Dad One. "I've got something in my shoe."

"He's stalling for time," one of his mates complained from the audience. "Don't take any notice of him."

"I can't run with something in my shoe."

"You can't run anyway, you fat bastard."

292

"Language!" said the coordinator. "Contestant number one is disqualified."

"You can't disqualify me," said Fat Dad One. "It weren't me what said it."

Adam straightened up again while coordinator and contestant argued the toss. Fat Dad One was allowed to stay in the race.

"On your marks . . ." the coordinator began again.

Chelsea and the fat dads assumed their positions. Adam dropped to the ground again.

"Get set . . ."

Adam rocked in his racing-start posture. Chelsea fixed her eyes on the fence at the far end of the Kidz Klub where her potato sack was waiting.

"Go!"

All four contestants left the starting line in a flurry of pumping legs and flailing arms. Adam was way ahead of the others within seconds. Of course, he was a runner back home. He'd proudly told Chelsea about his time in some half-marathon back when they were on friendly terms. Well, she may not have been a runner but Chelsea got to the fence second and managed to claw back some time by being quickest into her sack. A decade of struggling in and out of skinny jeans had left her with some transferable skills after all.

Moving in the sack was a little bit harder than putting it on; however, Chelsea had the edge here as well. Adam tried to shuffle forward, but Chelsea knew that the only way to cover ground and not get the sack twisted round your ankles was to jump. One of the fat dads gained a little on Chelsea and Adam with his own jumping technique, but it was Chelsea who was first back to where the race had started.

"Come on!" Jack shouted from his place by the starting line. As she scrambled back out of her sack, Chelsea found a second to give him a high five. "You're winning!"

One of the coordinators handed Chelsea her potato and spoon. As a child, Chelsea had taken part in plenty of egg and spoon races. Balancing an egg on a spoon was never as difficult as you expected. You just had to make sure that the wide part of the egg was in the wide part of the spoon. But balancing a potato?

"The rules are, if you drop the potato, you have to return to the start," the coordinator reminded the frantic adult competitors.

Chelsea took a moment to centre herself and properly place her spud. Alas, it was no dinky new potato but an enormous baker that was covered in misshapen knobs. Meanwhile, the spoon was an ordinary dessert spoon. There was no way that it would fit. Chelsea glanced at the other competitors to make sure they had no potato-based advantage. All three of the dads were struggling to get enough balance to even consider stepping over the starting line. Adam was the first to attempt a step. He managed to cover about a metre before his potato dropped to the ground.

"Back to the start!" a coordinator shouted.

"Shit," said Adam.

"Language!"

Finally, Chelsea seemed to have achieved the perfect balance. If she just took it slowly, she would be fine.

She stepped forward. One. Two. Three steps. The potato hit the ground.

"Back to the start!"

"Arse," Chelsea muttered.

"Language!" the coordinator screeched.

"Come on, Auntie Chelsea, come on," Jack cried.

"This is harder than it looks," Chelsea explained to her nephew.

"I know, but you can do it, I know you can."

Chelsea wasn't sure she could. While watching the children compete in the potato races earlier, Chelsea had assumed they were all just too young to understand the principles of balance, too eager to get to the finish line. Now she knew that they'd been set a close-to-impossible task. At least the children hadn't had to return to the start every time they dropped their potatoes.

"OK," said Chelsea. "Here we go." She took another deep breath. Adam was six feet ahead of her by now. She couldn't let him get too far in the lead. Chelsea stepped out again, spoon clutched in her hand, and soon she found herself passing Adam while he scrambled to retrieve his spud from the dirt for a third time.

At the other end of the track, Chelsea joyfully threw down her potato and spoon, and picked up her hula hoop. Here she definitely had the advantage. The hula hoops were all the same size, but Chelsea was three inches shorter than her nearest rival. She was the only contestant able to skip through the hoop without getting it caught on the top of her head. It was an unfair advantage, of course, but Chelsea made the most of it. The gap between her and Adam grew wider still.

Dumping her hoop, Chelsea stripped off her kaftan, threw it towards Jack for safe-keeping and ran over to the pool ready for the final stage of the race. She was grateful that she was wearing her sturdiest bikini that day. As a child, Chelsea had endured lessons at the local baths on a Tuesday afternoon, but she certainly couldn't claim swimming as a favourite activity. Since leaving school, she'd avoided it as far as humanly possible, only venturing near a pool if the air temperature was hot enough that she would sizzle upon getting out. As a result, her style was far from Olympian, based as it was on keeping her face and hair completely dry, but there was no time to ease herself into the pool inch by inch now. Her super-expensive Japanese smoothing process was doomed. Now at the edge of the pool, Chelsea took a flying leap.

Splash!

Chelsea struggled to the surface and began the swim of her life, spitting chlorine as Adam followed her in with a dive-bomb. Chelsea did not look back. She just fixed her stinging eyes on the end of the pool. Most of the time, her feet touched the bottom and she was able to adapt her swimming style to a sort of pool jog. She had no idea whether or not that was allowed. The coordinators hadn't said anything about it.

The Kidz Klub children were starting to get hysterical with excitement as the race entered its final stage. Even with the water in her ears, Chelsea thought she could hear Jack shouting her name. She pushed on

296

and on, though her lungs were ready to burst with the effort. She thought, not for the first time, that those people who did triathlons for fun must be truly deranged.

"Chelsea, Chelsea, Chelsea!"

It wasn't only Jack who was chanting Chelsea's name now. She reached the end of the pool and turned to start her final lap. She passed Adam on the way. One of the other dads was five strokes behind him. The fat dad who had almost been disqualified for his friend's swearing hadn't even bothered with the swimming part of the race. He was sitting in a plastic chair, fanning his face with a copy of the *Sun*. He'd done more than enough for the day.

"Chelsea, Chelsea, Chelsea!"

The chants of the crowd spurred Chelsea on. She was in the lead. All she had to do was hold on to her advantage. She had to find that final burst of energy. Getting to the end of the pool at last, she almost forgot that the race didn't end there.

"Auntie Chelsea!" Jack screamed. "You've got to ring the bell!"

The bell! Chelsea was panting so hard through exertion she felt as though the very fabric of her lungs was tearing each time she inhaled, but she managed, just, to haul herself from the pool like an elephant seal pulling itself onto a jetty. Groaning like an old woman, she got to her feet and ran, tripping with fatigue as she went, to find that bloody bell.

"Ruuuuunnnn!"

As Chelsea stretched for the bell, Adam was reaching simultaneously. Somehow he had caught her up. For a moment, it seemed as though the two of them were frozen in time, arms outstretched towards the bell but never quite getting there. Then Chelsea's hand slammed down on the dinger. Adam slammed his hand down at the same time, but Chelsea's hand was firmly underneath his. She had definitely got there first. The stinging slap Adam accidentally delivered her was well worth it.

"You did it! You did it! You did it!" Jack sang.

Chelsea was over the finish line. She had actually won the race. She swept Jack into her arms and they did a victory jig.

"You did it. I knew you would win it. You're the very, very best," said Jack. "You're the winner! You're the winner!"

Chelsea punched the air.

She didn't know when she had last felt so happy. Certainly, she had not felt quite so full of pure joy when she won an award for her journalism. This win was so unexpected and so sweet. Perhaps it was because she had made such an enormous effort. Chelsea sneakily glanced over her shoulder to where Adam was doubled over, winded by the hard work of that final sprint to ring the bell. Lily's face was creased with disappointment. Adam put his hand on her shoulder, but Lily shook it off.

"Loser," Jack mouthed as he made the "L" sign. Chelsea quickly brought the offending hand down.

"Jack, we have to be gracious in victory" she told him. "Though you're absolutely right. What a loser, eh?"

Chelsea wrapped herself in a towel and busied herself with accepting the congratulations of the parents who had not taken part in the race. One of the dads offered to email her a series of extremely unflattering photographs he had taken during the contest, which he showed her now on the back of his camera. Recoiling at the sight of the exertion on her face, Chelsea told him that she would rather simply remember the moment.

"I took some photos too," said Jack then, revealing that he had hacked into Chelsea's iPhone and used it to capture the moment himself.

"Great," said Chelsea. "I thought I told you not to mess with my phone."

"I wasn't messing with it. I was taking photographs."

Jack was especially proud of his picture of Chelsea carrying her potato and spoon. She was looking over her shoulder at one of the fat dads. His grimace reminded Chelsea of a cartoon character.

"We can send this one to Grandma and Mummy."

"That's a good idea. Shall I show you how?"

While all this was going on, Chelsea didn't notice that the runner-up was deep in conversation with two of the Kidz Klub coordinators. Eventually, the chief coordinator gave a blast on the klaxon that he sometimes used to bring the children to order.

"It's time for the prizes," said Jack, clapping his hands with joy.

Now fully dried off, Chelsea pulled on her kaftan and sauntered across to the Kidz Klub podium, though given how flimsy it was, she very much doubted the adults would be expected to climb up on it. Adam was already there. He looked oddly smug for a loser, thought Chelsea. The KKC looked nervous.

"Er, ladies and gentlemen, boys and girls, can I have your attention, please?"

Chelsea smiled at the crowd as everyone quietened down for her big moment. The coordinator continued, "I'm afraid there has been a disqualification."

Chelsea turned to look at him in confusion.

"Er, yes. I'm really sorry, but . . . it seems that one of the, er, audience saw the winner actually, er, *holding* her potato on her spoon."

"What?" Chelsea spat.

"I'm afraid we've got a witness who says you had your thumb placed so that you were actually holding your potato on your spoon to make sure it didn't fall off. That's not allowed. The rules of the race say there must be no 'steadying' of the potato."

"This is ridiculous! Who said I was steadying the potato?"

The coordinator looked at his shoes. One of the laces was undone. He took the opportunity to duck down out of the line of fire while doing it back up.

"Come on, who said I cheated?" Chelsea asked again. "If you're going to disqualify me on the basis of such slander, I want to know exactly who accused me."

There was an eerie silence around the Kidz Klub pool. It was never quiet around the Kidz Klub pool.

Everyone held their breath as Chelsea scanned the crowd, as though she might be able to tell just by looking at them who her accuser was.

"If someone wants to call me a cheat, they can call me a cheat to my face. Come on, which one of you did it?"

"I did," said Lily, suddenly stepping forward.

"Right," said Chelsea. "Well—" Her diatribe came to a sudden end. "If you say so, Lily."

Jack glared at his pigtailed nemesis. Meanwhile, Chelsea ducked down to make herself level with the coordinator, who had retied his loose lace three times. "Could I have a word?" she hissed.

Chelsea took the coordinator to one side. Jack followed them. "Don't you think it's strange that it's the daughter of the contestant who came second who decided I cheated in the potato and spoon stage? Which I absolutely did not, FYI."

"She didn't," Jack agreed. "She wouldn't. My auntie Chelsea never lies."

"And neither does my daughter." It was Adam.

"Of course not," said Chelsea, her voice heavy with sarcasm.

"She wasn't raised to lie. Or cheat."

"Neither was I," Chelsea retorted.

"It's a matter of your word against hers," said the coordinator.

Chelsea turned to Adam. "You put her up to this. Well, if it matters to you that badly to have the free beer vouchers, then you're welcome to them. I don't want to be in such an unfair competition. I'm disqualifying myself. Come on, Jack. Let's go and have lunch."

"We're not cheats!" was Jack's parting shot.

He was struggling not to cry.

CHAPTER
FORTY-TWO

Chelsea

Even during lunch, Jack was still outraged that his aunt had been accused of cheating. Lily was such a liar.

"We can't let them get away with it," he said.

"They have got away with it," said Chelsea. "He's got the free beer vouchers, and my good name has been besmirched. Still, we know I was the winner. We know the truth."

Jack speared a chip and regarded it thoughtfully. Chelsea could tell that something was on his mind.

"What are you thinking?" she asked him.

Jack shook his head.

"Come on," Chelsea insisted. "You can tell me."

Jack took a deep breath before he asked her, "Auntie Chelsea, *were* you cheating in the potato and spoon section?"

Chelsea looked away and pressed her lips together to contain a laugh.

"Yes!" she said at last. "Of course I was. For goodness' sake, there is no other way to keep a potato on the end of a spoon. It's impossible."

"Auntie Chelsea!"

"But I was only cheating a little bit, and Lily is still a snitch."

"Yeah!" Jack chimed in agreement. "Lily is a snitch."

"Plus, there's still one more competition to go, and I know beyond a shadow of a doubt that you and I have got this one in the bag. No cheating required."

Jack's eyes lit up. "Are we going to do the fancy dress?" It was the only competition left on the agenda for that week.

Chelsea nodded. "Darling, I work on a fashion magazine. I am fancy dress. We most certainly are going to enter the competition. Come on, finish your chips. We've got work to do."

The theme of the Kidz Klub fancy-dress afternoon was *A Thousand and One Nights*. Jack, understandably, interpreted the theme as "a thousand and one *knights*" and was disappointed when Chelsea told him that wasn't the brief at all. There would be no cross of St George and no clanking armour (though she had no doubt there would be plenty of parents at the Klub who misunderstood the theme as well).

"We're talking about *The Arabian Nights*," Chelsea explained. She gave Jack the lowdown on the classical fairy stories. "So I'm thinking you need to go as Aladdin."

Jack perked up again. He knew the story of Aladdin and his genie. He'd seen the Disney film.

"I like Aladdin," he said.

"Perfect. Now, what do you need to look like? Let's Google."

Chelsea got out her phone and together she and Jack pored over pictures of Aladdin for the best part of an hour. There was plenty of inspiration to be found online. The possibilities were endlessly exotic. The problem was how to translate that inspiration into a costume using only those items that could be found in the resort. While there was no official limit on how much you could spend, there was certainly a lack of variety to choose from. If only the theme had been "international football teams": they'd have had no trouble whatsoever fitting Jack out in the colours of any team from Arsenal to Zenit St Petersburg. But a costume fit for a prince? That was going to be hard.

First things first, Jack and Chelsea retired to their room and ransacked their cases to see what they already had. Jack had a pair of jogging bottoms that could be pushed up into knickerbockers. The fabric might not have been quite right, but it would give a good silhouette to build on, and Chelsea had a scarf she could tie round his waist to make a jaunty sash.

"It's got flowers on it," Jack complained.

"Aladdin was so tough he could get away with wearing flowers," Chelsea assured him. "Hmm. You need a waistcoat."

Perhaps the barman could be persuaded to part with his waistcoat for an afternoon? Chelsea suggested. He'd struck up quite a friendship with Granddad Bill. But before they took the step of asking him, they decided that his waistcoat wasn't really going to be colourful enough.

"I need something that goes with this scarf," said Jack. "Something red."

"I don't think we've got anything red," said Chelsea.

"This dress has got red in it."

Jack fingered the Mebus dress Chelsea had worn on the flight out to Lanzarote. The dress that day by day was getting less and less likely to clean up properly, as the blackcurrant stain was well and truly baked in by the heat.

"This is really colourful," he said.

"I know," said Chelsea, "but Aladdin doesn't wear a dress. I suppose you could go as Scheherazade . . ."

"Is that a girl?"

"Yes. A very beautiful girl."

"I'm not going as a girl," said Jack flatly. "But you could make the dress into a waistcoat."

"How?"

"With some scissors." Jack picked up the dress and made a snipping motion.

"Jack, I can't cut up this dress."

"Mummy cut up her dress when I had to be a king in the nativity play."

"I don't suppose her dress was by Mebus."

"It was *velvet*," said Jack.

"Yeah," said Chelsea. "That sounds nice, but, Jack, I still can't cut up that dress. It doesn't actually belong to me. Your costume will be OK without it. I assure you, it'll be the best."

"It might not be," said Jack. "I might look rubbish. I look rubbish now."

Chelsea adjusted Jack's sash. He had a point. The more Chelsea looked at him, the more he looked as though he was wearing a pair of jogging bottoms with a scarf round his waist and a hand towel round his head. Jack's face took on the expression of an unhappy spaniel.

"This is important to you, isn't it?" said Chelsea.

"We've got to beat Lily at something!"

"We will. Her costume will be terrible, especially if her dad makes it. Men can't sew," Chelsea said, though she of all people knew that was far from true. Male designers dominated fashion.

"Lily's costume won't be terrible. I heard her saying that she won last year. Her dad sewed her a fairy costume with actual wings. She said she could fly and everything."

"She definitely couldn't fly Jack. She made that last bit up."

"She said it was true."

"Yes. And she said that I cheated in the potato and spoon race."

"That was true as well," Jack pointed out.

Chelsea picked up the dress from where it lay on the bed. It was a thing of beauty. The person who designed that dress certainly knew how to spin a fairy tale. It was cut so well that a horse would have looked good in it, but it was the fabric itself that was especially wonderful. There was something very exotic about it. Chelsea could see the fabric's potential as well as Jack could. She fingered the stain, which had stiffened the silk. Chelsea could almost hear the fashion editor scream,

"What are the chances of that mark coming out?" She wondered for a moment whether her best tactic might be to say the dress had been stolen from her flat. No one need know that she'd worn it on holiday. The magazine's insurance would cover it, wouldn't it?

Jack was looking hopeful. Chelsea knew he thought she was softening.

"We've got to find some scissors," he said.

"I can't do it, Jack."

Chelsea replaced the dress on its hanger.

"Then we're going to lose," said Jack, as he ripped off his makeshift turban and sash. "Lily is going to win and then she'll have won everything."

"Jack, that's not necessarily the case."

"I don't want to be in the competition any more. I don't want to wear this stupid costume." Jack threw himself face down on his bed. "We'd only lose and I don't want to be a loser any more."

"Jack." Chelsea put her hand on his back in an attempt to comfort him. She felt utterly helpless in the face of his disappointment. "Jack, there are all sorts of things we can do to make your costume better. We'll go into the town, shall we? We might be able to find you a proper genie's lamp."

"I don't want to," said Jack.

"We could find you a sword. I bet there's a shop that sells swords."

"I don't care. I just want to go and see Grandma."

"OK," Chelsea sighed. "Let's go down to the pool."

"You don't have to stay with me," he told her. "You can just drop me off. I don't want to play with you."

308

Chelsea's mouth dropped open. It was the most hurtful thing that anyone had ever said to her. None of the occasions on which she had been dumped came close to this. Chelsea felt hollow to the pit of her stomach. Her darling nephew, Jack, didn't want to hang out with her any more.

CHAPTER
FORTY-THREE

Chelsea

Despite Jack's protestations that he wasn't interested in entering the competition any more, full stop, Chelsea decided she would find him that genie's lamp anyway, just in case he changed his mind. The resort was full of gift shops. One of them was bound to stock something that looked like an old-fashioned oil lamp. It was exactly the kind of everyday object that could be fashioned into perfect tourist tat. Stick a scented candle where the oil used to be *et voilà*! Indeed, Chelsea found the perfect genie's lamp within ten minutes of setting off on her expedition. She handed over her cash and the sales assistant wrapped it up. Chelsea was momentarily buoyed by the thought of Jack's face when he opened it, but that feeling soon passed.

The holiday was almost over. This time next week, Chelsea would be back at her desk. She would be back in her real life. Despite herself, she had really started to enjoy being in Lanzarote. That was in no small part due to the time she had been spending with Jack, of course. He was so open-hearted, she couldn't help but be uplifted. He took her mind off the way things were in London. She thought of the nightmare that lay ahead when she got back to Stockwell. She'd still be single and lonely. Her flat would still be too small. Her job would still be too badly paid given the stress that it caused her. She was especially dreading her first day back in the office. What was she going to do about the ruined dress?

As if the gods were out to punish her, at that exact moment, Chelsea received an email from Carola at work.

Chelsea, have you seen a Mebus dress? Fifties style. Red print. Erica wants to take it on the cover shoot in Venice. She is going ballistic.

Chelsea did the only thing she could do. She pretended her mobile was not working.

She sat down on a bench in the middle of the boulevard and juggled her phone from hand to hand.

"Hey! What's a beautiful lady like you doing looking so sad?"

Chelsea looked up and around her. Was the man in the doorway talking to her?

"Yes, I'm talking to you," he said, as if he could read her mind. "You can't look like that in Lanzarote. You are on holiday."

Chelsea gave him a wan smile, but this was her worst nightmare. Her English urge to be excessively polite even in the face of harassment was going to cause her trouble here. How could she get away quickly without talking to him and not seem chilly or rude? She started to stand up and gave a half-hearted wave that would, she hoped, conclude the interaction.

"I'm not going to let someone as beautiful as you slip through my fingers so easily," the man said. "Come and have a Diet Coke with me. It's cool in here." He gestured towards the inside of his shop, which as far as Chelsea could see was an ice-cream stand-cum-money exchange.

"I've got to be somewhere," said Chelsea. There was something about this man she really didn't like. There was definitely a very practised manner to his patter. She wondered how many times a day he trotted it out and how often he succeeded in persuading some poor cow to believe she truly was the most beautiful creature he'd ever seen. The idea that he thought she might be that gullible made Chelsea feel slightly sick. What with Jack's disappointment and now this slimeball, this really was turning out to be a bad day.

"You're on holiday," the man persisted. "You don't need to be anywhere fast." As Chelsea tried to walk by, he actually reached out and tried to take her arm.

"I have to pick up my son from the Kidz Klub," Chelsea lied.

The man shrugged, but he did, thank God, seem put off by the idea that Chelsea was a mother. He disappeared into the gloom of his shop without another word, like a lizard slinking back into its hiding place.

Chelsea hurried to the poolside. She felt as though she had walked through a shadow that wouldn't leave her. She needed the brightness of the pool. She wanted to hear children laughing, even if Jack was still in a sulk and affected not to notice her. Chelsea sat down by Sophie instead.

"You all right?" Sophie asked.

"Some awful creepy guy tried to chat me up," said Chelsea.

Sophie nodded in sympathy.

"What have you been up to today?" Chelsea asked.

"I was hanging out with a friend from the amusement arcade this morning. He asked me to go clubbing with him tonight, but Mum said I couldn't. She says I'm too young."

Chelsea clucked in sympathy. "I'm sure she's only thinking of your safety."

"I'd be safe. I'd be with my friend. Plus, I can handle myself," said Sophie.

"I bet you can," Chelsea agreed.

Nevertheless, the degree to which that man in the currency booth had unnerved her came back so vividly she felt her stomach lurch. Was this the time to tell Sophie that it can be far harder to get a man to back off than you imagine? Even in broad daylight, that slimeball had succeeded in making Chelsea feel vulnerable. It was as though a shark had brushed her leg in the children's pool. Chelsea could only hope that Sophie did not attract the same kind of idiots. She was probably in some way safeguarded by the fact that she thought anyone over the age of eighteen was ancient and to be avoided in any case.

"You know, your mum is only looking out for your best interests."

"Yes," Sophie sighed. "I get it. I understand."

"You could hang out with me tonight instead. Maybe your mum would let us go and have a drink together after dinner in one of the bars in town? How about that?"

"All right," said Sophie. "You're on."

"You can't have any alcohol, though."

"I know," Sophie sighed.

"You look very pretty in that dress," Chelsea said then. "It looks great with a bit of a tan."

"Do you think so?"

"Yes. The blue brings out the colour of your eyes. You should wear lighter colours more often. You look very grown-up and sophisticated."

Sophie beamed. "Really?"

Chelsea knew that her compliments probably carried slightly more weight than they should do because of what she did for a living.

"Can I ask you something?" Sophie said then.

"Of course," Chelsea replied.

"Do you think I've got what it takes to be a model?"

Chelsea took a deep breath before she answered. "I think you are beautiful," she said, "but the last thing I would ever want you to be is a model. They are all more neurotic than racehorses, and for the most part they stink of puke."

Sophie looked confused.

"From throwing up every single thing they eat," Chelsea clarified, recognising the irony as she said it. "So, yes, I think you're every bit as beautiful as any model I've met, but I think you'd hate it if you did it as a job."

314

Sophie seemed happy with that.

"Can I borrow one of your lipsticks?" she asked her aunt.

Chelsea delved into her bag and brought out three. "Take your pick."

"Which one suits me?"

Chelsea handed Sophie a Chanel Coco Rouge Shine in *"Fétiche"*. Despite the racy name, it was a natural-looking shade of pink. Hopefully Ronnie wouldn't go too bonkers if she saw Sophie wearing it.

"So, come on, what's he like?" Chelsea asked. "This local friend of yours."

Sophie blushed.

"He's really nice. He's mature, you know. Not like the idiot I was going out with at school. He pays me lots of compliments. He makes me feel good about myself."

"That's great," said Chelsea. "A boy should know how to pay a girl compliments." So long as he didn't grow up to be like the jerk in the currency booth, dishing them out like fish food. "You just have to remember that compliments are free and you don't have to do anything you don't want to in return."

"Auntie Chelsea," said Sophie, "I'm not stupid, you know."

CHAPTER
FORTY-FOUR

Ronnie

Ronnie felt she was on the verge of doing something foolish. She was certain now that Mark was shagging their neighbour. It would serve him right if she did the same. One of the barmen had given her the eye. She could easily get him into bed if she wanted to. And yet, wasn't the grown-up thing to do to confront Mark first and talk things through before she started an affair of her own? At one point, Jack saved her from herself by asking if he could play a game on her phone. Ronnie let him sit with her on her sunlounger and have a go at BrickBreaker. She was glad to have him next to her, but she was surprised that he didn't want to play with Chelsea any more.

Jack got bored of playing BrickBreaker after a while, though, and followed his dad to the snooker room for a couple of frames. Sophie was sunbathing alongside Chelsea. Granddad Bill was in the bar with Gloria.

Ronnie decided to go indoors to get a magazine. As she crossed the lobby, she saw her mum, newly returned from her coach trip.

"Had a nice day, love?" Jacqui asked. "How's Granddad?"

"He's all right," Ronnie reported. "That Gloria woman is still sitting with him. Weird, eh?"

"I know. But I'm not knocking it — saves me worrying."

"Mum—" Ronnie saw her chance to get her mother alone for a while — "do you think we could go up to your room for a minute?"

"What's up, love?" Jacqui asked.

What wasn't up? Ronnie told herself that she would tackle her mum's worries first, before she said anything about Mark.

"Let's just go upstairs," Ronnie insisted.

"Mum," said Ronnie, when they were finally alone. "I can't help noticing you've been a bit preoccupied this week."

"Really?" Jacqui tried to look surprised.

"Yes, really. Every time I've glanced across at you, you've been looking at me or Chelsea or the grandkids like you think you might never see us again."

"Have I?"

"You have."

Jacqui nodded faintly. So it had been obvious. Dave had warned her she was looking worried. She wished that he were with her now. Jacqui had the feeling that the moment she'd been dreading was finally upon them and she wanted to face it together with her husband. He would help her to say the right thing.

Ronnie continued, "I know it probably sounds ridiculous, but I can't help feeling you're hiding something from us: from me, Chelsea and Mark.

Something's bothering you. I want you to know that whatever it is, I'm ready to hear it. If there's anything I can do to make you less worried, I want to be able to do it, but of course, I can't help if you don't tell me what there is to worry about."

"Oh, Ronnie." Jacqui could not keep her eyes from moistening.

Ronnie grabbed Jacqui's hand. "Let it out, Mum. Please. Whatever it is," she said. "We'll get through it together. Chelsea can get access to the best doctors in London through the magazine."

"What doctors?" Jacqui was confused. "Why do I need to see a doctor?"

"Well, it might be a good idea," said Ronnie. "I haven't said anything to Chelsea yet, but I'm sure she'll know someone who can give you a second opinion." She took a deep breath and spat it out. "Mum, have you got cancer?"

"Oh God." Jacqui covered her mouth. "Oh God, no. Whatever gave you that idea? Oh, Ronnie Benson. The things you come out with."

"But you've been so weird. You keep hugging the children. You wanted us to go away as a family. You seemed to be building up to telling us something awful."

"And you thought I only wanted you all around me because I was ill?"

"Aren't you?"

"No, no, of course I'm not. I'm absolutely fine. I'm fit as a fiddle. You know that."

"But—" said Ronnie.

"Is that what we've come to? Our family? That you girls think I would only want you around me because I was dying?"

"It's not exactly how I meant it to come out."

"You girls and the grandchildren are the most precious people in my life. I would like to have you with me every single day, not just on special occasions. Nothing makes me happier than to have my family all together in one place."

"So why have you been so sad?" Ronnie asked.

"I haven't been sad," Jacqui protested.

"You have, and, look, I overheard you talking to Dad the other night. You said you had something to tell us."

"We do have something to tell you," said Jacqui, "but I don't know where to start."

Jacqui squeezed Ronnie's hands.

"You've won the lottery," said Ronnie, attempting to lighten the moment.

Jacqui shook her head. There was no way of lightening this particular moment for her.

"I wish . . ." said Jacqui. "I wish . . . You know, your dad should really be here for this." She looked hopefully towards the door, but of course there was no sign of Dave. Sod's law. He'd gone into town in search of insect repellent after Jacqui complained that something had bitten her during dinner the previous evening. "And Chelsea too. I wanted her to hear at the same time."

"I want to know now," said Ronnie.

"I can't tell you on your own. Chelsea has to hear it too."

"Hear what?"

"I can't tell you without her. It's not fair. You've got to hear in the same way at the same time. It's important."

"Then let's get her up here," said Ronnie, losing patience. "And Dad too. You can't leave me hanging on now, I've been worried stupid."

"But your dad's gone into town to find some bug spray," said Jacqui hopelessly. "Oh, maybe it doesn't matter if it's just you, me and your sister—"

"I'll get her up here." Ronnie was already dialling Chelsea's number.

CHAPTER
FORTY-FIVE

Jacqui

Chelsea looked a little anxious as she came into the bedroom. If she hadn't been worried about her mother before Ronnie's call, it was clear she was worried now. Like Ronnie, upon hearing that their mother had something to tell them, she immediately jumped to the wrong conclusions.

"Mum," she said as she entered the room, "what's going on? Please tell me you haven't got cancer."

"I haven't got bloody cancer," said Jacqui. "Sit down. Please."

The sisters flanked their mother on the tightly made bed in the centre of the room. Clasping each of them by the hand, Jacqui smiled nervously. Both Chelsea and Ronnie leant forward expectantly to hear what she had to say.

"Your dad and I . . ." Jacqui began. "Well, you both know that we were childhood sweethearts. We went out with each other when we were still at school."

The girls nodded. They both loved the idea that their parents had met as teenagers and never loved anyone else.

"And then you didn't see him again for nearly ten years," Chelsea picked up the story.

"That's right. After your dad left school, we had a nine-year break when we didn't see each other at all, but it wasn't just that I went off to work in Essex that kept us from staying in touch over those years. We didn't stay in touch because we were too upset by what happened when we were both seventeen."

Ronnie inclined her head. "What happened when you were seventeen?"

"Ronnie, Chelsea . . ." Jacqui squeezed her daughters' hands tightly as though to stop them from flying away. "Oh, I don't know how else I can say this."

"Say what?" Chelsea asked.

Jacqui hesitated. "I should wait for your father."

"Just spit it out, Mum. You can't not tell us now."

Jacqui took a deep breath.

"You've got a big sister called Daisy."

"Fuck," said Chelsea, as all eloquence escaped her.

Ronnie said nothing, but she slowly pulled her hand away and the flash of anger in her eyes was unmistakeable. Jacqui knew Ronnie too well not to notice.

"Fuck," said Chelsea again. "A big sister? I wasn't expecting that."

"What exactly do you mean, we've got a sister?" Ronnie asked.

"Just what I said. You've got another sister. A full sister. Me and your dad, we had another baby."

"But when?" asked Ronnie.

"Like I told you, when we'd just left school. I was sixteen and a half when I fell pregnant, seventeen when she was born —"

322

"Wow," said Chelsea. "Just wow."

"Where is she now?" Ronnie asked.

"That's the thing. We don't know. We had to give her up."

Chelsea shook her head, but Jacqui could tell from her face that it was more in disbelief and sympathy than disapproval. Ronnie, on the other hand—

"You gave her up?" Ronnie's voice was quiet. Unnervingly so.

"Yes. We did." Jacqui tried to stay calm. She had known there could be anger — she and Dave had discussed that very probable outcome — and Jacqui also knew, that when the whole story came out, it would likely be she who bore the brunt of any blame. Chelsea was still holding her hand at least. "We had to, Ronnie love. We put her up for adoption. We were only children ourselves."

"You were seventeen years old! I was seventeen when I had Sophie."

"Times were different," Jacqui told her. "There was no other way back then."

"Oh, Mum." Chelsea leant her head on Jacqui's shoulder. "It must have been terrible for you both."

Ronnie shook her head. Taking strength from Chelsea's reaction, Jacqui reached for her hand again. Ronnie wouldn't let her near.

"I don't want to hold your hand."

"Ronnie, please."

"Why didn't you tell me this before?"

"There hasn't been a right time," said Jacqui.

"You're so fucking hypocritical," Ronnie spat. "I can think of a perfect time. Why didn't you tell me this when I got pregnant? Don't you think it might have made a difference to know what you'd done in the same situation? You let me ruin my life, but you didn't let it ruin yours."

"Are you kidding?" asked Jacqui.

"You just gave that baby away and went on as if nothing had happened. You made me keep mine. I could have gone to university. I could have had a career. Instead, you near as told me it would be evil not to have the baby. After what you'd done?"

"Ronnie." Chelsea tried to intervene. "You can't talk to Mum like that. You have no idea what it must have been like for her."

"Don't get involved," Ronnie warned her.

"But I am involved. We're talking about my sister too."

"Then you should be as angry as I am that we've been lied to all these years." Ronnie turned back to snarl at Jacqui. "You let me throw away all my plans for the future because of your guilty conscience."

"You don't think my life was wrecked by what happened to me and your dad?" Jacqui responded. "You don't think I've spent the past forty-two years feeling like the lowest piece of scum on this earth for giving away my daughter?"

"I hope you have, because you are."

"Ronnie!" Chelsea protested.

"I didn't have a choice," Jacqui said again.

"There's always a choice," said Ronnie.

324

"I didn't know what else to do. They were different times, Ronnie. If you weren't married when you got pregnant, you had to give the baby away. If your parents wouldn't help you, you couldn't turn to social services."

"That's bollocks," said Ronnie. "You're talking about the early 1970s."

"And I'm talking about being part of a family that acted like it was still the 1870s. My parents were from a different age and they had different values. As far as they were concerned, if I kept that baby, I'd bring shame on their name."

"So you dumped her instead. You let her go just to save the family name? Just because your parents told you to?"

"I didn't have a choice. I couldn't do it on my own. I had no money. I had nothing."

"You had Dad."

"He didn't know."

"How could he have not known?"

"He was away on a training course in Scotland when I found out. He was just starting out in his career. My parents told me I'd be ruining his life as well if I went ahead and kept our child. I loved him so much I didn't want to mess things up for him. My parents were trying to persuade me to have an abortion, and the state wouldn't support us like they do nowadays. I couldn't have gone it alone."

"So you gave her away and went on to do exactly what you wanted?"

"What I wanted? I didn't get to do what I wanted. I just about managed to persuade my parents not to march me to the hospital for an abortion, but I had to leave home. I split up with your dad. I had to leave my family. You want to know why you never met your grandmother? It isn't because she died before you were born. She may still be alive and kicking for all I know. It's because I never spoke to her again after she made me give Daisy away. No one told me what happened to my baby. I never heard another thing after the day the social worker took her from my arms. You don't think that hurt? You don't think I wish every single day that I could hear from Daisy? I didn't choose the easy option, believe me."

"But why didn't you tell me all this when I got pregnant?"

"I didn't want to influence you. Your dad and I wanted you to have alternatives, Ronnie. If you'd wanted to have an abortion, then of course we would have stood by you. But if you really wanted to keep the baby, we wanted you to know that was an option as well. We had enough room in our home for another little one, and we could help you out financially. Nobody cares these days if a baby's parents are married. It certainly didn't matter to us that you and Mark never tied the knot. It doesn't matter at all."

But Ronnie was not softening. "You should have made me have an abortion. I was doing well. I could have stayed on at school and made something of myself. I'd have got a degree. I'd be living in London like Chelsea. I wouldn't be stuck in Coventry with a man who only notices what I do for him when he can't find the toilet roll. My life is shit and it's all because you forced me into having a child."

"We didn't *force* you," Jacqui persisted.

"You bloody did. You felt guilty because of what happened to Daisy and you tried to correct your own mistake through me."

"Ronnie, I don't know where this is coming from. We didn't force you to have Sophie. We talked about the alternatives for weeks. You've told me before that you're glad you became a mother. You love your children. They're the best thing you ever did."

Ronnie was already by the door.

"You lied to me and you let me ruin my life, all because I made one stupid mistake."

"Sophie's not a mistake," Chelsea piped up hopefully. "You're so lucky to have a family. Being a mother is the best—"

"Shut up," Ronnie spat at her sister. "Four days with your nephew and you think you know what my life is like. Well, you don't. I hate my life. I *hate* it."

Ronnie left the room in such blind fury she didn't notice her daughter running ahead of her down the hall.

With Ronnie gone, Jacqui and Chelsea just stared at the bedroom door as if it would reopen any second, but Ronnie did not come back. Jacqui finally let go of Chelsea's hand to wipe her eyes.

"Mum," said Chelsea, "it'll be OK. All this stuff, it's only because she's shocked. She will get over it. I know she will."

"Oh, Chelsea," Jacqui mumbled through her hands, "I wish I could believe you. I knew she would be angry, but not like this . . . Are you angry?"

"I'm a bit surprised," Chelsea admitted. "It's not every day you get a new sister. I wouldn't say I'm angry, though. It's not my place to be angry. You were the one who was forced to give up a child. I can't imagine what that did to you. When do we get to meet her?"

"You might never meet her," said Jacqui. "That's the ridiculous thing. I've upset your sister by telling her about it and it might not even matter."

"Have you been looking for her? For Daisy?"

"We don't even know her name. It won't be Daisy, that's for sure. Her adoptive parents will have changed it, and what they changed it to is confidential information. She can know our names but not vice versa. Adoption was a one-way street back then. The idea was you would never have contact with your child again."

"And there's nothing you can do?"

"We've been signed up to all the adoption registers for years but we'll never get to meet her if she doesn't decide to look for us. And the more time that passes, the more likely that seems. She'll be forty-two this year. Oh, Chelsea." Jacqui started properly sobbing. "You girls are the most important thing in the world to me. I can't lose both of you too."

"You won't lose us." Chelsea gave her mum a cuddle.

"I got so many things wrong," Jacqui sniffed.

328

"What are you talking about? You've been a wonderful mother to us. I'll go and talk to Ronnie," Chelsea offered.

"Will you? Please, Chelsea, please. Tell her that I love her, won't you?"

CHAPTER
FORTY-SIX

Chelsea

Chelsea wasn't sure how much point there was in talking to her sister right then — when Ronnie got angry, she stayed angry — but she knew she had to give it a go for their mother's sake. Ronnie was not in her room, and she had not gone back to the pool. In fact, there were no Bensons by the pool at all: Sophie had also disappeared; Bill was in the bar with Gloria; Dave was still on his mosquito-repellent mission and, as was typical, his mobile was switched off. What was the point of having a mobile if you never switched the stupid thing on? Meanwhile, Mark and Jack were playing snooker. They hadn't seen Ronnie since she went inside to talk to Jacqui.

"You look upset. What's the matter?" Mark asked.

Chelsea wasn't sure it was the right time to tell him their mother's news. "Nothing. Sisterly falling-out," she lied. "My fault."

"Oh, all right."

Of course that was feasible to Mark.

Where could Ronnie have gone? Chelsea decided to set out along the promenade and see if she could catch up with her sister there. To be honest, she also felt in need of a walk. Though she had reacted less violently to her mother's news, Chelsea found she was still vibrating with adrenaline. Jacqui's revelation had been such a surprise. The only thing that would have been more surprising would have been for her mother to announce that she was pregnant again right now.

Intellectually, Chelsea thought she understood why Ronnie felt she had more reason to be angry, but Ronnie's accusation that Jacqui had forced her into having a baby didn't ring true. As far as Chelsea could remember it, once she got over the initial panic, Ronnie had been delighted by the prospect of becoming a mother. She had certainly seemed to enjoy playing happy families with Mark and their new baby, while Chelsea was turfed out of their once-shared bedroom to sleep on the sofa downstairs. There were only two bedrooms in the Benson family's council house. Not having her own room — or even half a shared room — hadn't made revising for A-levels any easier. No one seemed to have considered how Chelsea might have suffered as a result. In those early days, everything in the Benson household revolved round Ronnie and Sophie. As she searched for her sister, Chelsea recalled the day she got her A-level results and confirmed her place at university.

"That's nice, dear," their mother had said, not even looking up from the bottle she was filling with formula.

Over dinner that night, Sophie's first proper words were far bigger news. Dave was the only one to comment on Chelsea's university triumph at all, and the only thing he said was that it would be great to have the sofa back. Yes, if anyone had a right to be angry with their parents, it was Chelsea. Ronnie got the support. Chelsea got a crick in the neck from spending almost two years sleeping on a sofa that was too short for her.

In a sense, though, Sophie's arrival had helped Chelsea to make her way in the world. When there was no place for you at home, you simply had to find somewhere else. Having long since learnt to do her own washing and cooking (or rather, making toast), compared to many of her contemporaries at university, Chelsea was well equipped to fend for herself. That was useful at least. She found living away from home blissful compared to being squashed into that tiny house with four other adults and a baby.

However, looking at her situation from a dispassionate point of view, nearly sixteen years on, Chelsea knew she had not been able to shake off her own need for attention altogether when Sophie came along. Was it possible that feeling unloved and ignored had been at the root of the vomiting thing? She still didn't have the guts to call it what it was: bulimia. It had started around the same time.

No, Chelsea knew she couldn't blame her family for that. Her parents had always done their best for her. And Ronnie. And Sophie. And Jack. That was why Chelsea had to find her sister now and ask her to find it in her to at least try to understand what their mum had been through. Chelsea knew that neither her mum nor her dad would have taken the decision lightly to let Daisy go. They were good people. Good parents.

Eventually, having walked for half an hour on her own, Chelsea did catch up with Ronnie. She was sitting on the sea wall about a mile away from the hotel. She was looking out to sea, concentrating so hard on the horizon that she didn't notice her sister until Chelsea touched her gently on the arm. Ronnie jumped.

"Mind if I join you?" Chelsea asked.

"Free country," said Ronnie.

Chelsea took up a spot on the wall. Ronnie resumed her sea vigil.

"You're really angry with Mum, aren't you?" Chelsea said eventually.

"Aren't you?"

"I'm certainly surprised. I can't say I'm angry."

"Well, you don't have as much to be angry about as I do. You're not the one who's ended up stuck in the town she grew up in, living like a slave for two kids and a useless fat-head of a partner."

"Wow," said Chelsea, "you *are* angry."

"Mum pushed me into having a baby because she gave her own child away. She wanted to fill some hole in her life by making a mess of mine."

"I don't remember it like that," said Chelsea. "I don't remember you being forced to do anything."

"Well, how do you remember it?" Ronnie asked. "You were only fifteen and a half."

"I certainly remember how it was when you found out you were pregnant."

It was Chelsea who found Ronnie crying in their bedroom that horrible afternoon after a third pregnancy test had proved positive. Chelsea didn't have to ask what was wrong. The last pregnancy-test box was sticking out from beneath the valance around Ronnie's bed, which was where Ronnie had inexpertly hidden it when she heard Chelsea and her parents come in from their shopping trip. Without saying a word, Chelsea sat down beside her sister and wrapped her arms around her. They stayed like that for several minutes.

"It's going to be all right, you know," Chelsea said eventually.

"How on earth can it be all right?" Ronnie asked.

"I'll help you," Chelsea promised.

It was a good job Chelsea was on the case. Ronnie was so distraught at the results of the test, she didn't know where to start. Perhaps they should have gone to their parents first, but Chelsea — with a teenager's logic — booked an appointment with the doctor for Ronnie to discuss a termination. Then she rang Mark and said Ronnie had tonsillitis and was too ill to see him or speak to him on the phone for a couple of days. She told their parents that Ronnie and Mark had fallen out. That was why Ronnie was red-eyed with distress, flopping around the house like a pre-Raphaelite beauty on too much laudanum.

Chelsea even went with her sister to see the doctor. She squeezed Ronnie's hand in a gesture of solidarity when the receptionist, who had known them since they were tiny children, asked, "Exactly what is it you want to discuss with Dr Swallow today?"

"It's confidential," Chelsea said. "We don't have to tell you anything."

334

The receptionist opened her mouth to protest.

"You know it's confidential," Chelsea repeated.

Once inside the doctor's office, Ronnie felt as though she was going to faint. Dr Swallow, who had always seemed so kind when they were kids, was curt and disapproving now. So Ronnie thought she was mature enough to be having sex but she hadn't been mature enough to think about contraception, eh?

"We're here for help, not a lecture," Chelsea told him.

Dr Swallow raised an eyebrow.

Ronnie was too late for the morning-after pill, of course, he said, but she was just within the nine-week deadline for a medical abortion. Dr Swallow described the procedure with what seemed to Chelsea like unnecessary relish. Two lots of tablets, two days apart. A bit of bleeding. *Dilation and curettage.*

"You'll definitely know you're having more than a period. It could take up to two weeks to complete. Now, let's get on with it. Time is of the essence."

Dr Swallow looked up the number of the specialist clinic Ronnie would have to be referred to. The wheels were in motion. In a matter of days, Ronnie could be taking the first of the tablets Dr Swallow prescribed. Her pregnancy would be over. Because of course, it was better that the pregnancy was over, wasn't it?

It was Chelsea, sitting next to her on a plastic-covered chair, who said, "Time may be of the essence, but you don't have to make any decisions right now, not while you're sitting here."

"You don't have for ever," said Dr Swallow.

"But she has at least a few days, doesn't she?"

"I thought you wanted a termination?"

Chelsea looked into Ronnie's face.

"Shall we go?" Chelsea asked.

The sisters left the surgery arm in arm.

"You want this baby, don't you?" Chelsea said, once they were outside. "I could see you weren't certain in there."

"Yes, I want this baby." Ronnie nodded. Her face broke into a smile for the first time in days.

"I'm going to be an auntie!" Chelsea shrieked.

Then the sisters went home and told Jacqui she was about to become a gran.

On the sea wall, Chelsea reminded Ronnie of the old story. It was the first time they had talked about that afternoon in Dr Swallow's surgery in years, certainly since Jack was born.

"You made up your mind before you even told Mum and Dad. Don't you remember? Dr Swallow was going to book you in for another appointment. You were completely white. I could tell you didn't want to go ahead."

"You got me out of there," Ronnie remembered.

"And when we got outside, you were so relieved. I asked you if you wanted to have your baby and your face just broke into this smile. You were even holding your stomach, protecting the little creature inside."

"Hormones," said Ronnie dismissively.

"Oh, Ronnie, it wasn't just that."

"I'm serious. You shouldn't have taken any notice of me, not with all those hormones making me crazy. Mum and Dad should have taken me straight back to the doctor."

"You wouldn't have wanted that. You were excited. We talked about every option that was available to you, but in the end, you knew you wanted to go through with the pregnancy. You told me it was going to be the making of your life. You would have your children early and take the world by storm later on. You could even take your baby into the boardroom."

"Yeah, but look at me now. No boardroom for me. I've completely screwed up. Every single day is the same: I get up; I make breakfast for three other people; I make sure they've all got clean clothes; I listen to them complaining because I've put the same thing in their lunchbox as yesterday. They leave the house without even stopping to thank me on the way. I've got a part-time job at a bloody undertaker's. When I get home, I don't think Mark would notice if I did the can-can topless, so long as the telly's on. I was ready to take on the world when I was seventeen, but I've ended up with nothing."

"You look like you've ended up with a whole lot to me. Ronnie, do you have any idea how much I envy you? I've always envied you. I told myself I didn't. I told myself I was much better off with my London life and my glamorous career than your life back home, but you've got so much love around you, Ronnie. You've got a partner who adores you—"

Ronnie snorted.

"—You're raising two wonderful children. Sophie is a really fine young woman — she's intelligent and beautiful — and Jack . . . Jack is something else. He's so funny and sensitive. Those qualities didn't just come from nowhere, Ronnie. It's you who helped nurture them. Your kids are a testament to exactly how much you've made of your life. If I could swap places with you and come home to Jack's smile every day . . ."

Ronnie nodded. Jack's smile was something truly special.

"Even to Sophie's grunts of hello," Chelsea joked.

Ronnie almost managed to laugh at that.

"I might end up missing out on all that," said Chelsea. "It's what Mum missed out on too, when she gave her baby away."

Ronnie's face hardened again and she looked back out to sea.

"Come on," Chelsea pressed on. "You know she's right that things were different then. She wouldn't have had any support if her parents weren't willing to give it to her. I don't think single women could even get their own mortgages."

"She should have tried harder."

"You know our mum, Ronnie. Don't you think she tried as hard as she could? Can you imagine what it must have been like? It must have broken her heart."

Though she was watching the waves advancing on the beach, Ronnie was back in Coventry, sixteen years ago. Though now she knew she must have imagined it — the pregnancy being so very new at the time — she had been sure that as she sat in Dr Swallow's office, she felt the tiny foetus turn a somersault. The connection between Ronnie and Sophie had been strong even then. How much stronger had it been seven months later? How painful would it have been to have that connection broken?

"Please," said Chelsea. "Let's go back to the hotel so Mum can tell us the whole story. She deserves that at least. So does Dad."

To Chelsea's great relief, Ronnie agreed.

Arm in arm, the sisters headed back to the Hotel Volcan to join their mother and father.

CHAPTER
FORTY-SEVEN

Jacqui

Forty-three years earlier

It was decided that it would be for the best if Jacqui left Coventry as soon as the pregnancy started showing. Thank goodness, her mother observed, it was fashionable that year to dress in shapeless smocks, so that even at five months gone, Jacqui didn't look all that different from her school friends. She didn't put weight on around her face or on her arms. Her parents' neighbour, Mrs Green, who was exactly the kind of person to be scandalised, didn't seem to have noticed a thing. She still asked Jacqui what she was planning to do after she got her exam results.

At five and a half months, however, Jacqui's mother started to get twitchy.

"I think it's time," she said. "People will start to talk."

So two days later, her father drove her to stay with her aunt near Chelmsford. They were mostly silent on the drive, but Jacqui felt sure she could hear accusation in his every exhalation. He carried her suitcase to the door. Jacqui had gone to carry it herself, but her father said, "Not in your condition," as if he were any proud grandfather-to-be, but of course he wasn't. He definitely wasn't proud.

After a cup of tea and some small talk with Auntie Pam, her father prepared to leave. Jacqui saw him to the door and reached out to hug him, but he backed away and squeezed her hand instead.

"It's not for long, pet," he told her. "Once this thing is sorted out, you can come home and everything will be back to normal."

Jacqui agreed, though she didn't see how it could possibly be true.

You can't imagine what it's like to be pregnant until it actually happens. Her parents were acting as though the baby were some kind of tumour, to be wished away and never spoken of again, but Jacqui's body hadn't taken on board the news that the baby wasn't staying. She had the same hormones as every expectant mother. She cupped her stomach protectively when walking through a crowd.

Auntie Pam did her best, but she'd never had children. Half the family said Pam *couldn't* have children; the other half said she'd never wanted to. Whatever the reason, Pam didn't seem to want to talk about the changes to Jacqui's body or the feelings churning in her mind.

"You just tell me when, you know . . ." Pam couldn't find the words. "I'll drive you straight to the hospital."

The day came. Jacqui's waters broke. Thankfully, she was in the bathroom at the time. She told her aunt she would be fine to clean the floor before they went to the hospital, but Pam was desperate for her share of the responsibilities to end. She insisted they go right away. Jacqui sat on a towel in the back of the car.

The small private hospital Jacqui had been booked into looked attractive enough on the outside, housed as it was in a mansion built by an eighteenth-century businessman to showcase his enormous wealth. On the inside, though, the building was as austere as any prison. Unlike the maternity ward at the general hospital, the corridors were largely deserted. There were no anxious husbands pacing for news, no prospective grandparents eager to help. Auntie Pam helped Jacqui to the front desk and left her there.

There were few kind words in the delivery room, as though the pain of labour was all part of the punishment for stepping out of line. Jacqui accepted it. She wasn't going to give the slab-faced midwife the satisfaction of seeing her pain and fear. She gritted her teeth. She'd faced worse. No, Jacqui decided five minutes later, actually, she had never faced anything as frightening as this. How she longed for Dave to be there, holding her hand.

The baby was born and immediately whisked away.

"What is it? What is it?" Jacqui wanted to know. Nobody would tell her. She was left alone with a bloody towel between her legs. Ten minutes later, she was back on the ward. She still didn't know whether she'd given birth to a girl, a boy or a kitten.

"Mrs Ross?"

Jacqui wasn't immediately aware that the ward sister was addressing her. Mrs Ross was her mother's name.

"Mrs Ross?"

"You mean me?"

"Who else do you think I mean?"

"I'm not Mrs—"

"I know," said the nurse, raising an eyebrow.

Later, Jacqui realised that the nurses addressed everyone as Mrs. Even the thirteen-year-old girl in the bed opposite who hadn't stopped crying since the moment she was wheeled back from the delivery suite.

"You can see your baby now."

Jacqui limped behind the nurse to a room full of cradles. She was allowed at last to hold her baby to her breast.

"Don't get too attached," the nurse told her.

Five weeks later, her father offered to pick her up and bring her back from the mother and baby home she and Daisy had stayed in since the birth. Jacqui had no real choice but to accept. This time, on the drive from Chelmsford to Coventry, her father was unusually chatty. He filled her in on all the gossip from their street. Mrs Green's cat had gone missing. She was convinced it had been stolen by a cat-sacrificing cult.

"Most likely it got knocked down on the dual carriageway."

Jacqui didn't speak. She watched the miles pass. Her body still hadn't quite said goodbye to Daisy. At the sight of a mother with a small boy, Jacqui's abdomen contracted painfully. Where had her baby gone? The social worker had taken Daisy away to her interim foster carers while Jacqui was having a bath one morning. Better that way, was the general consensus. No one tried to comfort her as she stood at the top of the stairs and screamed, with her hair still dripping wet. It would haunt Jacqui for the rest of her life that she had missed her chance to say goodbye. Were they looking after her? Were they holding her tight and keeping her warm? What were they going to call her?

Jacqui's mother had cooked her favourite meal for tea, as if this homecoming without the baby was something to be celebrated. Jacqui ate three mouthfuls and pushed her plate away.

"After all your mother's done for you!" her father snapped.

A week later, Jacqui left home for good. She left a note on the kitchen table saying she would send a forwarding address. She never did.

Dave never really stopped hoping that Jacqui would come back into his life. He had no idea about the baby. As far as he was concerned, Jacqui had dumped him on the advice of her parents and gone to Essex to pursue a secretarial career. He was convinced that one day she would change her mind about him. Admittedly, as the years passed, it seemed less likely, but it never felt impossible. Dave might have moved around the country in search of work, but his dad, Bill, hadn't strayed from the same old address. If Jacqui wanted to get in touch with him, all she had to do was call.

Then Bill announced that he was moving. Dave hadn't lived at home in years. The family home was too big without him. Bill liked the idea of downsizing to a bungalow and spending the money left over on a caravan. He'd always fancied having a caravan.

"But . . ."

They talked about the reasons why a move might not be a good idea. *The* reason.

"She hasn't been in touch for nine years, son," said Bill. "I don't think it's going to happen now."

Bill half-heartedly encouraged Dave to get back out there, find a new girl and get on with his life, though Bill knew more than anyone what it was like to have lost true love, having lost his own wife to cancer fifteen years before. Even so, he couldn't stay in a house that echoed around him just so that Jacqui would know where to post her Christmas cards.

"Whoever I sell the place to will just have to forward the post."

The night before Bill moved, Jacqui called.

There was no awkwardness in Jacqui and Dave's first meeting nine years after they'd last said goodbye and they soon made up for lost time. There was so much to catch up on. Within six months they were engaged. There was no need to elope. They were both more than old enough to chart their own destinies.

Eventually, Jacqui told Dave about the adoption. She told him everything. Dave vowed they would meet their daughter again one day — they weren't going to keep her a secret — but then the other girls came along and the concept of a sister who had been given away seemed too difficult to explain to a toddler or a five-year-old. Ronnie had enough trouble dealing with

345

being usurped by Chelsea. How would she react to the idea that she wasn't even the oldest sibling after all? It suddenly seemed better not to talk about it. In any case, Dave and Jacqui were increasingly aware of the possibility that their first child would never get in touch. As birth parents, they weren't allowed to access any of the details of their daughter's new identity. Everything was up to her.

The run-up to Daisy's eighteenth birthday was an especially difficult time for Jacqui. She knew that at eighteen, Daisy would be allowed to apply to see her original birth certificate and find out who her birth parents were. Jacqui felt sure she wouldn't have to wait much longer, but Daisy's eighteenth birthday came and went and still there was no news. Her nineteenth. Her twentieth. Her thirtieth. Her fortieth.

People at the adoption support group Jacqui joined online said that adoptees often decided to search for their birth parents after becoming parents themselves. Surely if Daisy was going to become a mother, she would have done so by now. Maybe she hated Dave and Jacqui for giving her away. Maybe she didn't even know she was adopted. Maybe, Dave dared to suggest one particularly sad year, maybe she was dead.

"She's not dead," said Jacqui. "I can feel she's out there."

For years Jacqui had listened to the wisdom espoused, even by Bill, that there was no point telling the girls about the existence of someone they might never meet, but as she approached her own sixtieth birthday, she wanted to unburden herself. She wanted her girls to know the full story. She wanted them to know why she was occasionally a bit too interested in their lives. Jacqui was tired of keeping the biggest sadness of her life hidden. People talked about miscarriages and still-births all the time these days. Jacqui wanted to talk about Daisy. Out loud.

"Oh, Mum," said Chelsea. "Oh, Dad." She put her arms round both their shoulders.

"That's why you two are so precious to us," said Dave.

"I always wanted to have another sister," said Chelsea.

"Yeah," said Ronnie, "but I bet you were thinking 'instead of' rather than 'as well' as me."

"That's not true," Chelsea insisted.

Jacqui held her arms out and Ronnie stepped into them. Parents and sisters squeezed together in a group hug.

"I wonder what she'd make of us?" Chelsea mused. "Daisy. I wonder if she thinks about us much."

"We're not allowed to look for her," Dave reminded his younger daughters. "It has to come from her."

"We might never get to meet her," Jacqui echoed sadly.

"Oh no, Mum," said Ronnie. "I've got this really weird feeling we will."

CHAPTER
FORTY-EIGHT

Sophie

The three women stayed in Jacqui and Dave's bedroom for another hour, going over Jacqui's astonishing news. Dave excused himself to the bar. It was all a bit too much for him. The idea of Jacqui all alone in the mother-and-baby home made Chelsea cry for her. Ronnie reared up when Jacqui told her that baby Daisy had looked just like newborn Sophie.

"I guess that gives us some idea of what kind of nightmare Daisy might have been as a teen," Ronnie observed in an attempt to lighten the moment.

There was much to talk about with regard to Daisy, but right then, the three Benson women had found a kind of peace. So much so that Ronnie felt able at last to share her other worries.

"I think Mark is having an affair," she blurted out.

Chelsea and Jacqui looked at each other in confusion.

"What makes you think that, love?" Jacqui asked her.

"I found a text message on his phone from Cathy next door. She said she was waiting for him to tell me something. Tell me what? It's got to be that he's leaving me, right?"

"No," said Chelsea. She'd met Cathy. She was a nice enough woman, but she had the voice and biceps of a long-distance lorry driver. "Never," she said. "Not Cathy next door."

"He's seeing her. I know he is. Every time he gets a text, he practically throws himself at his phone before I can get to it. He never used to get text messages. Now he's getting twenty a day and they're all from her. I'm going to tell him I know."

"Oh, sweetheart," said Jacqui, "don't you think you're jumping to conclusions?"

"Well, tonight I'll know for certain. I'm sorry, Mum. I didn't want to spoil your birthday holiday, but I'm going to ask him straight out, after dinner."

"Ronnie, love," said Jacqui, "I really think you've got the wrong end of the stick here."

"Well, tonight, I'll find out for sure, won't I?"

Ronnie wouldn't get the chance.

"Where's Sophie?" Mark asked Ronnie when the family reconvened for dinner in the Jolly Pirate. "What time did you tell her to be back here?"

"Half past six," she said.

"It's ten to seven."

"She'll be here in a minute. She's on holiday, Mark. You're the one who's always saying I should give her a break."

At half past seven, though, when the rest of her family took up their usual table in the restaurant, Sophie was still nowhere to be seen. Ronnie texted her four times and received nothing in reply. Everyone ordered their food. Eight o'clock came and went.

"Where the hell is she?" asked Mark, losing his cool at last. "She knows she's supposed to be here." The words were angry, but another emotion was written all over his face: anxiety. Sophie was his little girl. No matter that he had been talking about giving her more independence. No matter that she was fifteen and a half years old and as tall as her mother. She would always be his baby.

"Who saw her last?" Mark asked.

"I saw her by the pool this afternoon," said Jack helpfully.

"She went upstairs at about four o'clock," said Chelsea. "She was going to get a magazine. I didn't see her after that. I assumed she must have decided to stay in her room or go into town."

While Mark interrogated the rest of the family (with the exception of Granddad Bill, who was eating in the pizza restaurant with Lesley and Gloria that evening), Chelsea texted her niece. It was immediately obvious to her where Sophie had gone. She'd put on her best dress and borrowed her aunt's lipstick to go somewhere with the boy she'd been hanging out with that week. She had done exactly what she'd promised she wouldn't do. God only knew what excuses she was going to come out with, but the sooner she came back to face the music, the better.

Where the hell are you? Chelsea typed. Your mum is going crazy.

Nothing. No response. Chelsea could understand why Sophie might not respond to a text message from her mother, but she had been sure that she — the cool aunt — would get some kind of acknowledgement. She called and left a voicemail.

"I'm serious, Sophie. You're two hours late for dinner. I know it's not late as far as you're concerned, but if you don't get back to the hotel in the next five minutes, your mum and dad are going to have the police on your case."

The screen of Chelsea's iPhone remained resolutely blank.

Half an hour later, Mark and Ronnie were starting to panic in earnest. Dave was trying to calm them down. Jack was sitting on Jacqui's knee. Ostensibly, he and his grandmother were playing a game of noughts and crosses on one of the paper tablemats, but neither of them was fully invested in the task. Both were covertly monitoring Ronnie and Mark's conversation for developments.

"I really don't think we need to get too worried just yet. It seems pretty obvious who she's with," said Chelsea. "She's with that friend she made in the amusement arcade, the one who asked her to go clubbing."

"But I told her she couldn't go," said Ronnie.

"She clearly decided not to take any notice," said Chelsea. "It's not such a surprise. She's just like you were at her age. Remember? She'll turn up at ten and claim that she texted you to say where she was going but the text must have got lost in the system."

Ronnie was momentarily placated by the idea that Sophie might just be disobeying her.

"I'll go and look for her," said Chelsea.

But Sophie was not in the amusement arcade, and frustratingly, when the woman on the cash desk, who worked there from dawn to dusk, seven days a week, was shown a picture on Chelsea's iPhone screen, she claimed she had never seen the young English girl.

Perhaps she hadn't noticed her because she'd been part of a bigger gang of local children? Chelsea suggested.

"The local children do not come in places like this," the woman sneered, as though it were self-evident. The local children were angels who would never worry their parents by failing to turn up for a family meal on time.

"Fine," said Chelsea. "Of course they don't."

Chelsea walked up the street, quickening her pace to go past the currency-exchange booth. The last thing she needed right then was to have to get out of a conversation with that creep. Thankfully, he wasn't hanging around. In his place, a white-haired woman nodded over a gossip magazine.

Chelsea stopped everyone who looked vaguely familiar and showed them the picture of her niece on her phone. No one seemed to have seen her before. At least, they couldn't say for certain.

"Teenagers all look the same to me," said one elderly Englishman.

"Please look more closely," Chelsea urged him. "Something about her might jog your memory."

"My memory ain't what it used to be."

Chelsea stopped other teens and asked them too. She used her best broken Spanish on local children, who answered her in perfect English. No one had seen Sophie. No one had ever seen Sophie before. If they saw her now, they would of course tell her that people were looking for her, but for now, Chelsea was none the wiser. Her niece had quite simply disappeared.

CHAPTER
FORTY-NINE

Sophie

The hotel manager didn't seem overly worried. After all, they weren't talking about an especially vulnerable child; Sophie was not a toddler. The manager suggested it wasn't unusual for a fifteen-year-old to go AWOL. English teenagers were always hooking up with the local kids. Perhaps she had taken a romantic walk down the beach and lost track of time? The local kids had sex behind the ferry terminal, he added helpfully.

"My daughter is not a slut," said Mark, pulling himself up to his full height and towering over the small, moustachioed manager.

"Of course not," said the manager. "I wasn't suggesting that."

"Good, because if you were . . ."

Suddenly, the manager started taking Mark and Ronnie's distress much more seriously.

"She's an intelligent, sensible girl," Mark continued. "I just don't believe she's not telling us where she is because she doesn't know what time it is. Something is stopping her from getting in touch. She could be with anybody. She may dress like an adult, but she's still a child."

"Of course," said the manager. "Of course."

"Nothing," said Chelsea as she came back into the hotel restaurant.

While she had been walking the length of the town, Mark had been scouring the pebbly bay to the west, towards the ferry terminal. Ronnie and Dave searched the sandy beach to the east. Jacqui stayed at the hotel with Jack, attempting to distract him from the goings-on with a card game, but Jack was way too bright for that. He knew this wasn't just a matter of his sister being a little bit late any more. This was serious. He wanted to talk about it.

"Will we find her, Auntie Chelsea?"

"Of course we will," Chelsea told him.

"If you need to use my sonic screwdriver, you can."

"Thanks, Jack." Chelsea gave him a squeeze.

Eventually, all the adults returned to the hotel restaurant.

"No sign of her," said Mark.

"She must have got into a car," said Chelsea.

"Don't say that," said Ronnie, covering her ears as though even mentioning the possibility could make it true.

"We're going to have to ask for proper help," said Jacqui. "We've got to get the police involved. Sophie's a good girl. I don't believe she would scare us like this deliberately."

"She better not," said Ronnie. She punched another text into her phone.

"She might have lost her phone," said Chelsea.

"Or been mugged," said Dave.

"Don't say that either!" Ronnie exploded.

"Stay calm," said Jacqui.

"How can I be calm?" Ronnie asked. "My daughter's gone missing!"

This is all my fault, Ronnie told herself. This is happening because I got angry with Mum and accused her of forcing me to have my daughter. This is God's way of showing me what I've got to lose. God, if you can just bring Sophie back to us, then I promise I'll set everything straight. I'll settle down and be grateful for what I've got in my life. I'll be happy with what I have. Just please, please let my baby be safe. Let her come back to us in one piece. Don't let anybody have hurt her.

Ronnie felt her legs weaken as she even allowed the idea that someone might hurt her daughter to enter her mind. Chelsea wrapped her arms round her sister to hold her up.

"I just want my little girl back."

CHAPTER
FIFTY

Sophie

Sophie had heard everything. She had gone up to her bedroom to get a magazine to read by the pool, having resigned herself to the fact that she was not going to be able to go clubbing with Luca. A visit to a bar with Auntie Chelsea was as good as it was going to get. Still, Chelsea was pretty cool. Sophie was going to ask her more about her life in London. Sophie had already decided that she was going to London as soon as she could leave school. There was no way she was going to get stuck in Coventry like her mum and dad.

It was as Sophie was about to go back down to the pool that she heard raised voices from her grandparents' room. Sophie couldn't resist eavesdropping. But what's the old saying? People who eavesdrop never hear good of themselves.

At first Sophie was just outraged. How could her mother say such horrible things? And then the outrage turned into a thirst for revenge. Or, if not revenge, a decision to take full advantage of Ronnie's indiscretion to get her own way for at least that evening.

Sophie went back into her room, changed into her favourite outfit and slicked on some of her aunt's lipstick. Then she went out, slamming the door behind her, full of a feeling of righteousness that took her right to Luca's currency exchange. If her mother didn't care about her, then why should she be bothered if Sophie stayed out past her curfew?

Luca was only too pleased to see her. He had been expecting to have to start from scratch when it came to finding willing company for the evening. He welcomed Sophie into the back of the shop and fixed her a vodka and coke. And another. And another. And another.

The walls of the little dark room in the back of the currency exchange seemed to sway and pulse. Sophie found herself giggling uncontrollably as Luca took her glass from her hand and went to kiss her. Just as his lips were about to touch hers, she threw up all over his chest.

After that the mood quickly darkened. Luca went from Romeo to Wrong'un in a heartbeat. He yelled at Sophie, furious that his best shirt was ruined. She threw up again, missing Luca this time but covering everything on the desk. The mess was terrible. Luca's face was ugly and twisted with rage. He slammed a fist into the wall right by her head. That little part of Sophie's brain that was still functioning properly, told her to run and keep running.

Outside, she threw up once more. Passing tourists looked at her in disgust but nobody offered to help. British tourists could never hold their drink. With the logic of the inebriated, Sophie decided that she should go and sit by the sea. The breeze coming in off the waves would help her sober up. There was no way she could go back to the Hotel Volcan in such a state. Her mum and dad would kill her.

If they cared that much . . . Her mother had never wanted her.

Sophie had never been drunk before. She didn't recognise the ways in which the alcohol messed with her brain. She had gone through giggly and sick and now she was getting to maudlin. As she walked the length of the jetty, she replayed what she'd heard from her grandparent's room. Her mother had never wanted her. She'd wanted an abortion. Having Sophie had derailed all her plans. With half a pint of vodka still working through her system, Sophie was quick to conclude that she should never have been born.

The jetty was empty. During the day, a few tourists laid out their beach towels upon it and swam from there, preferring the sun-bleached boards to the gritty black sand, but now Sophie had it to herself. She walked to the very end of it and leaned against the wind. Tears streamed down her face. Nobody wanted her. Her parents didn't want her. Luca certainly didn't want her now. Harrison had thrown her over for Skyler. She would never amount to anything. Her auntie Chelsea had only told her not to become a model because she didn't want to have to tell her she wasn't pretty enough. If she'd been prettier and cleverer then perhaps her parents would have loved her more. Her mother wouldn't have shouted that having Sophie had ruined her life.

★ ★ ★

From a café on the promenade, Adam watched Sophie walk out towards the sea, while Lily amused herself by doodling on the paper tablecloth. Thank goodness for the emergency crayons. Adam recognised Sophie. He'd seen her around the hotel complex with Jack. And there was something about her that reminded him of Chelsea. She had the same chestnut-brown hair. The same heart-shaped face and cheeky eyes.

What was she doing on her own? She seemed to be crying. Adam briefly gave Lily his opinion on her latest drawing — "Brilliant, darling" — then went back to watching Sophie's unsteady progress. It was a death trap, that jetty. It had been allowed to fall into such disrepair. Some of the planks were almost rotted through. Lily had wanted to walk along it but Adam had refused. Now Sophie swayed from foot to foot as she avoided the holes. She looked ... she looked drunk! Really very inebriated. But hadn't Chelsea said her niece was only fifteen years old? Adam was allowing himself the small satisfaction of being absolutely sure that his daughter would never be allowed to run wild like that when, all of a sudden, Sophie disappeared.

The last plank of the jetty had broken beneath her weight and Sophie had plunged straight into the water as though through an open trapdoor. Adam leapt up and called the restaurant staff to help. The waitress who had been serving them that evening took care of Lily while Adam, the cook and a waiter raced out to the sea.

Sophie was ordinarily a reasonably strong swimmer but the alcohol in her system made her slow to react.

The posts of the jetty were out of her reach before she realised what was happening. She flailed against the waves to get back to them. She shouted for help. There was no one around.

But then, suddenly, Adam and the men from the café were there with a lifebelt. The cook and the waiter held onto the end of the rope, while Adam took the belt and dived in. With the belt under one arm, he powered through the water towards Sophie. Grasping her hand, he pulled her close and helped her struggle into the hard plastic loop.

"You'll be all right," he promised her. "Everything will be all right."

Two minutes later, Sophie was back on the jetty, spluttering and suddenly very sober. Adam sat beside her, panting from the effort, dripping and cold. Someone appeared with a couple of towels. Sophie cried and Adam shed a few tears himself, as he considered that he may have saved Sophie, but in the process, he could just as easily have orphaned his own daughter. It didn't bear thinking about.

"Thank you," Sophie whispered as he helped her towards the café. "Will you take me back to Mum and Dad?"

CHAPTER
FIFTY-ONE

Chelsea

Sophie's disappearance caused quite a stir at the Hotel Volcan. Once news spread that a child was missing, the hotel's guests could talk of nothing else. Several search parties were organised, though they never got any further than noisy meetings in the bar where the volunteers spent most of their time speculating as to what horrible end might have befallen the poor kid in the few hours she had been gone.

When Sophie, Adam and Lily got back to the hotel safe and well, a cheer went up that was almost as loud as the one heard in the bar when England won the Rugby World Cup in 2004. It was the perfect excuse for a celebration. Joachim, the barman who had tagged Granddad Bill as a lottery winner, was run off his feet providing liquid sustenance for the guests, who were, for the most part, very pleased there was a happy ending to the dramatic story they would have to tell their friends back home. Gloria threw her arms round Granddad Bill and smothered his bald, liver-spotted head with kisses.

Ronnie clasped her daughter to her chest and covered her head with tears.

"My little girl!" she murmured over and over. "My precious baby."

Sophie allowed herself to be held. Her legs were still shaking. For the moment, she never wanted to leave her mother's side again.

Jacqui and Mark both cried with relief. Even Dave wiped away a tear. The hotel manager brought out a bottle of champagne.

"Have a drink with us," Chelsea said to Adam.

"I should put Lily to bed."

"Let her stay up with Jack for a bit," said Jacqui. "I can keep an eye on them. Why don't you have a drink? You certainly deserve one."

Adam hesitated.

"She can be a bit . . . Well, difficult with people she doesn't know well."

"She'll be a good girl for me, won't you, Lily?" Jacqui got down to Lily's height. She opened her arms and, to everyone's surprise, Lily allowed herself to be picked up.

Jacqui carried Lily across to the table where Jack was setting up for a round of Go Fish. In the excitement of Sophie's reappearance, he had negotiated himself a later bedtime. He moved across to make space for Lily.

"Do you like *Doctor Who*?" he asked, without actually looking at his one-time enemy.

"I do," said Lily. "It's my favourite."

"Then you can have a look at my sonic screwdriver," said Jack, passing his precious toy across. This time he dared a tiny glance at her out of the corner of his eye.

"I think that might be the beginning of an entente cordiale," said Adam.

Chelsea and Adam didn't go to the hotel bar. They walked out onto the beach road to look for somewhere quieter. Adam told Chelsea what Sophie had confessed on the walk back to the Hotel Volcan about the alcohol and her local "friend".

Chelsea wasn't in the least bit surprised when Adam revealed the identity of the man who had given Sophie so much to drink. The creep from the currency exchange! Thank goodness Sophie had cut short anything too awful by vomiting, but there were still questions to be answered and Chelsea would make sure Sophie's "friend" answered them at the police station.

It had been the most extraordinary time, not least because of what her mother had revealed before Sophie's disappearance became the bigger issue. You didn't learn you had a new sister — or an old sister — every day.

So Chelsea was thoughtful as she and Adam searched for somewhere to relax. They chose the bar of a pizza restaurant. Adam ordered a bottle of Chianti. There was actually a choice of wine here.

"Thank you," said Chelsea. "You saved the day. I don't dare think what might have happened if you hadn't been in that café on the front."

"I'm glad I could help. It seems like the least I could do after . . . well, we've butted heads a few times this week, you and me. I've said some awful things."

364

"I just thank God you were watching my niece," said Chelsea.

"I hope it makes up for all those times I wasn't watching Lily earlier in the week.

Chelsea laughed.

"I guess it started before we even got off the plane. That dress you were wearing . . . it was expensive, wasn't it?" Adam asked.

Chelsea pulled a face that suggested he was on the right lines. In fact, her expression said, "You have no idea how expensive a dress can be."

"I thought so," he said. "I can tell when something's well made."

"Really?" Chelsea had yet to meet a man who could tell the difference between Prada and Primark. At least, not a straight man.

"Yes. I could see it in the cut and the fabric. I had a great teacher. My wife always dressed very well."

Wife? Dressed? The past tense? Chelsea let it hang in the air.

"My wife died," Adam explained in short order. "Nearly three years ago."

"I'm sorry. Was . . . ?"

"Was she ill for a long time? No. Thank God. She — Claire was her name — had an aneurysm. Apparently, it was waiting to happen — could have gone at any time. It was incredibly sudden and fast. It happened when she was at the office. She'd only been back at work for a week. I kept thinking about that. If it had happened a week earlier, she would have been at home with Lily."

Chelsea winced at the thought.

"As it was, Lily was with her grandparents. I don't know what I would have done without them. I was in pieces for months."

"That's understandable."

"But you have to carry on. Claire would have been furious if I hadn't pulled myself together. Lily was only just three years old and she needed me."

Adam was visibly distressed by the memory. Chelsea found herself reaching across the table to pat his hand. She halfway withdrew when she decided that was a lame gesture. Then she reached out again and this time she took his hand properly. After rescuing Sophie, the very least he deserved was a good listening-to.

Adam confirmed that he was grateful seconds later. "I don't talk about it much any more. People were very willing to listen at first, but when you've told the story a hundred times, you know they're just being polite when they tell you to call whenever you want."

"Well, I'm hearing this for the first time," said Chelsea. "You can talk for as long as you want."

"I don't know how much Lily remembers. Everyone told me that she was so young she would adjust and it would be as though nothing had happened, but she definitely feels a lack. I know it. I try to be everything to her. Sometimes I think I try a bit too hard. I find it difficult to get tough with her when she's being so spoilt. It doesn't help that none of her grandparents or aunts and uncles ever says boo to her. They always see her as the poor motherless child rather than the stroppy little madam she can be from time to time."

Chelsea was careful not to nod.

"Sometimes when she's kicking off about something or the other, I imagine Claire looking down on me and telling me I'm getting it wrong. I'm sure she would know exactly how to handle Lily's tantrums. I'm sure Lily wouldn't dare have them if Claire were still around."

"Don't beat yourself up," said Chelsea. "I used to think that parenting was easy, but I've had my eyes well and truly opened this week."

"Jack seems like a good kid."

"He is — he's lovely, and he's incredibly wise. He comes out with things that I can't imagine having even thought about at his age."

"They can be like that, children. Claire used to say that the under-sevens are like dogs — they pick up on everything. It's like they can read the flicker of an eyebrow you don't even feel. You can't hide anything from them. I think that as children get older, they start to close down to what other people are feeling, and by the time they're adults, they can be totally oblivious. It's a self-defence mechanism."

"It would be good to be oblivious from time to time," Chelsea joked.

"They teach you a lot about yourself, children," Adam continued.

"That's what my sister was always telling me. She used to say you aren't really a woman until you've had a child."

"I don't think that's entirely true," said Adam. "You don't have to give birth to benefit in some way."

"I know that. Jack has certainly made me think about a few things this week. I shall endeavour to have some of his patience, for a start."

"He's a very good loser," said Adam. "I mean, he's OK with being disappointed, unlike . . ."

He nodded towards her. Chelsea raised an eyebrow back at him. "Let's not talk about the parents' race, please."

"I'm sorry about that, but if you had any idea what I was expecting to have to deal with if I hadn't won . . . Anyway, you did hold on to your potato."

"And you didn't?"

Adam laughed. "Rumbled."

"I knew it was impossible!"

"You're right. *Potato* and spoon, I ask you. It simply does not work. Look, it's getting late. Are you sure your parents are OK with having both Jack and Lily?"

Jacqui had texted to say that she was putting both the children to bed in her and Dave's room so Chelsea and Adam didn't have to hurry back.

"I think Mum just wants to feel useful tonight," said Chelsea.

"In which case, I shall make the most of having my bedroom to myself. You have no idea how loudly a six-year-old can snore."

"Oh no," said Chelsea, "I do."

Adam picked up the bottle of wine they had shared. There was just an inch left in the bottom. He offered it to Chelsea, but she refused. He passed up on it too.

"Tomorrow's a big day," he reminded her.

Chelsea tilted her head to one side. She wasn't sure what he was referring to.

"The fancy-dress competition?" Adam reminded her. "You are entering the fancy-dress competition, aren't you? Last chance to prove you're not a—"

Adam made the "L" sign.

Chelsea flicked a finger at him. "You're on."

CHAPTER
FIFTY-TWO

Jacqui

Jacqui and Dave didn't mind having the children sleeping on cushions in their room, because going to bed was the very last thing they felt like doing. Instead, they sat out on the balcony, leaving the door into the room ajar so they could hear the slightest snuffle or movement. They talked to each other in hushed tones. There was a lot to discuss. The truth about their eldest daughter was out at last. It hadn't happened in the way Jacqui anticipated, but it was out there nonetheless. Ronnie knew. Chelsea knew. Mark knew. Sophie knew. One day soon, Jack would know as well.

"How do you feel?" Dave asked his wife again. Though it was very much his story too, he knew she was the one feeling the brunt of the day's events right then.

Jacqui assured him that she was OK. In truth, she felt exhausted. The row with Ronnie, Sophie's disappearance, her subsequent return to the family fold: the day had encompassed more highs and lows than the craziest roller-coaster a Disney imagineer could have invented. Facing Ronnie's anger, Jacqui had thought she might lose everything. Knowing that her granddaughter was safe, Jacqui had been on top of the world. A couple of hours later, she was feeling deflated again. She was thinking about how her life had been, all those years ago, when she discovered that she was carrying her first baby.

Dave knew the story, of course, but he was happy to let her tell it again.

"Ultimately," she said at last, "today has changed nothing. The girls know the truth, but I'm still the mother to a child I've never known."

"And the mother to two girls who adore you," Dave pointed out. "Two grandchildren who think you're the best gran in the world. And my wife. You're the wife of a man who will always love you."

"For ever?" asked Jacqui.

She buried her head in her husband's shoulder.

"For ever," Dave confirmed.

CHAPTER
FIFTY-THREE

Sophie

When everyone else had gone to bed, Ronnie and Sophie sat side by side in Sophie's room and talked through that day's adventures.

"You said you didn't want me," Sophie said flatly.

"Oh, sweetheart! That's not what I was saying at all."

"It is. You said you never wanted to have a baby and I ruined your life. I took away all your chances."

"You didn't," said Ronnie. She held Sophie tightly, but Sophie remained stiff within her arms, as though trying to keep herself from her mother.

"Why didn't you just get rid of me? You didn't have to do what Grandma and Granddad said."

"Because I didn't want to. We didn't want to. Your dad and me, we wanted to have you."

She protested so much that Sophie started to thaw. Then Ronnie told her about the moment in Dr Swallow's surgery.

"I felt you there inside me and I knew we could get through it all. When you were born, the feeling only got stronger. I would sit by your crib and watch you for hours. We both did, me and your dad. We'd hold hands and watch you while you slept. When you were awake, we'd fight over which one of us got to cuddle you first."

"Did you really?" Sophie asked her.

"We really did. And as you got older, it just got better and better. I can't describe how fabulous it was to see you take your first steps. You spoke really early. I was ever so proud of you. You were so sensitive and thoughtful. You made me proud every day."

"I don't make you proud any more?"

Ronnie sensed that Sophie was fishing.

"You make me proud all the time, you do. When you're helping your brother tie his shoelaces, when you're in the netball team, when you bring home your exam results. You've got a great future ahead of you. I know you're going to go to uni—"

"But you could have gone to uni if you hadn't had me," Sophie reminded her.

"I'd never have got into university," said Ronnie.

"That's not true. You would have got your A-levels."

Ronnie shook her head.

"And you could still get them, Mum. You know that, don't you?"

"What, now? I'm thirty-two years old."

"Age doesn't matter."

"Can you imagine how old I'd be when I finished a degree?"

"The same age you'd be if you didn't do a degree at all," said Sophie.

Ronnie blinked at her daughter's wisdom.

"You could totally do it, Mum. You could do it all at the same time as me. When I start my A-levels, Jack will be eight. He won't need so much looking after. You can go back to study. And then, when you've got your A-levels, Jack will be starting senior school. You'd definitely have time to do a degree then."

"You've got it all worked out, haven't you?"

"It's worth doing. That's what you've always said to me. It's worth getting a proper education. Why don't you believe the same for you? You know that Dad would support you every step of the way."

"Would he?"

"He told me he would."

"Did he? When?"

"Ages ago. Dad and I talk about lots of stuff. He loves you and he wants you to be happy. He hates that you have to do that job at the undertaker's; he's been doing everything he can to get more hours so you don't have to go there. He wants you to have the freedom to do something you really want to do."

"Does he?"

Sophie nodded.

It seemed so at odds with what Ronnie suspected of him after reading Cathy's text. She almost revealed her suspicions to Sophie, but decided her daughter had probably had enough family news to digest for one day.

Ronnie decided she would tackle Mark about their next-door neighbour when they were safely back in Coventry. She'd seen the way he'd swung into action to protect his little girl that night. Mark wasn't the type of man who would give up on his children easily. Perhaps that meant he wouldn't give up on Ronnie so easily either. Perhaps there was still hope.

374

Later that night, the screen of Ronnie's mobile cast a little square of light on the ceiling of the room she shared with Mark. She had a text. It was from Chelsea.

You OK, sis?

Well as can be expected.

You'll always be my favourite sister, Chelsea responded.

And you'll always be mine, Ronnie wrote.

"Who are you texting, love?" Mark stretched out his arm and laid it across Ronnie's stomach.

"Just Chelsea," she said. "I'm just letting her know that everything's OK. Everything is back to normal again."

"Mmmm."

Mark was half asleep. Ronnie turned off her phone and put it back on the nightstand. All Ronnie wanted to do right then was close her eyes and thank God that she had made it through the day. Her daughter was safe and well. She had her whole family around her. She just had to keep them together. That was the only thing that mattered now.

CHAPTER
FIFTY-FOUR

Chelsea

Friday

Adam's parting words about the fancy-dress competition had got Chelsea thinking. It was wonderful that he had turned out not to be such a smug dad after all, but his comment that Jack was a good loser had twisted in her gut. Yes, it was a good thing that Jack was a child who could be unusually gracious in defeat, but Chelsea did not like the idea the word "loser" being appended to her nephew at all. Not one bit.

The fancy-dress competition was important to Jack. No matter how much he had insisted he no longer cared enough to compete, Chelsea knew she could not let the competition pass by. There was only one person who could make sure Jack had a costume worth wearing.

Chelsea dug the little brass lamp out of the wastepaper bin. She rubbed it to clean it off, half hoping that a genie would come out. There was no genie, of course, but as Chelsea made the lamp shine, she knew at last where she was going to find the magic she and Jack needed. She pulled the Mebus dress out of the wardrobe and scrutinised it under the feeble light of the eco-friendly bulb. That blackcurrant stain was never going to come out, but perhaps Lily and Adam had done her a favour.

"Jack Benson-Edwards, you will go to the ball."

It was two o'clock in the morning, but Chelsea had no time to lose. She needed a pair of scissors and she needed a sewing kit. Where should she start? She didn't have high hopes for the hotel reception. The Hotel Volcan was the kind of place where the hairdryers were attached to the walls to prevent theft. It was very unlikely they would have any of those complimentary sewing kits going spare. As it turned out, though, they had something better.

The man looking after the reception that night was using the time to sew buttons onto his shirts. He didn't just have one of those sewing kits with the ready-threaded needles; he had a full-on sewing box with everything you could imagine inside it.

"It's my wife's," he explained with a blush.

"All the best men know how to sew," said Chelsea. It was a pity she had a fairly rudimentary concept of the ancient skill herself. Still, she knew a lot of people who could give her great instructions. Many of them would be asleep at that particular moment, but . . .

Chelsea telephoned a contact at a fashion house in Los Angeles. It was only seven in the evening there. Miraculously her friend picked up the phone.

"Ellie, I need a pattern for a waistcoat, big enough for a six-year-old boy, and I need it faxed through to Lanzarote right now."

"Lanzarote? What are you doing there?"

"It's actually a very culturally important island," Chelsea replied defensively.

"I know," said Ellie, "I love the place. But why do you need a waistcoat pattern?"

Chelsea explained the competition. "Look, could you do this for me? I promise you'll be heavily featured in the next issue of *Society*."

"Give me the fax number. I'll see what I can do. How tall is the boy?"

Chelsea made a guess. "And the waistcoat needs to have something of the East about it. The theme is *Arabian Nights*."

"Oh my God," Ellie exclaimed. "That's Angelo's inspiration for next season. This is fate."

"Maybe," said Chelsea. "Could you hurry up?"

"Your wish is my command. See? You've even got me talking like a genie. What's your fax number?"

The pattern came through to the fax machine in the hotel reception on four sheets of A4.

Chelsea hadn't picked up a needle and thread since she was thirteen years old and had to make a dirndl skirt of the type that hadn't even been fashionable when her mother was a child. She laid the pattern on the hotel's front desk. Because it had been faxed through, some of the pieces had to be taped together. It should have been easy but in Chelsea's hands, it was like one of the harder puzzles in *The Krypton Factor*. Eventually, with the help of the guy on reception, she thought she had it.

Chelsea smoothed out the dress, spread the skirt to maximise its area and started to pin on the pieces of the pattern. At last she was ready to make the first cut.

"Please don't let this be the worst mistake I've made in my life." Chelsea closed her eyes and prayed as she brought the blades of the scissors together.

The Mebus dress had been a goner anyway. After a week of marinating in blackcurrant juice, it was already beyond the help of even the very best dry-cleaners. Now it was fit for nothing but the rag bag. Or the fancy-dress box. Chelsea dreaded finding out how much she would have to pay to recompense the designers, but she dreaded Jack's disappointment more. Jack was right: the fabric of the dress was the very essence of *the Thousand and One Nights*.

Snip, snip, snip. Chelsea cut out the four panels she needed. She pinned them together as per Ellie's instructions and tacked them into place to make the actual sewing easier. The receptionist helped with the tacking before he went off-duty.

Slowly, the little waistcoat began to take shape. It needed a button. There was one on the back of the dress. That would have to do.

With the waistcoat finished, Chelsea fashioned a sash and a turban out of a wide swathe of fabric from the ruined dress's hem. The turban looked good enough, but it was missing something. She knew what it was: in the illustrations, a fabulous jewel always fastened Aladdin's turban. Chelsea opened her vanity case and pulled out the jewellery pouch she had hidden inside it. She knew she had something that would be perfect. She found a Lanvin necklace with a huge fake cabochon centrepiece. The necklace itself was a sort of fabric bib. It was easy to take apart. It wouldn't be so easy to put back together, but for now that was the least of Chelsea's concerns. She had a wish to fulfil.

It was six o'clock in the morning before Chelsea finished her mammoth task. She hung the little waistcoat over the back of the chair in her bedroom and placed the sash and the jewelled turban on the seat. The outfit looked as though it was awaiting the arrival of a fairytale prince, who would doubtless fly in through the window on a magic carpet. Chelsea couldn't help but grin at the result of her handiwork.

"I did it," she murmured, as she lay back on her dirty pillow and finally fell asleep.

Chelsea didn't sleep for long, however. She had left the window open for some air and it was less than an hour before the first of the guests gathered in the pool restaurant for breakfast. Their voices drifted in through the open window, pulling her from her dreams. For once she didn't mind. When she saw again the costume she had created, she couldn't wait to get up and find her young friend. She looked out. She could see Jack and Ronnie walking by the pool.

"Jack!" Chelsea shouted down from the window. Jack didn't look up. Either he hadn't heard or, more likely Chelsea thought, he was still in a mood about the competition.

Chelsea called Ronnie instead.

Ronnie did look up. "Don't hang so far out of that window!" she yelled back.

"Sorry." Chelsea took up a less precarious position. "Ronnie, can you bring Jack upstairs, please? I've got a surprise for him."

CHAPTER
FIFTY-FIVE

Bill

"Auntie Chelsea! You are the bestest of the very best!"

"That *is* pretty impressive," Ronnie agreed when she saw what Chelsea had created.

"Crikey," said Dave, who had joined them to see what the fuss was about. "Our Chelsea can sew. Perhaps she's not totally unmarriageable after all."

"Thanks, Dad."

Jack was busy climbing into his costume. Chelsea helped him to arrange the matching turban.

"It's got a real ruby," Jack gasped.

"It probably is real, knowing your auntie," said Ronnie. "Make sure you don't lose it."

Ronnie and Chelsea shared a look, but for once Chelsea knew her sister's comment was meant affectionately.

Like a veteran actor, Jack immediately inhabited his costume as though it were a second skin. He struck a pose in front of the mirror. "I need a sword," he said.

"Done," said Chelsea, handing him the sword she'd fashioned out of a piece of cardboard she had pinched from the reps' display in the lobby.

"Did Aladdin have a sword?" asked Ronnie.

"God knows," said Chelsea. "But it sort of looks right, don't you think?"

Jack drew the sabre across his body, fluttering the fingers of his free hand in the other direction. He crouched low.

"Would you look at Laurence bloody Olivier," said Dave.

"He needs a moustache," said Chelsea, brandishing a Chanel eyeliner pencil. Jack stood still while Chelsea drew him a moustache with a handlebar flourish at each end.

"Brilliant!" Jack breathed, when he saw his reflection. He wrinkled his nose to see the drawn-on moustache move.

"Thanks," said Ronnie. "You've really made his holiday."

"He's made mine," Chelsea admitted.

"I can't believe you cut up that dress, though. I bet it was really expensive. How much did it cost you?" Ronnie asked.

Chelsea shrugged. "It may yet cost me my job."

The fancy-dress competition was not to take place until the afternoon, before they all met up for Jacqui's birthday dinner. Chelsea managed to persuade Jack to take off the costume — "You don't want to ruin the element of surprise when you walk into the Kidz Klub" — but he insisted on keeping his moustache. He also insisted that he be allowed to draw some stubble on his chin.

"I could do with one of these pencils back home," Jack mused as he scribbled in some thicker eyebrows. Chelsea resigned herself to losing yet another item from her make-up collection — Sophie had kept the lipstick. Jack was delighted to be able to wear his new face down to lunch.

The rest of the family had already gathered at their usual table in the Jolly Pirate, but this time two interlopers had joined them.

"It's that horrible lady," Jack whispered. "The one who likes Granddad Bill."

"We've got to be polite," Chelsea reminded him.

"I don't want to be polite. I want to be truthful."

"If you can't say anything nice . . ." said Chelsea.

"Say it behind someone's back?" Jack suggested.

"That'll do for now," said his aunt.

There were just two spots left at the table. One was between Ronnie and Jacqui. The other was next to Gloria.

"Oh! Look at your funny face, Jack! You look ever so grown-up." Gloria patted the empty seat next to her as Jack and Chelsea approached. The boy's eyes grew wide in terror and he quickly skittered into the seat next to his mother instead.

"He'll get used to me," Gloria assured Chelsea, who had no choice but to take the empty seat next to her. "How has your morning been?"

"It's been lovely," said Chelsea.

It was about to get a whole lot worse.

Chelsea soon noticed that there were two bottles of cava on the table and a wineglass had been set at each place. That hadn't stopped her father and Mark from setting themselves up with beers, of course, but it still suggested that something strange was afoot. The Benson family were not great wine drinkers.

"Mark," said Gloria, "will you please open the *champagne* and pour everybody a glass? It's my treat."

Something was definitely up.

"Shall I do it now?" asked Granddad Bill.

"Wait until everybody has a full glass," Gloria instructed.

"Can I have some?" asked Sophie.

Gloria nodded. "Of course! Jack too, if he likes it. He can have a little sip."

"I don't want to," said Jack quickly. He turned his head away from her.

"He'll grow into having more refined tastes," Gloria assured Ronnie.

"Not if he takes after his dad," Ronnie replied.

"OK, everybody." Gloria clapped her hands. "Up you get, Bill."

Bill got to his feet. He'd been having a good couple of days, but still he swayed dramatically without his stick and had to grip on to the edge of the table to remain upright.

"Ladies and gentlemen, boys and girls," Bill began, "I've got an announcement to make."

Gloria beamed up at him. Her friend Lesley, who was sitting at the other end of the table, looked at her hands. Bill directed his gaze at his son.

"You know, David, how much I loved your dear departed mother."

Dave nodded slowly.

"Yes, Dad, I do."

Chelsea looked at her mother and sister. They were already both beginning to look seriously worried.

"There's no woman in the world could ever replace my dear Jennifer, not here where it counts, in my heart." Bill patted the right side of his chest.

"That's your pacemaker," said Mark.

Ronnie glared at her partner. This was not a moment for levity. Something serious was going on.

"Jenny was an excellent woman. She was *nonpareil*. She made it her life's work to make the people around her happy. She never had a bad word for anyone, right up until the end."

Jacqui took hold of Dave's hand and squeezed it. Dave's eyes were glistening at this emotional talk of his sweet dead mother and it was very moving. This was the longest sensible speech that Bill had made in years.

"Even on her deathbed, my Jenny was looking to the future for all of us. She said to me, 'Bill, you mustn't be sad without me. You and little David have got to keep on living. You've got to keep on loving, too.'"

"Oh God." Ronnie put her fingers to her temples as the penny dropped.

"I ignored that advice for many years. When I got to sixty, I thought my romantic life was over."

"Shit," said Sophie. "He's not—?"

"Sophie, ssssh," said Gloria.

"What's she shushing me for?" Sophie complained to her mum.

386

"Anyway, what I'm trying to say is" — Bill cleared his throat — "I've fallen in love again at last and I'm going to make Gloria my wife."

Gloria got to her feet and flung her arms round Bill's neck.

"Oh, Bill!" she cried.

"Oh, Dad!" Dave exclaimed.

"Oh God, no!" said Ronnie.

Chelsea just gawped.

"What's happening?" asked Jack.

"Great-Granddad Bill's getting married," said Sophie. "That is so gross. People his age shouldn't be allowed to get married. I want to be sick."

Gloria unwound herself from Bill's neck.

"Well, thank you very much," she spat at her prospective step-great-granddaughter. "That's charming, that is. Your great-grandfather has just announced he's getting married and all you can say is that you want to be sick. Well, you make me sick too," said Gloria, "every one of you. Look at the way you're all looking at me like I'm something you just picked up on the sole of your shoe. Can't you see that I make him happy?"

"Well, yes," said Jacqui, "and that's lovely, but—"

"In any case, if you're thinking about sticking your oar in and trying to stop us, you're too late. We've got the date set. We're getting married here next Wednesday. We've already been to the mayor's office and done the paperwork."

"Bloody hell, Dad!" said Dave. "Why didn't you tell me?"

"He didn't tell you because I told him you'd react like this, and I told him why you'd react like this an' all. I said to him you won't care whether he's happy or not. You'll only be bothered about how it affects you. I've seen you all this week, leaving him stuck in front of Sky Sports while you enjoy yourselves out in the sun."

"He likes Sky Sports," said Dave.

"It's a good job, isn't it? Distracts him from you lot spending his money while he's not looking. And now he's fallen in love with me, all you're really worried about is that there will be less to spend."

"What is she on about?" asked Ronnie.

Chelsea shrugged.

"I haven't been spending Great-Granddad's money," Jack piped up. "I've been spending my own pocket money. I saved it up 'specially."

"I don't think she means you," said Jacqui, giving Jack's hand a squeeze. "Look, Gloria, I don't know why you're so angry. Surely you must see that we care about Bill very much and we want him to be happy, but . . . This is all very sudden. You've got to see why that makes us a little bit nervous."

"He's your meal ticket and you're not going to share him, that's what it is."

"He's nobody's meal ticket. He's part of our family."

"And he's brought you on this fancy holiday."

"Er, *we* brought *him* on this fancy holiday," Jacqui corrected her.

"Trying to make him believe you love him for who he is, I'll bet. A small gesture ahead of your grand inheritance."

388

Jacqui and Dave looked at each other and snorted.

"What inheritance?" said Dave. "You're having a laugh."

"Oh yeah, you had it all worked out. You didn't bargain on him falling in love again so you'd have to share the cash."

"If there were any cash to share," said Jacqui.

"You wanted it for yourselves. You've probably already spent it in your heads. What are you having, Ronnie, liposuction?"

"I'll bloody—" Ronnie got out of her chair and pulled back her arm as though to take a swing.

"Ronnie, sit," Jacqui barked. "Gloria, we really don't know what you're talking about."

"But . . ." Gloria paused. "But . . . the lottery."

The entire Benson family stifled a guffaw as they realised poor Gloria's mistake.

"What's so funny?" asked Gloria.

"The lottery? Dad," said Dave, "when did you win the lottery?"

"I won the lottery the day I was born, son, because I've been blessed with this fabulous life: my wonderful family, my children, my grandchildren, my great-grandchildren—"

"And?" Having heard enough about the blessings of family Gloria prompted him to tell her when the money had arrived. "The real lottery? You said—"

"I won ten pounds a couple of weeks ago," said Mark.

"I've never won anything," said Jacqui, "and I've done it every week since it started."

"And I've never done it at all," Bill announced then. "Waste of bloody time. It's a tax on poor people, that's what the lottery is."

Gloria's face grew pale. She sat down heavily. Even under her spray tan, she started to look quite ill. Lesley had her hand over her mouth, but she was suppressing a laugh rather than horror.

"You told me you'd won the lottery," said Gloria weakly.

"I did. I won the lottery of life, and I win it again every time I look into your eyes." Bill pulled Gloria close and puckered up his lips for a kiss.

"Oh! Ugh! Get off me, you disgusting old man."

Gloria wriggled out of his embrace and stood up and away from him. The colour had returned to her face and now it was bright red with fury.

"You've all made a fool out of me," she said. "You let me think he was a millionaire when all he is, is a senile old idiot."

"Hang on," said Jacqui, standing up so that she and Gloria were nose to nose. "That's my father-in-law you're talking about."

"You've all had a right laugh, haven't you? Letting me entertain him while you got on with your holidays."

"Nobody held a gun to your head," said Ronnie. "Who were we to tell you not to hang around him? We thought you must find him amusing."

"Amusing? That old fart? You've made a fool of me," Gloria reiterated.

"We didn't make a fool of you, you silly cow," said Jacqui. "You did that all by yourself. If you'd asked us, we would have told you what he's like."

"They're right, Gloria," said Lesley.

"Don't you start! You knew about this, didn't you? You knew he wasn't a millionaire."

"I did think it was unlikely," Lesley admitted. "I mean . . ."

Ronnie and Jacqui both shot Lesley a look that warned her not to elaborate on their family patriarch's shortcomings.

"You let me kiss him!"

"Just one kiss," Bill started singing. He reached out to grab her again.

"Go away. Go away." Gloria swatted at Bill with her napkin. "Don't you dare bloody touch me."

"I take it the wedding's off, then?" said Mark.

"Oh!" Gloria spun on her wedge heels and disappeared into the hotel. Lesley followed right behind her, muttering an apology over her shoulder as she went. Mark and Dave could hardly breathe, they were laughing so hard. Sophie was mortified. Jack was bewildered. Ronnie, Chelsea and Jacqui instinctively gathered around Bill. Sure, the idea that any sensible woman would have wanted to take Bill off the Benson family's hands was perfectly laughable, but all the same, the women were aware there was probably some level on which Bill had been flattered by Gloria's attentions and would be hurt to discover they were not based on any genuine affection. Jacqui gave her father-in-law a squeeze.

"What a silly cow," she said.

"You're better off without her," said Ronnie.

"Are you OK, Granddad?" Chelsea asked him.

"Plenty more fish in the sea," said Bill. "Besides, I got a quick feel of her derriere before she popped the question, and when you get to my age, that's the equivalent of winning—"

"The lottery," the rest of the family chimed.

CHAPTER
FIFTY-SIX

Jack

Once Jack was back in his costume, he was back in character, and he was not about to come out of character on the way down to the Kidz Klub. The adults and older children around the pool gamely cowered as he waved his sabre over them. He perfected his scowl and a deep throaty growl of a voice. Well, as deep and throaty a growl as such a little pipsqueak could manage.

"OK, Jack," said Chelsea, as they paused outside the picket fence. "We're going in, and I think we've got a good chance of coming out with the prize, but what I want you to remember is that whether we win this fancy-dress competition or not, you will always be a winner to me."

"That doesn't count, Auntie Chelsea," Jack sighed.

"Fine. Just so long as you remember I said it. It may comfort you when you're old like I am."

Chelsea followed her sabre-toting caliph into the Kidz Klub enclosure.

"Don't forget your lamp."

A number of children were already gathering on the stage in preparation for their costumes to be judged.

Chelsea said nothing about her thoughts on the rest of the competition to Jack, but as soon as he climbed onto the stage, she was pretty sure he had won hands down. The other kids' costumes resembled Chelsea's earlier efforts, before she attacked the Mebus dress with the scissors. They had basically rolled up their trackie bottoms and borrowed their mothers' sarongs to make hopeless turbans. And, as predicted, there was one errant knight.

Jack's costume was in a different league. Chelsea hoped that wouldn't count against him in any way. It was funny to think she had been so concerned that her sewing skills weren't up to much. Now she worried just a little that the costume she had stitched together from that crazily expensive dress looked altogether too professional.

The fancy-dress competition was to be judged by the hotel manager. That too might count against Jack, Chelsea feared. After all the fuss about Sophie, Jack and Chelsea were well known to the hotel boss. Would he discount Jack as a possible winner for fear that people would think he was awarding him the prize to deflect criticism of the hotel's initial handling of Sophie's disappearance?

Jack was so obviously the rightful winner. He wasn't just wearing his costume; he was actually inhabiting it, like an actor on a world-class stage. The other children stood stiff as the mimes on the Playa Brava seafront, but as the hotel manager walked by, Jack animated the tableau with another hearty growl. The hotel manager sportingly stepped back as though in fear.

Chelsea crossed her fingers behind her back. Surely the trophy was in the bag?

"Hold on! Hold on!"

Adam and Lily came racing through the Kidz Klub enclosure gate. "We want to enter too." Adam panted.

The Kidz Klub coordinators conferred. The competition had been advertised as starting at three o'clock sharp and it was now almost a quarter past. The coordinators were keen on disqualification, but the hotel manager reminded the Kidz Klub team they were all about making sure the hotel guests had a wonderful holiday. Kidz Klub rules were made to be bent.

Lily was admitted to the stage, and much as Chelsea wanted to be magnanimous, her proud auntie heart sank.

"You didn't say you were a seamstress in another life," Chelsea said to Adam.

"I've learnt to be pretty much everything since Lily and I have been on our own."

Lily was dressed as a temple dancer. Sure, like most of the other children, she was sporting tracksuit bottoms instead of harem pants, but the rest of her costume was a marvel. Adam had taken the fairy dress that Lily wore on that fateful plane journey when Mebus silk met blackcurrant and transformed it into a cropped top and a diaphanous veil. The glittering belt that had circled Lily's waist now graced her forehead. Lily couldn't resist giving Jack a knowing look.

Jack growled. Lily responded with a very professional belly-dancer's shimmy. There were two horses in the race now.

★ ★ ★

Having walked the row of contestants several times, the hotel manager and the Kidz Klub team retired to the coordinators' desk to discuss the final decision. They seemed to be taking for ever. The tension was almost unbearable. Chelsea and Adam stood side by side, looking at their respective charges. From time to time, the two adults stole a glance at each other and smiled. As did Jack and Lily. Their night together under Jacqui's supervision had gone a long way to healing the rift that had begun on the slide all those days ago. All the same, Chelsea didn't like to think of the possible outcome of the hotel manager's deliberations. There was no way he could choose any child other than Jack or Lily. Their costumes were streets ahead of the rest. But whom would he choose out of those two? Maybe the best possible outcome would be a joint first place. There would be no need for anyone to be disappointed. Deep inside, though, Chelsea wanted Jack to be the outright winner. He needed it. He needed that shot of confidence more than Lily ever had.

The hotel manager got up from his seat at the coordinators' desk and walked back towards the waiting contestants. He looked solemn and serious. Anyone who didn't know what was going on might have thought he had been judging the Olympic gymnastics rather than a kids' competition.

"Come on," muttered Chelsea. "This isn't the Nobel Fancy Dress Prize."

Adam laughed, but Chelsea could tell that he too was anxious for the "right" result.

"Ladies and gentlemen, boys and girls," the hotel manager began, "first of all, we'd like to thank you for taking part in our Kidz Klub competition this afternoon. I have to tell you I've been judging the fancy-dress competition every week of the summer season for nearly five years now, but it's rare we see a field of contestants as well turned out as this one."

Chelsea and Adam shared a proud smile.

"Of course, that makes my job more difficult than ever. When everyone has put so much effort into his or her costume, how can I possibly say that one is better than the rest? The winner would be happy, yes, but everyone else who entered might think I didn't appreciate their hard work too."

They're going for a joint first, thought Chelsea.

"Still, there can be only one winner today at Kidz Klub. There is one child here whose costume is a cut above the others, someone whose costume incorporates the colour and the magic that we've come to associate with fairy tales."

Lily gave another little wiggle.

"Aaaah, how wonderful," said the hotel manager.

The prize was Lily's, Chelsea was sure.

"We're awarding first prize to . . ."

One of the coordinators flicked a switch on the CD player so that it played music from the judges' deliberations on *The X Factor*.

"Sheesh," said Adam. "Could they string this out any longer?"

Chelsea threw back her head and exhaled long and loud. So long and loud that she didn't immediately realise they were calling Jack up to the podium.

"Jack Benson!"

The crowd roared their approval.

"Jack Benson-*Edwards*, actually," said Jack, as he took his place.

"Jack Benson-Edwards it is."

The hotel manager placed a crown rather precariously on top of Jack's carefully made turban. He then handed him a silver-painted plastic trophy. Jack balanced the trophy on top of his lamp. He was not going to step out of character even to receive his prize. The hotel manager tucked an enormous packet of Haribo into the open cup.

"I'm sorry," Chelsea said to Adam when she saw Lily's face crumple with disappointment.

"We'll deal with it," said Adam bravely. "Got to start recalibrating her expectations somewhere."

Chelsea squeezed his arm. "Thank you. You know this is really important to Jack."

Jack returned to his aunt's side triumphant, holding his prize above his head.

"I'm a winner!" he said. "We're the winners, Auntie Chelsea!"

"Well done," said Adam, offering Jack his hand.

"Well done," said Lily. "Can I have some of your Haribo?"

Jack didn't dare refuse.

CHAPTER
FIFTY-SEVEN

Jacqui

Jack's triumph at the fancy-dress competition was the perfect start to Jacqui's birthday, which, she decreed, started at teatime because that's when she was born.

"So, how does it feel being ancient?" Dave asked his wife when four o'clock arrived.

Jacqui cuffed him round the ear. In all the years they had known each other, Dave had never ceased to be amused by the fact that his wife was almost six months older than he was. He made an especially big deal about it every time she had a birthday.

"I'm hardly your Mrs Robinson," she told him. "You'll be here soon enough."

At half past five, the whole family went in from the pool to get ready for Jacqui's birthday party. They were going to be eating early. Jack was tired after the previous night's excitement, and Bill always slept better if he ate before seven. That didn't mean they weren't going to make a proper occasion of it, though. With great reverence, Jacqui lifted out the dress she had brought all the way from Coventry for just this moment. She had actually bought it in the summer sales two years earlier, justifying the splurge to herself by saying it would be the perfect thing to wear if one of her daughters got married. Neither of them had, but now the dress was going to have an outing anyway. Jacqui wrapped the green floral number round her body and tied it with an extravagant bow.

"You are every bit as beautiful as the day I first met you," Dave assured her when she gave him a twirl. "Come here." He pulled her towards him.

"Get off," she said. "You'll crease me." Then she relented and let him hold her close.

Jacqui felt the tears spring to her eyes. She had managed to keep a stiff upper lip through all the drama of the past couple of days, but now she could hold it in no longer. The relief of having unburdened herself of her secret was enormous. The relief, too, of getting Sophie back safe and unharmed came rushing out now like a wave breaching a sea wall. Everything might have turned out so very differently. So very wrong.

"Come on," said Dave. "It's your birthday. You've made it to sixty. That's something to be happy about."

"You're right," said Jacqui, wiping the tears from her cheeks. She knew Dave. She knew he wasn't being in any way dismissive of the huge emotions she was feeling. He was just trying to help her get her game face on. Wasn't that one of the things she had always loved about him? His ability to pull her back from whatever precipice she found herself on the edge of? Dave was the one person who could always make her smile.

"You should probably touch up your make-up, though," he said. "Otherwise it'll look like there's an even bigger age gap between us."

"You sod." Jacqui made another playful swipe at his head. "You go on down, then. I'll catch you up."

She dabbed away the smudges of mascara and gave her nose another pass with the powder puff before examining herself in the mirror. Not bad for such a significant birthday. She walked out onto the balcony and looked down to the poolside restaurant, where they would be celebrating that night. Dave was already there with Bill and Mark. Sophie was sitting on the low wall that surrounded the restaurant. Texting, as usual. Ronnie had let Sophie have her phone until they could get her a new one back in Coventry. Ronnie was talking to one of the waiting staff. Chelsea and Jack were sitting at the table, engaged in a thumb wrestle.

"I am so lucky," Jacqui breathed to herself.

Jacqui wasn't quite so lucky with her timing when it came to joining her family. As the lift travelled down towards the lobby, it stopped at the third floor and Gloria stepped in.

Jacqui had not set eyes on Gloria since the engagement debacle that lunchtime. She had hoped she would get away with not seeing her at all before they went home to the UK. What was she supposed to do now?

Jacqui looked straight ahead at the lift doors. Gloria did the same. There was something about the way she stood that made Jacqui feel she was being judged. The cheek of it! As if it was her fault that the stupid woman's gold-digging plans had come to naught. Jacqui felt her blood pressure start to rise as the lift dropped. Just as the lift came to the ground floor, Jacqui opened her mouth to give the other woman a piece of her mind.

Gloria beat her to it.

"I just wanted to say I'm sorry about this lunchtime," she said.

"What?"

"You're a nice family," she added. "I could always tell that."

"Thank you," said Jacqui. The angry words she had intended to spew had disappeared altogether. The two women stepped out of the lift on the ground floor. Gloria caught her arm.

"And Bill . . ." Gloria hesitated. "Is he—?"

"He's not heartbroken, if that's what you're worried about," said Jacqui.

"Good," said Gloria. "I didn't want him to get hurt."

"I'm sorry if you felt misled," said Jacqui.

"Oh, I misled myself. I'm a silly old woman sometimes," Gloria admitted. "A lot of the time."

Gloria suddenly looked her age. Beneath the hair extensions and the warpaint, Jacqui recognised a contemporary. Before now, she would have put Gloria at any age between forty-five and fifty. Now Jacqui could see that Gloria had at least sixty years on the clock. What must it be like to be that age and have no one to look after you, in the way that she had Dave?

Taking both of them by surprise, Jacqui suddenly gave Gloria a genuinely warm hug. Gloria didn't seem like such an awful woman right then, just tired and worried and a bit vulnerable. And if nothing else, she

402

had given the family some entertainment. They would laugh about Bill's holiday romance for years to come.

"You made Bill happy," said Jacqui. "Fortunately, he won't remember how it ended."

"Thank God for that," said Gloria.

"Come and join us for a drink later on."

At last the Benson family sat down for Jacqui's birthday dinner. The manager of the hotel brought over a bottle of cava. The birthday girl had a dry Martini with lemonade. Ronnie had a Bacardi Breezer. Sophie asked for one too.

"No way," said Ronnie. "You're fifteen years old."

For once, Sophie didn't protest.

Later on, the chef brought out a birthday cake. He had somehow managed to fit sixty candles on top of it, even if half of them had been blown out by the sea breeze by the time he reached the table.

The family sang and Jack helped his grandmother to blow out the rest of the candles.

"Make a wish," said Bill.

Ronnie, Chelsea, Mark and Dave knew exactly what Jacqui would be wishing for. Chelsea gave Ronnie's hand a squeeze.

"I have had the best birthday ever," said Jacqui.

"Even with me going AWOL?" Sophie asked.

"Even with you going AWOL. Awful as it was at the time, it was the perfect reminder of how much we all mean to each other, wasn't it?"

Everyone agreed.

"Just don't do it again."

Jack proposed a toast with his glass of Coca-Cola. "I love my family," he said. It was the perfect sentiment.

CHAPTER
FIFTY-EIGHT

Ronnie

"Come for a walk on the beach," said Mark. "Your mum and dad will keep an eye on Sophie." Jack had already gone up to bed with his auntie.

"Are you sure?" Ronnie asked.

"I'm sure. In any case, I don't think Sophie's going to be doing anything too stupid any time soon, do you?"

"Let's hope not."

Ronnie followed Mark out of the hotel grounds onto the beachside path. He held out his hand to her. She took it and let him help her over the sea wall onto the beach itself. They took off their flip-flops. In the darkness, the sand, which had been too hot to walk on during the heat of the day, felt cool and damp. Ronnie commented on it.

"Are you sure that's not just where some dog peed?"

"Mark!" She playfully cuffed his head. "What a thing to say. I want to put my flip-flops back on now."

"Don't be silly. Come on, let's sit down here."

"Not on the wet bit. I'm not sitting on the sand."

"How about here, then?"

Mark lifted a sunlounger off the hotel's neatly stacked pile and opened it out so that Ronnie would not have to sit on the ground.

"You're such a gentleman," she said.

They sat down side by side. There was a chilly breeze coming in from the sea.

"Snuggle up," said Mark. He opened out his arm so that Ronnie could tuck herself in to his side and take advantage of his body as a windbreak.

"It's lovely here, isn't it? I can't believe we sat in the bar every night."

"*You* sat in the bar every night," she corrected him.

"I know," he said. "I should have made more effort."

"It doesn't matter."

"No, it does. I should have tried harder. Not just this week either."

Ronnie waved his mea culpa away.

"Last night was the worst night of my life," Mark continued. "I thought I was about to lose you both."

"Both?"

"Yes: Sophie and you. To be honest, I thought I'd already lost you."

Ronnie felt tears prick the back of her eyes. "I don't know what you're talking about," she said, hoping to avert the conversation altogether.

"We've let things slide, haven't we? Or maybe I should say I've let things slide. I know I haven't been the best partner in the world. I should have made more effort to keep you happy. I was so wrapped up in my own unhappiness with the way that things were going with work. I went out every night because I couldn't face seeing you looking so disappointed every time I got home. Getting so tired with the work and the kids. Stupid, isn't it? I should have just tried to help you. I wouldn't have blamed you if you'd run off with someone else. God knows there are enough men out there who fancy you."

Ronnie blushed. She was glad it was dark.

"I just tried to ignore what was happening. I did pretty much ignore what was happening until you started working again. I saw the way it boosted your confidence and the way men started to look at you. I knew then that I could lose you. I'd always taken you for granted. I even spoke to your mum about it."

"Did you?"

"She did her best to reassure me, but she also suggested I pull my finger out."

"That sounds like Mum."

"So I bought you this. I was going to take you out to dinner — just you and me on our own, while your mum looked after the children — but last night's events put the mockers on that."

Ronnie stared at the little blue box Mark had pulled out of his pocket. It was unmistakeable. Tiffany.

"How did . . .?"

"I afford Tiffany? I didn't. Cathy next door lent me the box. I thought it would be a laugh."

"Cathy lent you the box?"

"Yeah. The charm bracelet her Tony gave her for her fortieth came in it, and she's been breaking my balls about when I was going to ask you ever since. She got quite into helping me plan everything."

"Hence all the texts?"

"Hence the texts."

Mark opened the box to show Ronnie the contents. Sure enough, there was no Tiffany ring inside it; instead there was a cheery-looking plastic number with a luminous-pink rock the size of a boiled sweet. Ronnie was sure she recognised it as one of the prizes from last year's Christmas crackers. He must have saved it. Mark plucked the ring out of the box and held it towards Ronnie's finger.

"I didn't dare get you a real one in case I got the wrong one. I was going to ask you to choose something you liked when we got back home."

Ronnie let him slip the plastic ring onto her finger. "I quite like this one," she said.

"It'd save some money if you do," said Mark.

"But . . . does this mean—? I mean, were you—?"

"Going to ask you to marry me? Yes, I was. I've been thinking about it for years, especially since Jack was born, but I knew you would want a proper wedding. You deserve one. So I was waiting until I'd saved up the money to tell you that you could have whatever you wanted. Big dress. Big party. Even a bloody elephant to pull the bridal carriage."

Ronnie frowned.

"Not because you'd need an elephant," Mark back-tracked quickly. "Just because it's the most exotic thing I could think of."

Ronnie's face softened again.

"So I was supposed to be saving up, but as the years went by, it didn't seem to get any easier to put aside the money. Every time I managed to salt a couple of hundred quid away, we had an emergency. Then the credit crunch came and my hours got cut. I didn't want to ask you to marry me and then have to say, 'We're having the reception at Nando's.'"

Ronnie laughed. "The kids love Nando's," she reminded him.

"Yeah, but it wasn't what I wanted for *you*. You deserve to have a proper wedding, Ronnie. You deserve to be treated like the princess you are, and I can't treat you like a princess because I'm only a part-time kitchen fitter. I mean, look at us. This is the first proper holiday we've had since Jack was born and your parents had to pay for it. Do you know how small that makes me feel?"

"You're not small," said Ronnie. "You've always looked after us. Remember when Sophie was born? You were just a kid. We both were. You've done loads of jobs you didn't want to do just to keep a roof over our heads."

"I've always wanted more for you, that's all. Then you got your job and I started thinking that maybe it was going to take someone else to give you what you really need. Your mum told me not to be so stupid. She said I should ask you anyway."

"She's right. I don't need a big, fancy wedding. I don't need any of that. I just need you, Mark. I need you to stay by my side the way you always have done. Annoying and irritating at times, but ultimately always there."

"So, will you?"

"Will I what?"

Mark nodded towards the ring box.

"Oh, for God's sake, Mark! Ask me properly!"

And so Mark got down on one knee, managing, for once, not to complain about the effort it took to bend his aching joints into position. Ronnie handed him the ring box, closed again. Mark flipped it open in front of her, as though the plastic trinket inside were the twenty-carat diamond she deserved.

"Ronnie Benson," he said, "will you marry me?"

"Mark Edwards," said Ronnie, "I think I will."

Mark got to his feet. Ronnie threw her arms round his neck and he lifted her from the sand, twirling her round and round.

"For God's sake, don't put your back out before we've had a chance to go on honeymoon!" Ronnie scolded. But that night, for the first time in a long time, she felt as light as a feather. She was floating with happiness. From feeling she was about to lose everything, Ronnie realised on the contrary, she had all that she needed. Mark gently set her down on the sand and kissed her. He slipped the gaudy plastic ring onto her finger.

"This is the best moment of my life," he said.

"Mine too," Ronnie assured him.

CHAPTER
FIFTY-NINE

Chelsea

After the birthday party, Jack and Chelsea settled down to share a room for the final time.

"This is our last night together, Jack," said Chelsea, as she pulled the sheet up to his chin. Jack immediately wriggled free, as he had done every night. It was way too hot to be tucked in. Chelsea helped him fold the sheet out of the way properly then perched on the end of his bed to say goodnight.

"Have you enjoyed this week at the Hotel Volcan?" she asked him.

"I love it here. Have you had a nice holiday?" Jack asked in reciprocation.

"I have indeed," said Chelsea.

"I'm sad I won't see you after tomorrow."

"Of course you will."

"But you're going back to London and the last time you came to see me at my house was years ago."

"I won't wait so long again. I shall come to Coventry for your mummy's birthday — how about that?"

Jack calculated the date. "That's before I go back to school. Do you promise?"

"I promise."

"And do you promise me you'll be better when you come to see me again?"

"What do you mean, better?" Chelsea asked. "I'm not ill."

"But you've been sick every night that we've been here. I heard you."

Chelsea's heart sank. She had thought she was being discreet. She should have known after the first night they shared a room that Jack was a very light sleeper. But even if she had taken that on board, would it really have stopped her?

"If you need to go to the doctor, you must," said Jack. "That's what Mummy tells Daddy, but he's usually sick because he's been drinking. You mustn't be afraid, though, Auntie Chelsea. The doctor is there to help you."

"I know. I'll go to the doctor," said Chelsea. "As soon as I get back to London, I'll go."

"Good," said Jack. "Because I was frightened."

Chelsea drew him into a cuddle.

"I didn't want to frighten you," she said. "I promise you I'll be OK, and I promise you I will be a much, much better auntie from this moment on. I'll come and see you as often as I can. I'll come and see you so often that you'll start to get sick of me. You'll get sick of me anyway when you're a teenager. You certainly won't want to cuddle your old auntie Chelsea any more."

"I'll always give you a cuddle," said Jack.

"I hope so," said Chelsea. "Now, it's time for you to go to sleep. You've got to go all the way home to Coventry tomorrow."

"I don't want to go to sleep. I want to stay up all night and talk to you."

Jack didn't even manage to stay awake for another fifteen minutes. He nodded off as Chelsea was reading to him from the new Alex Marwood, editing out the really gory bits as she went. Unable to resist, she pulled the sheet up to his chin again. Before she got into her own bed, a sleeping Jack had flung off his sheet.

That night, for the first time in what seemed like a decade, Chelsea did not purge herself of her evening meal. It was difficult not to. She could feel the multi-layered chocolate birthday cake she had eaten because she couldn't possibly refuse, sitting in her stomach like a slab of damp cement. She so wanted to be rid of it. She curled into a ball beneath the sheet, making herself as tiny as possible, holding herself tightly as she waited for the urge to pass. It felt as though it never would. Inside Chelsea's mind, an argument was raging. She was desperate to be sick again, but she would not break her promise to Jack. She couldn't. She would find a way to beat this thing.

At about three o'clock in the morning, Chelsea was still awake, but she still hadn't purged. She got out of bed and crept to the bathroom door. It was crazy to stay awake any longer. When she got to the bathroom door, though, she realised that vomiting now would be pointless. Her body was already starting to digest the food she'd eaten that evening. She lay back down on her bed. Having resigned herself to the pointlessness of throwing up, she was surprised she didn't feel as anxious as she might have done. Neither did she look like a whale thanks to that one properly digested meal. Was this the way to do it? One meal at a time? Though she knew it would be tough, Chelsea felt a rush of optimism. As soon as she got back to London, she would bite the bullet and get some proper professional support.

Yes. She could do it. She was going to try to change her life. For Jack and for herself.

CHAPTER
SIXTY

The Family

Saturday

Everyone was subdued on their last morning at the Hotel Volcan. As the family took their places at their usual table in the dining room, they were all of them well aware of the fact that that very evening another family would claim the Bensons' table as their own. What would they be like, this new family? Would their holiday be as full of revelation as theirs had been?

Sophie arranged two fried eggs on her plate. She looked at her father as though challenging him to make a comment. Mark managed to behave. Jack had Chelsea make his sausage sandwich one more time and she managed to get it exactly right.

Even Bill seemed to have recovered from the trauma of his broken engagement.

"He's probably forgotten it altogether by now," Jacqui said to Ronnie, whose own engagement was already a much bigger story for the Benson clan.

Just an hour later, it was time for the majority of the Bensons to catch the resort coach to the airport. Everyone but Chelsea was flying back to Birmingham.

She would be returning to Gatwick the following day, thanks to having missed the flight out.

As the family's luggage was loaded onto the coach, Ronnie and Chelsea embraced as lovingly as the little girls who had once called each other best friends.

"You're not to be a stranger," Ronnie reminded her younger sister. "You're to come and stay with us as often as you like. I mean it. We're never going to fall out with one another again."

"I wouldn't go that far," said Chelsea, earning herself a playful cuff round the ear.

"All right," said Ronnie. "We'll stay friends as long as you don't say anything stupid."

"And as long as you don't overreact if I do," Chelsea replied.

"I never overreact," Ronnie protested.

"Mum, you always overreact," was Sophie's view. It hadn't taken long for Sophie to get over her wilderness adventure and rediscover her inner bolshy teen.

"Come here, Sophie." Chelsea demanded a cuddle. Sophie briefly pulled a face that suggested she could imagine nothing more embarrassing, but she gave in and wrapped her arms round her aunt's waist all the same. "And you." Chelsea gestured to Jack.

Jack had been standing apart from the women, with his father and his granddad. Chelsea was aware he had been slightly strange with her all morning. Now as she gestured towards him, Jack buried his face in his father's shorts and refused even to look at her.

"Come on, Jack." Sophie had decided that a ten-second hug was quite long enough and so Chelsea's

416

arms were free. Chelsea walked over to the men and sank down onto her haunches so that she was level with Jack's face.

"I won't see you again," he said.

"Of course you'll see me again — don't be silly. We're best friends now, aren't we? You and me. The winning team." She offered him a fist to bump.

Jack dared to peep out at his aunt. His eyes were wet and pink-rimmed.

"I'm not crying," he insisted when Chelsea reached out a hand to wipe away his tears.

"I know you're not," she said. "Your eyes are just leaking."

"Go on," Mark said to his son. "Don't be so moody. Give your auntie a hug."

Encouraged by a gentle push from his father, Jack at last allowed Chelsea to wrap him in her arms. Once he had done that, the waterworks were switched to full on. His eyes weren't just leaking now; a dam had burst.

"Jack," said Chelsea, "you have made this the best holiday of my life, ever. I will never forget how much fun we've had, but we're going to have more fun together, you and me. Right up until you're a teenager and you tell me you don't want to be seen with your boring old auntie any more."

"I'll never think you're boring."

"I'll remind you how you once said that when you do."

"What was your best bit of the holiday?" Jack asked then.

"I think it was seeing you get your trophy in the fancy-dress competition," said Chelsea, "but that wasn't just the best bit of the holiday. That was the best bit of my year."

Jack nodded. Chelsea could see he was pleased.

"I'll remember that every single day," he said.

"And me," said Chelsea. "I'm going to put the photo on my desk."

"Everybody for the airport on board now," said the driver. "It's time to go."

"That means us," said Mark, putting his hand on Jack's shoulder.

"No!" Jack protested. "No, I don't want to go!" He held Chelsea more tightly. So tightly she could feel his little fingers digging into her skin. Mark gently peeled Jack off. "I don't want to go," Jack cried again. Chelsea wiped a tear from her own eye. Every time Mark managed to prise one of Jack's limbs from Chelsea's body, Jack grasped her more tightly in some other way. One arm off. One leg on. It was like trying to remove a determined octopus. In the end, Chelsea had to somehow get to her feet and carry Jack to the coach herself, where his mother and grandmother performed a four-handed manoeuvre to free Chelsea of his clinging embrace.

"I love you, Auntie Chelsea!" Jack cried out.

"And I love you."

At last, Chelsea was back outside the coach and waving goodbye. She waved until the coach had rounded a corner and disappeared, leaving her standing alone on the pavement. It was hard to believe how

418

difficult it had been to say goodbye to Jack when she remembered how horrified she had been by his sticky hug on their first day at the Hotel Volcan. She smiled to herself as she remembered recoiling from Jack's ice cream-covered hands. Then she looked down and saw that he had left snot all over the front of her last clean T-shirt. And she didn't care a bit.

Airborne at last, Ronnie looked out at the island as it shrank away beneath them. As the plane gained altitude, she clutched Sophie and Mark by the hands. Across the aisle, Jack was in his element, tucked safely between his doting grandparents. Bill was already snoozing in his seat with his head lolling back and his mouth wide open. Her beloved granddad. Only Chelsea was missing from this gang of people whom Ronnie loved most in the world, and she knew that it wouldn't be long before they saw her again. If nothing else, Chelsea would have to come to Coventry for the wedding that Ronnie was determined to fix as soon as she got back home. She'd already Googled the Coventry registrar's office and discovered that you could organise a wedding in as little as sixteen days.

"What!" Mark had exclaimed. "You mean I've only got two weeks left as a free man?" He had winked at Sophie as he said it and then told Ronnie that even two weeks seemed too long to wait until she could be his wife.

"We're going to be a proper family at last."

Even Sophie refrained from saying, "That's lame."

Ronnie knew she had a second chance, and she was going to make the most of it.

CHAPTER
SIXTY-ONE

Chelsea

Chelsea had another day to kill before she needed to present herself at Arrecife Airport. It didn't seem right to be at the Hotel Volcan alone. The place was eerily quiet as the staff made preparations for a new influx of guests later that afternoon. For once, the pool was quiet enough to swim lengths in. Chelsea decided to try to do twenty.

She didn't get very far. Instead, she floated on her back right in the middle of the water, enjoying the contrast of the warm sun on her face and the cool water underneath. She thought to herself that she would miss Lanzarote. She would even miss the Hotel Volcan. It was unbelievable given how negative she had felt about the place when she first arrived, to find it sandwiched between the amusement arcade and the kebab stand. Maybe she would even come back . . .

Floating in the pool, Chelsea recalled the events of the week just past. It was still bizarre to think that there might have been three of them: three Benson girls. Ronnie would have been the middle child and Chelsea even more the baby than she'd always been. What would happen next? Chelsea wondered if this sister stranger ever thought about whether she had siblings. Would they ever meet? Would they like each other if they did? What a terrible secret for her parents to have kept through all those years. How painful it must have been for her mother as the anniversary of that uncelebrated birthday passed.

Chelsea promised herself she would arrange to go up to Coventry as soon as she was able. There was so much to talk about. Perhaps there was even something to be done to make the Benson family complete. She'd start investigating as soon as she got back to London.

Chelsea was just drying off on a sunlounger when a tall, man-shaped shadow blocked out the sun above her.

"I hoped we'd find you," said Adam.

Lily was beside him. She was carrying two Cornettos.

"Lily thought you might like one of these, because you didn't get to taste Jack's Cornetto the other day."

Chelsea took the ice cream graciously.

"That's very thoughtful, Lily. Thank you."

"And we wondered what you were planning to do for the rest of the day?"

"I thought you'd never ask."

So Chelsea spent her last twenty-four hours in Lanzarote with Adam and Lily. They hired a car and drove to all the beauty spots Chelsea hadn't found time to see. They lunched at a restaurant on the beach. Fresh fish and salsa. No radioactive-looking ketchup to be found.

That evening, they enjoyed the hotel's weekly entertainment. Lily insisted that Adam and Chelsea take part in a dancing competition, for which they won a voucher for a bottle of wine. They shared the wine on the balcony of Adam's room, while Lily slept inside.

They shared more stories too. Chelsea told Adam about the origin of the blackcurrant-stained dress and how, when she had finally confessed to *Society*'s fashion editor via email, attaching a picture of Jack in his costume for good measure, the fashion ed had gone crazy for the idea of a spread featuring the children of the rich and famous in fancy dress made from designer clothes.

"So I guess I'll have to resign rather than be fired."

Adam was also dreading going back to work but his office was based in South London.

"So perhaps, you know . . ."

"What?" Chelsea asked him.

"Perhaps we could meet up when we're back at home?"

Adam put down his wineglass and leant forward in his chair. Chelsea subconsciously followed.

"Go on a date?" Chelsea asked him.

"I suppose you could call it that," he told her.

Their lips were almost touching now.

"I think I'd like that very much," Chelsea murmured.

"Good," said Adam. "Because I would like that tremendously."

He leant a little further forward and their lips met at last.

CHAPTER
SIXTY-TWO

Daisy

As Dave turned the car into the driveway of their house, Jacqui took a deep breath. She had been away from home for just a week and yet it felt as though she had been through a lifetime's worth of changes. There had been moments when it seemed as though she was about to lose everything she valued. She had thought her daughters would turn away from her when they learnt the truth about their sister. Now she knew differently.

There was just one piece missing from the picture now. Acknowledging the secret that she and Dave had carried for so long had gone some way to lessening the ache in her heart, but only some way. Forty-two years was a long time not to know what had happened to the girl she had carried for nine months and known for just five weeks.

While Dave unloaded their luggage from the back of the car, Jacqui opened the front door. It didn't open smoothly. A small landslide of post had built up behind the door. Ordinarily, Ronnie would have been looking after the house, making sure no one knew they were away. Jacqui scooped up the post: bills, bills. The bills kept coming, even on your sixtieth birthday. Fortunately, there were some cards too. Jacqui opened those as she pottered about the kitchen, waiting for the kettle to boil. She laughed at a rude card from one of her cousins. Way too rude to be put on display now that Jack seemed able to read just about everything.

Then she came to an envelope addressed in handwriting she didn't recognise. She tucked her thumb under the edge of the flap and eased it open. Inside was a single sheet of A4, She pulled it out. At the sight of the address at the top, Jacqui's heart almost stopped. It was from one of the adoption reunion registers they'd signed up to so long ago. Jacqui held the letter to her chest.

"Dave," She called him into the kitchen, "Dave, quick. I think it's happened."

They sat opposite each other at the kitchen table, the letter between them in a circle of light. Jacqui couldn't look at it. Dave did the honours, though his hands were shaking as he picked it up and started to read.

"It's about Daisy," he confirmed. He reached across the table to take his wife's hand. "Our baby girl has decided she'd like to meet us."

Acknowledgments

This book has been through many incarnations and has passed through many hands. For all their efforts to bring *A Proper Family Holiday* to your beach bag, I'd like to thank the lovely team at Hodder, especially Francesca Best, Eleni Lawrence, Emilie Ferguson, Veronique Norton, Sarah Christie, Isobel Akenhead, and Harriet Bourton, and my agent, Antony Harwood. Thanks also to Victoria Routledge for listening to the endless mid-book moans. And they were endless . . . Finally, I'd like to thank Mark, for always being there. With tea. And my family, for being nothing like the family herein.

Other titles published by Ulverscroft:

WHAT I DID ON MY HOLIDAYS

Chrissie Manby

Sophie Sturgeon can't wait for her annual summer holiday. Not only will it be a week away from work, it will be a chance to reconnect with her boyfriend Callum. Sophie's spent a lot of time getting ready. She's bought a new wardrobe. She's determined she and Callum will have the best time ever. Then Callum dumps her, the night before they're due to leave. In a show of bravery and independence, Sophie says she'll go to Majorca alone — but in fact, she hides in her London flat. But when her friends, family, and even Callum seem so surprised and delighted at her single girl courage, Sophie decides to go all out and recreate the ultimate "fake break" . . .

GETTING OVER MR RIGHT

Chrissie Manby

Have you ever had your heart broken? How did you get over it? Did you delete his number and start again? Are you now friends with your ex? Perhaps you're godmother to his children? In which case, you're a weirdo and this book is not for you. But if you reacted with denial, begging or a spot of casual witchcraft, then you've come to the right place. This is one woman's journey from love to lunacy and back again. If you ever recall past heartbreaks with an urge to go into hiding, this will make you feel better. Sure, you may have sent his new girlfriend a bunch of dead roses, but did you spend a grand on psychic hotlines and a voodoo curse?

KATE'S WEDDING

Chrissie Manby

Thirty-nine-year-old Kate had almost given up on love when she met her fiancé. Now she's planning for the wedding she never dreamed she'd have. But things seem to be slipping out of her control. Diana, born on the day of the 1981 Royal Wedding, never doubted that one day she would find her prince. Newly engaged, and with daddy's credit card in her grasp, she's in full Bridezilla mode. Against the backdrop of the other couple getting married in April 2011, both women prepare for the most important day of their lives. But will each bride get her perfect day? Or will it all become a right royal fiasco?

THE FIRST PHONE CALL FROM HEAVEN

Mitch Albom

In the small town of Coldwater, Michigan, a handful of bereaved residents start receiving phone calls from beyond the grave. Some call it a miracle; others are convinced it's a hoax. Regardless of opinion, one thing is certain: Coldwater is now on the map. People are flocking to this tiny, remote town to be part of this amazing phenomenon ... Sully Harding's wife died while he was in prison, and he now cares for his young son — who carries around a toy cell phone, believing his mommy is going to call him from heaven. But Sully soon discovers some curious facts: the calls only come in on a Friday, and each recipient happens to have the same cell phone plan. Something isn't adding up, and Sully is determined to keep digging until he uncovers the truth ...